BOOKS BY DAVID HAGBERG

Twister
The Capsule
Last Come the Children
Heartland
Heroes
Without Honor*
Countdown*
Crossfire*
Critical Mass*
Desert Fire
High Flight*
Assassin*
White House*
Joshua's Hammer*
Eden's Gate
The Kill Zone*
By Dawn's Early Light
Soldier of God*
Allah's Scorpion*
Dance with the Dragon*
The Expediter*
The Cabal*

NONFICTION BY DAVID HAGBERG AND BORIS GINDIN

Mutiny!

*Kirk McGarvey adventures

ABYSS

DAVID HAGBERG

A TOM DOHERTY ASSOCIATES BOOK
NEW YORK

This is a work of fiction. All of the characters, organizations,
and events portrayed in this novel are either products of
the author's imagination or are used fictitiously.

ABYSS

Copyright © 2011 by David Hagberg

A Forge Book
Published by Tom Doherty Associates, LLC
175 Fifth Avenue
New York, NY 10010

www.tor-forge.com

Forge® is a registered trademark of Tom Doherty Associates, LLC.

Library of Congress Cataloging-in-Publication Data

Hagberg, David.
    Abyss / David Hagberg. — 1st ed.
        p. cm.
    "A Tom Doherty Associates book."
    ISBN 978-0-7653-2410-8 (alk. paper)
    1. McGarvey, Kirk (Fictitious character)—Fiction. 2. Terrorism—Prevention—Fiction.
3. Women scientists—Fiction. 4. Hutchinson Island (Fla.)—Fiction. I. Title.
PS3558.A3227A65 2011
813'.54—dc22

                                                                        2011007891

First Edition: June 2011

Printed in the United States of America

0 9 8 7 6 5 4 3 2 1

For Laurie, as always,
and for Tom Doherty, who provided the genesis,
and Bob Gleason, who helped shape the story

AUTHOR'S NOTE

Details about methods and capabilities of the National Nuclear Security Administration's Rapid Response Teams have been altered. The author does not want this book to become a blueprint for nuclear terrorism.

Anne Marie Marinaccio is the name of a real person, but she in no way is connected with the business deals described in this novel, which are completely fictitious products of the author's imagination.

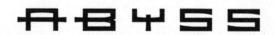

Of course for a long time our central dilemma hasn't been humanity's survival. Since the advent of agriculture, people have striven for advancement; huts instead of caves, horses to help with plowing and transportation—particularly after the wheel and axle were invented—and then the internal combustion engine and electricity, but this brought us up against the need for oil. And the explosion began.

In a very real way, however, our quest for the good life could well push us back to the horse-and-buggy days—if not extinction itself—given the greenhouse effects generated by the combustion of petrochemicals. In the race between climatic destruction and fossil fuel depletion, the outcome will be apocalyptic no matter which side of the coin comes up.

Still the solution has always been around us. In the major sea currents, in the endless winds that roam the land, and in sunshine from the sky.

The battle lines are being drawn for what could be the largest, most important struggle in human history.

April

The last day of the experiment was bright and warm on the Atlantic twenty-five miles off Florida's east coast, and Dr. Evelyn Larsen, who was thirty-six, slender, with short-cropped, sun-bleached blond hair, and overly tanned skin, was in a good enough mood now to grant the interview with Fox News after all. George Szucs, the young producer and his camera crew had choppered out to the National Oceanic and Atmospheric Administration research vessel *Gordon Gunther* in the early afternoon and they'd set up on the afterdeck, manned at that moment by only two crewmen operating the winch off the fantail. The sea was flat calm, and Eve, along with the other ten techs and three postdocs up in the main electronics compartment, was in high spirits.

"The damned thing works," Dr. Don Price, her chief assistant in his third postdoc year, said when the *Big G*'s generators were shut down and the ship's power came entirely from the sea—just one tiny impeller only three feet across placed forty feet down in the middle of the Gulf Stream.

Eve had smiled. "You had doubts?"

Price, who was tall, husky, handsome, and bright, nodded. "Sure, didn't you?"

"Not really," Eve said.

Eve found him attractive except for his ego, which Price could not control or acknowledge, no matter how much his colleagues complained.

He had not been supportive when Eve's paper was published in *Nature* eighteen months ago. Her conclusions were so controversial she was amazed NOAA had actually sprung for two weeks aboard the ship, and funding for the ship's crew as well as for her lab, postdocs, and techs. Someone brought out a couple of bottles of good champagne and toasted the Queen of the High Seas, because all of her postdocs and techies loved her easygoing nature, sometimes self-mocking sense of humor, and her absolute devotion to them and the project.

Eve had raised her glass, a tickle deep in her stomach, and a little dose of smugness just at the tip of her tongue. The damned thing works, she thought.

Growing up in Birmingham, England, with a father, three brothers, and assorted uncles and cousins, the public houses and markets and the fields of the Midland Plain had shaped her in some respects that she had tried to grow out of all her life. All the men in the family worked in the mills, leaving the women at home to do the washing, the mending, the babysitting, the cooking, and at night, briefly, the telly for some comfort, unless a soccer match was playing and money was so short the men couldn't watch the match at the pub.

Eve's destiny was to marry one of the mill-bound boys in her class, or perhaps one or two forms ahead of her, and settle into the domestic routine of her clan. Each evening before bed her mother would slowly read a few passages from the Bible, her finger tracing each sentence word by word, and Eve, sitting on her lap, following her finger and listening to the sounds of the language, had learned how to read.

By the time she got to school, she thought that she had died and gone to heaven because of the library and all the new books for her to read. The only books in her house were the Holy Bible and the union handbook. At first no one believed that she could read—and upside down and backwards at that—so her parents had been called to school to explain why their daughter was nothing but a liar who had learned some parlor trick that they had to work hard to undo.

That's when the verbal abuse began at home, at family gatherings, and especially at school, so that no place had seemed safe to her, and she'd rebelled, pushing herself to learn science, mathematics, philosophy, and languages, to superachieve.

The worst day of her life had been at church when she'd told the Anglican priest that the notion of some god with long hair and a beard, who walked on water, brought dead people back to life, and whose mother had conceived him through immaculate parthenogenesis was silly. She'd been sent home in disgrace, her father had beat her with his belt, and she'd been sent to a boarding school for recalcitrant girls in the country outside Penrith in the north.

And because of her brilliance, she had excelled for a time until the other girls became jealous. Her troubles and misery increased fourfold, pushing her into withdrawal, forcing her to hide her talent as best as she could, making her sometimes ashamed that she was smarter than the other girls, and even smarter, by the age of eleven, than her instructors.

At fifteen, graduating three years early, she had applied to Princeton in the U.S. on a lark, and she'd been accepted with a full scholarship after she'd passed the entrance examinations sent to her boarding school. The headmistress was so delighted to be rid of the girl that the school even helped with the money to get her to the States.

No one from her family came to see her off at the train station, or went down to Heathrow. After boarding the airplane she had not looked back.

In England she'd been considered a freak, but at Princeton she found herself in a community of students and teachers, many of them just as smart as she was. And she'd blossomed.

The low Florida coastline was nothing more than a smudge on the horizon marking the boundary between the gray-green Atlantic and the cloudless blue sky. The Big G rocked gently in the calm swell. Eve, dressed in white coveralls, NOAA's insignia on the breast, hesitated for just a moment before she turned back to the Fox News producer. Her mind had wandered, now that they had come this far. This was just the beginning. And before long the crap would truly hit the fan.

Eve to her friends, or Doc to her assistants, was NOAA's most brilliant climatologist and oceanographer. At this moment she was in her element and yet she felt as if she were trapped, because when they were done with this stage of the experiment she would have to search for funding. It was her least favorite part of real science. God, how she hated asking—begging—for money.

They stood on the work deck on the fantail of the 264-foot research ship that Eve's department at the Geophysical Fluid Dynamic Laboratory had borrowed from NOAA's Marine and Aviations Operations. At 2,328 tons the ship had been originally built as a T-AGOS spy ship for the

CIA, but that work was better done these days by satellite. Most of the sophisticated electronic instruments had been left aboard and the stubby ship bristled with antennas, radar, and GPS domes. Tomorrow morning she and the thirteen techs and scientists would be dropped off in Miami and the crew would take the ship back to her homeport of Pascagoula, Mississippi.

She'd been at it with the Fox News crew for the better part of an hour, and she was ready to get back to work, finalizing the week's data set, and getting the generator back aboard.

"Okay, Dr. Larsen, I'd love for you to sum up what you're doing out here," Szucs asked. "What you hope to accomplish and where it goes next? Maybe something of the long-term implications you told us about."

"By 2050 the world's energy needs are going to be double what they are today," she began. "But the fact is we'll run out of relatively clean fossil fuels to generate the electricity that we need long before that. There's only a finite supply. We have enough coal to last well into the next century, but if we went that route the air would become unbreathable. The entire planet would turn into Beijing on a bad day."

She pointed toward the coast. "Twenty-five miles away is the Hutchinson Island nuclear generating plant. In the next year permits will be given for at least thirty-four more facilities like that here in the U.S. and maybe several dozen more worldwide. That helps, but what are we supposed to do with the radioactive waste—thousands, eventually millions, of tons of the stuff?"

She shrugged and managed a slight smile. "And yet we need to go all electric. Electric cars, ships, and airplanes, electrically heated homes, electrically operated factories. If coal is out and nukes are too dangerous we'll have to look someplace else."

She was lecturing, but in the end she supposed it wouldn't matter. They'd either listen or they would trivialize her like her ex had, which in the end was why he'd become her ex. "Of course wind farms are helping, and so are solar cells, but those technologies have a long way to go before they become commercially viable—and they're not without their problems."

"How about T. Boone Pickens's suggestion that we switch to natural gas?" Szucs asked.

"It's marginally okay as an interim measure, but burning gas still produces carbon dioxide. We're in the middle of the Gulf Stream, which is a thirty-mile-wide ocean current that runs all the way up the U.S. coast and across the Atlantic to the UK as the Atlantic Drift. It's warm water, so there are palm trees in southwestern England, which is at the same latitude as Newfoundland. It never slows down—thirty million cubic meters per second in the Florida Straits and eighty million cubic meters per second by the time it passes Cape Hatteras."

"That's a lot of water."

"And that's a lot of energy," Eve said. "One-point-four petawatts— one-point-four followed by fourteen zeroes—of equivalent heat energy. More than one hundred times the energy demand of the entire world.

"If we can harness just a tiny fraction of that power, along with energy from the Humboldt Current along the west coasts of South America and North America and the Agulhas Current around Africa, our energy problems would be at an end. We'd have cheap, clean, renewable energy. All the electricity we'd need for centuries, maybe millennia."

"But the energy from the Gulf Stream has to be brought ashore," Szucs said.

She hesitated for just a moment, the toughest part yet to come. The part that she had been sharply criticized for not only by her fellow scientists, and especially environmentalists, but by senators and congressmen from states where coal or uranium provided the economic backbone, and of course by big oil.

"We've placed a small water generator fifty feet beneath us," Eve said. "A Pax Scientific impeller shaped almost like the agitator in a top-loading washing machine, or an auger, three feet in diameter. The Gulf Stream turns the impeller, which is connected to a shaft that runs an electrical generator. In our experiment the electrical current is brought aboard where it's used to run all of our electronics, air-conditioning, and even the bow and stern thrusters that keep us in place.

"When we get funding we'll place much larger impellers in the Stream with blades twenty-five feet in diameter, and run the electrical current generated ashore where it can be plugged directly into the already existing power grid—the high voltage lines you see leading away from power plants like Hutchinson Island. When the first few are up and running, Hutchinson Island can be shut down and dismantled."

"How many impellers?"

"Eventually thousands, maybe tens of thousands around the world," Eve said. "It'd be the biggest project ever undertaken in the history of the world. Thirty, maybe forty, trillions of dollars over a fifty-year period."

Szucs whistled in spite of himself. "What you're talking about could bankrupt us all."

"We can't afford not to do it," Eve said. "But there's more, something we haven't covered yet." The something her boss Bob Krantz, NOAA's chief of special projects, had expressly forbidden her to bring up.

"Make so much as a hint, and your career will be over," he'd told her more than two years ago ago. He was a large man who'd played football for Notre Dame and had not gotten too badly out of shape yet. When he wanted he could be physically intimidating.

They were in his book-lined Silver Spring, Maryland, office and although Eve had been standing while he was sitting behind his desk, she'd felt as if he were towering over her. She remembered her anger at that moment. Blind, frustrating. He had her paper in front of him, and she knew that he'd read it. The science was sound, and her results good, yet he was dismissing her.

"It's my career, Bob," she'd shot back.

"Not with NOAA if you persist."

"Are you threatening to fire me?"

"You won't have a lab and you won't have the funding to be on the water," he said, sidestepping the question, which was his style. He'd been a fair scientist who, in Eve's estimation, had risen to his level of incompetence.

"Then I'll get my own funding."

Krantz nodded sadly. "You're a brilliant scientist, Eve. Too brilliant to go off half-cocked. Power generation is an attainable goal, but not on the scale you want to achieve."

"We're not talking about that!" Eve had shouted, but immediately got control of herself.

"Let me finish," Krantz said. "Even Sunshine State Power and Light agrees that your water generators might be able to supply thirty-five percent of Florida's needs. Which is a good thing."

"One hundred percent," Eve said. "But that's still not the issue."

"No," Krantz said. He handed Eve's paper back to her. "Send this to *Nature* without convincing data, and at least two other climatologists who're willing to put themselves on the firing line, and you're done."

Eve focused again on Szucs. "We can control the planet's climate." It was the same thing she'd told Krantz that day.

"If you generate enough power so that coal- and oil-fired electrical plants can be shut down, it should have some effect on global warming."

"No, I mean *control*."

Szucs looked at her as if she were an alien from outer space who'd just landed.

She would be sending her research to *Nature* once she had the final data set from this experiment. Everything she'd seen so far verified her approach. Her peers might call her a lunatic, but they wouldn't be able to dispute the facts.

"The Gulf Stream is a closed system," she told the camera. "The sun powers it, and the Stream distributes the energy around the Atlantic Basin. Take enough energy out of the system and redistribute it as electricity and the transfer, if it's big enough, will have an effect on weather in this hemisphere. Take enough energy out of the Humboldt Current along the east side of the Pacific, and weather will be modified there. Balance the two, along with Africa's Agulhas Current, and others in the Arctic and Antarctic and we'll stop or diminish hurricanes and typhoons, whose main purpose anyway is the distribution of energy."

Don barged out of the electronics bay forward and two decks up and raced to the aft rail that looked down on the winch deck. "Eve!" he shouted.

She looked over her shoulder.

"We've lost it!"

"What are you talking about?" she called up to him. Even from here she could see that he was extremely agitated, which was completely out of character.

"The power spiked and then went to zero!"

Something at the main winch let go with a loud bang that instantly slid up into a sickening twanging noise as if a string on a huge guitar had suddenly snapped, and Eve knew exactly what it was. The eight-millimeter titanium-sheathed cable that held the impeller-generator in place and brought the power up to the ship had somehow snapped. But that was impossible.

"Get down!" she screamed, turning back in time to see the suddenly slack cable come rocketing back aboard like a deadly cobra. One of the crewmen was struck in the chest, ripping his upper torso in half, and flinging him back against the base of the derrick in a geyser of blood.

In the blink of an eye a loop of the cable tangled in the other deckhand's legs and recoiled, lifting the man up over the stern rail and into the ocean.

"Launch the tender!" Eve screamed. Unzipping her coveralls and peeling them off, she went to the rail where she pulled off her deck shoes, and, mindless of the Fox camera trained on her nearly naked body, dove overboard.

Don had been shouting something she couldn't quite make out as she plunged into the warm water of the Stream. She spotted the deckhand about ten feet below, moving incredibly fast to the north along the starboard side of the ship's hull. He was frantically trying to untangle himself from the cable that was dragging him toward the sea bottom two hundred feet down.

Kicking hard toward him Eve was caught up in the powerful Gulf Stream, moving in excess of four knots, understanding that if she missed him the first time she would be swept away with no possibility of getting back to him against the current.

She was a strong swimmer, and had free dived in the U.S. Virgin Islands to the pilothouse of the Rhone in sixty feet of water. But trying to make the angle to reach the deckhand was sapping her strength, tiring her faster than anything she could ever imagine, and for a moment she was frightened for her own survival and nearly hesitated.

The deckhand looked up toward the surface, a resigned expression on his face, as he stopped struggling and allowed the cable and current to drag him farther down.

Eve got to the man and grabbed him by the collar of his coveralls. Suddenly he came alive and tried to reach for her, but she pulled out of his grasp and went to where the cable was wrapped around his knees. As the deckhand desperately clutched at her hair, her neck, her arms, she managed to undo the slack cable, and a second later they were rocketing toward the surface, her lungs burning.

The deckhand convulsed once and then went slack just before they surfaced, and Eve was able to breathe, dark spots in front of her eyes, pinpricks of light flashing off in her brain as her cerebral cortex began to feel the effects of oxygen deprivation.

Don and a pair of crewmen, as well as Stewart Melvin, their medical officer, had launched the eighteen-foot RIB, the smaller of the *Big G's* tenders, and they were alongside within ninety seconds, the Honda four-stroke holding them against the Stream until the deckhand could be pulled aboard.

Melvin immediately began CPR as Don hauled Eve aboard. She'd lost her bra and the nipples of her small breasts were so erect they ached, another effect of near drowning.

Don put a blanket over her shoulders and she looked up. "Thanks," she said, and then she looked over as the man she'd saved suddenly coughed up a lot of seawater, his eyes fluttering.

"He belongs to you now," Don said.

"No thanks, I'm handful enough for myself," she said. "What the hell happened?"

"We'll know as soon as we haul the cable in, but the impeller and generator are gone. No way we're going to find them. And Parks is dead."

Eve's eyes narrowed. "He didn't have a chance. But the cable didn't snap from the strain."

"Manufacturing defect?"

"I don't think so, and neither do you."

They approached the boat, circling around to the port side davits, which would lift the tender back aboard. The Fox crew was at the rail.

Don managed a thin smile. "You'll make the national news. The Queen of the High Seas to the rescue. Maybe it'll divert their attention from our failure."

"Setback," Eve said under her breath.

Eve had debated sending the Fox crew ashore before the cable was brought aboard and they began their search for the generator set and the answers to what had gone wrong. But science was about openness, not secrets, a creed she had lived by her entire professional career. She wasn't about to start a cover-up now.

Bob Taylor, the rescued deckhand, was immediately hustled to the ship's infirmary. The body of Stan Parks, the other deckhand, had been covered but not moved on the Coast Guard's instructions. A crewman was hosing down the blood and gruesome bits of viscera, washing all of it overboard through the scuppers.

Eve hurried to her cabin to dry off and get dressed and when she got back to the winch deck the cable had been brought aboard. Hugh Banyon, the Gunther's captain, was holding the mangled end in one of his meaty paws. It was blackened, as if someone had taken a blowtorch to it.

"That wasn't cut," Eve said.

"No," Banyon said, looking up.

"We had a power spike in the system just before it went down," Don said.

"It'd take a hell of a power surge to fry the cable," Banyon said.

"A direct short could have done it," Eve said. She was sick at heart about this, especially about Parks's death. But there was no way the system could have shorted out naturally. They'd designed too many safeguards, much like fuses, against just such an overload. But unless they could recover the impeller-generator they had no way of knowing what had failed, and why.

She stared toward the west and the smudge of Florida's coastline. Finding the unit would be next to impossible. The Stream could have sent it almost anywhere to the north along a track that was thirty miles wide.

The thought struck her that someone had planned it that way.

She was supposed to fail here. Afterwards what little funding and support she was getting from NOAA would dry up, and it would be over.

"What do we do now?" Don asked.

The Fox camera was close, and a boom mike was just above them.

"Prove that this was sabotage, which makes Stan Parks's death murder, and look for the money to go all the way."

Don was shaking his head. "If you're right, this thing is out of control. We're done."

"We're just getting started," Eve countered.

May

Anne Marie Marinaccio and her mob had been cruising southwest along the European Mediterranean coast for the past two weeks, pulling in and docking at places like Iráklion, Palermo, Sassari, Cagliari, then Palma de Majorca. Except for her homeport of Monaco, where her motor yacht *Felicity* was nothing more than a bit over average, the stunning 402-foot German-built Blohm & Voss was the belle of the ball in just about every marina from Cyprus off the Turkish Coast to Spain's Costa del Sol. Every player's dream.

Finally, two days ago at Alicante she'd gotten tired of the endless, meaningless vacation, the drinking, the outrageous gourmet meals on deck, the stream of business wannabes with their investment schemes— hands outstretched, confidential whispers in her ear, portfolios, facts, figures, projections—and then the string of pretty girls—topless or nude, flawless bodies flouncing around, seemingly everywhere aboard, mind-lessly giggling from bed to bed—so she'd sent them all ashore.

Except for Captain Panagiotopolous and the crew of nine plus two bodyguards, she was alone now with her thoughts, and mostly her gut-gnawing worries. Everything she'd worked for was starting to fall apart, and she'd been like Nero fiddling while Rome burned.

Anne Marie was a player. Her Marinaccio Group, known simply as the MG, was run from offices in Dubai, but domiciled primarily as a discretionary macro oil futures hedge fund in Mauritius. The MG was valued at $498 billion, but heavily leveraged with actual investments, some through derivatives, of something under $50 billion, which was about three times the amount she'd taken from her investors in a mammoth U.S. real estate scheme six years ago. She'd been forced to leave her estates in the Hamptons, Palm Beach, and the Sonoma wine country to the feds and take her private jet to Dubai, whose sheikhs greeted her and her money—despite her gender—with open arms. She was their kind of wheeler-dealer.

Tall and fit-looking for a woman of fifty-two, Marinaccio's undyed salt-and-pepper hair, deep, expressive eyes, and somewhat chiseled features reminiscent of the Redgrave actresses, lent her the aura of success. Heads turned when she entered a room; men were intrigued and their women were instantly on guard, even if they didn't exactly know who or what she was. And it pleased her. It was in her nature.

She was a fighter, too, with a track record to prove it. But the world had gotten much smaller since her days stateside, when she had half a dozen senators in her pocket, along with twice as many representatives, all in on her mortgage-flipping schemes that had racked up some fabulous profits. She'd funded five top-ranked lobbyists who worked both sides of the aisle along with the Americans for Tax Reform to head off increasing scrutiny of the commercial banking industry that was making questionable loans, billions of which Marinaccio Group arranged through dozens of partnerships, mostly in the two prime housing markets— Florida and California.

She had figured that the boom had to end sooner or later and when it did banks would fail and a lot of important people, who had trusted her to continue making them even richer than they already were, would be seriously hurt. And when she saw it coming, smelled it in the wind on Wall Street, knew it in her gut, she had made one final push—leap, actually— and when she walked she was a multibillionaire, her money safe in the Saudi-run International Bank of Commerce in Prague, in Syria, and, of course, in Dubai, and lately MG's fortune in Mauritius.

It was those important people stateside who wanted to get to her. Which meant that for the past six years her travel had been restricted, and lately she had begun to chafe at the bit, thus this trip to test the waters in a way. And to take her mind off her latest set of troubles, because if her oil ventures failed—and there was a more than even chance now that they would, especially because of the money she'd poured into Iraq—the Middle East would be gone for her, leaving her Russia or China, in a worst-case scenario Cuba, or with her friend in Venezuela.

The Med was calm this afternoon. Standing in the ultramodern and expensively furnished Italian-designed saloon with a glass of Krug in hand, she could see the Marseille skyline far to the hazy north. This morning the captain had asked if they were returning to their berth at Monaco, but Anne Marie had merely shaken her head. She figured she would need at least a few more days to work out her next moves.

Run? If she did that she would be out of the business, possibly for good. On the surface it wouldn't be so bad to retire somewhere. She had plenty of money, and when she got back she would begin siphoning even more cash from the fund into a few untouchable private offshore accounts. Her investors, especially some of the Saudis, would send someone after her naturally. But she had the means to fight back, and if need be it's exactly what she would do, fight fire with fire. But her strike would be harsh beyond measure. It was something her father, one of the original hedge fund managers back in the late fifties and early sixties, would have done.

"The whole notion of minimizing risk at the expense of reducing profits is a load of pure horseshit," Thomas Senior stated flatly at his daughter's graduation from Harvard Business School. Anne Marie had inherited her dad's tall, slender frame and good looks, along with a few million when the old man had put a 1911A1 Military Colt .45 to his temple and blew his brains out. When he had been alive though the old man had never been shy about offering his opinions whether they'd been asked for or not. Anne Marie, who had followed in his footsteps, first with a BA in accounting from Loyola, her CPA from DePauw, and finally a Harvard MBA, had also inherited that trait.

"Al Jones got it wrong," Senior had told the group of MBA graduates gathered around him and his daughter on the Yard. Jones had been the financial wizard who'd created the first hedge fund in 1949, buying assets he thought would go up and selling those that he expected to fall. The man was hedging his bets. "That's the way the market works when pansies weak in the knees make their trades."

"And now?" one of the newly minted MBAs asked politely, even though they all knew what the answer would be.

Senior looked at them as if he were seeing a bunch of English lit majors who wouldn't be expected to know the difference between a high-water mark and a hurdle rate or a discretionary macro strategy versus a systematic macro—which in his opinion was no strategy at all. Letting computer software direct your buy-sells was for idiots and cowards.

"Profits!" the old man roared.

"At all costs?" the same young man asked.

And then Senior, realizing that his leg was being good-naturedly pulled, smiled. "Is there any other way?"

Anne Marie had been proud of her father that afternoon. Senior had been a player right up to the end when the markets crashed in '87, and although his funds had lost only 10 percent of their NAVs, or net asset values, it was enough because they'd all been leveraged to 90 percent. For every dollar his funds had lost, they'd wiped out nine. And it was over.

Anne Marie took the bottle of Krug out to the aft sundeck and sat back in one of the chaise lounges, a dark scowl on her features. She was dressed in a white lounging suit and she was aware that she looked good. But she couldn't keep her mind away from her troubles. Her situation was a lot more complicated, but she was heading toward the same net effect that her father had faced. This cruise had been meant to recharge her batteries, figure a way out, because she sure as hell wasn't going to put a pistol to her head. But she was lonely now. She'd had three high-profile marriages, the last one to a Hollywood star that had ended six years ago when she had to get out of Dodge and he refused to leave with her. She had her staff, but they couldn't be counted on to share a confidence; most of them would see it as a sign of weakness, typical for a female, and jump ship.

The only man she could count on was Gunther Wolfhardt, a former German intelligence officer who Anne Marie had been introduced to by a high-ranking assistant to the UAE's minister of finance, Sheikh Hamdan bin Rashid Al Maktoum, as a good man to have in one's employ. Especially in the sort of business ventures that Anne Marie might be interested in pursuing and, of course, because she was a woman in a man's world.

As a young KGB lieutenant, Wolfhardt had been a killer for the East when the Germanys were separate countries, and after they'd united, he'd headed farther east, ending up in Prague, where he somehow came to the attention of the Saudis.

The exact details of why Wolfhardt had suddenly fled the Czech Republic and turned up in the UAE, where he did the royal family favors from time to time, were fuzzy. Nor was Anne Marie interested in finding out. Instead she'd created what she called the special projects division of the MG, and gave Wolfhardt a healthy budget and free reign. Her orders were to fix things that needed fixing. If some investor somewhere got cold feet and wanted to back out, Wolfhardt and his string of freelancers would arrange an unfortunate accident, or perhaps a stroke or heart attack, and even the occasional home or business fire or terrorist suicide bomber.

Anne Marie had immediately connected with the German because they were of like minds; they were survivors, and nothing else mattered, though there was no love between them.

But Gunther wasn't here now, only the two bodyguards he'd arranged for were, so there was no one to talk to. No one to confide in.

Primarily the Marinaccio Group, with Anne Marie as the sole manager, dealt in oil futures, a lot of the risk propped up by derivatives among the oil suppliers, mostly OPEC and the refineries in the U.S., India, and China. It was nothing more than insider deals between the producers and the users who agreed to set a price and deliver a set amount of oil. The people who pumped the oil were assured of a market, the refiners were assured of a steady supply, and cash could be made on the promises.

All that had been fine, especially when oil had approached the $150 per barrel mark. But she'd made a few side deals, pumping a lot of the fund's money into China's industrial revolution. The higher China's per capita income rose, because of farmers coming into the cities to work in the factories, the more automobiles and trucks they would need, ergo an increased demand for oil.

The problems came one after the other: Americans reduced their driving when gasoline hit $4 a gallon and they vastly scaled back their discretionary spending when trips to the mall got too expensive, which sharply cut back the need for inexpensive Chinese products that were increasingly more expensive to ship to the U.S. Although oil dropped to under $100, then $50 per barrel—simple supply and demand—Americans were not returning to their gas-guzzling SUVs, nor were they returning to the malls, and China had to cut back its manufacturing outputs, and curtail building new factories.

The Marinaccio Group was hemorrhaging money, and Anne Marie had no real idea what to do about it.

"Be bold," her father would have advised. "Make an end run."

But look where that had gotten him. It was depressing.

Carlos Ramirez, one of her bodyguards, came from the saloon with a sat phone. He was a small, wiry man with a star soccer player's physique and the dark complexion of Pelé. He moved with the grace of a jungle cat and never raised his voice. "Sorry to bother you, Ms. Marinaccio, but you have a call."

"No calls," Anne Marie said.

"I think you need to take this one, ma'am. It's Abdullah al-Naimi."

Anne Marie hesitated for just a beat. Al-Naimi was the deputy director of Saudi Arabia's chief spy agency, the General Intelligence Presidency or GIP, and first cousin to the Saudi minster of petroleum and mineral resources. The shit was about to hit the fan much sooner than she'd thought it would. The Saudis were not interested in developing Iraq's oil fields. They didn't want the competition when the oil began to flow, principally to the U.S. They wanted to squeeze the market as hard as they could for as long as they could. And they definitely did not trust women in business.

She took the phone and Ramirez retreated back through the saloon. "Mr. al-Naimi, good afternoon. Where are you calling from?"

"If you look to the northwest you will see my helicopter," al-Naimi said. "Stop your vessel and prepare for me."

Anne Marie looked, and she could see it low in the distance. "We're at minimal staff, at the moment. And actually we're on the way back to—"

The connection was broken and for a moment Anne Marie considered ordering the captain to speed up and change course directly for Monaco, because for whatever reason the Saudi was coming out here to speak with her would not be pleasant. It was even possible that some of the important Saudi princes who'd secretly invested in the MG were getting pressure from the king to bail out, which would destroy the fund so that the remaining power hitters would be coming to Anne Marie for answers.

She'd sent Felicity's helicopter back to Monaco with the last of her guests, so the ship's landing pad was empty and she couldn't make that excuse.

Make an end run, Senior had advised. Well, if ever there was the time for something so dramatic it was now.

She picked up the ship's phone lying on the table beside her and ordered the captain to come into the wind, slow to idle, and prepare to board a helicopter.

Almost immediately the ship turned toward the southeast and slowed down. One of the crewmen came out of a hatch onto the landing pad two decks up and just aft of the bridge, and Anne Marie followed him up.

Within just a couple of minutes the sleek Bell 429 twin-tailed corporate helicopter with the Saudi coat of arms, a palm tree above crossed scimitars, flared opposite Felicity's starboard quarter and the pilot slid to a hover a few feet above the helipad and set down. It was a slick bit of flying, but the royals had the money to hire the best.

A rear door opened and al-Naimi, dark, sleek, slightly built, but with the characteristically large Saudi nose, dressed in Western business clothes, beckoned Anne Marie to join him.

"Tell the captain to hold here," she told the crewman, and ducking low she hurried across to the helicopter and climbed aboard. As soon as the door was closed and she'd secured her seat belt, the pilot took off and headed south.

Al-Naimi was a cautious man who never spoke about anything of consequence if he were in an environment that wasn't directly under his control. There could be, and in fact were, microphones and video cameras concealed in every compartment of the yacht. Sometimes Anne Marie found that it was in her best interest to see and hear what was going on with her guests. The surveillance and recording equipment had come in handy on several occasions, and Anne Marie knew al-Naimi well enough to figure that the man had to know, or at least suspect as much.

They'd first met five years ago in Dubai when Anne Marie had begun to attract the interest of several Saudi princes. The GIP had vetted her and the fund, and al-Naimi had come around to introduce himself. They'd met on several other occasions, at cocktail parties, and once in Monaco aboard a yacht owned by one of the royals. And their meetings had never really been friendly, nor had al-Naimi ever been cold, just neutral. But Anne Marie had been warned a couple of years before by her friend in the UAE's Ministry of Finance that she should always be on guard against al-Naimi's wrath.

"Do nothing to anger this man," she'd been told.

Now it was impossible to tell from al-Naimi's expression what his mood was. And Anne Marie thought that was an ominous sign. The professional poker player who held a straight flush had the same impenetrable look in his eyes.

"I'll not keep you long, Ms. Marinaccio," al-Naimi said conversationally. "I've just come to make a trade with you. One that you may not refuse, and the details of which are not negotiable."

Anne Marie just nodded. She had no idea where this was heading, except that she felt as if she were in the biggest danger of her life.

"I want no denials from you, no excuses, no explanations. We know about your Iraq oil development fund, and the names of our royal family members who have invested in the fund. For the moment we will take no action to stop you, though officially we cannot approve. You understand."

Anne Marie started to say yes, but al-Naimi gestured for silence.

"We also know of your investments in certain Chinese business ventures, and we approve. In time these will bring a good return. But we also know that your fund is heading for trouble because of the problems in the American mortgage market—some of which you helped create. High gasoline and diesel prices at the pump stopped people from driving, airlines raised their rates, and the cost to ship a standard container of products across the Pacific went from three thousand to nine thousand dollars, eliminating profits."

"One hundred and fifty dollars per barrel was the breaking point," Anne Marie said.

"Which is why you will help us raise the light sweet crude to three hundred dollars, perhaps four hundred per barrel."

Anne Marie almost laughed, but she thought better of it.

"We want you to make gasoline and diesel fuel far too expensive to use merely for transportation," al-Naimi said. "You will do this in such a way that my government cannot do, even with the help of the new al-Quaeda."

"I don't understand."

"The U.S. and eventually China will switch to electrically driven means of transportation, and your fund will encourage this."

Anne Marie spread her hands. "It's already happening. There'll be more nuclear power plants, solar farms, and T. Boone Pickens is pushing wind farms and natural gas."

"You will make those efforts unpalatable to the public, first in America and then elsewhere. Electricity will be generated by oil, which will be purchased from us, and from your Iraqi oil fields."

"I don't have that power."

"Perhaps not alone, but you will find a way. Make nuclear power unsafe. Another Three Mile Island could be arranged. Our trade will begin there. Later you'll concentrate on coal."

"It will take time."

"I've spoken with certain investors who will give you the time you need. We understand such things."

"In trade for what?" Anne Marie asked.

Al-Naimi picked up a handset and ordered the pilot to return to the yacht. He looked at Anne Marie as he might have looked at a child. "For your life, of course, Ms. Marinaccio. Could there be any better medium of exchange?"

Felicity put in at Monaco and Anne Marie took her Gulfstream IV back to Dubai that evening, landing at the Dubai International Airport at dawn where she was picked up by her limo and brought to her in-town residence, the penthouse at the Marina.

After she'd dismissed her bodyguards, she went out to the balcony where one of the house staff brought her a pot of Earl Grey with lemon, and she looked out over the waterfront, starting to get busy now. She'd gotten a few hours sleep on the airplane, but she was still dead tired, only she couldn't shut down her mind. She was three thousand miles from the Med where al-Naimi had issued his warning, and it seemed like a lifetime.

Her decision would pit her either against the Saudi intelligence apparatus, in which case the MG would almost certainly go under and her life be put in jeopardy, or against the U.S. Department of Homeland Security, in which case she would need plausible deniability. Nothing could point in her direction. Though what the Saudis wanted would probably still be impossible—four hundred dollar oil for electrical generation would put an untenable burden on the American economy. It was something that al-Naimi and whoever was directing him did not understand. Of course China and a rapidly emerging India could soon take over from the Americans, but it was the transition period that bothered Anne Marie.

In the end, there was no decision. Not really. Once she'd started down this path there'd never been the possibility of getting out cleanly, no matter how much she'd talked herself into believing she could. It was oil, after all, which had its tendrils in just about every corner of the planet. Almost no place on earth was free of needing it.

At noon, she finally telephoned Wolfhardt. "I'm back."

"I heard. Trouble?"

News traveled fast, and her chief of special projects had ears everywhere, including a satellite feed from the surveillance equipment on *Felicity*, aboard the Gulfstream, and inside her penthouse here, in Monaco, and her house on the Palm Jebel Ali man-made islands in the bay. He would know about al-Naimi's brief visit to the ship, but not what they had talked about in the air, though he knew what was going on more than anyone else in the fund, and was putting two and two together.

"I have a job for you, this one could be the biggest yet," Anne Marie said. "Get us a tee time."

"Already have. Two o'clock."

The Majlis eighteen at the Emirates Golf Club was the best in Dubai, green fairways snaking in and around the desert sand dunes, and it was the first grass course in the Middle East. Before then golfers played in what amounted to eighteen-hole sand traps.

Wolfhardt was waiting outside the pro shop with a cart on which he'd already loaded his own and Anne Marie's clubs. He was a short, stocky man of fifty-six, with broad, powerful shoulders and a round, almost cherubic face that had fooled more than one person who wanted to believe a man's smile was a mirror to his soul. In fact Wolfhardt was as ruthless as he was brilliant; driven, he'd once admitted, by some inner demon. He was a sociopath by birth, a killer who only valued money as a way of keeping score on his "jobs," as he called his assignments.

Since joining the MG he'd seldom pulled the trigger himself. Instead he'd arranged the hits, and sabotage and suicide bombings, with an exquisite precision he'd learned from the Russians at the KGB's School One outside of Moscow, from years of direct experience in the field, and from retraining at the Dzerzhinsky KGB Higher School and the Red Banner Yuri Andropov KGB Institute, both in Moscow.

He'd never been married, so far as Anne Marie knew, though from time to time he would disappear to somewhere in Europe, usually for no more than one week, and each time he came back it was clear he'd shed a little of his tension. But Anne Marie never asked about Wolfhardt's personal life or where he went and why.

"Good afternoon, Gunther," Anne Marie said, sitting down on the passenger side.

"Good afternoon," Wolfhardt replied, very little German accent in his deep bass voice.

He drove down to the first tee where they had to wait five minutes before the foursome ahead of them chipped on to the green. Play today would be slow, but Anne Marie didn't mind. Wolfhardt would either accept the assignment or he'd refuse. It wouldn't be about money, it would be about personal consequences, and before he agreed he would first have to see the entire operation as well as its aftermath in one seamless piece, with nothing reaching back here. Not simply plausible deniability, but complete and total distance, not so much as the hint of any connection, and Anne Marie thought it might take some time to bring Wolfhardt to that point.

The afternoon was desert hot and airless, but the golf cart was air-conditioned, and the small cooler just behind the seats held an ice-cold bottle of Krug and one crystal glass for Anne Marie and a bottle of Evian for Wolfhardt.

Both of them were indifferent golfers, though no matter how poorly Anne Marie played, she always managed to beat Wolfhardt, though they never actually kept score.

And Wolfhardt always kept his silence at times like these when it was obvious Anne Marie had something important on her mind. Nor did Anne Marie ever speak until she had worked out her approach. No cocktail party small talk, no banter between friends. This was strictly business.

Until the difficult 434-yard par-4 eighth hole, which required a long but precise drive uphill if there was to be any chance of reaching the tiny, sharply sloped green in two. Most golfers were happy to walk away with a double bogey, because even in two strokes it often took four putts to put it in.

They had to wait again for the foursome ahead of them, and Anne Marie poured a glass of champagne. "The job I have for you will be difficult," she began. "There will be consequences even more far-reaching than nine/eleven."

"The Saudis?"

Anne Marie looked at him, and for the first time wondered if the East German had become too powerful, too all-knowing, maybe omnipotent. But there was no way out now.

"Al-Naimi came out to see me. They want four hundred dollars per barrel."

"They'd lose the American market," Wolfhardt said. "Anyway what do they think we could do about it? You said another nine/eleven."

"The U.S. is switching to an electrical economy, or at least one that's hybrid, and eventually it'll catch on elsewhere. Europe first, eventually China and India."

"Nukes are back in, and wind and solar power are getting the press. What do the Saudis have in mind, because crashing airplanes into places like the World Trade Center or the Pentagon wouldn't help. Even if they destroyed the White House or—" Wolfhardt stopped in midsentence and an odd, calculating, even thoughtful look came into his round face. "Impossible to stop all that. There's plenty of natural gas, especially in the U.S. for the interim until the new nuclear plants come online. That'll be their main source."

"They want oil-fired power plants."

Wolfhardt smiled, obviously knowing what had been suggested to Anne Marie, and appreciating the grand sweep of the project. "Consequences indeed."

"We'll start with the nukes. Make them even more unpalatable then they were after Three Mile Island."

"Or Chernobyl."

"Can it be done on a large enough scale to make a difference?" Anne Marie asked, hopeful for the first time since she'd left *Felicity* in Monaco.

Wolfhardt shrugged, most of his attention elsewhere, planning, looking ahead, balancing odds, risk management. His concentration was one of the traits, besides his intelligence, experience, and ruthlessness, that had attracted Anne Marie.

"Nuclear power stations are vulnerable, especially in the States," he said, almost dreamily. "A nuclear accident would be difficult but certainly not impossible. Their Homeland Security is a joke. Even though they have some good people working for them, no one takes anything seriously. Their eyes are in the sky, not on the front door."

"Americans are leery of nuclear power. We need to make them frightened enough to be willing to shut them down, even when they know they need more electricity."

Wolfhardt focused. "It'll take more than an accident."

"Two, or three."

"Public sentiment. The public has to be swayed in a very large way by someone who is very good. Someone trusted to tell the truth."

Anne Marie didn't understand, and Wolfhardt could see it because he went on.

"Within a couple of years after nine/eleven Americans had already begun to resent security measures at the airports. They'd forgotten. You'll need to find someone with the means to keep in everyone's mind that nuclear power means death. Someone who can make it a cause. Someone charismatic, because if all you convince are the Greenpeacers and not the man and woman on Main Street, you will lose."

Anne Marie didn't need to give the suggestion any thought: she knew who was right for that job. The man who had the power, the connections, the means, the will, and the ability—as well as the motivation.

The golfers ahead of them had taken their second shots and were heading up to the green.

Anne Marie nodded, confident finally that she had found the means for her salvation, or at least the end run that would give her time to work her way free and escape with her money and her life intact. "I have just the man for that part. Can you manage yours?"

"Of course," Wolfhardt said. "Like you, I have just the man. But as you warned, there will be consequences."

"There are consequences to everything we do."

PART
ONE

Fourteen Months Later

⊡∩ᴇ

Brian DeCamp, forty-three, slender with thinning sand-colored hair, unremarkable in looks and stature, parked his rental Ford Taurus next to a tour bus in the visitors center of the Hutchinson Island Nuclear Power Plant on Florida's east coast eighty miles north of Miami. It was a few minutes before noon on a sunny day, but driving up along A1A, the highway that paralleled the ocean, he'd not really noticed the beaches or the occasional stretches of pretty scenery. Instead he'd mentally prepared himself for what was coming next.

Prepare first, shoot second, and you might just live to return to base. Never underestimate your enemy. Kill whenever, wherever the chance presents itself. Take no prisoners. Show no mercy. Wage total war, not police actions.

He'd learned those lessons from his days as a young lieutenant in the South African Defence Force's Buffalo Battalion.

The Battalion's primary mission had been to fight a brutal unconventional war behind enemy lines in Angola. And he'd been damned good, so that when he finally walked away seventeen years ago when the South African government had betrayed the unit by disbanding it and disavowing its tactics, he'd been one of the most decorated and youngest full bird colonels in any South African unit.

And he'd been a bitter man because he'd been forced to leave the intense camaraderie and esprit de corps of men who had shared the fighting and violent deaths with a sense of purpose; the holy zeal for the motherland, for the empire.

In the end the Battalion's ideal had arisen from a letter a Roman

centurion had written to a cousin back in Rome when the center began
to fall apart:

> Make haste to reassure me, I beg you, and tell me that our fellow citizens under-
> stand us, support us and protect us as we ourselves are protecting the glory of the
> Empire.
>   If it should be otherwise, if we should have to leave our bleached bones on the
> desert sands in vain, then beware of the anger of the Legions!

He got out of the car and headed across to the low building called
Energy Encounter that served as the facility's visitors center and he was
still surprised at how easy it had been to get permission for a tour of the
plant, though it had taken him the better part of the year to put everything together before he'd applied. It was silly, actually, after 9/11, for
Homeland Security and the National Nuclear Security Administration
to be so lax with such vulnerable targets that had the potential for destruction and loss of lives a hundred times worse than the World Trade
Center.

He'd gotten the first call eight days ago from Achmed bin Helbawi,
who'd reported that everything at the plant was in readiness. The Semtex and detonators were in place along with the weapons he'd smuggled
in piece by piece over the past weeks. The Saudi- and French-educated
New al-Quaeda operative had worked at the plant as an engineer in the
control room for ten months under the name Thomas Forcier, and already he'd built up a reputation as an intelligent, cheerful, and reliable
employee. Everyone liked Tom. He'd made no enemies.

DeCamp's application for a tour had required a social security number, which he'd supplied under the name Robert Benson, a high school
teacher from San Francisco. The name and the number were legitimate,
but Benson was dead, his disappearance not yet reported because he was
on vacation. In fact, that part of the op had been the most difficult to
figure out. DeCamp had hacked into the databases of several San Francisco high schools before coming up with a dozen possibilities—teachers
about the right size and build, who were single and lived alone. And it
had taken even longer to find out who would be leaving town at the
right time.

Benson, who was a homosexual, fit the bill, and two nights before he was scheduled to fly to Hawaii, DeCamp had followed him from a gay bar back to his apartment. Posing as an interested guy from the club, DeCamp got into the apartment without a fuss, had broken the man's neck, and then telephoned Delta Airlines to cancel his flight.

That same night DeCamp had sealed the body in a plastic sheet with duct tape so that no odors of decomposition would escape to alert the neighbors and stuffed the body in the bedroom closet.

He took Benson's identification and laptop to his hotel, where in the morning he went online to apply for a tour pass, which came three days later. After he'd altered his appearance with hair dye and glasses and then Benson's driver's license, substituting his own photograph, he'd left for Miami to wait for the final call from bin Helbawi giving the time and date that the next large tour group was scheduled.

The power plant's twin pressurized water reactors, housed in a pair of heavily reinforced containment buildings like giant farm silos, dominated the facility that sprawled over an 1,100-acre site on Hutchinson Island, which looked more like some manufacturing operation than an electrical generating station. A maze of buildings were interconnected by large piping, umbilical cords that sent nonradioactive steam from inside the containment domes to the turbines and generators, returning the cooled steam back to the heat exchanger attached to the reactor. Two wide canals brought seawater for cooling from the ocean just across the highway.

Producing 1,700 megawatts, the plant supplied a significant portion of Florida's power needs, and should there ever be an accidental release of nuclear materials, which would happen in about four hours, more than 140,000 people in a ten-mile radius would have to be evacuated or be in trouble.

That part of the operation was of no interest to DeCamp because by then he would be flying first class aboard a Delta jet back to Paris and from there by train to his home in the south of France where he could return to his flower gardens and pastoral existence.

It was just noon when he presented his visitor's pass and driver's license to one of the women behind the counter in the busy lobby of what looked like one of the attractions at Disney's Epcot. An animated model of the facility took up an adjacent room, and everywhere on the walls and scattered around the center were interactive flat-screen televisions, models of atoms and other displays where people, either not taking the tour or who had already been, were wandering. A group of middle school children and their chaperones were doing something at several computer screens, and overall there was a muted buzz of conversation. No one was speaking much above a whisper. Just out the door and through the secured area fences were a pair of nuclear reactors, practically atomic bombs in some people's minds, devices that were even holier and scarier than churches. This was a place of respect and awe.

The clerk compared the photograph to DeCamp's face then laid it on a card reader, which was connected to a nationwide police database, something DeCamp had already done. Benson had come up clean.

When she was finished she looked up and smiled. "You have a choice, sir. You can join the Orlando tour, which starts in ten minutes, or wait for the next regular one, which begins at two. You might want to wait because the two o'clock has four people booked. The noon has eighteen. And the one o'clock is just for the schoolchildren."

DeCamp nodded. "Actually I'm supposed to be in Jacksonville later this afternoon, so if it's okay I'll tag along with the Orlando group."

"Yes, sir."

She handed him a packet of materials containing cutaway diagrams of the plant's reactors, turbines, and generators, as well as a map of the site, all the buildings and their functions, including the main control room in the South Service Building, labeled, which was incredible, and DeCamp had to suppress a smile. He was here to damage the facility, and they had given him a blueprint of the bloody place.

"You'll need this as well," she said, handing him a bright orange visitor's pass on a lanyard. "Please keep it around your neck and in plain sight at all times. Our Barker security people get nervous otherwise."

"Of course," DeCamp said.

As well they should. It hadn't been difficult to dredge up profiles on most of the two dozen or so security people and any number of so-called security lapses over the past eight or ten years, including the shortcuts that guards on patrol routinely took, apparently because they'd wanted to get back inside and watch television. Early in 2003 some new fuel containers had been delivered to the plant aboard a flatbed truck, which was parked just outside the radiologically controlled area (RCA) fence. But the containers were sealed at only one end, and no one had bothered to search them before they were admitted too close to the containment domes and the RCA backyard and one of the fuel-handling buildings. And this had been going on for some time before that incident. The year before, Barker's people doing access control duty let an unauthorized visitor into the protected area of the plant where he somehow managed to get inside the South Service Building without an escort and without being challenged.

The only really good improvement was the closed-circuit television system, with cameras in a lot of the sensitive areas. That information had not been available online, of course, but bin Helbawi had sent him a detailed sketch map of the camera locations, which he memorized, and for a hefty price a Swiss engineer, with whom he'd done business before, had supplied him with a device that could freeze any camera for a few seconds at a time. Disguised as an ordinary cell phone, entering 000 then * would activate the clever circuit, yet the device actually worked as a cell phone.

The tour group people, most of them middle-aged men and women, not too different in appearance from DeCamp, were passing through an electronic security arch one by one, after first putting their wallets, keys, watches, and cell phones into little plastic containers that were sent through a scanner. It was the same sort of setup used in airports, and just as easy to foil.

Putting the visitor's pass around his neck, DeCamp joined the queue, where he placed his wallet, watch, cell phone, and money clip with a few hundred dollars into a plastic tray, and when it was his turn he stepped through the arch under the watchful eye of an unarmed security guard in uniform.

Besides the man seated behind the scanner examining what was coming through in the plastic buckets, two other security guards stood to one side as the tour group gathered in front of an attractive young woman dressed in a khaki skirt and a blue blazer with the insignia of Sunshine State Power & Light on the left breast. She was smiling brightly and DeCamp noticed the two guards watching her rather than the people in the tour group, and he thought that it was a wonder that this place hadn't been hit yet. No one here seemed to think that such a thing was possible, let alone feasible.

"Welcome to Sunshine State Power and Light's Hutchinson Island Nuclear Power Plant," the young woman said when DeCamp and everyone else had recovered their belongings from the scanner. "My name is Debbie Winger—just like the movie actress."

A few of the men in the group chuckled.

"I'll be your guide for this afternoon's ninety-minute tour. But before we get started I need to go over a few ground rules with you. This is a working electrical generating facility, and therefore some areas are strictly off limits—simply because they're too dangerous. So, rule number one, everyone stick together and no wandering off on your own. Once we go out the door behind me, you'll be given hard hats. So, rule number two is that you wear them at all times." Her smile widened even further. "If you have a question, please don't hesitate to ask. And the last rule is, enjoy the tour."

TWO

Gail Newby looked down from the executive gallery at the tour group on the main floor of the South Service Building. The security people at the visitors center had presumably checked their credentials before the young tour guide had brought them over here, and when she was finished with her short spiel she would be bringing them upstairs and down the corridor past the conference room to the big plate-glass windows that looked down on the complex control room where the real work of the station was accomplished.

"Craziness," Gail muttered, and she was reminded of her heated discussion last week with plant manager Bob Townsend about the recent spate of security lapses. As independent chief of security, which meant she did not work for Barker Security, Inc., but directly for the National Nuclear Security Administration, NNSA, it was her job to oversee the overall safety of the plant. In that she was second in command only to Townsend, a fact he had sharply reminded her of again yesterday.

At thirty-eight, she was a slightly built woman with short dark hair, coal-black eyes, and wide glasses framing her pretty, oval face. She'd graduated magna cum laude from the University of Minnesota with degrees in criminology and business, and then four years later graduated number three from Harvard's law school. And as one of her classmates whom she'd dated during most of her freshman year said, she was definitely a case of beauty and brains if he'd ever seen one. But driven. He'd called her "the Ice Maiden," which had stuck with her the entire four years.

Her assistant, Lawrence Wager, also an NNSA employee, came down the corridor from the conference room where he'd set up the security arrangements for the meeting of a bunch of SSP&L top brass and a NOAA egghead from Princeton, which had just started a couple of minutes ago.

"Looks like we're running Grand Central Station," he said, leaning on the rail next to her.

Wager, in his early forties, was an ex-New York City gold shield cop who'd been forced into retirement after he'd been shot during a domestic dispute on the Upper West Side. He and Gail got along very well because their ideas about security were practically the same. They both had the cop mentality, his from twenty years on the force, and hers because she'd been raised by her father, a Minneapolis cop who'd been killed in the line of duty, and because of her background with the FBI.

She glanced up. "You got Townsend and everybody settled in?"

He nodded. "Could be blood on the table before it's done. She wants to close us down."

"Never happen."

"Why's that?"

"First rule of business—never screw with a moneymaking concern."

Wager, who was even shorter than Gail with a featherweight boxer's build and the square-jawed, no-nonsense television docudrama profile of the quintessential cop that in fact had landed his face in police recruitment posters and literature all through his career, had to laugh. "Until somebody decides to build a better mousetrap. Anyway, this place gives me the willies."

"Yeah, it affects a lot of people that way."

"But not you."

She shrugged. "The chances of getting hit by lightning are ten million times greater than this place turning into another Chernobyl. Our guys already know how to build the better mousetrap."

"How about Three Mile Island?"

"Different type of reactor, along with what was probably sloppy management," Gail said.

Because whatever disagreements she'd had, and in some ways still had, with Townsend they were never about operations, he had a first-class staff of engineers and safety experts here. But security had become a big enough concern in all 104 nuclear power plants in the U.S. that the NNSA had hired people like her and Wager for oversight. These tours were her one bone of contention with Townsend, who had bent under pressure from Homeland Security to allow public tours in order to prove that there was nothing to fear from a terrorist attack.

The New al-Quaeda had some sophisticated people out there looking for the right opportunity to strike the U.S. in a way that would be on par with 9/11. The CIA had been warning the director of U.S. Intelligence that the terrorists had become almost frantic in their efforts to hit us, because since bin Laden had faded from sight al-Quaeda had lost its luster. The opportunity was ripe for something to happen, even though the Agency was expending a great deal of its resources to stop such an act, which in itself was worrisome to Gail. The CIA had blinders on, paying too much attention to the evolution of bin Laden's followers instead of monitoring the bigger picture, looking for our weaknesses, watching for the unexpected attack to come from a completely unexpected direction.

It was the same mistake her father had made that had cost him his life. He'd been working street crimes, and he and his partner had been tracking the small-time drug dealers, trying to follow the links up to the big suppliers. The night he was killed in downtown Minneapolis near the old Greyhound bus depot, he had been dressed as a hustler in a flashy suit and gaudy gold jewelry, talking with one of the small-time street dealers, pressing the kid for a big score. So big it would have to go to one of the suppliers.

A bus had dropped off a load of passengers and as some of them began to straggle out of the depot, a street bum came up behind an old woman struggling with her suitcase, knocked her to her knees, and tried to grab her purse.

Gail had heard the story from her dad's partner at the funeral, but it wasn't until she'd become a cop herself that she'd been able to see the file. The woman had screamed for help, and her dad, figuring being a Good Samaritan was better than being supercop, turned away from the drug deal to help the woman.

But the street bum, who'd had a long record of petty thefts, public drunkenness, and urinating in front of a school bus loaded with kids, was armed with a .38 Midnight Special, which he pulled and fired, one shot hitting Officer Newby in the heart, dropping him on the spot.

Before the bum got three steps, Officer Newby's partner shot and killed the man, but by then it was far too late.

It was a mistake that had cost him his life when Gail was nine years old, and every day of her life since she had been angry with him for leaving her so soon, leaving her to a mother who became a drunk and who'd slept with any man who would have her until sclerosis of the liver ended her life. And every day of her life she'd desperately wanted to prove that she was a better cop than he had been. Her near-manic drive had put off just about every man she'd ever met, except for one, and he'd been the exception. Perhaps he'd even been a father figure. But he had been in the middle of dealing with his own personal tragedy, so she'd known even though she'd thrown herself at him that they could never have a real relationship. And maybe she'd been punishing herself again.

Christ, there were days like this when all that past came roaring at her like a jumbo jet, so that she had trouble not despising who and what she had become.

The tour guide pointed toward the open stairway from the entry hall and she started her group that way.

"Want me to tag along with them?" Wager asked.

She had gotten up on the wrong side of the bed this morning, and now she was bitchy. It was nothing more than that. She shook her head. "We have to put up with this sort of thing, no getting around it."

Wager knew her moods. "I'll keep an eye on the monitors," he said. "But from here they look harmless."

"Yeah," Gail said. "If you need me I'll be outside, seeing how our guys are doing." She often wandered around the facility, carrying her FM communications radio that not only kept her in touch with the Barker guards, but could also monitor any of the closed-circuit television cameras. Since she'd started her unannounced patrols the security force had definitely sharpened up, not that they were all that bad before.

Wager went back to the security suite at the far end of the corridor, and Gail waited for the tour group to come up to the second floor and walk past her. The tour guide nodded and smiled.

"Good afternoon, Ms. Newby," she said brightly.

Gail nodded, but kept her eyes on the nineteen people in the group. Most of them were from the Orlando Chamber of Commerce, but four of them were add-ons, whose names and backgrounds Homeland Security had vetted. Ordinary-looking people. No Arab males with serious five o'clock shadows. No one wearing bulky clothing that could conceal explosives. No one who looked away, or looked frightened, or nervous or ill at ease. No one who looked the slightest bit suspicious.

But she couldn't relax, couldn't just go with the flow. It was one of the parts of who she was that she didn't find appealing. A friend had once said that being around her for any length of time was like biting on tinfoil. It probably wasn't an original line, but it had made Gail wonder that if her friends had that sort of an opinion of her, what sort of image was she projecting? When she thought she was smiling, maybe in fact she was frowning. A defense mechanism against hurt?

When the group had passed, she put on her hard hat and headed downstairs.

THREE

The group stopped at tall plate-glass windows that at this moment were closed by blinds on the inside, and DeCamp glanced back to where the woman had been standing by the rail, but she was gone. It was the expression in her eyes, the way she had scrutinized everyone, frowning a little, clearly disturbed about something that had attracted her attention.

He hadn't risked looking at her for more than a split second, nor had he taken the chance to read her name tag, but he was fairly certain she was security, possibly NNSA. And had she remained at the rail, watching them, it would have made things difficult. It would have been risky to slip away at this point, he would have had to wait until they were outside before he could change badges and go around to the back of the building. Every mission contained the possibility of the unexpected. It couldn't be helped.

The tour guide pushed a button on a small remote control device and the blinds opened on a room below on the main floor about fifty feet wide and twice that long that looked like something out of science fiction. Rack-mounted equipment with dozens of monitors and controls covered the front wall, faced by a pair of horseshoe-shaped desks, each manned by two men dressed in spotless white coveralls. The desks were equipped with several computer monitors and keyboards that were used to control the reactors.

A supervisor dressed in a dark blue blazer stood near his own desk directly below the window and between the two control positions. He was talking on the telephone.

"This is the heart of our facility," the tour guide began.

DeCamp had remained at the back of the group throughout the tour so far, and no one had paid much attention to him. Directly overhead, one of the closed-circuit television cameras, its red light illuminated, was angled toward the people standing in front of the viewing window.

He turned his head as the camera panned from left to right so that whoever was watching would not get a good frontal image of his face.

"Both of our nuclear reactors are controlled by the four operators and one supervising engineer you see on duty below. The room is manned twenty-four/seven as you can imagine, and the primary purpose of most of what you're seeing is safety."

The camera panned back to the center of the group and came to rest, the red light still on. Someone was looking for something or someone, and DeCamp thought it might be at the orders of the woman at the rail. But if she'd become suspicious, even had a hunch, she would have either stopped the group and asked to see their IDs, or she would have turned everyone back. To do otherwise, especially in this building, would have been more than foolish.

"The panels on the back wall look complicated," the tour guide was saying. "And they are, but put simply they're each divided into three parts. The first controls the reactor itself, along with the coolant, in this case seawater, and the steam generator, which you will see a little later. The second is used to operate the steam lines that feed the turbine, which generates the electricity we produce. We'll be going to the turbine room, and believe me, you'll be impressed. And the third set of gauges and monitors is in many ways the most important, because they control the reactors' emergency coolant systems."

She turned to look at her group. "You've probably heard the term scram, or scraming a reactor. Well, that's something called a backronym, which comes from the first nuclear reactor in 1942 in Chicago. In case there was a runaway nuclear reaction, which would have caused a meltdown, one man with an axe was ordered to cut the ropes that held the control rods in place. That would have immediately shut down the reactor. His job title was Safety Control Rod Axe Man—SCRAM. And of course every one of those systems has its own alarm in case anything goes wrong."

"Has anything ever gone wrong?" one of the women in the group asked. She seemed nervous.

"Sure," the guide said, smiling. "All the time, but that's what the panels on the back wall take care of. If one of the reactors gets a little too frisky, a few control rods automatically drop into place."

Another in the group started to speak, but the guide held him off.

"Nothing serious has ever happened in the more than thirty years we've been in business," the guide said. "Let me put it this way. Back in 2003 the Nuclear Regulatory Commission, which oversees our operations, extended our license on reactor one until 2036, and until 2043 for number two." Her smile broadened. "Even I will be an old lady by then."

A few of the guys chuckled, and DeCamp had to wonder if every American male thought through his dick, or was it just the men in this group?

In France it was different, subtler, but with an ever-present sexual tension that seemed to hang in the air. It was his world now, with Martine in their hillside home above Nice. Different than when he was growing up alone on the streets of Durban, Port Elizabeth, and Cape Town, places of stiff formalities among the whites and an almost feckless abandon among a lot of the blacks.

He was eight years old when a man shot his father to death in a waterfront bar over an argument about money. He could see his mother's face after the cops had come to the door of their Durban apartment to tell her what had happened. She'd become instantly angry, not hysterical that her husband was dead, but mad that she was being stuck with the bills and the responsibility for raising her only child. She'd railed at the cops, who'd finally turned and walked away.

And DeCamp remembered the look on their faces as well; they'd been surprised at first, but that had changed to something else, that even an eight-year-old could clearly understand. It was disgust written in their eyes, on their mouths, and pity, too. Later, when he'd become streetwise enough to pick just the right mark to rob so that he could eat, he realized that the cops weren't feeling any pity for his mother or for him, they had been feeling pity for the poor bastard of a husband who'd lived with a woman like that.

In the morning she was gone. No note, no money, just the furniture and dishes and a little food in the fridge and the cupboards. It took two days before the landlord realized what was happening, that the husband was dead and that the wife was gone, leaving an eight-year-old to fend for himself, and he called the authorities.

When DeCamp had spotted the cop car pulling up outside, he'd grabbed a jacket and ran out the back door into the alley and disappeared. His father had never trusted the coppers, and they were the ones who'd brought the news that he was dead, so he wasn't going to let them take him to jail. They probably did things to little kids in those places.

The following months were a blur to him, though he had been raped by a gang of boys on his second night on the street, and he remembered being hungry all the time, and cold and afraid. But gradually he learned to take care of himself, to run if possible or to fight back if need be.

He was a street-hardened kid of eleven when he'd come to the attention of Jon Frazer, a retired SADF lieutenant colonel, whom he tried to rob at knifepoint early one evening. That had been in Cape Town, and before he knew what happened he was on the ground, his right arm dislocated at the shoulder, and the knife skittering away down the alley.

"Lad, before you go up against a bloke, the wise tactic would be to study him first," the colonel told him.

"Fuck you," DeCamp said.

"An interesting proposition," Frazer, who as it turned out had been in charge of the school that trained special forces units, replied. "I'm in need of a batman, and you can have the job if you want it."

DeCamp said nothing. He hadn't known what a batman was, and lying there in the alley with the deceptively harmless old man who had disarmed him standing over him, he realized that there were a lot of other things he hadn't learned. Living in one of the shantytowns for whites, and working the streets for his existence, left no time to do anything except survive.

"Either that or we'll just pop round to the police barracks and let them take care of you."

"What's a batman?"

"What's a batman, sir," the colonel said. "An officer's assistant, and you'll fit the bill if you want. A place to live, three hots per day, and if you behave, a little money, and perhaps school." The colonel shook his head. "On second thought you wouldn't fit in. No, it'd be tutors."

The next eight years had not been without trouble, but DeCamp had learned to keep his mouth shut, his inner thoughts to himself, and he'd learned languages, history, mathematics, physics, and chemistry from a series of tutors, as well as the basic principles of weapons, explosives, combat, and hand-to-hand techniques from the old man. But he'd never forgotten the lessons he'd learned on the streets, mostly self-reliance, nor did he ever learn why the colonel had taken him in like that, except the old man had never been married and never had children and he liked to have sex once a month with his batman.

The last two things the colonel had done before he'd died of a massive coronary were to enroll DeCamp in the South African Military Academy at the University of Stellenbosch in the West Coast town of Saldanha, and ask some of his friends still in the SADF to watch out for the kid. "He'll make a hell of a fighter. Ruthless and smart."

DeCamp had graduated at the top of his class with a bachelor's in military science in the field of natural science, which was the most prestigious of studies.

The colonel's friends made good on their promises, and he was sent to a series of specialist schools in various combat styles, weapons, explosives, field tactics, infiltration and exfiltration, and HALO parachute jumps in which the fully kitted-out soldier jumped from an airplane at a very high altitude, to escape detection from someone on the ground, and stayed in freefall almost all the way down until making a low opening.

It wasn't long after that he was assigned to the Buffalo Battalion, and his real life had begun. For the first time he had a purpose, and he'd reveled in it.

The tour guide stood flat-footed with her silly grin. "Now if there are no other questions, we'll head downstairs the back way and go over to the turbine building."

No one said a thing.

"No questions? Good, then if you'll follow me."

DeCamp stepped aside as if he wanted to take a last look at the control room as the blinds closed, allowing the tour guide and her flock to pass him. He casually reached in his pocket and pressed 000* on his cell phone, which temporarily froze the closed-circuit camera just above the window, before he turned and fell in behind the last people in the group.

The corridor branched to the left past several offices, most of the doors closed, accessible only by key cards, to the stairwell and they headed back down to the ground floor, where DeCamp again used his cell phone to shut down the camera mounted high near the ceiling.

"You'll be issued earmuffs before we go into the main turbine hall," the tour guide was saying at the exit door. "It's the loudest place any-where in our facility. Even louder than the cafeteria on a Bucs game day."

She went outside first, and before the last of the group was out, and before the closed-circuit camera came back to life, a door to the left opened and bin Helbawi was there.

"Everything set?" DeCamp asked, keeping his eye on the outside door as it swung closed.

"Yes."

DeCamp slipped inside, the security door shutting behind him.

F O U R

The box lunches were tuna sandwiches on white bread or ham and cheese on rye, a small bag of potato chips, a pickle, and a bottle of Evian. The same sort of lunches Eve Larsen had been eating as she talked to scientists, energy people, and journalists around the country for the past fourteen months, trying to drum up acceptance if not support for her project. But it had become a tough sell once oil slid below the magic number of $70 per barrel, which is when interest in alternative energy sources began to fade.

It would be no different here today, she could see it in the bored faces of the eight men and one woman—all VIPs of one sort or another with Sunshine State Power & Light, which owned and operated this facility. But at least they'd been willing to listen, in a large measure because she'd promised to supply SSP&L with practically free electricity. An in-triguing thought, even though most of them had heard of her and knew something about the experimental work she'd done just offshore last year. Work that had ended in one death and a near drowning, that Eve—though no one else—had claimed was sabotage. And in another measure SSP&L had agreed to let her speak here out of a certain amount of wishing to get to know a potential enemy sooner rather than later. Don had called her "The Queen of the High Seas." The Fox crew had picked up on it that day aboard the *Gordon Gunther*, broadcast it as part of the mini-documentary, and it had stuck.

"Queen of the High Seas comes to the daring rescue of a crewman. Brains, beauty, and fearlessness. Who can say no?"

The nine people seated around the table in the spartan second-floor conference room in the Hutchinson Island South Service building that's who, she thought, as Bob Townsend, the plant manager, got to his feet to introduce her to the eight others. He looked more like a roustabout than the guy in charge of a highly complex and potentially dangerous facility, but he'd been in the business in one way or another all his career, and had a solid reputation.

"Dr. Evelyn Larsen has come here today to tell us a little more about her intriguing project to not only help solve our energy problems, including the dangers of nuclear energy, as well as our continued dependence on foreign oil, but how she plans to modify the weather worldwide." Townsend smiled. "For the better, we presume."

Eve smiled faintly, not rising to the same bait that had been thrown at her from the beginning.

"By way of a very brief background, Dr. Larsen comes to us from the National Oceanic and Atmospheric Administration–funded Geophysical Fluid Dynamics Laboratory at Princeton where she has been conducting her research into what she calls the World Energy Needs project.

"Her reputation and solid academic credentials of course have preceded her. I don't think anyone missed the *Time* magazine article on her two years ago in which it was suggested that she was short-listed for the Nobel Prize in Physics. So it is a distinct honor to have her with us today."

Everyone was looking at her as if she were a bug under a microscope. In some ways a dangerous, disagreeable bug, and it was the same look she'd gotten practically everywhere she'd given her presentation. She was getting tired of trying to explain herself, and of trying to raise awareness and therefore money.

"You've all received background information that Dr. Larsen was kind enough to send us in advance of her visit today, and if you've had a chance to look at the material you'll have a better handle on what she has to say."

Townsend was a nuclear engineer by training and Eve's project, which threatened to make nuclear power plants obsolete, ran opposite of everything he'd worked for his entire career, and it showed in the tone of his voice, his demeanor, and his entire attitude, one of barely concealed contempt. And fear?

He continued. "From my left around the table are Sarah Mueller, Sunshine State Power and Light's nuclear programs manager; Dan Seward, our vice president for environmental affairs; Thomas Differding, SSP and L's top engineer and chief of operations; David Wren, the company's assistant chief financial officer; Alan Rank, our vice president; Craig Frey, a member of SSP and L's board of directors; Eric Utt, vice president in charge of new plant development, and our own Chris Strasser, whose job here at Hutchinson Island is chief engineer."

Each of them nodded politely as they were introduced, but with no warmth, only a little curiosity that they were meeting the Queen of the High Seas.

"Dr. Larsen," Townsend said, and he sat down at the opposite end of the mahogany table from her.

She kept a neutral expression on her face, and promised herself that she would not lecture, nor would she let her anger get out of hand like it had done before. "It's counterproductive," Don had warned her. "You're the scientist—one of NOAA's most respected, so that's how you need to come across."

"They don't listen," she'd responded, knowing Don was right.

"Hell, even Bob Krantz won't listen and he's seen the data, he understands the conclusions, and he knows that the science is sound."

"It's all politics," Eve had said bitterly. Just as it was here in the Hutchinson Island boardroom.

"Damned right," Don had said. "So you better start acting like a politician if you want funding."

Eve got to her feet and managed to smile and actually mean it. These people weren't her last hope, but without SSP&L's cooperation she would have to move the first stage of her project elsewhere. But Hutchinson Island was ideal, and the experiment last year had proved it.

"Good afternoon," she said. "And thank you for agreeing to hear me out. If you've read the material my lab e-mailed you two weeks ago, I won't have to go over in any detail the science of my proposal, except to tell you some things that I'm sure you all know. By 2050 the world will need twice the energy we're producing now. Which is why more than thirty permits will be granted for the construction of new nuclear power plants in the U.S. alone."

"We've applied for several of those permits," Sarah Mueller said. "And our funding is already coming together."

"That's good to know, because the need for new power is acute, and of course it will take two decades before any power from those new stations will hit the Eastern Interconnect. And that's only one of the problems; there is a larger issue with using nuclear energy to generate electricity."

"Spare us the dangers of the ten-thousand-year half-life of spent fuel rods," Townsend said, obviously holding his anger in check. Without doubt he'd been hearing that argument for years, and was sick of it.

But Eve had known it would come up. "Not that at all," she said. "The problem is the huge amount of cooling water you have to bring in from the sea. Nuclear reactors generate a bunch of heat, and a lot of that energy is lost. It's the same with coal-fired plants where energy is lost up the stacks and into the atmosphere. Combine that loss, which is as much as fifty to fifty-five percent, with the ten percent loss from transmission lines made of aluminum wire, and more than half the energy you produce here is wasted."

"You're quoting Jeff Sachs now," Seward, the VP for environmental affairs, said. "But he was talking about fossil fuel emissions. His implication was for more nuclear stations, not less."

Dr. Jeffrey Sachs, who ran Columbia University's Earth Institute, was an economist who had argued in *Scientific American* that government-mandated cutbacks in carbon dioxide emissions from burning oil, natural gas, and especially coal, would create an economic blow to an expanding global economy so severe that billions of people would be adversely affected.

"You're right," Eve agreed. "But he was also warning that cutting back on carbon dioxide emissions *before* we develop new, cleaner, renewable energy sources, and technologies is the real culprit that could send us into a worldwide depression and very possibly war.

"Tom Wigley, who's a climatologist at the National Center for Atmospheric Research, wrote a paper for Nature a couple of years ago along with a political scientist at the University of Colorado and Chris Green, a McGill economist. Those guys argued that instead of mandating tougher emissions standards, we need to mandate the development of new technologies."

"Clean technologies, which Fermi did with the first nuclear reactor in 1942 in Chicago," Mueller, the company's nuclear programs manager, said. "As a result we got the bomb, but we also got Hutchinson Island and the other hundred and three nuclear-powered generating stations in the country, which I might remind you supply twenty percent of this nation's energy needs, do just that. Generate electricity cleanly."

"But not efficiently," Eve shot back. "And the new generating stations won't come online until it's too late. Even you admit that much."

"We've looked over the material your lab sent us," Utt, SSP&L's new plant VP, said. "We understand what you're trying to do, and your project is as intriguing as it is expensive, with no guarantees that it will work in the long run. Or, even if you do generate the power you say is possible from your water impellers without the wholesale killing of sea life or severe dangers to navigation, maybe the effects on the climate will be the opposite of what you expect."

"I'll be happy to send you all the data we've collected, along with the mathematics supporting my work," Eve said. "It's compelling. From just one impeller three feet in diameter—which did absolutely no harm to sea life—trailed behind my research ship last year, we were able to generate all the power our research vessel needed not only for navigation and communications equipment, but for the scientific gear, the galley, the air-conditioning and lighting and the electric bow and stern thrusters, which kept us in one place over the bottom against the nearly four knot northward current of the Gulf Stream. And we had energy to spare."

"It didn't work," Seward pointed out. "You had an accident in the second week when your transmission line parted and there were casualties. And that was with a three-foot impeller. What you're proposing is to place generators more than eight times that diameter, and hang them from oil platforms in the Gulf Stream. Am I correct?"

"Yes, to a point, but—"

Seward interrupted her. "If a cable large enough to support genera-tors of that size should break, you'll suffer more than a couple of deaths. And putting hundreds, or as you propose, even thousands of these rigs in the Gulf Stream, would pose more than a danger to navigation, they would be a blight on the horizon."

A number of the others around the table obviously agreed.

Eve held her temper in check. "Only one oil rig out in the Gulf Stream, twenty-five miles from here, with four impeller-generator sets that would be built by GE. It would be merely the second stage of my experiment, and my calculations imply that the power generated would amount to a significant percentage of what one of your nuclear reactors produces. When the full project comes online the impellers would be anchored to the seabed, fifty feet below the surface, where they'd pose no hazards to navigation."

"You're still left with a hell of a safety issue," Strasser, the plant's chief engineer pointed out, not unkindly. Of all those around the table he'd seemed the most interested, and the most sympathetic.

Eve wanted to say that there were safety issues in any power-generating station, and that the mandatory wearing of hard hats here would not do much if one of their reactors had a meltdown. She nodded instead. "You're absolutely correct, sir, but for two points. The first is that the safety issue would be ours, not SSP and L's until the experiment suc-ceeded. And, the incident aboard my research ship was not an accident. It was sabotage."

"That's not been proven," Alan Rank, the company VP, said.

"You're right, but if you'd like I'll send you the lab findings, which show that a massive power spike melted the cable. But that would have been impossible with the safety features built into the design. The only explanation was that someone had sabotaged those features before the impeller-generator was sent overboard."

"Someone from your staff, or the crew of your research ship?" Rank asked.

"It's possible, but I suspect it happened before the set got to us."

"Didn't you check it?" Strasser asked.

"Of course," Eve said, making sure that she was speaking in an even tone. "We think that one of the seals may have been tampered with. Everything worked within design specs for two weeks before the spike. Time for seawater to slowly breach the system until one or more of the safety checks were affected."

"You think," Townsend said.

"Yes, I think. In the meantime, the reason I'm here is to offer any power that we might generate to SSP and L essentially free of charge for the first year. We would be responsible not only for the generators, but for bringing the power ashore on undersea transmission lines. Your only expenditure would be building the connection point between our cable and your transformer yard, a cost that you would certainly recoup in the first month, selling free energy to your customers at the usual rate."

Sarah Mueller turned to the company VP. "We'd have to put this before the NNSA, to get their take."

"I've already approached them," Eve said. "In principle they see no problem."

"Who'd you speak to?" Rank asked.

"Deputy Secretary Caldwell." The NNSA was a division of the U.S. Department of Energy that was headed by Joseph Caldwell. "In fact it was his people who suggested I come here to speak to you."

Still she wasn't sure she had their interest even now, mentioning Caldwell and the DOE's tacit approval, though it was a powerful gun. It had been Don who'd suggested that end run, and her relationship with him over the past couple of years had in some ways given her the strength to cope. He helped her to be herself, to be strong without the nuisance of being possessive or any sense of ownership.

Their relationship was vastly different than the one she'd had, briefly, with her theoretical physicist husband, whom she'd married just after graduating with her second PhD.

"Let's think about starting a family," he'd said out of left field one morning on their way into their offices at Princeton.

She'd been surprised, though secretly pleased, but she'd turned him down. "Not yet, Sam. Maybe in a couple of years."

"It's the climate thing of yours."

"I think I might be getting close."

He glanced over at her. "Your math is spot-on so far, but I don't know if it supports the kind of conclusions that you're suggesting. A little far-fetched."

Dr. Samuel Larsen's doctoral thesis attempted to reconcile Einstein's relativity with quantum mechanics using a modified form of string theory to bridge the gap. He had his sights on the holy grail of theoretical physics—the TOE or Theory of Everything—which would explain the workings of the entire universe, large and small.

He was the only man she'd ever met who was smarter than her. But just then he'd pissed her off. "Far-fetched?"

He'd shrugged. "I didn't mean to make you mad. It's just that I'd like to start a family."

"Two years."

"Two wasted years."

Their marriage didn't last that long, nor did his work pan out. Two many flaws in both, too many dead ends, and out of frustration he'd practically ordered her to drop what he called her "nonsensical" work, come back to dry land, and become the mother that a beautiful woman like her was destined to be.

But for her, being a scientist was like being a Catholic nun; she was the bride not of Jesus Christ, but of her data and her concepts, stuff from which she could not simply walk away.

She'd told him the same thing that was on the tip of her tongue at this moment in the Hutchinson Island boardroom: Go screw yourself. Thank the gods for Don, because with her husband gone, her parents and siblings all still back in Birmingham and lost to her, she had no one else to turn to.

"We'd need more information, technical specifications, reliability predictions with the appropriate data sets, assuming you plan on first doing a test run for ninety days," Strasser, possibly sensing something of her angst, suggested.

"Six months, actually. We'll have dummy loads, and we will have the capability of controlling the actual outputs of our generator sets."

"We're interested in where your funding will come from," David Wren, the company's assistant CFO, said. He looked like a chief financial officer, his eye forever on the money trail. His implication being that if sponsors for the project were in any way competitors with SSP&L no deal with her would be possible.

And she began to calm down. She had their interest after all. "It's the second part of the project I wanted to discuss with you today."

FIVE

□

By now DeCamp was dressed in white coveralls, an employee name tag around his neck, and he stood with bin Helbawi at the door from the engineers' locker room to the corridor across from which was the door to the control room. At this time of the day, with lunch in full swing, those personnel not on duty were over at the cafeteria and wouldn't be expected back here for another half hour. Plenty of time to get in, accomplish the mission, which was quite simple actually and would only take a couple of minutes, then get out.

They were armed with 9mm Austrian Glock 17 pistols equipped with suppressors that bin Helbawi had smuggled in and hidden at the back of his locker. Each of them carried a spare nineteen-round magazine of ammunition in their pockets along with satchels that contained three one-kilo bricks of Semtex plus a half-dozen electronic detonators that had been modified so that once they were in place they could not be disarmed and if moved would automatically fire.

DeCamp looked at him. "Are you clear?"

"*Jie haan.*" Bin Helbawi said yes in his native Urdu with an almost dreamy expression in his wide, deep black eyes. His narrow, bony shoulders drooped and he stood as if he were in the beginning stages of some kind of a religious trance.

DeCamp had seen the same look on a mission he'd carried out for a lieutenant general in the ISI, Pakistan's military intelligence service, a few years ago in the Hindu Kush along the border with Afghanistan. His job had been to find a pair of CIA field officers quietly searching for bin Laden and kill them before they got to the ailing al-Quaeda leader and put a bullet in his brain. As long as bin Laden remained elusive, Pakistan's government could maintain the illusion that it was a staunch U.S. ally and continue receiving American military aid.

DeCamp had staged his push into the mountains from the city of Peshawar, which was the first decent-sized city on the east side of the Khyber Pass, with a pair of deep cover ISI field officers who knew the rugged tribal areas and who were smart but in the end expendable.

The day before they were to leave, DeCamp had been coming out of the hotel when a young man—perhaps in his early twenties, only a couple of years younger than bin Helbawi—had come across the street, clutching at his padded jacket. He'd had the same look in his eyes as bin Helbawi did now; what amounted to the same religious fatalism in the set of his shoulders and his gait. At that moment DeCamp understood what was about to happen and he ran off in the opposite direction, managing to get fifty or sixty meters away where he ducked around the corner of a stone building when the massive explosion destroyed the entire front of the hotel.

The young man had been a suicide bomber, willing to give his life for the cause. But whether or not DeCamp had been the target had been impossible to know, and after his successful mission, after he'd killed the two CIA officers as well as the two ISI agents assigned to him, and he'd returned to Nice one million dollars richer, he'd remembered the look in the young man's eyes, and swore he'd never forget it, because recognizing it had saved his life.

And now bin Helbawi, who'd been sent to him by the same ISI general, had the same look as if he were preparing his soul for paradise and not escape. It was a look that he'd carefully concealed during his training in Syria and evidently for the past ten months here, because in addition to being a dedicated missionary he was bright.

He'd gotten his initial education, and militant Islamic radicalization, as bin Laden had, in Jidda, Saudi Arabia, at the King Abdul Aziz University where he'd studied physics and mathematics. Al-Quaeda, needing bright new minds for another spectacular push after 9/11, had brought him from Pakistan and had footed the bill for his BS. After graduation they'd sent him to Paris for eighteen months to learn French, and then to the International School of Nuclear Engineering at Saclay, and finally the Kestner Division of GEA Process Engineering in Montigny, which provided engineering solutions for nuclear power stations where he learned more engineering and perfected his French.

By the time he reached New York, on a French passport under the name Forcier, with an impressive résumé, the first headhunter he'd approached got him the Hutchinson Island job in less than twenty-four hours. Nuclear engineers were in short supply.

Such a waste, DeCamp thought. All that education would end in a couple of hours because bin Helbawi knew damned well that he'd never get out of the control room alive. Or, if by some miracle he managed to hold out until just before the explosives destroyed the scram panels for both reactors, and if he could get to his car and make it through the gate and drive away, he wouldn't have the time to get outside the radiological damage path. He would take a heavy hit of rems that would sicken and eventually kill him.

Either way, he would not survive this mission and he knew it; he'd probably known it from the beginning, as did his ISI general. His willingness to die for the cause—not such a rare trait among Islamic extremists—plus his intelligence were the very reasons he'd been selected.

Afterwards, his mother, three sisters, and one brother in the tiny town of Sadda on the Afghan border would get some serious financial help, enough so that his brother could be sent to a real school in Islamabad, or perhaps even Jidda. A way out for them.

All that had passed through DeCamp's head in the blink of an eye, and he simply didn't care about any of it. He was here to do a job and then go home. There were no other considerations.

DeCamp keyed his cell phone, temporarily freezing the camera in the hall and, making sure that no one was coming, let bin Helbawi cross the corridor first and use his key card to unlock the control room door.

DeCamp had spent thirty days with him at an al-Quaeda camp in the desert outside of Damascus where they'd gone over, in detail, every step of the mission. Bin Helbawi was a lot brighter than the average terrorist, even brighter than most of the upper-level planners who'd worked with bin Laden and knew what they were doing, so he'd caught on very quickly.

The door opened and bin Helbawi hesitated for a moment, then they both went inside. There were no cameras in the control room.

Before Stan Kubansky, the supervisor, leaning up against his desk, realized that someone had come through the door, bin Helbawi disabled the card reader so that no one could get in, and DeCamp pulled out his silenced pistol and marched all the way into the room.

One of the operators glanced up and started to say something, but DeCamp put one round into his head, the force shoving him against the man seated next to him at the first console.

Kubansky turned, his eyes wide, his mouth half opened, and reached for the telephone, but bin Helbawi fired three times, one round hitting the engineer in the neck just below his jaw, and he lurched sideways, his hand going to his destroyed neck, blood pumping out in long arterial spurts.

"The blinds," DeCamp said, his blood singing again like it had in the old Angola days, and he shot the engineer in the head.

"Son of a bitch!" one of the operators shouted, and he reached for his keyboard, but DeCamp shot him in the head.

Still moving toward the two consoles, he shot the remaining two men, one round in each man's head, and the control room was suddenly silent.

Bin Helbawi was standing behind one of the consoles, a lot of blood on the computer monitor and keyboard and splattered across the desk, not moving as if he were in a trance.

"The blinds?" DeCamp prompted.

Bin Helbawi glanced at him. "Locked."

At the training camp in Syria, bin Helbawi showed DeCamp photographs and diagrams of how most nuclear power station control rooms were configured—the monitors, the safety devices, and their controls and most important the scram panels. Hutchinson Island was similar, but last week bin Helbawi had faxed several sketches, which showed the differences and exact layout, and DeCamp had committed them to memory while he waited in Miami.

The plan was simple. First they would destroy the panels that controlled the coolant systems, which would cause each reactor to overheat. Next they would destroy both scram panels, which would have sensed the overheat and automatically shut down the reactors. Once the Semtex was in place and fused, the only way to prevent a catastrophic meltdown would be to pull the panels apart and rewire them so the coolant and scram controls could be manipulated manually.

Bin Helbawi would remain behind until the last minute to make sure there would not be enough time for such a fix.

"I could do this thing myself," he'd said the night before he'd left Damascus.

They'd been sitting at a sidewalk café just off Azmeh Square downtown, the evening soft, the streets busy and noisy. "It's better if I come," DeCamp said, sipping tea.

"But I'm the nuclear engineer, not you. It's what I know. I can do this."

DeCamp nodded. "It's what you know. But my expertise is killing people. Are you an expert in this as well?"

"I can shoot a gun and mold plastic explosive," bin Helbawi had argued stubbornly.

"By the time this happens some of those people may be your friends."

"Never," bin Helbawi had replied angrily. He had gotten himself worked up, and DeCamp had reached across the table and laid his right hand over the boy's.

"No one doubts your dedication, Achmed, least of all me. I know what you're capable of doing. It's why you were sent to me. But you'll need patience, too. And trust. We'll work as a team. You'll see."

Bin Helbawi had looked away and remained staring at the passersby for a long time, as if he were trying to memorize the scene, knowing that he would probably never see it again, and DeCamp had allowed him his peace for the moment.

When he'd turned back, he nodded. "I was told that you were an expert, and that I should listen to you and obey your orders."

"Instructions," DeCamp had corrected. "You taught me about nuclear power stations and I taught you about weapons and explosives. We will do this together."

Careful not to step in any of the blood, DeCamp stuck his pistol in his belt and went around the computer desks to the panels and consoles on the back wall that controlled reactor one. He set his satchel on the floor, took out one of the Semtex bricks, removed the olive drab plastic wrap, and plastered it against the reactor coolant panel, his movements precise.

Bin Helbawi remained standing in front of the supervisor's desk, looking down at the dead man. He glanced over at DeCamp. "Stan interviewed me for this job," he said, his voice strained.

"Forget him, you have work to do. Get on with it."

"Bastard," bin Helbawi said, and DeCamp thought the remark was meant for him and he reached for his pistol, but bin Helbawi fired one round into Kubansky's body. "*Salopard.*"

"Enough," DeCamp said.

Still bin Helbawi hesitated for a few seconds, until finally he came out of his angry trance, laid his pistol on one of the computer desks, and came around to the panels and consoles for reactor two, and began setting the Semtex bricks on the controls for the reactor coolant pumps and the scram unit, finishing just behind DeCamp.

"How long would it take to rewire just the two scram panels to bypass what we've done here?" DeCamp asked.

"At least an hour, maybe a little longer," bin Helbawi said. He seemed to have steadied down. "They'd have to be careful not to disturb the plastique."

"The detonators are set for two hours, so once they're cracked you'll have to hold out here for seventy-five minutes. Can you do that?"

"Of course. *Insha' Allah.*"

It took less than two minutes to place the detonators and activate them.

"Seventy-five minutes," DeCamp said. He took off his coveralls and employee badge, and tossed them aside, then laid his pistol and spare magazine on one of the consoles.

"I know."

"Jam the door lock after I leave."

Bin Helbawi was staring at Kubansky's body, and he nodded but didn't turn around as DeCamp went to the door and opened it a crack to make sure no one was in the corridor. He keyed his cell phone, shutting down the camera, and without looking back stepped out of the control room, went down the hall, and out the back door where he headed over to the visitor's center, a bland expression on his face. The reactors would melt down in two hours and no one would be able to do a thing about it.

SIX

□

Gail was in the driveway between condenser building two and its turbine building when Karl Reider, one of the Barker security people at the visitors center, called her FM radio.

"One of the people on the noon tour just showed up here. He's leaving. Says he's sick."

"Are you holding him?" Gail asked, worried for reasons she couldn't define at that moment. But then Wager maintained that worried was her normal state of mind, while she thought it was nothing more than a matter of being a stickler for detail. A precision freak.

Reider hesitated for a moment. "There was no reason for it," he said. "He just walked out the door so he's probably still in the parking lot, do you want me to bring him back?"

Ever since she'd come aboard, discipline at the plant had definitely tightened up. She'd fired a couple of security people in her first ninety days, which had sent a definite message to everyone else: Don't cross the bitch. They were on their toes, no one wanted to get on her bad side.

Just now no one was around, and except for the heavy industrial whine of the turbines and generators, the day was bright, warm, and at peace, yet she had to force herself to keep on track, because she'd never believed in intuition—feminine or not. "No reason for it," she radioed. "What'd you say his name was?"

"Robert Benson," Reider said. "I pulled up his tour app, he's a schoolteacher from San Francisco. Short guy, slight build, light hair."

The security team had definitely sharpened up in Gail's estimation, and she remembered the man in the second-floor corridor as the tour group had passed. He'd been at the rear and had glanced at her briefly before looking away. Guilty secrets? Or just so nervous at being so close to a pair of live nuclear reactors that he had already been getting sick?

"Good job, Karl," she said. "I'll take it from here."

"Yes, ma'am. EE out."

She switched channels and pulled up a page showing the closed-circuit cameras around the plant, scrolled down to the single camera under the eaves of the visitor's center that was pointed at the parking lot and hit Enter. A black-and-white image of the half-filled lot came up on her FM radio's small screen. One car was just turning into the driveway from the beach road, A1A, and as it went left she spotted a lone figure just getting into a dark blue Ford Taurus parked next to the Orlando tour bus, his back to the camera. Moments later the car backed out of its spot, turned and went out to the highway and headed south.

He hadn't been in a hurry, and he definitely hadn't acted like a man who was nervous either because of his surroundings or because he had done something wrong and was making a getaway, and yet something about him bothered Gail. She couldn't put her finger on it, except that he had seemed almost too self-assured for a man who'd gotten sick and had to cut the tour short. On the way to his car he hadn't looked around nervously or over his shoulder to see if anything was happening behind him.

The screen on her FM radio was too small for her to make out the license number, but that would show up on the recordings in security, and there'd been something about the incident that made her want to follow up.

She switched back to the main calling channel as she turned and headed around the corner to where she had left her golf cart. "Post one, this is Newby," she radioed.

"Post one, Reider."

"Did you talk to this guy?" Gail asked.

"No, that would have been Deb Winger, the tour guide."

"I meant there at the center. Who checked him in and out? Who talked to him?"

"Monica checked his ID and gave him his package, but no one

checked him out. He just came in, laid his badge and hard hat on the counter, said he was sorry, but he had to leave, he was sick, and he walked out the door."

Gail got in the golf cart, made a sharp U-turn, and headed over to the visitor's center. Something wasn't right, damn it, she could practically taste it, smell it in the air. She really didn't believe in intuition, but sometimes she had hunches. "Is she still there?"

"She's on her lunch break."

"I'm on my way over, I want to talk to her," Gail said. "Newby out."

Some schoolkids and their teachers from Vero Beach were still in the visitors center, working with the interactive displays. They were scheduled for the one o'clock tour and had probably eaten their lunches on the bus on the way down. Reider came over when Gail walked in the back door. He was a big man, a high school football standout who'd never made it in college, so that now at thirty-one he could only hope for a supervisory position with the security company one day. But he'd sharpened up over the past year or so, and he never seemed to resent his job.

"Monica's waiting in the break room for you. Is there something I should know about?"

"I'm not sure yet," Gail told him. "But you did the right thing to call me. I don't like anything unusual to happen around here, if you know what I mean."

"I hear you."

Gail nodded at the other security officer and woman standing behind the counter and went back to the break room where the greeter who'd checked Benson in was seated at one of the tables. She was a middle-aged woman, slightly round, with a pleasant face but frizzy hair, and just now she looked nervous, most likely because Reider had filled her in about the Ice Maiden who ran security. She started to rise, but Gail waved her back down.

"Monica?"

"Yes, ma'am."

Gail shook her hand. "Look, this is probably nothing, but I just wanted to check out something with you, if that's okay."

The woman nodded and wet her lips. She looked as if she were about ready to jump up and run out the door.

"You've done nothing wrong, I just need to ask you about the guy you checked in. The one who came back a couple of minutes ago, said he was sick, and left."

"Mr. Benson. He didn't look sick when I processed him. He was sort of calm, and pleasant. Nice manners, soft-spoken."

"Did he say why he was taking the tour? He was a schoolteacher, maybe he was doing this so that he could bring something back to his classroom. Did he mention anything?"

"No. He just told me that he had an appointment later this afternoon so he'd join the Orlando tour. I offered the two o'clock because it was a much smaller group, but he turned that down."

Gail had another thought. "How often does something like this happen? Someone getting sick and leaving in mid-tour?"

"I've been here three years and it's never happened while I was on front counter duty."

"Has the tour guide been notified?" Gail asked.

"I don't know."

Gail went to the door and beckoned for Reider, who came over. "Has anyone told the tour guide that she's missing one of her flock?"

Reider looked sheepish. "No, ma'am. You're the only one I told."

"You'd better let her know."

"Shall I call her back in?"

"That won't be necessary," Gail said sternly. "But I want to see her in my office as soon as she's done. Damn sloppy."

"Yes, ma'am."

Gail turned back to the desk clerk in the break room. "Is there anything else you can tell me about Mr. Benson? Anything, any little detail that might have caught your attention? You said that he was soft-spoken, nice manners. Southern?"

"No, he was English, maybe Australian, or something like that. I don't think I've heard the exact accent. But it was nice."

"A foreigner?"

The woman shrugged. "He had a California driver's license."

Even easier to forge than a passport, Gail thought. "You said he told you something about needing to take the noon tour because he had an appointment? Did he mention where?"

Monica brightened. "As a matter of fact he did. He said he had to be in Jacksonville."

For a split second it just didn't sink in, but when it did Gail's heart tightened. The car had turned to the *right* on A1A. To the south, toward Miami. Jacksonville was to the north.

"Christ," she muttered, and she went back through the visitors center in a rush, ignoring Reider who'd looked up in alarm, and out the back door to her golf cart and headed back to the South Service Building as fast as the cart would carry her.

Steering with one hand she keyed her FM radio. "Security Center, this is Newby." They had a copy of Benson's driver's license, but before she called the Florida Highway Patrol, she needed the license number on the blue Taurus. She had an incredibly bad feeling about this situation.

"I was just going to call you," Wager came back. He sounded excited. "We have what might be a developing situation in the main control room."

"Shit, shit," Gail swore. She keyed the FM. "What?"

"No one's answering the phones, and the observation blinds have apparently been locked from the inside."

"I'm on my way."

SEVEN

DeCamp got off the island highway at Jensen Beach a few miles south of the plant, and once on the mainland headed for I-95, keeping a few miles per hour over the speed limit, while at the same time clamping a lid on his feelings of triumph.

It wasn't the money, exactly, though two million euros was significant, it was the almost rapturous feeling of accomplishment he felt when an operation of his design worked. It was almost like a drug to his system, really, and it was something he'd never shared with anyone before, not even with his comrades in the Buffalo Battalion, not even after a battle from which they'd emerged victorious, everyone pumped with adrenaline.

No deaths had been necessary this time, except, of course, for the four engineers and their supervisor plus bin Helbawi in the control room, and for the other people in the power plant when the reactors melted down, releasing a lot of radiation into the atmosphere, and for possibly tens of thousands directly downwind, but he'd not had to go in with a squad strength force of specialists like in the old Battalion days and risk casualties.

He had no ill will toward the local authorities who would have been involved in just such a firefight, but the operation this afternoon had been clean; it had been even elegant in its simplicity. And that was something he'd admired ever since the colonel had taught him the concept, simple moves in hand-to-hand, simple moves in the field, no wasted efforts, no unnecessary casualties to reach an objective. And it all had made perfect sense to him then as it did now.

Merging with traffic heading south on I-95, he took an encrypted sat phone from his bag on the passenger side floor and speed-dialed a number that connected him with an automatic rerouter in Amsterdam that would use a different satellite to connect with a number in Dubai. The two-second delay in transmissions was nothing more than a minor irritation.

Gunther Wolfhardt answered in English on the first ring. He'd been expecting the call. "Yes."

"One hour, forty-five minutes."

"Troubles?"

"None."

"The operation has taken longer than we originally expected."

This type of questioning was something new, bothersome. "It is what it is."

"And what of your team?" Wolfhardt asked. Although DeCamp never discussed his methods, or the names and qualifications of any team members he used—if any—the German had to believe that the operation was more than a one-man job.

"Untraceable."

Wolfhardt hesitated for a few seconds beyond the delay, and DeCamp, who'd met him only twice before this assignment, still knew him well enough to see the man's wrinkled brow because he'd not gotten the answer he wanted. "Dead?" he asked, his tone mild.

"Untraceable," DeCamp replied.

Again Wolfhardt hesitated. "You are aware of the consequences of failure," he warned.

"Certainly. Are you?"

"When I see the news on CNN your account will be credited. And there will be further assignments."

"For which I'll need more time."

"These will be of a simpler nature," Wolfhardt said. "But perhaps equally as important."

"We'll see," DeCamp said, and he broke the connection and laid the phone on the passenger seat. Wolfhardt's attitude was completely different this time. He'd never pressed for details until now, nor had he ever issued any sort of a warning. He'd come to DeCamp because of a recommendation from General Jan Van Der Stadt who'd been a close personal friend of DeCamp's mentor Jon Frazer, and who had been the Buffalo Battalion's commandant at the end, so there'd been no need to present bona fides or make silly promises or answer stupid questions.

But then it came to him that Wolfhardt, or perhaps the man or men he represented, was frightened. Because of the fourteen months it had taken to pull off this bit of business. But a man of the German's obvious background—there was no doubt in DeCamp's mind that Wolfhardt had been East German Stasi, the stamp was practically a scarlet letter on his broad Teutonic forehead—would know what planning and training had been necessary. He would understand the delicacy of such an operation. It was one thing to go into a situation—a bombing, an assassination, an act of sabotage—with no expectation of coming out alive but something completely different otherwise. And such operations took time.

Wolfhardt had evidently been under pressure to produce results. In a timely fashion because . . . of what? DeCamp asked himself. Money was a possibility, though where the profit would be in destroying a nuclear power plant was a puzzle. Certainly the German was not allied with an

Islamic radical organization, there was no fit there that made any sense. Nor had Wolfhardt ever made even an oblique mention of his employer.

They had met the first time by arrangement in Paris at the touristy sidewalk café Deux Magots, on Boulevard Saint-Germain across from the Saint-Germain-des-Prés church. The place had been crowded and in fact DeCamp, who'd arrived a half hour early to look over the situation, had waited twenty minutes before getting a table. When Wolfhardt had walked across the street from the church, and not from a cab or the metro, it had struck DeCamp that the man had also arrived early as a precaution.

"It's a good thing to be cautious," DeCamp said as the German sat down.

The waiter came and he ordered a café au lait and waited until it was set before him before he got down to business. "You've come highly recommended."

Nothing was required for DeCamp to say.

"I have a job for a man of your skills. An assassination."

DeCamp relaxed and he nodded. No doubt the German had made his preparations, careful to make absolutely certain that no one could hear their conversation. The area had been swept for bugs and listening devices, and the man's operatives were certainly nearby, otherwise he would not have spoken so openly

"I make no kills on French soil."

"This would be in Berlin," Wolfhardt said. "A German businessman who is a principal in the Frankfurt Stock Exchange. He has a lake house outside the city."

"Would there be family, staff, security?"

"Yes, all of that."

"And they would have to be eliminated as well?"

Wolfhardt shrugged, the gesture suggesting a near-total indifference. "That would be up to your discretion. For your own protection. But I will offer five hundred thousand euros for the man. Nothing for the others."

"Two fifty now, and the rest on completion."

"Agreed," Wolfhardt said, and he took a CD in a jewel case out of his jacket pocket and handed it across the table. The disk was labeled *Beethoven Sinfonien 2 & 8, the London Classical Players, Roger Norrington.* "You may need time to study the material before you accept the primary payment."

"That's not necessary," DeCamp said. He took a plain business card, no name, address, or phone number, only two sets of numbers—the first with nine digits, the second with ten—and slid it across to the German. "I'll begin immediately after the initial deposit."

Wolfhardt nodded curtly. "You'll have the funds within twenty-four hours," he said, and he rose to leave.

Driving toward Miami, DeCamp remembered that first meeting clearly. Up until the end, the German had been coolly professional, but just before he'd walked away, he'd said one more thing, his tone at that point almost congenial, almost friendly, one comrade in arms to another. "Good hunting," he'd said.

The businessman's name was Rolph Wittgen, and as it turned out the house staff had been dismissed early, and the security cameras and devices switched off. The only other person there that night was Wittgen's mistress. Killing both of them in the act of lovemaking and getting away had been simple, and two days later the second payment had shown up in his Channel Islands account. The entire affair from the meeting in Paris until the final payment had taken less than one week.

They'd met once again for a similar assassination, and then again fourteen months ago at a different café in Paris, and that time Wolfhardt had presented the same coolly professional demeanor as before, not questioning DeCamp's abilities to carry out the assignment—that of sabotaging the Hutchinson Island reactor—despite the size and complexity of the operations.

No questions, ever, neither before nor after an assignment, not until just now over the sat phone. It was puzzling, and DeCamp disliked puzzles unless they were of his own making. But as long as the money arrived as promised he decided not to take Wolfhardt's changed attitude as a sign of anything other than the unexpected length of time the assignment had taken.

Yet DeCamp had the disquieting feeling that the men he had worked for seventeen years ago had displayed the same change of attitude just before the Buffalo Battalion had been disbanded. They had been cutting their losses, disassociating themselves with the very men they had directed into battle. The war in Angola had been terminated, to no one's satisfaction, and the Battalion had been dismantled and swept under the rug, its continued existence a potential embarrassment to the South African government.

"If it should be otherwise, if we should have to leave our bleached bones on the desert sands in vain, beware the anger of the legions!"

Anger indeed, he thought. They had no idea what he was capable of. Always had been. Setting the LED counters ten minutes back, for instance. No mercy. No prisoners. No quarter.

And now there was the possibility of more assignments. More money.

EIGHT

Kirk McGarvey, dressed in jeans, deck shoes, a white long-sleeved shirt, and a khaki sports coat, got out of his rented Chevy and walked inside the National Air Guard's main hangar at Homestead Air Force Base a few miles south of Miami, pretty much in the same bad mood he'd been in for the past eighteen months. He was a tall man, in very good physical condition because he'd worked out just about every day of his life, and more than once that regimen had save his life. In his early fifties, still not too slowed down or mellowed even after a twenty-plus-year career with the CIA—mostly as a black ops field officer, which meant killings, but for short stints as deputy director of operations and director of the entire Company—he was alone as he'd never thought he would be at this stage of his life.

His partner, Alan Lundgren, slightly built with wire-rimmed reading glasses and a buzz cut, was formerly an FBI counterterrorism special agent. He had arrived on base a half hour earlier and was explaining the facts of life to a group of seven National Nuclear Security Administration Rapid Response team recruits gathered around him just to the left of the open service doors, about the distinct possibility of facing a terrorist one-on-one, which could develop into a hand-to-hand, life-or-death situation. All of them were nuclear scientists or engineers, not combat specialists, who'd signed on with the NNSA to help stop terrorist nuclear attacks on the U.S. Their eyes were wide; this was something completely new for them, and they were paying attention to what they were being told, and no one noticed that someone without credentials around his neck had come in.

It was an opening act that McGarvey and Lundgren had used at all the other training sessions like this one, their special ops assignment to bring all twenty of NNSA'S Rapid Response teams up to real-world speed.

A couple of mechanics were working on an F-15D Eagle jet fighter on the far side of the hangar, and parked in the middle of the big space was a MH-60G Pave Hawk helicopter, its rotors drooping, nobody around it just now.

McGarvey hung back to give someone a chance to spot him, and in that brief few moments of inaction his thoughts were drawn back eighteen months and a horribly black haze dropped over him like a dense smoke cloud from an oil fire. His last assignment as a freelance field officer for the CIA before he'd quit for good—he hoped—when the organization he'd gone up against had murdered his son-in-law, Todd Van Buren, who'd been codirector along with McGarvey's daughter, Elizabeth, of the CIA's training facility outside Williamsburg. Todd been on his way back there after meeting with an old friend in Washington when a pair of gunmen forced him off I-95 in broad daylight and shot him to death, putting a final insurance round into the back of his head even though he had already been dead.

But that wasn't the end of it. McGarvey had struck back, and in retaliation the same group had buried an IED in the road at Arlington Cemetery's south gate where McGarvey's wife, Kathleen, and their daughter, Elizabeth, were leaving after Todd's funeral, killing them both. And just like that he'd been alone; everything he'd worked for all of his life wiped out; the real reason, if he was being honest with himself, that he had made a career in service to his country was that he'd wanted to make America safe not simply for Americans, but specifically for his family, for the people he loved. And he knew a lot of people over at the CIA and National Security Agency and every other U.S. intelligence agency who felt the same, because it sure as hell wasn't about the money, or for most of them not even the thrill of operations, of being in the know.

Nothing was the same for him after that day. Todd's death had hardened his soul, but killing Katy and Liz had eliminated it. His enemies, America's enemies, any enemy had become fair game. Any method reasonable. No trials, no plea bargains, no deals, just destruction. He'd been an assassin for the CIA, his operations sanctioned, or at least most of them after the fact, but now everything was different. Simply put, he'd become a killing machine, and the job he'd been hired to do by the NNSA was to train its rapid response scientists how to recognize and deal with such a person, which had been a good thing for him, because at least for now he was in the role of a teacher and not of a killer.

Just lately, however, he had begun to chafe at the bit. Tough times and rough beasts were gathering for a strike. He could feel it in his bones, sense it in what for him had become like a strong electrical charge in the air, and his heart had begun to harden further.

Still no one in the group Lundgren was talking to had looked up, and this is how it was every other time, even though word must have spread from the other teams. It was a sloppiness that could get them killed one of these days, and stop them from preventing an act of nuclear terrorism, and it pissed him off.

He pulled his Wilson Tactical Supergrade Compact .45 ADCAP pistol out of the holster at the small of his back under his jacket and strode the last thirty feet to where the nearest man in the group stood listening to Lundgren tell them to make sure to maintain a peripheral awareness at all times and jammed the barrel of the pistol into the man's temple.

Before the man or anyone else could react, McGarvey cocked the hammer. "You're dead," he said, and he pulled the trigger, the firing pin slapping on an empty chamber.

"Jesus H. Christ." The man reared back, almost going to his knees.

McGarvey withdrew his pistol, ejected the empty magazine which he pocketed, slapped another into the handle, and charged the weapon before he reholstered it. "You weren't listening."

"We're not some fucking cowboys here!" the group's team leader, Dr. Stephan Ainsle, shouted. He was a youngish, curly-headed man with a prominent Adam's apple and intensely dark eyes, and he was shaken, too.

They all were. But Lundgren had warned them from the get-go to keep on their toes, to expect the unexpected; it was a vital part of the job they would be expected to do once they were fully trained.

"Then you'd better learn to get on the horse, Doctor, or else you'll be worthless to the program."

"We'll see about that," Ainsle said, and he started to turn away, more frightened than he wanted to admit than angry.

"You're not in the program until we sign you off," McGarvey said, holding his temper in check. He'd seen guys like this coming out of the Farm, with attitudes that got them killed or at least burned within their first ninety days in the field. It wasn't the training, it was the certainty that they were superior to the trigger-pullers. They were the intellects who would solve every problem with their minds, with superior reasoning. And such a line of thinking was common among these types.

Ainsle looked at the others on his team, still not convinced to open his mind. "I don't need this shit."

"But we need you, Doctor," McGarvey said. "You signed on to the program because you obviously thought so, too. If you'll listen up maybe we can teach you how to survive long enough to find and disarm a nuclear weapon before it detonates, maybe in downtown Washington or New York."

It had become a matter of face now, Ainsle's education versus a pair of men he took to be nothing more than well-connected thugs, even though he might know something of McGarvey's background. But unless he was convinced that he and his entire team would be scrubbed, which, in McGarvey's estimation would be too bad, he would walk away now. They'd left the safety of academia, for whatever reasons, to volunteer for some tough training, and at least a two-year commitment to serve their country in a potentially hot zone. They were definitely needed.

"I know why you guys are here, and it sure as hell isn't for the glamour or big bucks; you won't have a new theory named after you, at least not while you're with us. Nor will your names ever get in the media. No awards, no Nobel Prizes, no advancement at your labs." McGarvey managed to grin. "Hell, you probably won't even get women out of this."

One of the younger scientists smiled and shook his head. "I knew it," he said. He glanced at Ainsle and lifted a shoulder.

Still Ainsle, who was currently working on a government-funded fusion research project at Cal Tech, hesitated, and McGarvey wanted to go over to him and wipe the smug, superior expression off the man's face. But he loosened up, so that they could all see it.

"Come on, Doc, make my day," McGarvey said.

"Dirty Harry," Ainsle said, and the others laughed. "All right, so I'm an asshole. But I'm a goddamned smart asshole and I want to help stop the bad guys."

"Good enough," McGarvey said. "Because from this point on I want you to keep two things at the front of your minds. It's not a matter of if an attempt will be made to conduct an act of nuclear terrorism on American soil, but *when* it will happen."

"And the second is to expect the unexpected," Lundgren said from behind them. He'd slipped away while the team had given McGarvey its full attention. It was a part of what he called his and McGarvey's dog and pony show.

They turned around.

Lundgren stood over a medium-sized aluminum suitcase that contained a Russian-made compact nuclear demolition device. The cover was open and a single red light flashed beneath a LED display that was counting down, and had just passed sixty seconds.

Ainsle was the first to recover. "That's a realistic-looking mock-up."

"You willing to bet your life that it's a fake?" McGarvey asked. In fact it wasn't a mock-up, though its physics package had been removed. The Russian-made gadgets leaked a lot more rems than ours did.

"We have equipment that can neutralize the firing circuits," Ainsle said. "We've gotten this close, the rest is easy."

"Fair enough," McGarvey said. "Do it."

Ainsle glanced toward the Rapid Response team van parked just outside. "Our stuff is in the van."

"Get it."

"Fifty seconds," Lundgren said.

"You're running out of time," McGarvey prompted.

"I'll get it," one of the team members said, but before he could move, McGarvey pulled out his pistol and pointed at him.

"Holy shit, that's loaded!"

"Yes, it is," McGarvey replied reasonably.

"Forty-five seconds!" Lundgren suddenly screamed.

The mechanics working on the jet fighter glanced over, but then went back to what they were doing. They had been briefed.

"*Allahu akbar!*" Lundgren screamed. He picked up a short stock version of the AK-47 and fired a short burst of blanks into the air, the noise impressive. "Infidels! Die!"

Ainsle made to move toward the suitcase nuke but stopped short when Lundgren aimed the AK at his chest.

"Are you willing to die for your country, Dr. Ainsle?" Lundgren asked. "Thirty seconds."

"Are any of you?" McGarvey demanded.

No one moved. No one said a thing. And it struck McGarvey that they were like sheep being led to the slaughter, or more like rabbits who froze rather than ran when they knew they were about to be spotted by the hunter and killed.

"Fifteen seconds," Lundgren announced.

"Anyone?" McGarvey prompted.

"Ten seconds," Lundgren said. "Nine . . . eight . . ."

At 00 the red light stopped flashing and the LED went blank.

"What happened?" McGarvey asked, but it was a rhetorical question and Ainsle and the others knew it. "You didn't expect the unexpected and none of you were willing to give your life to try to stop the bomb from detonating."

"We would have given our lives for nothing," Ainsle said.

"In this case you would have been right. But you didn't come here prepared to win."

"All well and good for you to say with blanks in the rifle, and with a device that was a dud," Ainsle said. "In the field, facing an actual nuclear threat, it'd be a little different."

"He knows from firsthand experience," Lundgren said. "Believe me the man knows."

A look of recognition came into one of the team member's face. "Holy shit, you were the guy in San Francisco. I was in grad school and my dad who's FBI told me about it. Not the whole thing, but some of it."

"What's he talking about?" Ainsle demanded, though he was clearly impressed.

"Later," McGarvey said. "Right now we're going to take this scenario step-by-step so that you can save your own lives long enough to save everyone else's. Are you on board?"

"Yes, sir," Ainsle replied sincerely and without hesitation.

NINE

Gail took the stairs up to the second floor of the South Service Building two at a time, her heart racing as fast as the thoughts in her head. On the way across from the visitors center her imagination had jumped all over the place, out of control for the most part, but now that she was here, at the scene of the possible trouble, she was calming down. It was almost liberating. Now she could get on with doing the job she'd been hired to do. Accidents and terrorism were on the minds of everyone who worked in or near nuclear power stations. Since 9/11 those kinds of fears had become deeply embedded in everyone's subconscious, hers included.

She'd said nothing to the pair of security officers at the front entrance. Wager hadn't spread the word yet, but they knew something had to be going on; the Ice Maiden never ran around like this unless something was in the wind. And she could feel their eyes on her back.

At the top she glanced toward the windows that looked down on the control room, the blinds closed now, as they usually were, then turned left and hurried down the corridor to the security offices at the opposite end of the corridor.

Alex Freidland, chief of South Service security, was just coming out of the monitoring center where all the images from the closed-circuit television cameras around the power plant were fed, watched, and recorded by a pair of operators 24/7.

He was a local from Port St. Lucie, and one of the few black men Gail had ever supervised. Except for his attitude of expect no evil, see no evil, which was sometimes frustrating, he was a damn fine officer, dedicated and bright, and a real pleasure to work with. He was one of the very few men Gail had ever met who could make her laugh, and that was saying something.

"Still no word from the control room?" Gail demanded.

"They've probably got their hands full with something," Freidland said. "Happened before."

"Bullshit," Wager said, coming out of the monitoring center. "At least three of the cameras in this building were on what looks like a sixty-second loop. Frozen. I didn't have time to check the others, but the first is up here in front of the observation window and the other two lead right to the control room door."

"The guy who got sick in the middle of the tour," Gail said. This wasn't about a control room crew too busy to answer the damn phones; this was the big one. "Has anyone tried to override the control for the blinds?"

"Dave Bennet's on his way over," Wager said. Bennet was the plant's chief electrical and electronics facilities manager.

"What did you tell him?"

"That the blinds don't work and we need them up and running before the next tour group."

Gail suddenly remembered the school group over at the visitors center. "There are a bunch of kids waiting to take the one o'clock tour. Get them out of here," she told Freidland. "And there's another group in mid-tour wandering around somewhere, get them back on the bus right now, and then close the visitors center, and send all those people home."

Freidland hesitated for just a moment, but then headed down the corridor as he got on his walkie-talkie to start issuing orders.

"Get someone on the front gate," Gail called after him. "No one gets in without my clearance."

Freidland stopped and turned back to her, his eyes wide. "Are you going to evacuate the plant?"

"I'll know in the next five minutes."

"I'm on it," Freidland said and he hurried away.

Gail turned back to Wager. "Where's Chris?" Chris Strasser was the facility's chief engineer.

"He's at the meeting in the boardroom."

"Get him, but let's do this low-key for the time being," Gail said. "In the meantime has anyone tried to get inside the control room from downstairs?"

"The card reader has been locked from inside."

"Shit," Gail said. "I'm calling the hotline, see if they can send us a team. Soon as you get Chris back here, dig out the remote camera, and call Bennet and have him bring a drill with a diamond bit. We're going through the observation window, I want to see what the hell is going on down there."

Like Freidland, Wager hesitated for just a beat, apparently unwilling to take the situation to the next step, admit that they were probably in the middle of a terrorist attack on the plant. "Do you think this is it?"

"We'll see as soon as we get through the window," Gail said, and she went into her office where she speed-dialed the NNSA's hotline in Washington. The one man she wanted with her at this moment was somewhere out in the field, and even if she knew how to reach him, she didn't know if she wanted to admit she needed help. It was that stubborn streak that her father had once warned would get her into a peck of trouble.

"It's okay to hold out your hand for a lift now and then," he told her, Minnesota thick in his voice. She could hear him at this moment, and her stomach knotted. The two most important men in her life; one got himself killed in the line of duty, and the other had always been, at least by reputation, a dangerous man. And eighteen months ago he'd become a damaged man, volatile in the extreme, yet thoughtful, kind, sometimes patient, and above every other trait, he was steady. He was a man who could be counted on in an emergency, like now.

"Hotline."

Gail turned back to the phone. "This is Gail Newby, Hutchinson Island Nuclear Power Station. We have trouble of an unknown nature developing. We haven't been able to raise our control room crew for the past twenty minutes, nor has an attempt to override the security lock on the access door been successful."

The rapid response team concept had been developed to counter the threat of a nuclear attack by terrorists, by detecting the arrival of nuclear materials and/or complete weapon assemblies primarily by ship, but also by airplane, by car or truck, or even by foot or horseback across the Mexican border, or by snowmobile across the nearly three thousand mile, mostly unguarded border with Canada. It had not been designed to counter an attack on a civilian nuclear facility. After 9/11 the thinking had always been that such threats would come from the air.

"Are you under attack at this moment?"

"All I know is that our control room crew does not respond."

"Can you shut down the reactors from elsewhere?"

Gail could see the man sitting at a desk in Washington, the Situation Book open in front of him. But so far as she knew this scenario wasn't there. "I think so. But if the reactors go critical a lot of people will get hurt. A lot of civilians downwind."

"Stand by," the hotline supervisor said, and the line went dead.

"Come on," Gail muttered impatiently. Two security technicians monitoring the closed-circuit television monitors were looking at her. They hadn't been told exactly what was going on yet, but they had eyes and they could see that the Ice Maiden was agitated about something.

The hotline super was back. "I'm dispatching our team from Miami. They should be with you shortly. In the meantime contact your local authorities, and prepare to evacuate the facility."

"What about the FBI?" Gail asked, allowing herself a small bit of relief. Something was being done.

"I'm on it."

Gail broke the connection and speed-dialed Larry Haggerty, who headed up the small unit within the St. Lucie County Sheriff's Department that was tasked to protect the plant in case of an emergency, but mostly to coordinate the evacuation. Like the NNSA, everyone had expected an attack to come by air.

"We have a possible situation developing here."

"Okay," Haggerty said, and she could see him suddenly sit up. They'd worked together since Gail had been assigned to plant security, and although his persona and drawl were of the southern cop, he was sharp. "You have my attention."

"We've been locked out of our control room, and there's been no response so far. One of our rapid response teams is coming up from Miami, but I'd like you to stand by in case we have to bug out of here."

"I'm on it. What else?"

"If there's an actual problem, I might have a suspect for you."

Wager came back with Strasser.

"On site now?"

"No, but I'll get back to you with a license number as soon as I can. But first we're going to try to take a look at what's happening down there."

"Talk to me, darlin'," Haggerty said. "What's your gut telling you?"

"I'm worried, Larry."

"Keep me posted."

"Will do," Gail said and she broke the connection.

"What's going on?" Strasser asked.

TEN

McGarvey said the same words he'd been saying for the past eighteen months. It was as if he were in a tightly scripted play that was so well rehearsed he wasn't listening to himself, not even gauging the reaction of the seven rapid response team recruits standing around the suitcase nuke.

The picture of his wife's tearful face as she said goodbye to him at Arlington National Cemetery after their son-in-law's funeral was permanently etched in his brain. She had been just perfect to him at that moment, her eyes red and moist but still expressive and beautiful, clear windows into her sweet heart.

Less than five minutes later she and their daughter, Elizabeth, were dead, and the following weeks in which he went berserk, in which he'd become a killing machine—something he still was—had passed in a blur. But he'd extracted his revenge, and it was enough; it had to be enough because he was alone more completely, at a much deeper level than he'd ever been alone. And now this work with the NNSA was something like a balm to his spirit, so that at times like this he could switch to autopilot and simply cruise.

"But what you're talking about is racial profiling," Ainsle protested and he glanced at the others to back him up.

"You're damned right he is," Lundgren said. "Little old ladies with white hair usually aren't the ones who go around blowing up airplanes or smuggling nuclear materials into the country. It's why we take a closer look at men in their early twenties to mid-forties, heavy five o'clock shadows, maybe Muslims, maybe not, because chances are if you're looking for a terrorist he'll be in that group."

"Okay, how do we stop a nuclear attack?" McGarvey asked.

"By disarming nuclear devices. We have some pretty neat gadgets that can interfere with firing mechanisms. Shut the weapon down even if it's gone into countdown mode."

"But first you have to find it."

"We work with customs and with air marshals and the Coast Guard," Ainsle said, a little more sure now that his argument was the correct one. "It's not perfect, but we can put detectors aboard airplanes that will pick up radiation signatures from a couple thousand feet up."

"You have to have to have a reasonably good suspicion that there might be a nuclear device let's say in Boston's south side, or maybe somewhere in the Mall in Washington. You can't simply fly over every part of every city twenty-four/seven," McGarvey said, trying to keep a reasonable tone. But it had been the same with just about every group he and Lundgren had trained. Scientists were bright, a lot of them so bright they were starry-eyed idealists.

"That's the job of the CIA overseas, and the FBI's counterterrorism people here in country."

"So you're saying that your only job is to detect and disarm nuclear devices that someone else will tell you are here and point you in the right direction," Lundgren said.

"What are we doing here today?" McGarvey asked. "What can we say that will make your jobs a little easier, make you a little more effective as a team?"

Ainsle shrugged. "I don't have the faintest idea, none of us do, except that we were ordered to meet with you if we want to be on one of the teams."

"Fair enough," Lundgren said. "So listen to the man. We've already established that he's faced this sort of a thing before in such a way that none of you read about it in the newspapers. If you open your minds you might learn something that'll save a lot of lives, possibly your own."

It was busywork, McGarvey had to keep reminding himself. The Company shrinks said that he needed to keep his mind occupied if there was to be hope he wouldn't go around shooting people. But all the bad guys weren't dead. There would always be a never-ending supply trying to knock down our gates.

"We're here to sell you on a mind-set," McGarvey said. "A way of looking at your environment—your *entire* environment, not just your electronic equipment—while you're on assignment in the field where the opposition might not play by the book, or by any rules of engagement that make any sense to you at that moment."

"You're telling us to stay loose, stay flexible," Ainsle said. "And you're right, we saw that when you showed up out of nowhere and pointed a gun at us. Won't happen again. We've learned that lesson."

Christ, McGarvey thought. They all came from the same mold. "Four points not negotiable," McGarvey said. "These are the new rules. One: in the field you most definitely will use profiling as one of your most important tools. Not only racial profiling, but profiling of the kind that will make you notice the one person in a crowd who seems nervous, the one wearing a bulky jacket on a mild day, the one who won't look you in the eye, the van with heavily tinted windows coming around the block for a second time apparently looking for a parking spot when several are available, the one person who doesn't seem to fit."

"Paranoia," one of the young scientists muttered.

"Right," McGarvey replied. "Two: you're bright people, and very often you have hunches, in the lab, at home in the middle of the night, driving to or from work. The eureka moments when you suddenly have an insight. Gut instincts. Trust them in the field. If something doesn't seem right to you, it probably isn't."

"We're scientists, not trained FBI agents," Ainsle said. "We don't think that way."

"You will after we're finished here," Lundgren told them.

"Three: you will be issued weapons and will be given the training to use them," McGarvey said. "In the field you will shoot first and ask questions later."

"I won't—" Ainsle started, but McGarvey cut him off.

"If you want to be on a team, you will be armed. Four: give no quarter. Which means if you draw your weapon, you will keep firing until the suspect is down and unable to shoot back or trigger any device he may have intended to detonate. Center mass."

"I could kill him doing that," Ainsle said.

"That's his problem, not yours."

"Or her problem," Lundgren added.

All of them looked a little green around the gills, but some of them were beginning to see the light, McGarvey could read it in their faces. It was a tough world out there, and no one had asked permission if they could fly airliners into buildings, and no one apologized afterwards. The only way in which they could have been stopped would have been to profile them and shoot them dead before they got aboard the airplanes.

McGarvey's cell phone vibrated in his pocket. The NNSA's hotline came up on the caller ID. Lundgren was getting the same call, and McGarvey felt the instant stirring that something was happening or about to do so.

"Excuse me," he told the group and he answered the call. "McGarvey."

"This is the hotline OD, we have a potential class one situation at the Hutchinson Island Nuclear Power Station."

"What's the nature of the problem?"

"A possible incursion, by a person or persons unknown. Security gets no response from the control room."

"Has Gruen been notified?" McGarvey asked. Carlos Gruen was Team Miami's leader, and one of the fair-haired boys with the program manager, Howard Haggerty, up in Washington. He did everything by the book—exactly by the book—which meant that he had his nose so far up Haggerty's ass that it would probably take him all afternoon to extract it, gather his team, and actually make the decision to head up to Hutchinson Island.

"He's in the process of getting his people and equipment together."

"Stand by," McGarvey told the OD, and he turned to Lundgren, and nodded toward the Pave Hawk helicopter. "Round up the pilot, we need a ride."

"I'm on it," Lundgren said, and he broke the connection with the hotline and headed over to the ready phone by the door.

"Have the local authorities been notified?"

"In the process."

"The Bureau?"

"They're sending teams from Orlando and Jacksonville, but you'll probably be first on site."

"We'll take it," McGarvey said, and he broke the connection.

The scientists were watching him. "What sort of a problem?" Ainsle asked.

"Someone may have taken over the control room at the Hutchinson Island Nuclear Power Station."

A minute later a pickup truck came through the doorway and screeched to a halt near the helicopter. A pair of ground crewmen jumped out and started prepping the bird; removing the rotor tie-downs, disengaging the safety locks on the tail rotor, racing through their engine checks and walk around.

Lundgren came over. "The flight crew'll be here in three minutes. Have you called Gail?"

"Not yet," McGarvey said. "She'll have her hands full at the moment."

A squat tow truck came into the hangar, hooked up to the chopper, and once the wheel chocks were removed towed the machine outside.

"This scenario isn't in the book," Ainsle said.

"It will be tomorrow," McGarvey said, and he and Lundgren followed the helicopter out the door.

ELEVEN

□

"Break down the control room door, now," Strasser demanded. He was primarily a nuclear engineer used to tidy, if sometimes complex, solutions.

"Not until we find out what's going on," Gail told him. At this moment the safety and security of the facility were in her hands, and she still didn't know what was happening. Time had seemed to slip into slow motion. "I need you to tell me if the reactors can be scrammed from somewhere other than the control room."

"Yes, but it would cause a very large disruption on the grid, and we wouldn't be able to get back up into full operations for a considerable amount of time. Damage would be done."

"I'll take the responsibility," Gail said sharply.

"The company could lose a serious amount of money." Strasser was a large, shambling bear of a man with a heavy German accent. He was from Leipzig in the former East Germany, and had escaped over the wall with his parents when he was a teenager. He'd got his schooling in nuclear engineering at the Polytechnic in Berlin and then at the Julich Division of the Fachhochschule at Aachen, before coming to the U.S. to work at Los Alamos. He was a very bright man, but he had never outgrown his stiff-necked German precision.

They were standing in her office, the doors to the monitoring room and the corridor open. So far there was no panic because very few people inside the plant knew that anything was wrong, but that wasn't going to last much longer. In the meantime she felt like a small child being admonished by her elder.

"Do it," she told him.

Strasser glanced toward the corridor door. "Townsend should be informed."

"Just how much damage could a terrorist do in the control room?"

Strassser's eyes widened, and Gail saw that she had gotten to him.
"More than you want to imagine." He picked up the phone and called Bob
Holiman, the day shift chief operating engineer who at the moment was
working on something in turbine building two. "Strasser. I want you to
initiate an emergency shutdown on number two."

Gail could hear Holiman shouting something.

"On my authority," Strasser said. "But it has to be done on site, there
is a problem in the control room. Cut the power to the control rod HMs."

Control rods suspended above a reactor's core would drop down,
once a signal that something was going wrong was transmitted to the
HMs, or holding magnets, that kept the rods in place, immediately shutting down the nuclear reaction by absorbing massive amounts of neu-
trons. That was a function operated from the control room where
computers monitored everything from the state of the reactor to the
coolant systems and even the electrical power output. If anything went
wrong in the system the signal would be sent and the reactor would be
scrammed. In this case, where the control room was apparently out of
the loop, power could be cut manually, shutting down the HMs, which
would allow the weight of the control rods themselves, aided by powerful springs, to do the job. Shutting down the reactor would theoretically
take four seconds or less.

Gail used her cell phone to find Wager who answered on the first
ring. "I have the camera and I'm on the way up. Is Bennet there with the
drill yet?"

"No. Call him again and tell him to get his ass over here right now!"

"I'm on it."

"I'll hold," Strasser said, and he put a hand over the phone. "It'll take
a minute or two to start the procedure."

"What about reactor one?"

"Let's try this first, and see what damage is done."

"Specifically what trouble can we get into from the control room?"
Gail asked, even though she knew something of it, if not the exact extent.

Strasser glared at her, not in the least bit comfortable with even thinking about it; his lips tightened. "Much trouble."

"Come on, Chris, I need to know what we're facing."

"It could be as bad, maybe even worse than Chernobyl."

"An explosion?"

Strasser shook his head. "That's not possible, but the reactors could go into a catastrophic meltdown if the cooling controls were disabled and the scram panels damaged. A great amount of nuclear material would be released into the atmosphere."

"Everyone in the plant would be in serious trouble."

"Yes," Strasser said heavily, as if he regretted his own assessment.

Wager came down the corridor on the run, with the remote camera bag slung over his shoulder while speaking on his cell phone, presumably to Bennet, and Gail stepped out of her office to meet him as he broke the connection.

"Where the hell is he?" she demanded.

"He's on his way," Wager said. "He didn't know the situation so he wasn't in any hurry. He knows now."

"Ms. Newby," Strasser called from her office and Gail went back inside to him and her stomach flopped when she saw the expression on his face. He looked frightened.

"What?"

"We cannot scram from outside the control room. The circuitry has been blocked."

"Can't the power be cut?" Gail asked.

"No. But he's on his way over to reactor one to see if it's the same."

"It will be," Gail said, no longer any doubt in her mind that the man who'd dropped out of the tour, claiming to be sick, was somehow involved in what was developing. "Has anything else been affected yet?"

"Everything appears to be operating within normal limits," Strasser said.

"Can we monitor what's happening to the reactors from outside the control room?"

"We can watch our power outputs, and watch that the flow of cooling water isn't interrupted. But once that happens it will be only a matter of minutes before the situation would start to become unstable."

Wager had come into the office. "Look, how about if we cut off electricity to the control room. The lights will go out and their computers will go down."

Strasser started to object, but Gail held him off. "They could have rigged explosives to some of the panels that might react to a power failure. We just don't know."

"Wouldn't work anyway," Strasser said. "For obvious reasons all the key equipment in there is on a self-contained backup power system."

Make a decision and stick with it, McGarvey had told her during her training last year. But whatever you do, don't do nothing. If a situation arises, react to it immediately.

"Even before you have all the facts?" she'd asked.

"As you're gathering the facts." He'd smiled wistfully in that sad way of his, which she had found bittersweet and immensely appealing at the time. Still did. "Most of the time you won't get all the details until later when everything is over and done with."

"Until Bennet gets here, I want you to alert all the section heads to start moving out their nonessential personnel," she told Wager. "No panic, no sirens."

"What about Townsend at the rest of the brass in the boardroom?"

"Them, too. I want everybody to get as far away from here as possible."

"What do I tell them?"

"Anything you want. It's just a precautionary measure. But not a word about the actual situation to anyone other than Townsend. Clear?"

Wager nodded, handed her the camera bag, and went into his office to make the calls.

Gail turned to Strasser. "Stick with me, if you would, Chris. Once we get through the window and get a look at what's happening inside, you'll be a better judge than me what condition the computers and panels are in."

Bennet showed up with his tool bag, all out of breath and red in the face. The stocky fifty-one-year-old electrical and electronics technician had retired from the Air Force after a thirty-year career dealing with and eventually supervising the same sort of work around nuclear weapons storage and maintenance depots, including a stint at Pantex in Texas where nukes were constructed. In the time Gail had worked here she'd never seen the man in a hurry, or flustered, and who could blame him for keeping calm? After working around nuclear weapons, some of them hydrogen bombs, a nuclear-powered electrical generating facility was tame. But right now he was agitated.

"Why not use the card reader?" he asked. "I can bypass the lockout."

"Because we don't know what's going on down there," Gail told him. "I want you to put a hole in the lower corner of the window, the farthest away from the control consoles, and with as little noise as possible. I want to thread the camera inside. Can you do that?"

"Sure," Bennet said. "But it'll have to be slow."

"How slow?"

"Ten minutes, maybe fifteen."

"All right, get to it," Gail told him and when he left she stepped around the corner to the monitoring room where the two on-duty security officers had been listening to what was going on. "You spot anything usual, and I mean *anything*, feed it to me," she told them. "But I don't think this situation is going to last much longer before I order the evacuation." She started to turn away, but had another thought. "Look, guys, if you want to bug out I won't blame you, or order you to stay. Okay?"

"We're staying," one of them said, and the other nodded.

They were both so young that Gail almost told them to get out, but she nodded. "Good show."

Back out in the corridor Strasser had followed Bennet to the observation window, where the technician was setting up his drill. Satisfied that they were working that particular problem, she called Freidland on her FM radio. "Alex, copy?"

"Yes, ma'am.

"Where are you?"

"Just heading to the visitors center to make sure everybody got out. Has the situation changed?"

"I want you to round up as many security people as you can find and standby for a full evacuation. I don't want any panic. But if it happens everyone'll have to get as far away as quickly as possible. Haggerty will be sending his people as soon as I know exactly what we're in the middle of. But I expect we'll know within the next fifteen minutes. Stay loose."

"Are you aware that people are already heading out?" Freidland asked.

"Right. Nonessential personnel."

"Well, a lot of those nonessential folks don't look too happy. Matter of fact they're scared."

"We'll have to deal with whatever comes our way."

"I hear you," Freidland replied.

Wager came out of his office. "The word's gone out."

"Alex says the exodus has already started, and so has the panic," Gail told him. "Bennet says it might take as long as fifteen minutes to get through the glass. Go let Townsend know what's going on, and it's his call but he might think about getting those people out of here. In the meantime I'll get Haggerty in gear."

Wager glanced down the corridor toward the observation window. "I never really thought it would happen this way, you know."

"Nobody did, Larry," she said, and went back into her office to call Haggerty again to get the local cops and emergency responders rolling. NNSA would have already alerted the FBI and as soon as she knew the exact situation she would be calling the governor in Tallahassee for help from the National Guard. It was a mess and for the first time in her life since her father's death she was frightened to the core.

TWELVE

The conference was beginning to wind down, and Townsend had managed to get beyond his prejudices and really see that Eve Larsen's project did have merit, even if it seemed far-fetched, especially the bit about modifying the weather. Yet that was the part that most intrigued him.

He'd worked the big coal-fired stations out in Nebraska and Montana and for a time in West Virginia and he'd seen firsthand the effects the emissions had on the air quality, even with the new electrostatic precipitators to take out the flue ash, and in some places stack gas scrubbers, which used a pulverized limestone wet slurry to clean up the exit gas pollutants. To this day, electrical generating stations were responsible for more than 40 percent of carbon dioxide emissions.

Just eliminating the coal-fired plants, which supplied half of all the electricity in the U.S. would have a massive impact on the weather, even on a global scale.

He wanted to believe in her science, and the impact it could have, and he could see that a few of the others around the table were beginning to get what she'd been driving at here.

The major stumbling block, of course, would be funding the next stage of her project, and David Wren, SSP&L's tightfisted CFO had suggested going to the oil companies themselves and ask them to give or sell her an abandoned Gulf oil drilling platform. At first she'd been startled, but Townsend had seen the glint in her eyes and the glimmerings of a plan as that notion began to strike her. The fact that Wren was only half serious meant nothing to the woman, and Townsend was damned thankful that she wasn't into nukes and working for him. She would definitely be a handful. Brilliant, yes, but almost certainly difficult.

Someone knocked at the conference room door and Townsend looked up, irritated as Wager came in. Eve Larsen was in mid-sentence and she stopped talking.

"Sorry to bother your meeting again, but could I have a word with you, Mr. Townsend?"

Townsend had been only mildly interested when Chris had been called out a few minutes earlier; they were generating electricity here and the chief engineer was always on call. But this interruption now, and the look on Wager's face, was troublesome.

"Excuse me, Dr. Larsen," he said, getting to his feet.

The others, especially Tom Differding, the company's chief of operations, gave him questioning looks, but there was nothing he could say, because he didn't know if there was any trouble, or what it might be, though he had a feeling whatever Wager wanted was serious.

"Please continue with your presentation, I'll just be a minute," he said, and he stepped out into the corridor with Wager, but waited until the door was closed before he asked what the hell was going on.

"Gail wanted me to call you out of your meeting," Wager said. "We have a developing situation that might mean evacuating the facility."

Townsend glanced down the corridor toward the security offices and beyond to where Chris Strasser and Gail were watching someone doing something to the observation window, and a little shiver of anticipation made the hairs on the back of his neck stand up. "Tell me."

"We've had no answer from the control room supervisor or crew in nearly a half hour, and Gail thinks that it's a real possibility someone has taken over down there. The card reader on the door has been blocked, and when Chris had Bob Holiman try for a remote scram on two it couldn't be done."

"Scram?" Townsend said and he was suddenly more frightened than he'd ever been in his life.

"Gail wanted to give you the heads-up, and she suggested that you finish up the meeting and get those people out of here. We're already evacuating nonessential personnel, and it's beginning to get ugly outside."

Townsend brushed past him and went down to the observation window. It was Dave Bennet on a knee drilling a hole through the glass, but slowly, making almost no noise, and just that fact was ominous.

Gail and Chris looked up, and he could see the concern and fear on their faces, even though Gail was trying to hide it.

"Okay, what's the situation? Larry told me something about it, but fill me in. You tried to scram two remotely?"

"It was locked out from inside the control room," Strasser said. "That's not supposed to happen, but somehow they tampered with the HM circuitry."

"I asked Chris to order it as a precaution," Gail explained. "It would have caused damage and cost the company a lot of money. But the alternative could be much worse."

"I understand that," Townsend replied curtly, his anger in part because of his fear but also in part that he'd not been informed until now. His input had not been asked for something so massively important not only to the well-being of the facility, but to its employees. "But what brought you to make such a unilateral decision?"

"No one answers from inside," Gail said, and he could see that she was getting angry as well.

"That's happened before. They may have their hands full."

"But they wouldn't have blocked the door lock, nor would they have tampered with the remote scramming mechanism."

"Has there been any changes on the status boards?" Townsend asked his chief engineer.

Strasser shook his head. "Everything's within the proper parameters."

"I didn't want to bother you until we had more information," Gail said. "Once Holiman told us that number two couldn't be shut down, I had Larry call you out of the meeting. I've already notified the NNSA hotline, and they're sending a team up from Miami. They've contacted the FBI by now and I gave the heads-up to St. Lucie County's emergency response people."

Townsend couldn't believe this was happening, didn't want to believe it. Troubles with coal-fired plants could and sometimes were bad, but nukes were the worst, because when they went bad a lot of civilians within the damage path could be hurt, the effects serious for the remainder of their lives; leukemia as well as a dozen other cancers could show up anytime, even as long as twenty years after an accident. The Russians knew all about that kind of a horror.

But he calmed down. "I assume you have a good reason for drilling a hole through the window."

"We want to thread a remote camera head inside past the blinds and take a look at what's happening down there."

"And?"

"We'll know when we get though," Gail said. "Dave?"

"Ten minutes, maybe less," Bennet said without looking up.

Townsend had developed a grudging respect for his chief of security in the year or so she'd been here. Although technically she was employed by the NNSA, and not Barker Security and therefore not for him, this was his facility, and in her first few months here he had come close to sending her packing. Generally she had been a pain in the ass—just the same as he imagined Eve Larsen would be, and for about the same reasons; they were both highly intelligent and independent women, nothing at all like his wife of twenty-seven years who was strong when strength was called for, and compliant when that was needed. His life was neat, private, and above all orderly.

The shades covering the observation window were closed, and he was about to ask why she just didn't open them, when he realized that function had probably been blocked from inside. The conclusion he was coming to was the same as Gail's, and he had to admit to himself that were he in her shoes he would have taken the same steps.

"We can't reverse engineer this thing?" he asked Strasser.

"The circuitry has been blocked from inside."

"That's impossible."

"Nevertheless that's the situation. Someone has managed somehow either to rewire the scram override panels, or rewrite some of the computer code."

"I understand," Townsend said. "But that couldn't have been accomplished in a half hour, could it?"

"No, sir," Bennet said, still not looking away from what he was doing. "Whoever did it knew what he was doing, and probably did the thing right in front of one of the shift supervisors."

"We're talking about someone on the inside. One of our employees."

"Yes, sir, a real pro."

A sudden strangely bleak expression came into Gail's face as if she'd just thought of something completely disagreeable, even horrible, and she looked at Townsend and Wager behind him.

"What?" Townsend asked.

"I think we need to start the evacuation right now," Gail said. "Immediately. Get everybody the hell away."

"I thought you wanted to wait to see what's going on down there first," Wager said.

"They're all dead, that's why they haven't responded."

Townsend had the feeling that someone or something was walking over his grave, but he also had the hollow feeling that she might be right, and he hated her with everything in his being for just that instant, until he came to his senses and knew that it wasn't her who had stabbed him in the heart, it was she who was trying to stop what was happening.

"I'll start it," Wager said, and he turned and rushed back to security where the code red would be broadcast everywhere throughout the facility, as well as to every law enforcement and emergency response agency within twenty-five miles.

"Get your people out of here, Bob," Gail said. "And make it quick, because once the sirens blow there will probably be a fair amount of panic."

"What about you?"

"We'll know the situation in a few minutes. Just get the hell away."

"I'll be back," Townsend promised, and he went to the conference room.

Everyone looked up when he came in, and most of them could see that something was wrong, and it showed in their faces.

"Ladies and gentlemen, a situation with one of our reactors is developing and merely as a precaution we're evacuating all nonessential personnel," he told them

"My God," Sarah Mueller, SSP&L's nuclear programs manager, said, getting to her feet. "Are you scramming the reactor?"

"Not yet," Townsend said. "But that may be next. For now I'd like everyone to get out of here."

"Where are you sending your people?" Differding, the company's chief of operations, asked.

"As far away from here as possible, Tom."

Everyone except for Eve Larsen was on their feet, and heading for the door. She was calmly putting the material she'd been using for her presentation into her attaché case.

"You too, Doctor," Townsend said.

"Are you in trouble here?" she asked.

He started to tell her no, that everything would be fine, but he couldn't lie to her. She was too bright, and she didn't seem the type to panic. He nodded. "Could be serious, we just don't know yet. Get away from here."

"Preferably upwind?"

"Yeah, something like that."

"Good luck," she said, and walked out.

Leaving Townsend listening to his own inner voices that ever since he'd gotten into nukes had been speaking to him about the inevitability of an accident. Three Mile Island had been bad, and Chernobyl much worse. This today could be catastrophic. And there would be others, because no matter how safe they engineered and built these things, they were nuclear engines after all. Not quite bombs, but damned close.

He picked up the conference room phone and called his wife. Their home was on Jupiter Island, just a few miles away.

THIRTEEN

□

Air National Guard left seat pilot, Captain Frank Henderson, flew the Pave Hawk helicopter low and at maximum throttle, generally following I-95 north along Florida's coastline that bulged a little bit to the east, out into the Atlantic, before turning due north and then northwest. Lundgren had gotten on his laptop and pulled up a site map of the nuclear plant, and showed it to McGarvey.

"The control room is on the ground floor in the South Service Building," Lundgren pointed it out.

"How about security?"

"Same building, second floor. I'm sure that Gail is right in the thick of it."

"No doubt," McGarvey said, and he glanced out the window at the interstate highway. Traffic was heavy, as it usually was on a weekday, but twenty miles from St. Lucie there still was no noticeable difference southbound than there was north. If a full-scale evacuation had been ordered the first ripples had not reached this far yet. But when it did, he figured it was going to get messy down there.

Since they'd gotten the call from the hotline he had gone over in his head the possible scenarios they would be walking into, none of which seemed the least bit attractive. Contrary to popular belief, nuclear reactors were not inherently unstable or even dangerous. Crashing airliners into the containment domes would probably cause a lot of damage, but not enough to guarantee a release of nuclear materials into the atmosphere. But the right team in the control room, willing to give their lives in exchange, could cause a great deal of harm, a catastrophic meltdown if the reactors were not allowed to be scrammed and the cooling pumps shut down or sabotaged. It would be many magnitudes worse than Chernobyl.

And Lundgren was correct, Gail would be right in the middle of it, chastising herself for allowing the incursion to get this far. It's one of the first principles he'd drummed into her head last year: prevention came first. Stop the guys from getting in the four airliners in the first place before they killed the crews and took over the flight controls. By then very little could have been done in the very short time once it was realized what was about to happen.

She'd allowed someone into the control room of her nuclear plant and she would be raving mad, beside herself, seething with a rage that she would not allow to show up on her face, in her actions, in her voice. She was the Ice Maiden on the outside, but still a lonely woman from Minnesota who in many ways was still mad at her father for getting himself killed, and therefore angry with just about every man she'd ever met.

Save one.

And there was a time when he'd been even more vulnerable than her. His wife, daughter, and son-in-law were all killed, leaving him to take a horrible revenge, and in the end he was a damaged, haunted man who had been open to the loving kindness of a woman. But almost immediately he began beating himself up for his weakness, and he still did for that weakness and his sometimes barely controlled anger. He didn't know how or where it would end for him. Or when, if ever.

The tops of the Hutchinson Island power station's containment domes appeared on the horizon right on their nose. And traffic on the interstate was beginning to pick up, most of it heading south.

McGarvey was wearing a headset. "Find a place to set us down inside the fence," he told the pilot.

"Their heliport is just off A1A north of the visitors' center," the pilot said.

"Inside the fence, Captain."

"Someone might take exception, sir."

"I don't care."

Lundgren showed the pilot the site layout on his laptop. "Get us as close to the South Service Building as you can," he said, pointing out the building that sat in front of and between the containment domes. "Looks like a staff parking lot."

"Whatever you say," the pilot said and he banked the helicopter off toward the island.

Lundgren shut down his computer and set it aside, then pulled out his pistol, a fifteen-round 9mm SIG-Sauer P226, and checked the load, before reholstering it high on his waist on the right side.

He caught McGarvey watching him and shrugged. Early on he'd admitted that he didn't like the idea of shooting someone, anyone, but if it came to a gun fight he wasn't going to rely on his less than perfect aim using something like McGarvey's seven-shot pistol. He wanted to pull off a lot of shots as quickly as possible without stopping to reload. And fifteen rounds beats seven, he'd argued.

McGarvey had never taken exception with Lundgren's tradecraft. He'd never once faltered, no matter the job that was set before him, and in the time they had worked together they had not really become friends—that was still difficult for McGarvey—but they had become trusted allies. McGarvey could count on him, and he was pretty sure that Lundgren felt the same about him.

The two bridges from Hutchinson Island to the mainland just south of the power plant were starting to jam up, traffic nearly at a halt. Police units were converging on the problem, but it was going to take a fair amount of time to clear up the situation, and that, McGarvey figured, was exactly what a terrorist bent on causing the greatest loss of life would have wanted. They would have wanted to wait until after the plant was evacuated and people were stuck on the roads before blowing the place.

The problem was the geography. Hutchinson Island's Nuclear Incident Evacuation Plan was the same as the county's Hurricane Evacuation Plan; the only way off the island, other than by boat or helicopter, was A1A—the narrow highway, more like a neighborhood street actually—that ran north and south, with only three bridges to the mainland, two a few miles to the south, and one to the north. It was a two-headed bottleneck that was already clogging.

"It's starting to get bad down there," he told the pilot. "Can you transport people out, somewhere upwind?"

Henderson and his copilot, Lieutenant Jim Reilly, nodded. "If those are your orders, sir."

"Good man, but I don't know how long the situation is going to remain stable. This place could blow at any minute. So it's your call if you come back for more."

"We normally carry a crew, including gunners, of six, plus a dozen fully equipped troops and their gear," Henderson said. "So we can probably manage twenty-five or thirty people each load." He glanced at his pilot. "We'll come back as many times as we're needed, or until you wave us off."

People were streaming out of the various buildings throughout the plant, including the visitors center and the South Service Building where there seemed to be some panic developing.

As the pilot flared over the middle of the big parking lot, several uniformed security people, realizing that the chopper was going to land, began herding people away as best they could. But it still took several long minutes before Henderson could set the Pave Hawk down.

As soon as they were grounded, McGarvey and Lundgren jumped down, and waved a pair of security people over, one of them a tall, black man who seemed completely unflustered despite all the chaos.

"Alex Freidland," he said, shaking their hands. "I'm chief of South Service Security. You guys from the NNSA?"

McGarvey nodded. "The whole team should be here shortly. For now I want you to take charge here. We're going to start moving people to high ground right now. Can you do that for me?"

They had to shout to be heard over the rising noise. People were still streaming out of the building and either racing to their cars and motorcycles or out the main gate to the highway where they hoped to catch one of the emergency buses that were supposed to be en route in this sort of situation.

"The bridges getting bad already?"

"It's going to be a major mess shortly," McGarvey said.

"Can do," Freidland said. "And if you're looking for Ms. Newby, she's straight up the stairs."

Some of the people were beginning to see the helicopter as a quicker way out and they started to storm it, but Freidland and several more of his officers held them back, picking out only those who had no transportation and were depending on the buses.

McGarvey and Lundgren fought their way through the crowd, roughly elbowing people out of the way, to South Service's main entrance in time to see a slender, deeply tanned blond woman carrying an attaché case struggle out the door. Before she could get five feet a half dozen or more people, men and women, burst out of the door, knocking her to the pavement, and raced past, even more people streaming out the building as the evacuation sirens began to wail.

Panic was nearly full-blown now. This was a nuclear plant and sirens were the last straw, and people crawled over each other to get as far away as fast as possible before the entire place went up in a pair of mushroom clouds. Only a handful of employees at any nuclear power plant were actually nuclear engineers. The vast majority were hourly workers from electricians and plumbers, to janitors and security officers and tour guides; these were people who were happy to have well-paying jobs, while at the same time believing in their heart-of-hearts that they were working under the threat of another Hiroshima or Nagasaki, especially after 9/11.

And now they wanted to be gone from this place as quickly as was humanly possible.

Another woman and a man were knocked off their feet just as McGarvey and Lundgren reached the blond woman.

McGarvey helped her to her feet as Lundgren was helping the other two, shielding them as best he could from the last of the employees leaving the building. And suddenly it was just the five of them at the entry.

"Get them out of here," he told Lundgren. "I'm going to try to find Gail."

"I have my own car," the blond woman said.

"I'll make a deal with you, Dr. Larsen, if your car isn't glowing in the dark by tonight, I'll make sure that you get back to fetch it. Right now I want you gone. Deal?"

Her mouth opened for just a moment, but then she nodded. "Deal," she said.

McGarvey spun on his heel and headed into the building.

"What's your name?" Eve called after him, but then he was inside, racing up the stairs.

FOURTEEN

☐

The main entrance security officers were gone, presumably outside helping with the evacuation, so there was no one to stop McGarvey from
going up to the second floor, taking the stairs two at a time. The building definitely had the air of not only desertion and emptiness, but of a
dark, dangerous cloud hanging just overhead; a crisis was in full bloom
here, and he could practically smell it in the air.

Gail was halfway down the corridor to the right with four men, one
of them on his knees in front of a large plate-glass window.

A large man who looked to McGarvey like a roustabout in a business
suit glanced over his shoulder as McGarvey came out. "Who the hell are
you?" he demanded.

"Kirk McGarvey, NNSA. Who are you?"

"Bob Townsend. I'm the manager."

Everyone turned around, and Gail's face lit up. "My God, Kirk, I thought
you were in Washington," she cried.

"Miami. Gruen is getting his team together. What's the situation?"

"Someone's locked us out of the control room," Gail said. "We're going through the window with a remote head video camera to see what's
happening down there."

"Why the evacuation?" McGarvey asked. "A lot of people are panick-
ing, and someone's bound to get hurt."

"We tried to remotely scram the reactors, but those circuits were
locked out as well." She shrugged, almost like she was back in training
with him and was waiting for his approval. "It was my call. Just to be on
the safe side."

"How many people are inside?"

"Five, a shift supervisor and four operators. But someone else could
have gotten in. I don't know how, and I'm not even sure it happened, but
my gut is singing." She explained about the man in one of the tour

groups, who'd claimed he was sick and had left. "He was up here on this level, and his group went down the back stairs and down the north corridor to the rear door over to the turbine buildings. The control room entry is off that corridor. He would have passed right by it. Ten minutes later one of my security people at the visitors center said the guy dropped off his pass and hard hat and left. When I brought up the camera in the parking lot he was just getting in his car, and when he got to A1A he turned right, to the south. But he told the people at the visitors center that he had an appointment in Jacksonville. To the north."

"Good call," McGarvey said. "How soon before you get through the glass?"

"Almost there," Bennet said.

Wager had set up a laptop computer and plugged the remote camera into it. The sharply defined image, displayed in color on the monitor showed the corridor they were standing in. The camera head itself, about the size of a pencil eraser, was at the end of a five-foot flex cable that could be controlled, left to right and up and down from the laptop's keyboard.

Bennet's diamond-tipped glass-cutting drill bit made very little noise. "It's not likely anyone inside will have heard anything," Gail said, watching.

McGarvey studied her profile, everything about her at this moment intent and tightly focused. She was doing her job the way she'd been trained by the NNSA, in part by him, and so far as he could tell she'd made all the right moves and for all the right reasons. She wasn't relying on happenstance. But he wondered if she still had a chip on her narrow shoulders for most men because of her father. When she'd turned around and saw him standing there, she'd seemed genuinely pleased, and not ashamed to let that emotion show for just second or two. And for just those seconds he was forced to reexamine his feelings about her, only he hadn't come to any conclusions. The situation was developing too fast for that sort of thinking, and anyway he wasn't ready. Later.

"Does anyone know who's supposed to be on duty down there?" he asked.

"Stan Kubansky is the shift super," Strasser said. "And if there really is a problem, it sure as hell wasn't him that caused it. I know the man personally."

"For how long?"

"Ever since I hired him five years ago."

"What's your position here?"

"Chief engineer."

"Good," McGarvey said. "You're just the man we'll need to evaluate the situation."

"We're in," Bennet said. He withdrew the drill and moved aside to let Gail insert the camera head, which she did with great care so as not to ruffle the blinds.

McGarvey and the others watched the computer monitor as the camera lens slowly cleared the blinds, the first images of the ceiling and light fixtures, until Wager flexed the cable to slowly pan the camera down.

Blood was splashed on one of the control panels along the back wall, and Townsend glanced at the observation window as if he didn't want to believe what he was seeing on the monitor was actually the control room.

"What is it?" Gail asked, sensing the reactions behind her.

"It's blood on the secondary cycle systems board for number two," Strasser said.

"I don't see any damage," Townsend said.

Leaving the camera cable in position, Gail came around to the monitor. "That's a lot of blood."

"Pan farther down," McGarvey told Wager.

The image on the screen slid down the panel to the edge of one of the horseshoe-shaped desks.

"Left."

Wager moved the camera head to the left until he stopped it on the image of the two technicians obviously shot to death, one of them slumped over his position, the other sprawled on the floor.

"Jesus," Wager said softly.

McGarvey looked closer. Both men had been taken out by a professional, a single shot to the head, but the backs of their white coveralls were splattered with blood. Someone else's.

"Any damage to the equipment at that position?" he asked.

"Not that I can see," Strasser said, his voice shaky.

"Left."

Wager panned left, and stopped a few feet away at the body of a man in a blue blazer. He'd been shot in the neck, the bullet probably severing a carotid artery that had pumped out a lot of blood. But he'd also been shot in the head. Two shooters, McGarvey figured. First the neck wound by an amateur then the head shot by the pro.

"Mother of God, it's Stan," Strasser said.

"Left," McGarvey said.

Kubansky's body crumpled on the tile floor in front of his desk, his right hand outstretched as if he were signaling for help or trying to reach for something, slid to the right of the screen, the image shifting now to the two technicians at the reactor one control position. Like the others, they'd been shot in the head and died before they could sound the alarm.

"They're all dead," Townsend said.

The shooter had to have been first class, McGarvey figured, but he also had to be well under Homeland Security's radar, otherwise he would not have been able to get inside, even with a false ID. Most hit men that good were on a lot of international watch lists, usually with fairly accurate descriptions, and in many cases fingerprints and even DNA on file, so the kinds of jobs they took required stealth, not openly walking into a secured facility somewhere.

But there was more. He was sure of it. If it was the guy who'd gotten sick in the middle of a tour, the one Gail had spotted driving away, but in the wrong direction, he would have done more than just somehow get into the control room, gun down the supervisor and four technicians, and leave. He had a plan and help. *Inside* help.

"Any damage to that control position?" he asked Strasser.

But the engineer shook his head. "Move the camera up," he said and Wager panned up, the image of the control panels along the back wall coming into view.

"Shit," Gail said, and everyone saw it.

A lump of plastic explosives, probably one kilo, was molded to one of the panels. Wires coming from a detonator were connected to a small device, about the size of a cell phone, with a LED counter.

"Is that an explosive device?" Townsend asked.

"Plastic, probably Semtex," McGarvey said.

"Well, if it explodes we can kiss all of this goodbye," Strasser said. "That's the primary control unit for all the reactor coolant systems. It monitors everything from the steam generator to the reactor coolant pumps and even the control rod indicators."

"Tighten the focus," McGarvey said, and Wager adjusted a control so the LED counter filled half the screen. It had just passed the sixty-minute mark, the numbers decreasing from 59:59.

"We have one hour to figure out how to get in and stop this from happening," Townsend said, when a blurred image passed on the monitor, momentarily blocking the LED counter.

Everybody had seen it.

"Someone's still alive down there," Wager said.

"Pull back," McGarvey told him.

The image broadened to include the entire control panel, but no one was in the frame.

"Left," McGarvey said.

The image of the LED slid to the right to another panel with another LED device. Wager tightened the focus. This counter was at 59:42.

"That's the scram panel for reactor two," Strasser told them. "With the coolant controls gone, and our ability to scram destroyed we'll go into a massive meltdown."

"How soon?" McGarvey asked.

"It'll start to happen within minutes once the coolant pumps stop functioning."

"Pull back again and go left," McGarvey said.

Almost immediately a man's image in profile filled the screen, and Wager pulled back a little farther.

"That's Thomas Forcier," Strasser said in wonder. "He's one of our engineers. Worked for Stan when he first got here."

But his words were choked off when the man they knew as Forcier turned directly toward the camera, and they could see that he was just finishing strapping two blocks of Semtex to his chest. He inserted detonators into both blocks and calmly began to wire them together, an almost saintly expression on his face, in his eyes, in the set of his mouth. He was a young man bent on making preparations for doing something good, even heroic.

"For Christ's sake, talk to him, Chris," Gail said.

The kid was connecting the wires to a simple switch, like the handle and trigger of a pistol.

"Does St. Lucie County have an evacuation plan in place?" McGarvey asked, watching the screen. He'd seen the same sort of look on the faces of terrorists he'd dealt with in Afghanistan. Bin Laden's acolytes, their religious zeal.

"Yes," Gail said. "But an hour won't do much for us. We're talking a hundred and forty thousand people in a ten-mile radius. The plan was designed to get away from a slow-moving hurricane."

"Nevertheless, get them started," McGarvey said.

Gail nodded tightly. "Right," she said, and she took out her cell phone and walked a few paces down the corridor.

"Gail," McGarvey called after her.

She turned around.

"Call the local weather bureau and find out the wind direction."

FIFTEEN

On the day the two pickup trucks filled with armed mujahideen warriors came into the ramshackle town of Sadda, one hundred kilometers southwest of Peshawar on the border with Afghanistan, Achmed bin Helbawi, known now as Thomas Forcier, was fourteen years old. Everyone was aware of Uncle Osama and the holy struggle against the West, but down here the war had passed them by. Mostly.

It was a school day and the children, all of them boys, ran out into the dusty street to see what the commotion was about, but when the teacher saw the guns he quickly herded the children inside. All except for Achmed, whose mother worried about him since he'd learned how to read at the age of six. "Your curiosity will be your undoing," she harped at him.

He was curious now, but not afraid. He was just a boy: and what could mujahideen with guns want with a boy?

A battered Gazik, which was one of the jeeps that the Russians had left in Afghanistan when they'd crossed the bridge, followed close behind the pickup trucks that, to Achmed's complete amazement, stopped in front of his parents' house. And suddenly he was afraid.

His father was gone, tending the sheep, and when his mother came to the front door of their hovel to greet the mullah who'd gotten out of the Gazik, Achmed ran home as fast as he could. His young brother Sayid was up in the fields with their father, leaving only their mother and three sisters alone—to face a man and two truckloads of armed warriors.

But by the time he reached them, his mother had begun to cry with a very large smile on her face.

Closing his eyes for just a moment in the control room, his right hand on the switch, he recalled that morning in exact detail. He'd been truly frightened, perhaps his mother was going crazy, crying and laughing at the same time, but then after the mullah had explained why they had come to Sadda, he was confused, deeply saddened, and overjoyed all at the same time.

"Achmed, we have heard very good things about you," the mullah, a very tall, stern-looking man with the traditional head covering said through his thick, gray beard, and the mujahideen followed his every word with rapt attention, as if they were listening to an important sermon. "Even in Peshawar."

Sayid had been removed from school when he was ten, because he was needed to help tend the sheep. But Achmed had been given special attention, even been taught from special books on algebra, the premier invention of Islam, geometry, physics, chemistry and languages—mostly English and French. And he was very good at his studies. He wasn't a genius, but he was bright, something unusual for a boy in this town, and after that day fearless.

The New al-Quaeda had gone searching for bright boys like Achmed, to take them from their homes and to educate them. He'd been sent first to Saudi Arabia where he lived with a devout family while he finished his secondary schooling, again with the emphasis on math and physics, then to the King Abdul Aziz University.

Once a year he was visited by someone from the Peshawar region who brought him news of his family. "They are well, Achmed. And if you continue to excel in your studies we will continue to provide for them."

Achmed agreed, of course. Really he had no other choice, and by the time he'd finished his second year at the university he was as fully radicalized as any other student—including Uncle Osama himself—had ever become there.

"You are now the hero of Sadda. Your people expect great things of you, as do we."

But very often there'd been long stretches of no laughter. He remembered that clearly now, holding the trigger. No fun, no games; there'd never seemed to be time even to play soccer in the street like he'd done as a boy at home. Nor did he much care for the limited television they were allowed to watch, though from time to time he did listen to music on the stereo tape player one of the other students had managed to smuggle into the dorm. It was Western and forbidden by the religious police, but not every student was there under al-Quaeda's direction, and the rich kids whose fathers were Saudi royalty were the most irreverent. Nothing would happen to them.

He opened his eyes and turned to look at Stan Kubansky's body lying in a pool of blood, his hatred and contempt rising so hard and fast that he could taste the bitterness of bile at back of his throat. The supervising engineer had been among the worst of the Americans Achmed had met, so profane and so proud of his atheism that sometimes he would talk and laugh at the stupidity of war—of religious war.

"And for what?" he would practically shout. "Ragheads killing Jews. Ragheads killing Hindis. Ragheads killing Brits, and French, and Germans, and Danes, and crashing airplanes here. Why?"

The first time Achmed had heard Kubansky's tirade he'd been struck dumb, his jaw dropping, and he'd almost stepped back, afraid that Allah would strike the infidel and anyone near him dead on the spot. But he had maintained his composure as he'd been told he must—his life and the mission would depend on it—but the deepest hatred he'd ever imagined possible had begun to smolder inside of him.

Each training shift he'd pulled with Kubansky hardened his heart further and he'd begun to pray in the evenings for the chance to kill the heathen, even as he was making subtle changes to the computer programs that ran both reactors, locking out any possibility of remotely scramming them, and smuggling in the Semtex, detonators, controllers, and the weapons and ammunition.

It was different after Saudi Arabia, when he went to France—first Paris where he studied French literature to perfect his language, and then to Saclay and Montigny for his nuclear training. And by then he had become fully integrated into French society, and there were even times, especially in Paris, where he'd had fun. He'd learned to appreciate jazz and smoking and drinking alcohol and dancing with girls who wore no head scarves, all activities his handler from Peshawar, who continued to visit him once a year in the spring, insisted on.

"Outwardly you are no longer a son of Islam," he was told. "In France you have your Saudi passport, but in the U.S. you will become a French nuclear engineer, and that is where your work for Allah will begin."

Finally, before he was to assume his new identity and travel to New York, he was sent to the Syrian training camp in the desert, well away from Damascus. The nearest settlement was the town of Sab Abar twenty-five kilometers to the southwest, and the camp was remote and desolate, another planet from France, but one he understood from growing up in Sadda.

He turned again and looked at the LED counters running down. If he truly wanted to survive he could try to leave here now. There wasn't enough time to disconnect the explosives or rewire the panels, or even to reprogram the computer. The main alarm indicator was flashing, indicating that the facility was being evacuated. It meant that the engineers, probably Strasser, had figured out something was going wrong, and when they couldn't reach the control room they may have tried a remote scram. All of that was inevitable, and the reason why he'd stayed behind.

And when his mortal body was destroyed, his soul rising to Paradise, al-Quaeda would help his parents, brother, and sisters to a far better situation; enough money to move into Islamabad where Sayid could get a real education, and life would become easy.

It was a way out for them, a real future, and a way to his salvation for the sins he'd committed since leaving Jidda.

At the camp his eyes had been completely opened for the first time; he'd finally been told the reason he'd been nurtured since boyhood. He was to become an al-Quaeda operative, a tool in the jihad against the West. He had a purpose.

And it was at the camp one evening, when a helicopter bearing the Syrian army markings brought General Mohamed Asif Tur, the Pakistani ISI officer who'd been behind his training, and Brian DeCamp with whom he would go on a mission.

Where General Tur was a dark, completely intense man who seemed to be in constant motion even when he was seated at a table, DeCamp was fair-skinned and calm. Achmed remembered his first impression of the former South African as a man who might have known all the secrets of the world, and had accepted everything, including his place in it. DeCamp was timeless, and that impression had not changed for Achmed during the thirty days in the desert, or at their last meeting in Damascus before he'd flown to London under the Forcier identity and from there to New York.

General Tur had taken Achmed aside that first night at the sprawling training camp, which appeared from the air to look like a Syrian army basic training center, and assured him that although Brian DeCamp was not a believer, neither was he an infidel in the ordinary sense of the word.

"This man is our friend," the general had said. "He is an expert at what he does, so pay special attention to him."

"An expert at what, sir?" Achmed had asked, but the general had smiled, not offended by the question.

"He will explain that to you, along with everything you will do together. Trust him, as I trust you. And may you go with Allah."

"And you," Achmed had replied.

All through his days at the training base, learning about weapons and explosives from DeCamp, who in turn learned about nuclear power stations from him, Achmed had asked himself the same question each night before sleep: I'm not angry. Why?

A deep anger seemed to lie just under DeCamp's calm exterior, General Tur was a man at war, and his handler from Peshawar was angry with the West, as were all of the al-Quaeda–financed kids at the university. Achmed thought it was the way he should feel. He'd accepted al-Quaeda's message about the evils of the infidels, but that had simply been at an intellectual level.

But it wasn't until he'd arrived here that he truly understood the nature of what Kubansky had branded as *radical Islam*. He was a soldier now, finally ready and willing to give his life for the cause. Not only that he thought that he understood the necessity, even the urgency of the jihad. The continued existence of Islam depended on winning a war in which the infidel West had vowed would stamp out all Muslims everywhere on the planet, would make the belief in a merciful and just Allah illegal, and would brand all of the Holy Land with the stigma of the Jews.

And ironically he'd learned almost all of that from Kubansky.

He closed his eyes again and he could see the hills and mountains behind his town; he could hear his mother's gentle voice instructing his sisters on their duties and responsibilities; he could hear his father and brother talking as they came down the street from the fields where the hired boy would remain with the flock for the night, and they sounded happy; and he could see the schoolroom so well that he could count the cracks in the walls, in the ceiling, and the swirls of dirt on the floor, and hear his teacher's voice calling his name.

But something was wrong, and Achmed's heart missed a beat, and he opened his eyes.

"Tom, Mr. Strasser wants to talk to you."

He didn't know who was speaking, and the voice was loud but distorted and it came from above, behind the observation window.

"Will you listen?"

And then Achmed saw the tiny camera head poking out from behind the blinds and he knew immediately what it was because similar remote video cameras were used to inspect the inside of reactor chambers.

It was time.

He smiled and took a deep breath and leaned backward.

SIXTEEN

□

Gail had finished her telephone call and came back as Wager, holding a bullhorn against the glass, was trying to talk Forcier down. McGarvey, watching the image on the computer monitor saw the sudden look of religious ecstasy on the young engineer's face and he knew what was about to happen.

"Down!" he shouted, and he turned and shoved Gail to the floor as a tremendous explosion blew out the observation window, cutting Wager to pieces and throwing Strasser back off his feet.

The tinkling of the falling glass raining down on them seemed to last forever, and McGarvey had been in this sort of a situation before so that he knew to keep his head down, his face shielded until it stopped.

"No one move!" he shouted.

Someone was swearing and McGarvey thought it was Townsend, the plant manager, and then it was over, and he looked up.

Strasser was sitting down against the opposite wall, a thin trickle of blood oozing from a cut on his chin. He seemed dazed, but his face and especially his eyes seemed to be okay.

"See to your engineer," he told Gail, and he went to Wager, but it was no use. The man was lying on his back a few feet from Strasser, his left foot folded under his right leg, the entire front half of his face and skull missing, splattered against the wall behind him. The force of the blast had driven the bullhorn into his head, followed by glass shrapnel. He wouldn't have felt a thing.

McGarvey turned to Bennet who was down on his knees, blood streaming from dozens of wounds on his face, neck, and chest, fragments of glass sticking out of his eyes. "Can you move?"

"Yes. How bad is it?"

"You're not going to die," McGarvey said. "No arteries were hit."

"What about my eyes?"

"I don't know."

Townsend wasn't hurt, but he was so angry he was clenching and unclenching his fists, and he was shaking, muttering something under his breath.

"Get out of here," McGarvey told him, helping Bennet to his feet. "And take him with you."

Townsend came out of his daze. "What the hell are you talking about?"

"You'll be needed to get this place put back together and organized. We're expendable, you're not. Now, get the fuck out of here. Out of the damage path as fast as you can."

Gail had helped Strasser to his feet, and she was staring at Wager's devastated body, her mouth tight, a hard look in her eyes.

"He's right, Bob," Strasser said. He was a little shaky on his feet.

McGarvey handed Bennet to Gail, and went to the blasted open window, not bothering to see if Townsend would really leave because he didn't give a damn.

The control room was in better shape than he expected it would be. Most of the force of the blast had been directed outward and upward. The son of a bitch had aimed his chest at the observation window meaning to kill at least the one trying to talk to him. As a result, his body, parts of which were splattered across the control desk for reactor one, had partially shielded the control panels behind him. The Semtex and LED counters were still in place, counting past 54:30.

Strasser joined him.

"Do you see anything obviously unfixable?" McGarvey asked the engineer.

"Just the explosives on the coolant and scram panels."

"I'll get you inside so you can take a closer look. Maybe he forgot something."

"How?" Strasser asked.

But McGarvey had already stepped up on the sill, and balancing for just a second leaped up catching one of the open aluminum trusses that held up the low ceiling. It bent slightly under his weight, but he hand-walked out to the middle of the control room, away from the pools of blood, and dropped the ten or twelve feet to the floor, rolling with the hit.

He had banged up his knees in the fall, and he had to hobble over to the door, but the electronic locking mechanism had been disabled so it wouldn't open. No time.

He pulled out his pistol and fired two shots into the back of the card reader, which sparked and the door lock cycled.

Gail was there with Strasser, her pistol out, but when she saw it was McGarvey she lowered her weapon. "We heard the shots, and I didn't know what the hell was happening."

He turned and went back to the control panels on the back wall and took a closer look at the LED counters, which had counted down to 50:00.

"My God, we need to call an ambulance," Strasser said.

"They're dead," McGarvey replied sharply. He understood the detonators that looked like pencil stubs stuck into the Semtex, but the LED counters were out of place. There was no need for them, or at least not something as big and as complicated as they seemed.

"Do you recognize the setup?" Gail asked at his shoulder.

"No," McGarvey said. He knew a fair bit about explosive devices and the means with which to detonate them, but this was something he'd never seen before.

"Can you disconnect the damned things?"

"I don't know. This is probably some sort of a fail-safe. Tamper with them and they'll blow." McGarvey looked up as Strasser eased one of the bodies away from the computer monitor for reactor two.

"Cutting out the ability for us to remotely scram the reactors was probably done here," the engineer said. "Maybe he rewrote the code. I need to get into the system to see what he did." He sat down, squeamish at first because of all the blood, but then he took out a handkerchief and wiped off the keyboard and pulled up the master program, which was a directory of all the control documents that were used to operate the reactors, the coolant and steam generators and condensers, the turbines and scram functions.

McGarvey glanced at the LED, which had passed 45:00. "You have about thirty minutes before we'll need to think about getting out of here."

"What can I do?" Gail demanded. "Goddamnit, I feel so fucking helpless, and guilty."

McGarvey thought that in a large measure it was her fault for not running a tighter security setup, even though this scenario wasn't in the playbook, but it wouldn't help to say it. The exact details of 9/11 had faded from the collective consciousness and a lot of people were walking around with blinders on. "You remember Alan Lundgren, from Washington."

"He's working with you now. Former Bureau counterterrorism man."

"An Air National Guard chopper brought us up from Miami, Alan's outside helping organize the evacuation, so he'll be nearby. But he's the explosives expert, I need him in here. You can take his place."

"At the heliport?"

"No, right outside in the parking lot."

It was obvious that she wanted to stay, torn between following McGarvey's orders, and wanting to help fix this problem. But she nodded grimly. "I might be able to retrieve an image of the guy who left the tour. The monitoring station is upstairs, just down the hall from the observation window."

"Later," McGarvey said.

Gail looked over at Strasser, whose fingers were flying over the keyboard. "Good luck," she said, and she left.

"Are you coming up with anything?" McGarvey asked the engineer.

"Nothing so far," Strasser said without looking away from the screen. "The remote scram control seems to be functional from here."

"Keep digging," McGarvey said, and he took a closer look at the explosives molded to the other three panels. Nothing complicated, in each case just a one kilo brick of Semtex molded between an in-the-wall-mounted unit about the size of a fifteen- or sixteen-inch flat-panel television set and a smaller panel of brightly lit push buttons beneath it. If the plastic went off, it would take out both panels and probably do a lot of damage to some of the other controls and indicators within a eight- or ten-foot radius, and then they would be in deep shit.

Like Gail, he was beginning to feel helpless. As the counters passed 40:00, he took out his cell phone and took several close-up photos of the LED devices then speed-dialed Otto Rencke's number at Langley.

Rencke was the CIA's oddest duck genius, on a campus filled with such people, and was in charge of Special Operations, which meant he thought about things that no one else had dreamed up. And whenever he came up with something, perhaps something new the Chinese were doing, or defeating a new computer supervirus, or predicting a likely military or terrorist operation aimed at us somewhere in the world—and he was never wrong—the director and everyone else on the seventh floor of the Old Headquarters Building sat up and took notice.

He and McGarvey had worked together for years, and over that time Otto and his wife, Louise, who worked at the National Security Agency, had become family to Mac and his wife. When their daughter and son-in-law were assassinated, leaving behind a three-year-old daughter, Otto and Louise took the child in as their own; no hesitation, no questions asked; it's what family did for each other.

Rencke answered on the first ring. "Oh, wow, Mac, is it you?"

"I have a problem I need your help with."

Rencke always wanted to talk about what was going on in McGarvey's life, about Audie, about Company gossip, and McGarvey almost always went along. But this time was different. "What do you have, kemo sabe?"

"I'm sending you some photographs," McGarvey said and he hit the Send button, as the LED timers passed 38:00.

"Okay, got 'em," Rencke said. "Oh, wow, you're in the control room of a nuclear power station, and you're in trouble."

"Hutchinson Island, Florida," McGarvey said. "It's Semtex and an electric fuse, but I've never seen timers like these."

"Not just timers. Probably remote controls too, maybe even monitors listening in to what's going on," Rencke said. He sounded out of breath as he usually did when he was excited or worried. "Who's with you?"

"For now, Chris Strasser, the chief engineer, and Alan Lundgren, who's been working with me at the NNSA."

"Okay, I'll run these downstairs to Jared, get his take. In the meantime I wouldn't screw around. That shit could blow at any minute and when it does it'll take out more than a couple of control panels, it'll take out whoever's standing in the way."

"One of those panels initiates a scram if something goes wrong."

"I see that," Rencke said. "And I think the other panel looks like coolant controls, and if these people were any good they would have screwed with the remote scram capabilities."

"Probably from the computer at the monitoring positions. Can you hack into them?"

"Nada. It's a closed system, they're not online," Rencke said. "I'll get back to you in the next couple of minutes."

"We don't have a lot of time."

"I see that," Rencke said, and the connection was cut.

SEVENTEEN

□

The LED counters passed 33:00.

McGarvey went around the control console for reactor two and watched over Strasser's shoulder as the engineer tried to figure out what had been done to his system. But he was a nuclear engineer, not a computer systems or programs expert.

"We're running out of time," McGarvey said, and Strasser looked up at him and shook his head.

"I'm getting nowhere with this," he said, frustrated and just a little frightened. "Whoever did this was damned good."

"What about the control panels themselves? Can we take them apart and rewire the circuits so that those functions can be accessed away from here?" McGarvey said. He wanted to light a fire under the engineer's ass; the man knew his stuff, but he was ponderous

"It's possible. But it'd take time."

Lundgren showed up at the door and pulled up short. "Jesus Christ, what a mess," he said, but then he spotted the Semtex and LED counters and went to the first panel.

"What are they?" McGarvey said, starting around the console.

"Stay the hell away," Lundgren said, his nose an inch from the LED counter. "This is practically a cell phone," he muttered. "Dual purpose.

A timed trigger, but it looks like it'll accept a signal input. The antenna is built-in. Definitely cell phone frequencies."

"No time to get a bomb disposal squad here," McGarvey said.

"I can see that, so we'll have to do it ourselves," Lundgren said. He looked over his shoulder at Strasser. "Are you the chief engineer?"

"Yes," Strasser said, getting to his feet. He was in some pain and it showed on his face.

"What are we dealing with here? What'll happen if these panels are destroyed?"

"The nuclear reactors will overheat and there will be a catastrophic meltdown that the containment vessel might not be able to completely handle."

"Will there be a radiation release?"

"Potentially massive," Strasser said.

"Carlos and his people just showed up," Lundgren told McGarvey. "From what I saw he only brought two of his team along. But Marsha is one of them, and she has her tool kit. If they'll just stop talking to the plant manager."

It was a bit of good news. While Carlos Gruen and his Miami NNSA team were highly trained to disarm nuclear weapons, Marsha Littlejohn was their expert on all kinds of explosive devices and detonators, easily on par with Lundgren. And although her personality was irrelevant at this moment, McGarvey remembered her as a cheerful optimist, the exact opposite of Gruen who found fault with everything and everyone. In advanced training, which McGarvey and Lundgren conducted at a weeklong workshop at Quantico, the team had been faced with a series of increasingly difficult tasks—everything from finding and disarming a nuclear device, to dealing with as many as ten armed and highly motivated FBI instructors playing the role of al-Quaeda fanatics—during which Gruen grumped his way, giving up when it became obvious the team was meant to fail. But Marsha never quit trying, always with a smile on her petite round face.

Lundgren pulled out a Swiss Army penknife, unfolded the one-and-a-half-inch blade, and probed one corner of the Semtex, digging out a tiny piece of it, and smelled it. "Good stuff," he said absently, turning his attention back to the LED timer, which was passing 27:00.

"I suggest trying to open the panels and rewire them," McGarvey said.

"We don't want to do that," Lundgren said. "Not until we know what we're dealing with. Could be motion sensitive, among other things. Might even react to body heat it someone touches it." He was studying the three wires leading out of the counter and up to the fuses. "Two of them complete the circuit, but I don't know about the third." He looked up. "But we caught a break. We're between the morning and evening land and sea breezes. Nothing's moving out there right now. So if this thing pops any radiation leaks should stay fairly close to home."

McGarvey's sat phone vibrated. It was Rencke.

"The LED units are almost certainly comms devices. Most likely on cell phone frequencies."

"We got that much, what else?"

"Is Lundgren there?"

"Yeah, and Marsha Littlejohn will be here soon."

"You've got good people with you, but make damned sure they understand that the detonation signal could come at any time."

"Stand by," McGarvey said. "Otto's on the line, and I sent him pictures of the detonators," he told Lundgren. "The Company's science and technology directorate is helping out. Anything you need to know?"

"What the hell's the third wire for?"

McGarvey relayed the question.

"The best guess here is a seismic sensory circuit," Rencke said. "Depending on what kind of a reading the unit receives from elsewhere that particular explosion will go off in a timed sequence with others. Jared thinks it's the kind of setup sometimes used to hunt for dinosaur bones buried too deeply for other means, and for oil exploration. The detonator reads the seismic returns from other explosions in the chain and decides what to do next."

"Why here?"

"Move anything in the wrong way, and the detonators will fire."

"You mean like another panel?"

"Yeah, and probably the control units that could maybe reroute cooling water. Just take it easy, Mac. Janet says your best bet will be disabling the LED counters."

"Alan thinks they could be heat sensitive," McGarvey said.

"Hang on," Rencke said. He was back almost immediately. "Probably not. But go tenderly."

"Will do," McGarvey said. He broke the connection and explained what Otto and the Company's S&T directorate had come up with.

"That's just fine," Lundgren said, disgusted.

"We can't touch anything in here?" Strasser demanded.

"No."

They all looked at the counters, which were just passing 23:20.

"What can we do?" the engineer asked.

"You've done all you can, it's up to us now. Get out," Lundgren told him. He glanced up at McGarvey. "Go pull Gruen's head out of his ass and get his team in here ASAP. Marsha's got the equipment we need."

"We're here," Gruen said from the doorway. "And I'm taking over this case as of now."

EIGHTEEN

Carlos Gruen was a roly-poly man, with a round, perpetually red face and the defensive attitude that many men who stood barely five feet two seemed to wear like a suit of armor. He was considered the fair-haired boy up in Washington, and his goal was to one day take over the entire NNSA, which was not out of the question. He had the credentials for the job: a Ph.D. in nuclear physics from M.I.T., an MBA from Harvard, and a lot of friends in the Department of Energy.

He carried two aluminum cases, each about the size of a medium-sized overnight bag, his glasses on top of his head, the collar of his powder blue coveralls properly buttoned up. He stopped all of a sudden when he saw the bodies and the gore, and the blown-out observation window above.

This was exactly the sort of situation McGarvey had been trying to drum into the heads of all the Rapid Response team personnel, but he'd suspected all along that no one actually believed they'd ever encounter something like this. They were scientists and technicians, not combat troops, and he could see dawning realization of what had happened, was happening here, in the momentarily sick expression in Gruen's pale eyes.

Marsha Littlejohn, tall, whip-thin, pale blond, a leather satchel slung over her narrow shoulders, stepped around Gruen, her expression tightening when she saw the bodies and the blood. But then she spotted Lundgren at the scram panel, and went directly over to him, ignoring McGarvey and Strasser for the moment.

"What's the situation?" she asked, and Lundgren explained what they up against, including the CIA's opinion.

Gruen's second team member stopped just inside the doorway. He was young, probably in his twenties, with the physique of a college football player, and like his boss he carried two aluminum cases that contained the equipment for detecting nuclear weapons, and for electronically interfering with the weapons' firing systems.

"This looks like your sort of work," Gruen said to McGarvey. "But since the shooting seems to be done with, why don't you get the fuck out of my incident scene."

"Nice to see you too, Carlos," McGarvey said. "Well equipped for the job at hand, and on time as usual."

Marsha had set her satchel on the floor and was pulling out some tools, and other equipment including a stethoscope and several small electronic devices each about the size of a pack of cigarettes or cell phone.

She looked up. "Oh, hi, Mac," she said pleasantly, a little smile on her full lips. If she was feeling any tension it wasn't showing. "You guys might want to get out of here, because we could screw this up."

"She's right," Lundgren said, and he too was calm. Behind him the LED counter was passing 22:00. "We're going to attempt to take the detonator circuit apart and disable the power supply, and it's going to get a little dicey. Somebody accidentally bumps into something and we could be in trouble."

Strasser was looking helpless, confused, and angry. This was his facility; he was responsible for the operation of the reactors and everything else of a nonbusiness and nonadministrative nature, and a dagger had been stabbed into his heart. Men he knew and trusted were dead, one of them the killer, the saboteur, and it was all too much for him.

"Leave now," McGarvey told him. "Find your plant manager and figure out what you'll have to do if we disarm the explosives, but more important what you'll need to do if we fail."

Marsha looked over her shoulder. "Everybody out. Now," she said.

Strasser left, but Gruen with his second team member remained at the door, just as frustrated as the chief engineer was. But this situation was out of his hands. Nothing he could say or do was going to help, and he knew it, and it made him angry. He needed to be in the center of things, he needed to be in control, and his attitude had always been the same: The road to the directorship was paved with good field decisions, good management of his resources, and innovative solutions, and he wasn't afraid to tell anyone who would listen.

"Do you need anything for backup?" he asked.

But Marsha didn't respond. She turned the LED counter on the coolant control panel over on its back, her movements slow, careful, precise, and she began to hum a tune from the back of her throat. She'd once explained that she was always frightened practically out her mind—spitless, as she put it—and humming distracted that automatic part of her fight-or-flight instinct so that she could do her work with a steady hand.

Lundgren was paying close attention to what she was doing, and copying each of her moves, his hands just as steady as hers, as he worked on the LED counter attached to the scram panel for number two.

The counters passed 20:00.

"I'll be right back," McGarvey said. He glanced at his wristwatch; it was a few minutes before 1:40 P.M. By 2:00 P.M. the situation would be resolved one way or the other, and for the moment it was just as much out of his hands as it was out of Gruen's.

"Doug and I will be out in the corridor," Gruen said. "If you need anything I'll be within earshot."

They went outside and McGarvey followed after them. Gruen badly wanted to say something, take a parting shot, but he just shook his head.

"They don't have a lot of time," McGarvey said. "So it's just a suggestion, but you might want to stay out of their way. Cut them a little slack."

"Get out of here," Gruen said.

McGarvey hurried down the hall and took the stairs to the second floor, past the blown-out observation window and Wager's body, and back to the security suite, deserted now, as he hoped the entire facility was.

A pair of offices—Gail's and Wager's—were down a short corridor from the reception area, and across from a small room with banks of closed-circuit television monitors built into a long horseshoe shaped console with positions for two operators. Behind them, another door opened to a room filled with a dozen or more racks of digital recording units.

Mac took a few precious minutes figuring out the system so that he could access the camera watching the visitors center. He brought the image up on one of the monitors. The lot was deserted of civilian personnel, and only a single St. Lucie County sheriff's unit was parked diagonally across A1A. The legend at the bottom of the screen showed a camera number and a date-time block.

Some of the other cameras showed various places within the facility, all of them deserted except for the parking lot directly outside, where the Air National Guard helicopter was just setting down. Strasser emerged from the building and headed over to a knot of a half dozen people, one of whom McGarvey recognized as Bob Townsend, the plant manager, getting ready to board the chopper.

McGarvey went into the recording room, where it took another minute or two to locate the unit that corresponded to the visitors center parking lot camera, pop the disk out, and pocket it.

Back out in the corridor across from Gail's office, he hesitated for a brief moment, wondering what he would find inside, what new measure of her he might discover, and in the next moment he wondered why he cared.

The answer came to him reluctantly as he hurried out into the main corridor and headed toward the observation window, Wager's blood splattered against the opposite wall, and pooled up under his body. He'd cared for someone all of his life, and those kinds of feelings were like unbreakable habits reinforced each time he entered a relationship. At this stage with his wife, daughter, and son-in-law dead, the habit was still alive and active inside of him, perhaps stronger than ever, and he couldn't help from wondering about Gail; couldn't help wondering about himself.

He glanced at his wristwatch, it was coming up on 1:50 P.M., as he reached the observation window. Still moving, he glanced down. Lundgren and Marsha had shifted over to the rigged panels for reactor one, and were hunched over their work. Both LED counters on reactor two lay on a tray beneath the panels, their batteries disconnected, as was one of the counters for reactor one, and for the first time since he'd arrived he had genuine hope that they'd come on time because there was still ten minutes left on the last LED counter.

He was just past the window when a bright flash caught the corner of his eye, and he turned his head as the explosion disintegrated Marsha's and Alan's upper torsos and heads in a single haze of blood, and metal parts, and dust from somewhere.

It was so fast that McGarvery had no time to react, no time to move a muscle, no time even to stop in his tracks, or to feel anything beyond surprise.

Gruen was shouting something that McGarvey couldn't make out over the ringing in his ears, and in the next second or two with the sounds of metal and bits of glass falling around the control room, he ran for the stairs to the back corridor and control room door.

"Get out of there!" he shouted, taking the stairs down two at a time, nearly stumbling and pitching headfirst, the images of his wife's and daughter's bodies destroyed beyond all hope of salvation, beyond even recognition, rising up in his eyes like a bitter gorge choking his breath.

Gruen, standing at the open door with his other team member, Douglas Vigliaturo, looked around, his movements in slow motion, as McGarvey hit the first floor running. "There was still ten minutes on the counters!" he shouted. "You saw it, too."

"It was a trap," McGarvey said. "Whoever set this up meant to kill anyone trying to disarm the explosives. We have to leave now."

"I need to recall our transportation," Gruen said, still shouting, panic showing in his eyes. "It'll take too much time."

"You can ride with me, but we have to get out of here."

Gruen looked inside the control room, uncertain what to do next. "What do I tell Marsha's husband?"

"Christ," McGarvey said. "Stay if you want, but I suggest you move your ass." He headed the rest of the way down the corridor, out the back door, and around to the front of the building, sirens wailing everywhere throughout the nearly deserted facility.

∏I∏ETEE∏

They were the last to head away from facility. As soon as McGarvey came around the corner, Gail didn't need to be warned, she knew what had happened. She got on the radio and began notifying Haggerty, who was on site, along with all the other emergency responders what was about to happen, and to get away—and far away—as quickly as possible.

She, Townsend, Strasser, Bennet, and a number of other station personnel were already climbing aboard the Air National Guard chopper when McGarvey reached them.

"Both reactors?" Gail asked.

"Just number two," McGarvey said, not too gently hustling her aboard.

Gruen and Vigliaturo came across the parking lot in a dead run, and Gail exchanged a glance with McGarvey.

"No one else?"

"That's it."

"You say they were unsuccessful to stop the explosions on one?" Strasser shouted over the roar of the chopper's engines and the heavy thump of its main rotor.

"That's right, but I think only one of the panels was destroyed," McGarvey told him, and Townsend looked mad enough to kill someone.

Police and fire units started to pull away from the station, some heading south, but most heading north on A1A by the time Gruen and his team member reached the chopper and climbed aboard. They'd left their antinuclear device equipment behind.

A St. Lucie County EMS tech was in the back of the chopper with Bennet, cradling the electrician's head, and he looked up. "I've called an ophthalmic specialist at Miami General. He's standing by. We need to get this man down there as soon as possible."

McGarvey waited a full minute to make sure that no one else was coming, and he turned to the pilot and pumped his fist, and motioned out to sea. The helicopter lifted off, made a sharp dipping turn to the left, and headed directly east away from the power plant.

"Have a Dade County medevac chopper head north up the coast. When we can set down we'll radio our position," McGarvey shouted.

Gruen started to object but McGarvey just glared at him, and he sat back. He was still deeply shaken by the death of one of his team members, which was obvious from his expression, and yet it was equally obvious that he was working out a way in which he could somehow either blame the situation on someone—almost certainly McGarvey—and/or turn it to his advantage.

"We need to go now—" the medic insisted, but Strasser overrode him.

"It's starting," he said. He was looking out the window on the opposite side from the still open hatch.

Townsend was crouched next to him. "Mother of God," he said. But the angle was wrong. The helicopter had already crossed A1A and was out over the water, the facility almost directly behind them.

McGarvey had to shout twice to get the pilot's attention and he motioned for him to turn the helicopter broadside to the coast, while still heading away. The helicopter banked a little to port, then slewed left, almost skidding, the coast sliding into view from the open hatch and then the facility dominated by the twin containment domes.

Gail was right there with McGarvey at the hatch, and Townsend, Strasser, and the others crowded around, looking over his shoulder. At first nothing seemed out of the ordinary, except for the traffic. The facility was deserted, and from their altitude of about five hundred feet they could see a long way up and down the coast and across the Intracoastal Waterway on the west side of the island to the mainland and down toward the town of Stuart, civilian cars and a lot of police and emergency responder vehicles streaming away.

Massive traffic jams blocked the bridges off the island, one to the north and two to the south, and it would be hours before they were cleared. Farther inland the turnpike and I-95, which ran parallel within sight of each other, were packed with wall-to-wall traffic both ways. The warning had gone out on radio and television and the public's remembrance of 9/11 spiked and with it the mindless, absolute terror of nuclear power and they were running. Three Mile Island and Chernobyl—Hiroshima and Nagasaki in some people's minds—conjured up visions of mushroom clouds hanging over Hutchinson Island.

Then McGarvey and the others saw what Strasser had already seen; a slight shimmer was causing the air over the containment dome for reactor one to waver and rise like summer heat from a black-topped road in the distance; like a halo of death hanging over the domed cap, it came to McGarvey. The bodies of Wager and Marsha and Alan were down there, and it was possible that the South Service Building would become their mausoleum for a very long time.

"There!" Strasser shouted over the noise, and the chopper slowed and stopped, hovering where it was a mile or so offshore.

A dark line seemed to crawl from about halfway up the side of the dome, widening as it accelerated, and steam, white by contrast, began to leak from the crack, a little at first but then more of it, rising up into the cloudless blue Florida sky.

"Is it radioactive?" McGarvey asked, without looking over his shoulder, his eyes glued to the dome, and the plume rising above it.

"Probably not," Strasser said. "It's coming from the steam generator, or the loop. As long as the reactor core container doesn't breach, we'll be okay."

"What are the chances of that not happening?"

"Depends on which panel they saved."

A geyser of water shot from near the bottom of the crack, slamming into the South Service Building like a stream from a fire hose.

"The primary coolant loop just opened," Strasser said.

"Goddamnit, Chris, what about the emergency diesel?" Townsend demanded. "It should have been pumping water into the core by now."

"I don't know," Strasser admitted. "More sabotage?" The remorse was thick in his voice. It *was* sabotage, and not only in the control room. His nuclear power generating station had been mortally tampered with, and it had taken months to do it, and it had happened on his watch, right under his nose. He should have seen it.

Gruen pushed forward so he was right on McGarvey's shoulder. "Christ," he muttered, but everyone heard him.

A second crack, this one wider and moving faster, branched off from the first, and headed at a wide angle from the top third of the dome, like a broad slice of pie, and the concrete began to take on a rosy glow, hard to see in the bright daylight, but growing.

"The core is overheating now," Gruen said in awe.

"He's right," Strasser said.

"Any possibility of an explosion?" McGarvey asked. "Even remotely?"

"No—" Gruen said, but Strasser cut him off.

"Not a nuclear explosion."

The massive piece of concrete pie began to glow brighter now, moving up the scale from a rose to a deep red and it began to slump toward the right, in slow motion, opening a big hole in the side of the dome. Suddenly another geyser of water and steam burst straight out of the breach, heaving pieces of concrete and other debris out into the open air, the heavier materials raining out as far as the shore and the lighter stuff roiling upwards.

"We'd better back off," Gail said.

No one could take their eyes off the terrible sight, and McGarvey remembered the pictures of Chernobyl right after it happened in 1986, but something else began to dawn on him as he watched the steam plume rise over the dome—the wind had shifted from the west. The radioactive release was heading out to sea. They had caught a break.

"It's coming this way," Gruen said.

And Townsend and the others saw what was happening. "Thank God," the plant manager said.

"Don't you think we should get the hell out of here?" Gruen asked.

The side of the containment dome slumped even farther, but the damage seemed to be slowing down.

"The reactor is finally scramming," Strasser said. "Your people saved that panel. Thank God."

McGarvey motioned for the pilot to get them out of there, and the chopper began a wide, swinging arc off to the south, away from the plume, as Gail got on her cell phone to contact the authorities on the ground, and Gruen got on his own phone to the NNSA hotline.

"You guys are going to have to deal with that," McGarvey told Townsend and Strasser. "Will it be impossible?"

"It's no Chernobyl," Strasser said. "But it'll take the better part of a year or more to get back online."

"If ever," Townsend said bitterly. "We're going to be faced with public opinion. Especially if any civilians get hurt." He looked away, overwhelmed for just that moment by the enormity of what had just happened, what was happening. He'd worked with nukes for the better part of his career, and this was in lieu of his gold watch and twenty-five-year service pin. He and Strasser would not be remembered so much for leading the cleanup efforts, but for the fact such efforts had been needed in the first place.

Nuclear power was unsafe, the headlines would blare. Worldwide.

If not for Lundgren and Marsha it would have been much worse, but McGarvey had the unsettling feeling that this incident was just the beginning. Hutchinson Island had been sabotaged, and he knew in his gut that this incident was only one part of something much larger.

TWENTY

It was ten in the evening in Washington when President Howard Lord entered the main conference center in the complex of offices that was collectively called the Situation Room, on the ground floor of the West Wing. Already seated around the long cherrywood table were the director of the CIA, Walter Page, who had been a Fortune 500 company CEO; the National Security Agency Director, Air Force General Lawrence Piedermont, who was short and slender with thinning hair and a titanium stare, and who was said to be the most brilliant man in Washington; FBI Director Stewart Sargent, who was tall with a stern demeanor, who'd worked his way from a New York street cop to chief of the entire agency, while at the same time acquiring a Ph.D. in criminal science; the president's adviser on national security affairs, Eduardo Estevez, who'd been deputy associate director of the FBI, specializing in counterterrorism; Director of Homeland Security Admiral Allen Newhouse, who'd been commandant of the Coast Guard; and Department of Energy Deputy Secretary Joseph Caldwell, who'd been in nearly continuous conferences all afternoon and early evening with Joseph S. French, who ran the NNSA's Division of Emergency Operations. The only key player missing was Director of National Intelligence Avery Lockwood, currently on his way back from Islamabad.

The main flat-panel television screen on the back wall facing the president's position was running scenes from the Hutchinson Island disaster, as the media had dubbed it, and it was immediately obvious that the meltdown could have been much, much worse.

Everyone got to their feet.

"Good evening," Lord said. At six-six he was the tallest U.S. president ever, a full two inches taller than Abraham Lincoln, and he'd been a decent basketball player at Northwestern, though the team was lousy. He was also one of the brighter men ever to sit in the Oval Office, but with that intelligence came a fair amount of arrogance that sometimes got in the way of his accepting advice from members of his staff who he thought weren't as smart.

The vice president, who sometimes sat in on emergency meetings such as this one, had been sent to Offut Air Force Base in Omaha along with several key members of Congress and two Supreme Court Chief Justices. After 9/11 no one was taking anything for granted; Hutchinson Island had been hit, and it was possible that more attacks would be forthcoming, maybe even here in Washington.

"Good evening, Mr. President," Admiral Newhouse said. "I'll be giving the briefing." He was a short fireplug of a man with a dynamic personality, and he was one of the men in the room whom Lord genuinely respected and liked. During a particularly disastrous hurricane season a few years ago, the Coast Guard, under Newhouse's direction, had been the only federal organization that actually knew what it was doing.

"What's the word on casualties?" the president asked, taking his seat at the head of the table. The preliminary briefing book was on the table in front of him, but the information it contained was already two hours old, and he ignored it.

"We caught a couple of breaks," Newhouse said, moving to the podium to the right of the main monitor. "Nine people were killed inside the plant, counting the suspected terrorist—"

"He blew himself up," Stewart Sargent said. "I think that makes him more than just a suspect."

"But he probably had help," Newhouse said, obviously disliking the interruption, and Lord motioned for him to go on, thinking that although Sargent was a good fit at the Bureau, he never knew when to keep his mouth shut.

"Two of the casualties—Alan Lundgren and Marsha Littlejohn, both of them National Nuclear Security Administration Rapid Response team members—managed to disarm the explosives on one of the reactors, preventing its meltdown. But they were too late to completely disarm the second one. Apparently it had something to do with defective detonating units. The explosives were triggered as they were working on the detonators, killing both of them instantly."

"They were true heroes," Joseph Caldwell said. "I never personally knew them, of course, but the public should be made aware of their sacrifice."

For which the DOE would take the credit, Lord had the nasty thought. "We'll hold on that for the time being," he said, and Caldwell wanted to protest. "We don't want to announce our abilities to the enemy."

"Yes, Mr. President."

"What about civilian casualties?" the President asked.

"A few cuts and bruises during the evacuation of the facility, and a fairly high number of traffic accidents on the highways within a twenty-mile radius, but reasonable considering that more than one hundred thousand people tried to get away from the possible damage path."

"Deaths?"

"Only three, Mr. President, which is remarkably low," Newhouse replied. "The biggest problem authorities on the ground are trying to deal with is convincing people at least five miles out to return to their homes. The winds all day were mostly out of the west, which pushed the bulk of the relatively small radiation leak harmlessly to sea."

"How soon before the cleanup operation can begin?" Lord asked. No one enjoyed briefing this president, because he hammered the presenter with an almost continuous barrage of questions.

"Actually some cleanup operations have already begun," Newhouse said. "A fair amount of debris, mostly concrete in sizes ranging from eight to ten pounds all the way down to dust, along with some metal slag, and water fell in the immediate area around the containment dome and the South Service Building where the control room was located. We're dealing right now with the outside areas, along with about one mile of A1A—that's the only highway on the island."

"How long before the plant is back up and producing electricity?"

"That's up to the nuclear engineers and waste disposal people. Could be a year, could be a lot longer."

"Could be never?" the president asked, already thinking ahead to the trouble the industry would face as the more than thirty permit applications for new nuclear-powered generating stations were ruled on. Granting any of them would be almost entirely dependent on public sentiment.

Newhouse nodded. "No one wants to admit the possibility, Mr. President, but I think we need to consider that Hutchinson Island may never reopen. It may have to be capped, and the immediate area evacuated and quarantined, much like Chernobyl."

"How many families would be affected?"

"I don't have that number yet."

"Get it by morning," the president said. "Include it with your overnight update."

"Yes, sir."

"What about the radioactive material that fell into the sea? How much of it has or will drift ashore?"

"That was another break," Newhouse said. "It looks as if the bulk of the material is migrating into the Gulf Stream, which will carry it north while at the same time vastly diluting its strength. Shipping interests have been notified to stay clear, which will cost them money, of course, since they won't get the boost from the Stream, but the effects shouldn't last long. Perhaps less than a week."

"What about damage to marine life?"

"It's too soon to tell, but it's my understanding from Loring that NOAA is addressing the possibility." Ron Loring was the secretary of commerce, of which NOAA was a department.

Lord glanced at the Hutchinson Island images on the big flat-panel monitor at the other end of the room. It hadn't been another 9/11, but it could have been. It had been meant to do the U.S. even more harm.

"Is there any reason for us to consider this as anything other than a terrorist attack?" he asked. "An incident with a national backing?"

"The CIA has no direct information of such a possibility," Walter Page began. He was well dressed as was his custom, and looked as if he had just stepped out of a Savile Row ad in *The Times*. "But a former director of the Agency was on site, and was apparently instrumental in saving some important people."

"Kirk McGarvey," the DOE's Deputy Secretary Joseph Caldwell said with a smirk. "A loose cannon if ever there was one."

"You hired him," Page shot back. "And yes, he's a loose cannon, but he's done some spectacular things for this country."

Lord knew of McGarvey, of course, everyone around this table did, and while he could see that Page had a great deal of respect for the man it was a view he didn't share. McGarvey was of an old, dangerous cold war school; the sort of a figure who approved of places like Guántanamo Bay and Abu Ghraib, and renditions, even assassinations. He'd done good, even great things for the U.S., but he'd also caused a lot of serious frustration and embarrassment for previous administrations.

"What was he doing at Hutchinson Island?"

"He was in Miami training one of our new Rapid Response teams to deal with actual face-to-face encounters with a terrorist or terrorists," Caldwell said. "But to this point he's been more bother than benefit. It's highly unlikely that our people would ever find themselves in such a situation."

"This time they did," Page said.

"Are there any current or developing threats against us or our interests that have recently come to light? Any possible connections to this attack?"

"Nothing that's not already on the table," Page said.

"We've picked up nothing recently," the NSA's Director General Piedermont said.

"For the time being the incident will be publicly treated as an accident," the president said.

"We may be too late for that, Mr. President," Newhouse disagreed. "Too many people were on site in the middle of it—several of them senior SSP&L officers. And those people definitely will not want to support any claim of an accident. It would give them a black eye."

"Get me a list of names, and I'll talk to each one of them personally."

"Yes, sir," Newhouse said, and he glanced over his shoulder at the monitor, and the president and everyone else in the room saw the CNN graphic comparing this event to 9/11.

The genie was already out of the bottle, and Lord's anger spiked, but he contained himself. "So, we've passed that point already. Has anyone claimed responsibility?"

"No, sir," the admiral said.

"In addition to the cleanup efforts, the next steps are clear. We find the bastards who did this to us, and take them out." Lord said and he looked each of his people in the eye. "Priority one."

"It could be helpful if we also found out why," Page said. "This attack could be an isolated incident, but it could be the opening shot of something much larger."

"I agree, Mr. President. Al-Quaeda and some of the other terrorist organizations have gotten a hell of lot more sophisticated since nine/eleven. We need to find out what's going on."

"I'll coordinate that effort," the president's national security adviser Eduardo Estevez said.

"We'll need to put someone in overall charge in the field," Page suggested.

"Do it, but quietly," Lord ordered. "This will not end up as another nine/eleven media circus."

But everyone in the room, including the president himself knew that an incident of this magnitude could not be manipulated. The American public had become more savvy since 9/11 and things like this always seemed to take on a life of their own.

TWENTY-ONE

It had come to her in a dream three days ago that something awful was about to happen, and that because of it she would be in a great deal of personal danger. She'd awakened at three in the morning, drenched in sweat, alone as she had been for the past five years since her divorce, and she'd gotten up, walked to the window, and looked out over the city of Caracas, goose bumps on the back of her neck and on her arms.

But it wasn't until late this afternoon when flash traffic from CIA Headquarters alerting all station chiefs worldwide about the attack on Hutchinson Island's nuclear power facility, that chief of CIA Station Caracas, Lorraine Fritch, suddenly put together most of the bits and pieces of information her people had been gathering over the past four months into one big—and to her—terrifying picture.

She'd had an epiphany, and she'd convinced herself it was because of Hutchinson Island. The connections had become crystal clear in her head, but not so clear that she would be able to convince her boss, the deputy director of operations, and especially not the DCI, by e-mail, no matter how detailed, or even by encrypted phone. This she had to do in person.

She'd messaged her boss, Marty Baimbridge, that she was flying up to Washington with something even more important than flash traffic could convey. This was something, she'd told him, that would have to be face-to-face. The one word reply had been: "Come."

It was late evening by the time she climbed into the backseat of an embassy Escalade, her driver and bodyguard in front, and they left through the front gate, and merged with steady traffic on the Avenida Miranda and headed out to the Aeropuerto Internacional de Maiquetia Simon Bolivar. Ordinarily embassy personnel, including CIA officers, were supposed to fly commercial, and coach at that. But Continental flights left first thing in the morning, and, stopping in Houston, didn't get to Baltimore until nearly midnight, so she'd chartered a private Gulfstream that would fly directly to Miami where it would refuel and then onward to Reagan National Airport in Washington, getting there first thing in the morning.

She could sleep on the flight, if she could sleep at all, which considering her state of mind at the moment was highly doubtful. It was one of the many reasons her husband had cited for their divorce: When she was engaged in something, she was superengaged to the point of completely tuning out her family, sometimes for days or even weeks at a time. Another of the reasons, of course, was the fact she couldn't discuss her work with her husband, and she would often drop everything and fly off to somewhere in the world at a moment's notice, again without telling him where she was going, what she would be doing when she got there, and how long it would be before she got back.

She was engaged now, and she was flying out, but the only one she'd had to inform was Ambassador Turner, who hadn't cared to demand a detailed explanation before she spent the money for the flight. It was her station's budget, not the embassy's.

It had began for her four months ago when she'd accidentally overheard a chance remark during a lunch at the Tamanaco Inter-Continental Hotel with a pair of advisers to President Chávez, who knew who and what she was, and were pushing her to make a mistake. They'd met with her on orders to find out what the CIA was up to, and she to get a hint of just how much SEBIN, Venezuela's intelligence service, knew or guessed about what was going on right under their noses.

It was a little before 12:30 P.M., and they'd just sat down and ordered drinks when a man, medium build with a mustache, his hair graying at his sideburns and temples, with lovely dark eyes, walked in with a pair of men just as expensively dressed as he was. Lorraine thought that he was extraordinarily handsome and vaguely familiar, but she couldn't dredge up a name though she thought it would be in her best interest if she could.

One of the men at her table looked up, and did a double take, and said something in rapid-fire Spanish to the other adviser.

It was too fast for Lorraine but she did catch the name, Señor Octavio, and it came to her that he was Miguel Octavio, Venezuela's richest man, and one of the most reclusive multibillionaires in the world—even more so than Howard Hughes had been. His was oil money, of course, but the fact he was here like this was nothing short of extraordinary, and she'd had the thought that only something very important could have brought him out in public.

"Do either of you recognize the two men with Señor Octavio?" she'd asked, and the two advisers looked at her with genuine fear in their eyes, and told her no, that they were strangers to them. Of course she hadn't believed them.

And it might have ended there, nothing more than a curiosity except that the obsequious maître d' led Octavio and his companions to a window table, passing within a couple of feet from where Lorraine was seated. They were talking, in accented English, their voices low but not so low that she couldn't guess that at least one of the men was an Arab speaker, and hear the initials UAEIBC mentioned, and her stomach had done a flip flop.

Lunch had been made difficult for her because she wanted to get back to the embassy and start working out what connection Octavio had made or was making with the United Arab Emirates International Bank of Commerce, which had been long suspected of funding a number of terrorist groups, including al-Quaeda, Hamas, Hizballah, and the lesser known group Islamic Jihad and their front cells and ancillary organizations—or at least funneling money from various Islamic fund-raising organizations into the groups. The bank had no direct connection with the UAE government in Dubai, but its books and client list were more closely held than any offshore bank in the world.

None of that had been proven yet, but consensus among top-ranking people in U.S. and British intelligence services compared the UAE bank with the Luxembourg-registered Bank of Credit and Commerce that had been funded by the government of Pakistan, likely through its intelligence service the ISI. The BCCI, which had collapsed in the nineties, had engaged in money laundering, bribery, and tax evasion, plus supporting some of the same terrorist organizations that the commercial bank in the UAE was supporting now. The BCCI had even dealt in arms trafficking, as well as brokering the sale of nuclear technologies. In the end the BCCI had collapsed under its own weight, its officers walking away with $20 billion that had never been accounted for.

That afternoon she'd set her assistant chief of station Donald Morton to the task of finding out everything he could on Octavio's financial connections outside of Venezuela. Don was a Harvard MBA, and had been sent to Caracas to keep his ear to the ground in the oil ministry. Because Venezuela was the fourth largest supplier to the U.S., keeping track down here was of vital importance.

"I want his background as well," Lorraine had ordered. She was finally on the hunt of something worthwhile and she'd already begun to love it. That trait in her had been the reason the CIA had snapped her up from her small, but exclusive, law practice in Beverly Hills fourteen years ago.

"Family history, education, stuff like that?" Morton had asked. "Just Google him, no need to use up our resources."

"I want his real background."

"Ah, a skeptic among us," he said. Although he was barely out of his twenties he was a portly man who in a business suit could pass for what most people pictured a banker or Fortune 500 looked like. But he was a lot smarter than most of that type. "I have a friend in the DI at Langley who owes me a favor, I'll get her started." The DI was the Company's Directorate of Intelligence, where all sorts of research was conducted on, among other things, international economic activities and the people involved.

"But quietly," Lorraine had cautioned him. "I want this as low-key as possible, because this guy carries a lot of weight around here, and it would be too bad if we tipped something nasty over and word got back to him, we could all be in some deep shit."

The first surprise had been how open the facts of his background were. What Don's friend in the DI had dug up on the oil billionaire exactly matched what was published on Wikipedia: his family was old money, able to trace their lineage back to the early Spanish sugarcane and tobacco fields, and, of course, oil. Octavio the younger had been educated at Oxford, specializing in international business and law, spending his vacations skiing in Switzerland and Austria, gambling in Monaco and Las Vegas, and romancing his way across Europe, his photographs on the front pages of tabloids everywhere. Until he turned twenty-five when he practically disappeared.

"Except in the business world," Morton had reported. "Miguel Octavio set out to become the richest man in the world, but very quietly, because some of his business deals were too sweet to be one hundred percent legit."

That had been two months ago when Don laid a thick file on her desk.

"Give me a couple of for instances," Lorraine had prompted.

"He's either the shrewdest or the luckiest man in the world, or—and this one's my best guess—he has had a whole lot of insider info. He was in on the dot-com boom in the States in a big way, investing in everything from Microsoft to Google, and sticking with them, but he also spread a couple hundred million in a bunch of other IPOs that went ballistic, and then sold them at the peak, before they crashed. And he walked away with his first billion."

"A few moves like those would have made him a smart investor," Lorraine agreed. "Did he ever fail?"

"Not once, and it was more than a few calls. More like three dozen."

"Any common thread?"

"Threads," Morton said. "And it's all in the file. Primarily three major U.S. banks where he has close personal friends on the boards of directors. They couldn't directly profit from what they knew, and more important when they knew what they did, but Octavio sure as hell could and did."

"Any of that money make it back to his pals?" Lorraine asked.

"Yeah, but that's the slick part. The guy bet the entire billion—or at least most of it—in the U.S. housing boom, the bulk of it in Florida and California, through Anne Marie Marinaccio."

"The FBI wants her."

"That's the even more interesting part," Morton said. "Marinaccio bailed when the housing market started heading south, and she took a few billions of her investors' money with her where she set up shop in Dubai under what's called the Marinaccio Group. Lots of derivatives, most of which she managed to dump in time. But the curious part is that Octavio bailed at the same time Marinaccio did. Pulling out more than two billion which was legit on the surface."

"What about these days? Either of them been hurt by the recession?"

"I don't know yet about Marinaccio, although there've been rumors about her oil investments, especially in Iraq, getting shaky, but Octavio is apparently in great shape."

"So why is he involved with the UAEIBC?" Lorraine had asked, and now heading out to the airport she remembered that question and Don's answer with perfect clarity.

"I'm working on that part, but it's almost certain that the Marinaccio Group is heavily involved in the bank, and of course Octavio and Marinaccio had a fabulously successful financial relationship. So there's that, along with their shared interest in oil, and one other intriguing tidbit that I'm still trying to run down."

"Intrigue me."

"The Marinaccio Group has it's own security division, headed by Gunther Wolfhardt, ex-East German Stasi. Rumors are that Wolfhardt might have been somehow involved with the heart attack of one of Marinaccio's rivals, and the terrorist bombing of another's office buildings. In each case Marinaccio came out on top financially. And there are other rumors."

"If all that's true, it means Marinaccio is a ruthless bitch who'll stop at literally nothing to protect her investments."

"That would be to Miguel Octavio's best interests as well."

"Keep digging," she ordered.

Last week Don had connected the Marinaccio Group with at least one probable assassination and one likely bombing as well as a direct connection with several of the UAEIBC-supported terrorist organizations, and a rumor floating around that al-Quaeda was planning another spectacular strike somewhere in the U.S.

Marinaccio equaled oil interests, equaled terrorism and terrorists, equaled Octavio. And then Hutchinson Island happened. Make nuclear-generated electricity unpalatable, and oil and natural gas would be ready and able to step in because coal was coming up against the increasingly powerful global warming lobby, and wind and solar technologies weren't ready yet to fill the gap.

She didn't have all the proof, but it was enough in her mind to make a damned good case for the CIA to spend some of its resources to take a closer look.

Two motorcycle cops pulled up beside them and waved them over. They were on the highway now, the airport within sight a few miles across an open field.

Lorraine didn't know if she should be alarmed yet. The plates on the SUV were diplomatic and even though she was CIA, her embassy title was Special Adviser to the Ambassador, which gave her diplomatic immunity. But Venezuela was Miguel Octavio's country, and just now President Chavez was acting particularly unkindly toward the U.S. And things happened down here.

"Were we speeding?" she asked the driver as he slowed down and pulled over to the side of the busy road.

"About ten miles over the limit, ma'am, the same as everyone else."

"Better get your passport out, Mrs. Fritch," her bodyguard said. "This is probably just a routine hassle. Been happening a lot lately."

When they were stopped the driver powered down his window as one of the cops came over, while the second came around to the passenger side as Lorraine's bodyguard lowered his window.

"Is there some trouble, Officer?" the driver asked.

Lorraine opened her purse, looked at her 9mm Beretta for just a second, but then grabbed her passport. Normally she didn't travel armed, but this time she was spooked.

The first gunshot was so loud in the confines of the car that she was so startled, so distracted she didn't realize for the first instant that her bodyguard's blood had splashed her face. She looked up as the second shot was fired, this one hitting the driver in the forehead, and then she was looking into the muzzle of a very large pistol, a SIG-Sauer, she thought, before a billion stars burst inside her skull.

TWENTY-TWO

☐

All the way back up to Washington the next morning McGarvey had the feeling that nothing in his life had ever been meant to last. Not his work in the Air Force, not his career in the CIA, not with his wife and daughter and certainly not his retirement from the field.

Getting out of the cab with Gail in front of the three-story brick-and-glass building that was home to the operational division of the National Nuclear Security Administration in Tysons Corner, just outside the Beltway, it struck him hard that his days as a teacher and Rapid Response team adviser were finished, and had come to an end the moment he and Lundgren had responded to the Hutchinson Island call.

The morning was bright and fresh, the countryside southern and lush, but McGarvey wasn't noticing any of it, he was so tightly focused. And he had to ask himself if he was glad for the chance to get back into action, or regretful. He thought he knew but he didn't want to admit it to himself, not yet, anyway, but the call from the Division of Emergency Operations Director Joseph S. French had been straight to the point: Drop everything and get up here as soon as possible, and he had responded without hesitation.

"I'm sorry about Alan," Gail said. "He didn't deserve it." She'd come up here to make her report to her boss, Louis Curtley, the operations manager in charge of in-place security operatives, the position she'd held—still held—at Hutchinson Island.

"None of them did," McGarvey said, and he really looked at her for the first time since yesterday afternoon.

She was ragged, her oval features pinched with stress and fatigue. No one had gotten much sleep in the aftermath, but right now she seemed to be more affected than she should have been, almost beside herself.

He stopped her halfway up the walk to the front entrance. "It wasn't your fault."

"It was exactly my fault," she said angrily, her black eyes wide, haunted. And he knew what she was seeing. "I was in charge of security. I let the bastard get into my control room six months ago, and I let the other just waltz into my facility like any fucking tourist."

"You're not an engineer, so there's no way you could have known about the sabotaged systems. That was Strasser's job. And it wasn't yours to vet every person who ever took the tour."

She looked up into his face, her anger like a halo. "He walked right past me, Kirk. And I knew something was wrong, I could feel it, but I did nothing. Like you said, it wasn't my job to vet those people. But it was most definitely my responsibility to follow my gut. And that's something else you said. Remember?"

She was on the verge of tears now, and McGarvey wanted to reach out for her, but he knew that she would resent anything like that, figuring that he would take her for being a weakling.

"I remember," he said. "That's how we learn."

"But at what terrible cost," she said bitterly.

"We keep going. You keep going."

"And do what? I'm practically out of a job until—or if—Hutchinson Island gets rebuilt. Or do you think Curtley's going to give me a new assignment as a reward?"

"Prove your plant was sabotaged, find out who did it and why, and go after them."

She said nothing.

McGarvey could see that he'd told her something she hadn't expected. "You know that the engineer inside the control room was a part of it, and you have a suspect who you saw get in his car and drive away. It's a start."

"The monitoring system is probably fried. The South Building took a big hit of radioactive water and steam."

"It may not have gotten inside the building," McGarvey said, and he took out the disk he'd taken from the monitoring station. "The visitors center parking lot camera." He'd planned on giving it to Otto to work on, but he suspected that Gail needed it.

"You went back," she said, taking the disk from him.

"I figured I owed you that much."

"You paid your debt, Kirk, and then some," she said with emotion. "If it hadn't been for you taking charge and keeping Carlos from screwing things up, a lot more people would've been hurt."

"Well, it could be a lead, especially if you can lift the license number," he said with more gentleness in his voice than he felt. The security lapses at Hutchinson Island were only a small part of the real problem, starting with Homeland Security that in some ways still believed the major threat to the U.S. was by air, just like 9/11.

"Eric can do it," she said, a hint of her old sparkle and excitement back in her face. Eric Yablonski was the NNSA's resident computer geek, and served in a similar function for the administration as Otto Rencke did for the CIA. And now she had something to do that had merit, worth, and it was enough for her. A lifeline.

Joseph French had one of the corner offices on the third floor, and although this division of the NNSA had been pulled out of the DOE's headquarters in the city, technically banished from the seat of power, he didn't seem to mind. Out here, he'd once explained to McGarvey, he had a free hand.

He was a short, tightly built man in his late fifties, with an athletic grace that came from playing racquetball twice a week, and the thousand-yard stare acquired from his naval career from which he had retired as a two-star rear admiral. He had been boss of a Sixth Fleet battle group, which should have qualified him for a more important position in the DOE, but he was an action man who was perfectly happy to spend his retirement years out of the bustle of Washington and especially away from the bureaucracy of the Pentagon.

"You were right and everyone else at the DOE was wrong," he said when McGarvey walked in. "Coffee?"

"No thanks on the coffee," McGarvey said. "And the other is no consolation. We lost some good people."

"It could have been worse," French said, his mood unreadable. He'd been black shoe navy, and had never been able to completely trust the sometimes maverick tactics of special ops forces, including the Navy SEALs, and definitely not the CIA's black ops officers—such as McGarvey had been. Yet he freely admitted that he considered Mac an asset too valuable to dismiss. He motioned to a chair.

"There are one hundred and three other nuclear plants out there, just as vulnerable."

"We're putting things in place."

"I'll bet you are."

"The White House wants this thing to be handled low-key for now," French said.

"Why's that, Admiral?" McGarvey wanted to know. "The president doesn't want to start a panic by letting people know we haven't a clue how this happened, why it happened, who made it happen, or if it's likely to happen again?"

"The FBI is working the case, so is the CIA. Anyway, you signed on to help with just that, remember?"

This was a morning for remembering. "Nobody's listening," McGarvey said, wondering about the depth of his bitterness.

"You're wrong," French countered. "I'm sorry about what happened in Florida. We all are, and not for the reasons you think—not for the negative PR impact. You came to me with a chip on your shoulder, and I understand that, too. Losing your wife and daughter. And I even understand your background, your deep background before you became director of the CIA. But here we are, and we need your . . . particular set of skills. And that comes directly from the White House via Walt Page who thinks like I do that you're a loose cannon, always have been. But it's a loose cannon we need."

"As you said, the FBI's working the case," McGarvey said. "And I'm sure Caldwell didn't sign off on me."

"He had no choice, and before you dismiss him as just another bureaucrat, take a hard look at the man's record. In two short years he's managed to jump-start the alternative energy field despite the low oil prices. He's an ass, but he does get the job done. On top of that, Homeland Security is in high gear, as is every other intel and LE agency in the country—just like after nine-eleven."

McGarvey knew what was coming next, and he had known it the moment French had called him up here. And nothing had changed in his mind about going back into the field versus simply turning his back and walking away, and yet he'd been intrigued since the call from the hotline OD. Even more intrigued now that Page had brought up his name.

French was watching him closely, but he was bright enough to hold his piece. He'd said what had to be said and now the ball was in McGarvey's court.

"I'll need a free hand."

"I'd expect you to work outside the system, especially independently from this office, but you'd have our resources at your disposal."

"But quietly."

"Yes."

"That part won't last, and you have to know it and understand why."

French nodded after a moment. "As I said, I saw your file before I hired you."

"I want Gail Newby to help out, and maybe Eric Yablonski."

"You can have them if they'll go along with you. This is a strictly volunteer operation. The way it was explained to me, the Bureau and everyone else will be beating the bushes for evidence and making a lot of noise doing it. Reassure the public. In the meantime you're to do what you've always done; go through the back door and the hell with the niceties."

"People are bound to get hurt."

"I imagine they will," French said evenly. "Do you have any ideas yet?"

"This was done by professionals. The very best, which means the most expensive. Considering what they tried to do—kill a lot of people—narrows down the list of organizations with that kind of money."

"Al-Quaeda?"

"It's a start," McGarvey said. "But this time we're not going to war, because I think the answers, when we find them, aren't going to be so simple. Something else is going on."

"Find out what it is," French said.

"I'll try," McGarvey promised, and he got up and walked out.

Back in the field, he thought, just that easy. And in some ways he was feeling something new, a new emotion, almost relief to finally be doing something worthwhile. He supposed he carried the same look now that he had seen on Gail's face when he'd handed over the video disk, only with one added burden—people were going to die before this was over, and he was going to kill them.

TWENTY-THREE

Gail's boss Louis Curtley, who was possibly the most disinterested and uninteresting man she'd ever known, had dismissed her out of hand when she'd reported to him on the Hutchinson Island situation, stopping her before she'd really gotten started. He'd told her that he had been sorry to hear about Larry's death, insincerity dripping from just about every word, and about the other deaths, but whatever theories she might want to run past him would have to wait until she had all the facts. Not only Forcier's true background, but the name of the man she'd seen leaving the facility and concrete proof that: A. he knew Forcier; B. that he had actually gotten inside the control room; and C. and D., who, if anyone, he was working for and some sort of motive that made sense as to why he'd wanted to sabotage the plant.

"When you have your facts come back and talk to me," he'd told her.

He was tall, dark, and slender, handsome, almost beautiful, but she'd always thought he looked and acted like a toad.

"And since there's nothing for you to do at Hutchinson Island— leastways until it's back up and running—finding the facts is your new assignment. Your only assignment."

And now she was downstairs in the data center adjacent to operations with Eric Yablonski, a man who, if complete opposites actually existed, was Curtley's counterpoint. Short, dumpy, homely, only a whisper of fine gray hair on his pink head, he was the kindest, nicest, and brightest man she'd ever met, with an open, generous heart, an easy laugh, and a sarcasm that had never fooled anyone—not her, not his staff, and especially not his wife and eight doting children.

"Curtley didn't want to hear what you had to say so he kicked you out and sent you down here," he said. "What makes you think that I'm any different?"

His office was separated from the main floor of the data center by a plate-glass window to the right, which in turn was separated from operations, which was called the Watch—the same as at the CIA—to the left by another large window. Four computer experts in the data center compiled and analyzed the real-time information gathered by five specialists in the Watch 24/7. It was all about threat assessments, what was coming at the U.S. right now, or what was developing somewhere—perhaps an intercepted telephone call or calls shunted over from the National Security Agency, or satellite images from the National Reconnaissance Office showing increased activity at some camp on the Syrian desert, or perhaps a field report from a CIA agent somewhere in the Middle East, Russia, or just lately South America.

"*Veni, vidi, vici*," Yablonski had once said, gazing out the windows at what he considered was his private domain, because everything flowing from the Watch to the data center was his to ponder, to rearrange, to fit into patterns that no one else was seeing, and translate the patterns into real-world events. His job was to penetrate the haze to find what was happening and why.

Only he and everyone else had missed Hutchinson Island, and he'd been beating himself up about it all night, so that now he looked like a train wreck in progress, his tie askew, his dress shirt rumpled, and his jacket dropped in a heap on top of one of the lockboxes.

"I never saw it coming, but I should have," Gail said, sitting down across from his desk that was dominated by a pair of wide-screen monitors.

"If it's any consolation, neither did I, sweetheart," Yablonski said, and his face fell a little. "I'm sorry as hell about Larry. I didn't know him, personally, but if he was a good enough man to work with you down there then he must have been first class."

"Thanks, but the entire control room crew was killed and one of Gruen's people was taken out too, along with Kirk McGarvey's partner.

It was a screwup from the moment it started, and I was the administration's hotshot who was supposed to make sure shit like that never went down."

Yablonski gave her a hard, critical stare then nodded. "Yup, you did screw up, but that particular scenario wasn't in your playbook."

"It should have been."

"So you're taking all the blame, is that it? Instead of analyzing what you let happen, how to guard against it ever happening again, and finding out who did this to us and why, so I can chase down some leads and find out how I screwed up, you're going to wallow in self-pity?"

She looked away. "Shit," she said. Mac had said almost the same thing to her, and just as bluntly. And he had handed her a lifeline, which she had temporarily blocked out of her head. She turned back and actually managed a slight smile. "But that was a nice speech."

"I worked on it all morning, soon as I found out you guys were on the way up."

Gail took the disk out of her jacket pocket and handed it to him. "This is what we recorded from one of our video cams at the visitors center's parking lot." She came around behind his desk so she could watch the video.

"Do we maybe have a suspect?" Yablonski asked, bringing the disk up on one of his monitors. It was nighttime and the parking lot was empty.

She explained about the man on the tour she'd seen at the control-room observation window. "A few minutes later one of my security people called and said a man showed up back at the visitors center, claimed he was sick and drove off. A little bit after twelve."

"Same guy who caught your attention?" Yablonski asked, fast-forwarding the video.

"I didn't know it at the time, but I had my suspicions, so I talked to the people at the visitors center who checked him in under the name Robert Benson, a schoolteacher from San Francisco. Same description. He'd told them earlier that after the tour he had an appointment up in Jacksonville. But when he left, he headed south. The wrong way."

Yablonski had gotten to the section of the recording that showed a man walking across the parking lot to a blue Ford Taurus. "That him?"

"Yes. Can you get the tag number?"

Yablonski paused the disk and magnified the image, centering on the license plate. "Florida, Dade County, Z12 5LS." They watched as the man got into the car, pulled out of the parking lot, and turned to the south on A1A.

"Didn't look sick to me," Gail said.

"Or guilty," Yablonski said. He pulled up a search program, got into Florida's Division of Motor Vehicles for Dade County and brought up the tag number. "Hertz, Miami International," he said. Next, he hacked into the Hertz computer system. "Okay, rented yesterday morning to Robert Benson, San Francisco. Your guy."

"Has the car been turned in yet?"

"Two thirty yesterday afternoon."

"Shit," Gail said. "It's not likely he left any forensic evidence for us."

"Probably not. Anyway the car went out this morning on a one-week rental," Yablonski said. "But we're not done yet." He pulled up San Francisco's Motor Vehicle Department, and brought up Robert Benson's driver's license, which included an address, a thumbprint, height, weight, and a photograph.

"That's not him," Gail said. "So what the hell happened to the real Benson?" But she knew damn well what had happened to the man, who in all likelihood was lying dead in a field somewhere, or maybe at the bottom of the bay. "Check the city police files."

"Don't tell me how to do my job, dear girl," Yablonski said, already headed in that direction. But they came up blank. Next he hacked into the school district's mainframe, bringing up Benson's file. "He's on vacation, not due back until the fifth."

"He's never coming back," Gail said. "The son of a bitch killed him."

Yablonski looked up at her. "I'll go along with that assumption for the moment. But why him, why that particular man?"

"He had a timetable, so he went looking for someone about the same height and weight, and killed him for his identity."

"That's a stretch even for a cop. I mean how the hell does he pick out the one poor sap in the entire country who he's going to pose as?" Yablonski shook his head. "Either your guy is brilliant or he knows something we don't. And by now he's long gone, certainly not back to California."

"Australia or maybe South Africa," Gail said. "The clerk at the visitors center said he spoke with an English accent—but she didn't think it sounded like he was a Brit."

Yablonski glanced toward the plate-glass window, and picked up his phone. "It's okay, let him in."

Gail turned as McGarvey said something to one of the clerks, then came across the data center, and walked in. He nodded to Gail.

"Mr. McGarvey, I presume," Yablonski said. "Good job at Hutchinson Island."

"Not good enough," McGarvey said. "My friends call me Mac."

"Mine call me Eric," Yablonski said and he rose to shake McGarvey's hand. "Let me guess, French assigned you to find the terrorists, you asked to have Gail help, and he tossed me in to the bargain."

"Do you know Otto Rencke?"

Yablonski grinned. "Never met the man, but everybody in my business knows him or knows of him, and we're all in a bit of awe."

McGarvey nodded. "He can be a little scary sometimes. I'm going to ask him to give us a hand, and if you'll agree, I'd like you to work with him."

"Absolutely," Yablonski said without hesitation.

Gail explained what they had come up with so far, tracing the man on the video as far as San Francisco, where they'd run into a dead end.

"Not quite," McGarvey said. "At least you've established that he had taken someone else's identity. Makes him our prime suspect, along with Forcier."

"But why San Francisco?" Yablonski asked. "Why not Denver, or Chicago, or Indianapolis. According to Gail the people who talked to him said he had an English accent, maybe Australian. So why not Sydney or Melbourne?"

"When we find him, I'll ask. Do we have any images of his face?"

"Not on this disk," Yablonski said. "But he took a tour inside the plant, at least as far as the control room observation corridor. He'll be on some of those disks."

"If the radiation hasn't fried them and if we can get in to retrieve them," Gail said. "But I got a pretty good look at his face so I can give a description to a police artist. Maybe we'll get lucky.

"What about Forcier? Was he scheduled to be on duty?"

"No, but he had the proper ID card to get inside. It's likely he met our Aussie and let him in."

"Could this guy have gotten a weapon or the Semtex past security in the visitors center?" McGarvey asked.

"Not a chance," Gail said. "But Forcier could have brought the stuff in. Nobody checks the employees. We run a pretty vigorous background check on our people before we offer them a job. I don't remember Forcier specifically, but he was fully vetted for work in the control room, which meant his background investigation had to have been rock solid."

"Obviously somebody missed something, so keep trying with the Australian and Forcier. In the meantime I'll get Otto started, and then take a run out to San Francisco, see what I can dig up."

"Do you want me to tag along?" Gail asked.

"No. For now just stick it out here," he told her. "I'll have Otto call you and you can pool resources. But my guess is that this guy isn't Australian; you might try South African ex-special forces or the SASS, their secret service."

Yablonski's phone rang and he picked it up, but the call was for McGarvey. "Dr. Larsen."

"You're a hard man to track down," Eve said when McGarvey got on.

"That's not necessarily a bad thing," McGarvey said. "You took a tumble yesterday, are you okay?"

"Just fine," she said dismissively. "I'm here in Washington, and I'd like to buy you lunch if you're free."

"I'm busy."

"This is important, at least to me it is. The Watergate at noon? Then I won't bother you again."

McGarvey glanced at his watch. It was just past 11:30 A.M. "I'll meet you at the bar."

"Good."

"NOAA's Doctor Larsen from Hutchinson Island?" Gail asked when McGarvey hung up.

"Yes. She wants to talk to me."

"About what?"

"Haven't a clue," McGarvey said, and he missed the quick expression of anger on Gail's face.

TWENTY-FOUR

McGarvey had no real idea why he had agreed to meet Eve Larsen for lunch except for the fact she'd been at Hutchinson Island yesterday, right in the middle of the attack, and he'd never trusted coincidences.

Last year she'd been short-listed for the Nobel Prize in Physics, her picture on the cover of Time: RADICAL DOC TOO RADICAL FOR STOCKHOLM? She hadn't gotten the prize, which was probably a good thing. People who blew up nuclear energy plants might not hesitate to kill the high priestess of alternative energy.

Dressed in a charcoal gray pantsuit with flaring legs, and a plain white blouse that practically fluoresced against her deep tan, she was seated at the half-filled bar in the Watergate Hotel, sipping a martini.

She was absorbed with something on the television screen behind the bar and didn't notice McGarvey until he sat down next to her, and when she looked at him she smiled warmly, though he could see that she was worried, or at the very least had something she considered to be very important on her mind.

"Hi," McGarvey said.

"Have you seen that?" she motioned toward the television that was tuned to CSPN, a stern-faced woman announcer reporting on something apparently grave. The sound was off, but her words appeared as a crawl at the bottom of the screen. A high-ranking U.S. embassy employee and her driver and bodyguard had been assassinated on the airport highway in Caracas, Venezuela.

An incident like that was bound to happen down there sooner or later, but something about the photograph of the woman, which flashed on the screen, was familiar to McGarvey and when her name came up on the crawl he realized that he knew her.

Eve was looking at him. "Did you know her?"

"I'm not sure. It was several years ago."

"You were with the CIA?" Eve asked. She glanced up at the television, but the announcer was back to reporting on the Hutchinson Island meltdown, which had dominated every newscast since yesterday.

"Yes, but you called me. What can I do for you?"

"Did she work for the CIA?"

McGarvey had to remind himself that he was dealing with a woman a lot smarter than the average scientist, and by her attitude now and her questions, a lot more aware of her surroundings outside the lab. "Even if I knew that, which I don't, I couldn't tell you. But if she was working for the Company the media will out her sooner or later."

"Because if she was a CIA officer, don't you see a coincidence with what happened at Hutchinson Island?"

"Where are you going with this?"

Eve shrugged, and glanced up at the aerial view of the power plant on the screen. "Anything else going on in the world? You were the director of the Agency, if anyone would know something like that it would be you, right?"

"Not much just now."

"Well, nothing's been on CNN in the past twenty-four hours except for the attack on Hutchinson Island, and now this assassination, which was supposedly carried out by something called the Earth Liberation Front. They want to topple the Chávez government so that they can use the oil revenues to fight for a clean environment. They want to put themselves out of business by squeezing the price of oil so sharply they'll make it impossible to keep using it for gasoline."

"Where's the connection?"

"I know about these people, and a thousand other groups like theirs. They're the ones who want people like me to succeed. They not only want to shut down our consumption of oil, for any purpose, they want to stop the use of coal, reduce our carbon emissions all the way back to preindustrial days."

"Hutchinson Island isn't clean enough for them?

"A nuclear plant emits more heat into the atmosphere than just about any other type of power plant. They might consider that just as big a threat to the environment as carbon dioxide."

"That's a stretch, isn't it?" McGarvey asked, though he wasn't so sure. And it depended on what Lorraine Fritch was doing in Caracas.

Eve was thoughtful. "Maybe," she said. "But I don't like coincidences and I'm especially suspicious of hidden connections. Hidden motives."

McGarvey smiled. "You'd make a good detective."

She returned his smile. "I'll take that as a compliment, but being a scientist is just about the same thing."

"I'll look into it," he promised her. "But you said you wanted to talk about something that was important to you. Was that it?"

"Related," she said, even more thoughtful than a moment ago. Worried? McGarvey wondered. "What usually happens when someone or some group goes on the attack?"

"Someone fights back."

"Right," Eve said. "And who would have the most to lose by closing down, or at least restricting, Venezuelan oil production?"

She was leading him, but McGarvey didn't care because he knew where she was going, and why she might be at least concerned for her own safety. "The other oil producers."

"And who would have the most to gain by making the public believe nuclear energy was so unsafe we might as well shut them down."

"Big oil."

"And then there's my little project. Tapping the sea for energy, so we can get rid of nukes, as well as coal, oil, and gas-fired plants."

"Something every energy producer would want to fight," McGarvey said. "They're all against you."

"Now that the evil genie is out of the bottle—now that they've struck in Venezuela and Florida—maybe the war has begun in earnest, and I might be next."

"What can I do for you?"

"You must still have connections over at the CIA. Maybe you can find out if something is coming my way."

"I'm working the Hutchinson Island attack, but I'll see what I can find," McGarvey said. "No promises."

"None expected," Eve told him. "But I have a hunch something's just around the corner. And I always like to follow up on my hunches."

"How long will you be here in Washington?"

"Just for today. I'm giving a speech over at the DOE in a couple of hours. If I can get them on board it'd be a good thing."

"Not commerce?"

"No."

"Fund-raising?"

Eve's lip curled. "I hate it with a passion."

"But it's part of the game," McGarvey said, and he realized that being with her was easy and pleasant. She was good-looking and very bright.

She smiled. "I don't suppose you have a spare billion or two for the cause?"

That Afternoon

The Department of Energy's auditorium was large enough to seat two hundred, and the hall was packed this afternoon: people from the department, of course, and environmentalists and earth scientists, but people from Homeland Security too, which Eve supposed was because she'd been at Hutchinson Island yesterday; the Coast Guard, because of her work in the Gulf Stream, also coincidentally just offshore from the nuclear power plant; representatives from the White House and the State Department, because what she was proposing would cost in the trillions; a few executives from ExxonMobil, BP, Royal Dutch Shell, Chevron, and others, and a couple of senior analysts from the Natural Resources Defense Council and the Department of the Interior, which controlled oil drilling and mining and the Department of Commerce which ran NOAA.

And a rep from the International Energy Agency, who stood up and told the group that an investment of one trillion dollars per year would be needed through 2030 just to keep up with the demand for conventional energy.

That had opened the debate after Eve's familiar forty-minute talk about not only the need for alternative energy sources and her solution, but the need to control greenhouse gas emissions, which would effect global weather patterns, and with her broader, thus more controversial, proposal to control the weather.

But looking out at her audience, all of them smart people, many of them the top minds in their governmental departments, think tanks, and universities, she was struck once again how much they were not hearing. As with just about every other group she'd talked to over the past fourteen months, these experts had only heard what their field demanded they hear.

"If you're talking about dumping oil and especially coal to produce energy in favor of ethanol, we'll run into a big problem right off the bat," an alternative energy expert from the University of Manitoba argued. "Just to replace oil we would have to plant corn on seventy-five percent of all the farmland on the entire planet."

To which one of the oil reps got up and reported that his company was cutting all of its investments in hydrogen, solar, and wind power in favor of biofuels.

While the vice president of another oil giant told the audience that his company was scaling back its alternative energy research and returning to its primary goals of finding more oil reserves and more efficient means to pump it out of the ground, and how to better refine and use it.

"The point is," Eve broke in, keeping her anger in check as best she could, "we all have to agree that natural gas and especially oil are not renewable resources. We will run out sooner or later—probably sooner."

"With present technologies, and what's on the drawing boards, that won't happen until well into the next century," the same oil executive argued, and Eve could see a general agreement among a sizable portion of her audience.

"And greenhouse gases, and global warming?" she asked, though she suspected her question was rhetorical here. "Those issues will not go away. I don't think there can be much argument about that basic premise, which is why my proposal for a World Energy Needs program is so important."

She stood at the podium at one side of the small stage, while the diagrams and some calculations she'd brought with her had been projected on the big flat-panel monitor to her right. The DOE had been gracious enough to allow her to make her presentation, and had been in some ways even more cooperative than Commerce.

Her boss, Bob Krantz, had come over from Silver Spring, and was seated at the back of the auditorium. She'd gotten the proof she'd needed from her work last year in the Stream, and despite the accident—sabotage hadn't been proved or disproved—he'd finally agreed to let her publish her findings.

"But you'll need a lot more," he'd warned her. "You'll have to convince a lot of people to go along with your scheme—not only other scientists and environmentalists, but the politicians and administrators."

"I know," she'd agreed. "And the oil people."

"They're the ones with the big bucks, and the ones whose throats you want to slit."

He hadn't painted a very pretty picture, and this far away from him now, even though she couldn't really tell the expression on his face, she knew damned well that he was thinking: I told you so.

Don Price had been seated next to Krantz, but he was gone, and for some reason his absence bothered her.

"Look at the science and the data and draw your own conclusions," she told them. "For the next stage of my research I need money to purchase an out-of-commission oil drilling platform, refurbish it, and have it towed to a spot in the Gulf Stream just offshore from the Hutchinson Island power station. I need money to commission General Electric to build four Pax Scientific impellers, just like the ones aboard the *Gordon Gunther*, only these need to be eight meters in diameter, deliver them to the platform, and hook their generators by underwater cable to the Hutchinson Island power connection."

"Hutchinson Island will probably be down for a long time," someone in the audience said without standing up. "Could be years."

"I spoke by phone earlier today with Sunshine State Power and Light's chief engineer who says the power connection would most likely be feasible in one year or less, and it will take us that long to prepare the rig and the generators and run the cable ashore."

"You have claimed that your original Gulf Stream experiment was sabotaged, which resulted in the death of one of your crew members, and the near drowning of another," someone else from the audience spoke up. "And Hutchinson Island may have been sabotaged. So now aren't you concerned that if you go ahead with your experiment that you'll become a target again?"

"I've considered that possibility. Yes."

"Yet you're willing to gamble your life and perhaps the lives of your crew to test your hypothesis?"

"I think solving our energy needs and reducing the intensity of destructive storms around the planet is worth the risk," Eve said.

"Who's behind the attacks on you and on Hutchinson Island?" the same man asked. She thought he was one of the reps from the White House, but she wasn't sure. "No group has come forward to claim responsibility."

And it was the sixty-four-dollar question she'd hoped wouldn't be asked, but had expected. Here and now, however, was not the time or place to give them the answer that was on the tip of her tongue, had been on the tip of her tongue since she'd evacuated from the power plant. Oil interests, she wanted to tell them, and their reactions would be as predictable to her as they would be inevitable. Preposterous. No evidence. Certainly no proof. And she would be cutting her own throat, as Krantz had warned. Blaming big oil, or the financial organizations that most profited from the manipulation of oil exploration, market development, and the futures and derivatives that resulted, would completely cut her off from funding by them. Even though it was for a project that would guarantee the future of their companies.

Think beyond oil production, she wanted to tell them. Think energy production instead. From her project, from wind farms, from solar mining.

But in the end what she most wanted to say to them was that once the impossible was eliminated, whatever was left—however improbable—would be the truth.

Don Price came in from the rear of the auditorium, said something to Krantz, and then headed up the aisle to the stage, with such an over-the-top look of excitement on his face that he practically ran the last few feet and leapt up the stairs to her side.

"Excuse me, Doctor Larsen," he blurted.

And something in the way he said it—he never called her Doctor Larsen—was alarming. But it wasn't bad news. She didn't think.

"I'm sorry to interrupt," he said into the microphone on the podium. "But this is important." He looked at Eve and smiled in the way she found devastating.

"What?" she asked.

But he turned back to the audience. "I got word just a few minutes ago that Dr. Larsen had received an e-mail at her lab from Oslo, Norway, informing her that she has been awarded the Nobel Peace Prize for her work on energy and climate change."

Eve was rocked back on her heels. The physics prize she had expected, though not for several more years, perhaps even a decade or more—because most Nobel laureates were a hell of a lot older than her. But the Peace Prize, and just now?

For just a few seconds no one moved, no one said a thing, until Krantz got to his feet and began to clap, which started everyone else applauding, some with more enthusiasm than others.

Whenever Don wore a tie, it was almost always loose; some sort of a rebel statement he was making, but for some reason she noticed that he had snugged it up.

The applause didn't last long, and when it died down, Don continued.

"She'll be presented with the gold medal and diploma at Oslo's city hall, on December tenth," he said, and he turned to her again, and held out his hand. "Let me be the first to congratulate you," he said, loudly enough for those in the front row to hear.

And then they shook hands, hugged, and he kissed her on the cheek.

"You beat the bastards after all," he said in her ear.

She didn't know how she felt, except that she was on the verge of tears, which she would not allow to happen. Not here and now. So she grinned. "Not yet," she told him. "But it's a start."

"Yeah, the damn thing works."

Although Department of Energy's Deputy Secretary Joseph Caldwell had not attended Eve's presentation, someone from his staff who was there, had called him with the Nobel Prize news, and he showed up as Eve was making her way up the aisle accepting congratulations and handshakes from just about everyone within reach. He was at the back of the hall, smiling broadly.

"Congratulations, Doctor," he said, shaking her hand. "This must be a wonderful vindication for your work."

"And a surprise, Mr. Secretary," she said gracefully. She hadn't met him before, although of course she knew of him, because he had given his initial blessing to approach SSP&L with her project. He was one of the Washington insiders who was on his way up.

"You were mentioned a couple of years ago for the Prize," he said.

"Physics," she said. "But thank you, and thanks for the use of your auditorium."

"Yours is an important project, and I suspect that the Peace Prize will stand you in greater stead than a scientific prize, especially with the people who you'll want to help with funding."

"You were one of the first people I was going to approach, after my boss at NOAA."

His smile was neutral. "The department cannot fund you, but I certainly can direct you to some folks who might be able to help. Perhaps Exxon or BP would be willing to give you one of their retired or soon-to-be retired oil platforms I know people over at Interior."

"I don't believe I have many friends in the oil industry," Eve had said.

"You don't understand how things work in the business world; this has nothing whatsoever to do with friendship. It has to do about appearances. Most of the oil producers are backing away from alternative energy research."

"Just what I mean."

"But they're taking heat in the media because of it, and because of the BP Gulf spill. Giving you a piece of hardware that they're no longer using would cost them nothing—hell, it would even save them the money they'd have to spend at a breaker yard. And this way they'd get the benefits of some good PR for a change." He shook her hand again. "I'll see what I can do."

Eve and Don followed Krantz up to his office in Silver Spring and for the first ten minutes neither of them said a word, especially not Eve who was so caught up with the Nobel Prize thing that she could not think of anything else. She realized at one point that what she was feeling was a legitimate sense of wonderment or rapture, perhaps even the Rapture, but instead of meeting Christ at the midway point down from heaven, she was seeing her project actually happening. As Krantz had told her before they left the DOE auditorium: "It'll be hard to say no to a Nobel laureate."

Don finally looked over at her. "You'll have a lot of crap facing you in the next few days. I didn't say anything back there, but the FBI wants to interview you about what you were doing at Hutchinson Island."

"Begging for them not to laugh me out of there," she said.

"Debbie said this guy sounded serious."

Debbie Milner was the general office manager at NOAA, and it was she who'd also taken the e-mail from Oslo through Eve's lab at Princeton. Nothing got by her.

"I'll talk to them," Eve said. "But we have a lot of work to do, and probably less than a year to get it done, because I want to be ready to plug into Hutchinson Island's power connection once it's up and running."

Don laughed. "You're not thinking straight, Eve."

She looked at him, really looked at him this time. He was an arrogant, conceited, irritating man, a prick at times, but at thirty-one he was one of the most intelligent men, other than her ex, she'd ever known, and she'd known a lot of bright guys. His Ph.D. thesis at Princeton three years ago was on possible methods of controlling the planet's climate, and its sheer brilliance and clarity were among the main reasons she had considered him for postdoc work, even though she hadn't been his thesis adviser. The fact she'd found him attractive had almost, but not quite, made her drop him from consideration, but in the end she'd hired him, and was still very glad she had done so.

"The Nobel Prize thing?" she asked.

"Right from the get-go; they're setting up a party for you in the boardroom, but that's just the start. Debbie says the phones have been ringing off the hook, and our Web site is damn near in gridlock with people wanting to talk to you. Mostly the press, but M.I.T., Cal Tech, Harvard, and a bunch of other department heads, plus the environmental geeks want a piece of you, too. She didn't have time to tell me everything, but on top of all that you're going to have to come up with a statement for the media—a sound bite that won't put everyone to sleep—and beyond that you'll need to start work on your acceptance speech."

She had to laugh with him, because of course he was right. And she'd never understood until just this moment why just about every writer or scientist complained that getting the Nobel Prize had kept them from their work. But Krantz was right too, when he assured her that it would be tough to say no to a Nobel laureate. Look what it had done for Al Gore; taken him from a failed presidential candidate to a respected, even renowned world figure who'd spoken at the U.N. And she relaxed a little, knowing that she would have to start learning how to go with the flow.

Sensing her new mood, Don reached over and patted her on the knee. "That's better."

"As long as they don't try to put my face on Wheaties boxes," she said.

That Evening

Anne Marie Marinaccio had buried herself in her work over the past year plus, each month that passed with no news driving her ever deeper into a funk that seemed at times to be bottomless. Ominously she'd not been pressured by al-Naimi or anyone else from Riyadh or any of the royals who'd invested, and continued to invest with the MG. And in some ways their new investments, many of them quite heavy, in the range of several hundreds of millions U.S., were even more troublesome to her. It was as if they—collectively—knew something that she didn't. And at times she'd been afraid that some sword of Damocles was about to drop down and chop her head off.

But except for the dismal state of the economy, worldwide, during which the MG had continued to invest not only on shorted oil issues, in secret as much as that was possible given the volume of money she was hedging, nothing seemed to be lurking around the corner. Al-Naimi had kept the wolves at bay as he had promised for fourteen long months.

And suddenly it was as if the dam had burst. Gunther had called her yesterday around ten in the evening. "It's been done."

And she remembered her feelings of relief mixed with a bit of awe at what she had set in motion, and the reasons for it as well as the consequences. Especially the unintended consequences, the even more important thought that came into her head as she watched the CNN news reports on the scene, and listened as the commentators explained that although the incident was bad, circumstances had made the meltdown and release of radiation far less disastrous than the Three Mile Island incident more than three decades ago, and especially less disastrous than the more recent Chernobyl accident.

A National Nuclear Security Administration official was the first to use the term *sabotage*, but that for two NNSA teams on the ground at Hutchinson Island the incident would have been nothing short of catastrophic. When pressed for details the official cited national security concerns, leaving the newscasters, and a few nuclear energy experts from industry as well as academia to their explanations of emergency shutdown procedures that included automatic scramming and coolant water dumping and why they did not work as designed.

Which, of course, led to even more intense speculation about the safety of the other 100-plus nuclear power stations in the U.S., and the call for more security, and it reminded Anne Marie of the hue and cry over airport security in the wake of the 9/11 disaster.

Then early this morning she received a telephone call at the same encrypted number Gunther regularly used, this one from her friend and longtime heavy investor from as far back as the dot-com boom, that a situation in Caracas had been successfully handled.

"I wasn't aware that there was a situation," she'd told him. And Octavio had chuckled, his voice low and in her estimation his accented English very sexy.

"I didn't want to bother you with something you could do nothing about, or until things began to get out of control."

She'd been alarmed, this call coming so soon after the Hutchinson Island business. "Tell me."

So he had explained about the CIA's chief of station who'd been snooping around him and his business dealings, presumably involving not only there in Venezuela but elsewhere, which would have included Anne Marie. "I was told that she had chartered a private jet to fly her to Washington." And the timing on the heels of a certain event in Florida was enough for him to take action.

She'd been afraid at that moment, because Octavio was talking about the assassination of an important CIA officer, an act that U.S. authorities would investigate with extreme vigor, but also because he'd made some sort of a connection to her and Hutchinson Island.

"How could you have been sure that the CIA was investigating you?" she'd asked, almost using the pronoun *us* instead.

"I wasn't one hundred percent certain, but after reading the documents that she meant to carry to Washington, I was glad that I followed my instincts," Octavio said. "And you should be glad of it as well, because not only were you and I linked, but the woman was making a case for a connection between you and me and the Florida business."

"Me, by name?" Anne Marie had asked.

"Yes," Octavio said. "But my security people assure me that this connection may have only been speculation, *un teoria*, a theory, because there have been no attacks on any of my online accounts, looking for information. Have your security people detected anything?"

"No," Anne Marie had assured him, and afterwards she had called Gunther to alert him of the possibility and he too had assured her he'd detected no increase in interest.

"Did you admit anything to Miguel?" Wolfhardt had asked sharply.

"No."

"He didn't press you about Hutchinson Island?"

"No."

"Good."

And finally her encrypted phone chimed again less than one hour ago, and Jeremiah Thaddeus Schlagel was practically shouting like he did in his sermons. "If I'm reading this right, it's about time," he'd bellowed. "I'm here, at the Raffles. Meet me in that whorehouse of a bar upstairs at eight."

She'd gotten dressed in a simple black Versace pantsuit and a plain white silk blouse, and riding over now to Dubai's newest and most famous hotel in the back of her Mercedes Maybach. Some of the fear she'd felt after Octavio's call had begun to fade, because the next phase of her operation for al-Naimi and the Saudi royals was about to begin.

About time indeed. Fourteen months ago after she'd set Wolfhardt on the task of creating a nuclear power station meltdown, proving nuclear energy was far too vulnerable to attack and far too dangerous a method with which to generate electricity, she'd contacted one of her largest investors back in the States and invited him to come over to Dubai to talk.

"Money's getting a bit tight, darlin'," he'd told her in his fake rural Kansas drawl. "Unless you got something interesting. Something I could set my teeth into."

"You're an ambitious man, Jerry," she'd told him.

"Yes, I am, I admit it."

"And you would make a fine president."

For the first time since she'd known the man he'd had nothing to say.

"But you would need a cause. Something you could get behind on your television and radio networks. Something the religious right, your flock, could become enthused about. Wildly enthused, enough to push you to the top."

"I'm listening," Schlagel had said that day, his Kansas drawl replaced by his flat Midwest accent. He'd been born and raised in Milwaukee, and whenever something unexpected overtook him, the Wisconsin in him came back.

"Not yet. But when it happens it'll be deadly, with a promise of more to come unless the right man is there to lead the charge."

"Something like al-Quaeda? Another nine/eleven?"

"Bigger," she'd promised.

"When?"

"This'll take a bit of work, so I want you to remain patient. But I also want you to get your organization geared up to be ready to move at a moment's notice. Tell them you had a revelation that something stupendous is in the wind. God spoke to you, and commanded you to get your flock ready, because they'd be needed."

Schlagel had chucked. "Not bad, darlin'," he'd drawled. "Not bad at all."

Her chauffeur dropped her off in front of the hotel built in the style of an ancient Egyptian pyramid in glass and steel instead of limestone, with the apex completely sheathed in windows so patrons of the city's most famous drinking establishment, the China Moon Champagne Bar, could see the entire city right out to the edge of the desert.

Inside the mammoth lobby one of the white-gloved attendants scurried over and escorted her to the elevators, a service the hotel provided for everyone who walked through the doors.

It was a weeknight, but Dubai was a business city, so the lobby was bustling, a half-dozen people riding up in the elevator with her, at least two of them speaking with German accents, and another speaking French with a Chinese woman and an Arab male dressed casually in jeans, an open-collar shirt, and a khaki jacket.

Schlagel was seated in a high-backed red upholstered chair at a low table in the far corner of the large room, and when he spotted Anne Marie coming over he got to his feet, a big grin on what she'd always considered was a broad peasant's face, perpetually filled with cunning and deceit. And except for his crudeness, almost total lack of manners or social graces, he was an extremely bright man, a good judge of human nature, and a shrewd investor, who at her last financial reckoning was worth at least two billion dollars, much of that hidden in offshore banks, including the UAEIBC here in Dubai, against the inevitable day his empire collapsed and he had to run.

"No way I'm going to end up like Brother Jim Bakker," he'd told her once. "Just hedging my bets like you and your old man before you." He'd done his homework on her as she had on him before she took any of his money.

Finding out about him, the real man behind the public image, hadn't been easy because he'd been very good at covering his tracks and inventing a new persona for himself, but Gunther had put the right people on the project about eight years ago and slowly most of the pieces came together.

His real name was Donald Deutsch, and he'd been born to a working-class family from the wrong side of Milwaukee's tracks; the one bit of his public background that wasn't far from the truth. He'd left home when he was seventeen or eighteen and joined the army where he learned how to take care of himself physically, and where he used his street smarts to run several illegal operations at each base he was assigned to; gambling and prostitution rings as well as trafficking tax-free booze and cigarettes from the PX, which he sold on the black market in Europe.

But he'd apparently run through the money he'd made, and after the army he'd ended up broke and busted in San Francisco at the age of twenty-one. Newly released from the county lockup he'd stumbled into a small storefront church that fed the homeless, and it was there, according to Gunther's researchers, that Deutsch found his salvation—his financial salvation.

Changing his name, he took up the old-time religion, which initially included faith healing, to conceal the exact amount that his growing flock of believers invested in God through the Reverend Jeremiah. He opened storefront churches all up and down the California coast, raking in money by the tens of thousands at first and then into the hundreds of thousands.

And Schlagel was not only very good at his preaching, he was a charmer, Gunther wrote in his report. Parishioners gave him money, which he supposedly invested for them, giving them a good return and only keeping a tithe for the church. In actuality he'd been running a highly successful Ponzi scheme that depended on the continual growth of his ministry and investors, and the provision that if a member left the church, his or her investments would remain with the church—to do God's will.

Eventually he sucked in beat cops, then police chiefs, local businessmen, and finally the mayors of some of the small towns where he preached, as well as state legislators.

He bought his first radio station in Fresno in the late eighties, then another in Port Angeles, Washington—by then he had branched out to a half-dozen western states, so that he was raking in enough money from ordinary contributions that he was able to pay off the last of his Ponzi scheme investors.

Then eleven years ago Schlagel moved his ministry to McPherson, a small town in western Kansas, built a huge church and television studio and started his own Soldiers of Salvation (SOS) Network that was initially based on Pat Robertson's 707 Club on the Christian Broadcasting Network. Within five years, his television and radio networks, as well as newspapers and magazines across the country, made him not only one of the most popular preachers on air, but brought him to the attention of presidents, and just three years ago *Time* magazine had named him Man of the Year, and called him, "America's man of God, the spiritual adviser to the White House."

Besides money and the good life he led in secret, Schlagel's chief ambition had become the same as Pat Robertson's; he wanted to be

President of the United States, and he was willing to do whatever it took to get there.

They shook hands when she reached him, and she smiled. She was going to get him the White House, and Hutchinson Island would be his start as well as her salvation.

"You're looking particularly chic this evening," he told her. He was dressed in a smartly tailored charcoal gray suit, and the look on his face was that of a man who was supremely confident that he was about to be handed the universe.

"Thanks," Anne Marie said, and they sat down.

Schlagel had already ordered a bottle of Krug champagne, and he poured her a glass. "It's your favorite," he said. "I remembered, though when I'm alone I prefer a cold Bud. Simple tastes for a simple man."

Anne Marie had to laugh at his disingenuousness. "Bullshit, Donald," she said softly, and he became suddenly wary, like an animal who figured he was being backed into a corner and wanting to get out rather than fight.

"Interesting name," he said, his smile fading.

"Maybe it wasn't such a good idea you coming here. We shouldn't be seen together."

"After tonight we won't be," he said. "But something like this cannot be trusted to some Internet connection, or satellite phone, even if it's encrypted."

"What do you want?" Anne Marie asked.

"Is Hutchinson Island the opening gun?"

"Yes," Anne Marie said, and she watched as the ramifications of the disaster began to hit him, what it could mean for him, and how it could be manipulated to his advantage.

"What's in it for you?" he asked.

"I want you to turn public sentiment against nuclear energy. It's your new cause. You had your revelation that something like this was going to happen, and now it has. Nuclear energy is against the laws of God and nature, and should be damned. The devil's business."

"Never preach to a preacher," Schlagel said. "All I want to know is what's in it for you, because I don't even want to hear how you pulled it off. Where's the gain for you, 'cause sure as hell you can't believe that simply shutting down the hundred or so nuclear power plants in the States will have any serious effect on the price of oil. Anyway you've been selling short, so you've made money on the way up and on the way back down."

"Never talk financial dealings with a Harvard MBA and a hedge fund manager who has no risk of going broke anytime soon."

Schlagel laughed. "But Hutchinson Island is just a start. I can make it something my people will believe in, but there'll have to be more."

"Even if it was possible to cause another meltdown, it's too risky."

"Haven't you been watching the news?" Schlagel asked. "You ever heard of Eve Larsen, an environmental scientist working for NOAA?"

Anne Marie shook her head. "Should I have?" she asked, but something in Schlagel's change of attitude all of a sudden was bothersome.

"Yes, because she's just become my new cause. Hutchinson Island is good, the timing is perfect, but Dr. Larsen has become even better."

"What are you talking about?"

"She's been preaching alternative energy sources. She wants all the nukes to be shut down, but she also wants to shut down coal-fired electrical plants as well as natural gas facilities and she wants all cars to run on electricity."

"Won't happen anytime soon," Anne Marie said. "People hammering away at that idea are a dime a dozen. Everyone listens, but just to be polite. Oil is here to stay at least through the end of the century." But even as she said it, something in the way Schlagel was watching her made her afraid.

"She wants to buy an oil platform and put it in the Gulf Stream, and stick some sort of paddle wheels into the water to generate electricity. She says she can supply all the electricity we need without burning coal or gas or use nukes."

"Wouldn't work."

"Wait, there's more," Schlagel said, his deep brown eyes flashing. He was into a sermon, but he was enough in control to keep his voice low. "And it keeps getting better. Where do you think she wants to put her rig? Right offshore from Hutchinson Island. She wants to send her power through underwater cables to the plant's electrical distribution system, and shut down the reactors."

Anne Marie had heard nothing about this, and she knew she should have. "Coincidence?"

"Doesn't matter. She's promising not only cheap electricity to power our trains, planes, trucks, and cars, but she's preaching that she'll change the weather. Get rid of all those nasty hurricanes and such." Schlagel's grin broadened. He was reaching his point. "Now that's God's work she's setting herself to do. Her own private little God project."

Anne Marie's anxiety eased a little. "The woman is a crackpot."

"Well, the crackpot has just gone and won herself the Nobel Peace Prize, what do you think about them apples?"

Anne Marie sat back, trying to see the advantages, because surely they were there, hidden somewhere in the clutter. "She'll have to fail," she mumbled half to herself, but Schlagel picked up on it.

"You're damned right. Hutchinson Island will be my rallying point, but the woman's God Project will be my battle cry, and I'll need as much time as possible to get my people behind me—to get the entire country so up in arms against nuclear power, and against the kind of tinkering she wants to do on God's playing field that our oil will be king. At least through my lifetime."

"And afterwards?" Anne Marie asked, though for the life of her she had no idea why.

Schlagel laughed. "Haven't you grown up enough, darlin', to realize there ain't no hereafter?" He leaned forward. "I want you to get one of your good old boys to give the little lady her platform, and maybe help with the money for her waterwheels. And you can leave the rest to me."

It was never about anything else but timing, of course. In that Schlagel was right. Nuclear energy had to become unpalatable to the public, which he would help bring about, and Dr. Larsen had to fail, for which she would arrange for a little insurance just in case something happened to the good reverend.

She raised her glass of champagne. "The God Project," she said.

"Leave it to me," Schlagel said, clinking glasses.

That same evening back at her penthouse apartment, Anne Marie telephoned Wolfhardt, and explained everything to him.

"I'll call on Mr. DeCamp, immediately," he said.

"Yes, do that."

"But I don't think waiting for her to actually get her oil platform and perform her experiment is such a good idea. She needs to be assassinated."

"It could come back to us," Anne Marie said. She was thinking about al-Naimi, and she almost said the Saudis, but she held off.

"Nothing would reflect on your oil interests, I can practically guarantee as much."

"Who then?" she asked, but she suddenly realized that Wolfhardt was only stating the obvious; when fingers were pointed they would be toward Schlagel and his people. She chuckled, the noise coming all the way from the back of her throat. The irony would be delicious, actually pitting her and the reverend—two allies— against each other. Actually in concert with each other. Asset multipliers, such operations were called.

"I think you know," Wolfhardft said.

"Of course," Anne Marie agreed. "And I trust you implicitly, but with care, Gunther, and with fail-safes and contingencies."

It was two in the morning when she called Schlagel's encrypted phone. He was still at the Raffles and after five rings when he finally answered she could hear at least two women giggling in the background. "This had best be very good, darlin'," he said, and he sounded drunk.

"Can you talk?"

"I can always talk. What do you want?"

"I want you to start now."

Suddenly Schlagel was sober, and he sounded guarded. "Something happen?"

"Let's just say I had an epiphany," Anne Marie told him.

"I'm all ears."

"Go after Dr. Larsen right now, sharp and hard. Send a couple of your soldiers after her. Shoot up her car, burn down her apartment, attack one of her lab assistants, maybe smash some of her scientific equipment. I don't care what."

Schalgel was silent for several beats, and Anne Marie could almost see him figuring the angles, working out the percentages. "I want the bitch aboard the oil platform."

"I agree. Don't kill her, just shake her up."

"Why?"

"I want to slow her down," Anne Marie said. "She'll get her platform, but I want your people to hound her all the way to Oslo. Make her know that she's vulnerable."

"Vulnerable people make mistakes."

"And if she starts making mistakes—I don't care what sort of mistakes—everything else that the woman says or does will become suspect."

Again Schlagel was silent for a beat, but then he chuckled. "You are one gloriously devious woman, darlin'," he said. "And I can't tell you just how much I love you."

"Because we're cut of the same cloth," she managed to tell him though her gorge was rising. "We're winners."

"Amen."

PART

TWO

Through December

TWENTY-FIVE

☐

When McGarvey showed up at the CIA's front gate, a pass was ready for him, and although normally visitors to the Agency had to be met here by someone authorized to act as an escort, he'd been the DCI. His was a special case.

"Welcome back, Mr. Director," one of the security officers said pleasantly.

"Just here for a visit," McGarvey said, and he drove up to the parking area in front of the Old Headquarters Building, the morning sunny and warm, nothing like his mood.

Rencke was waiting for him in the main lobby, and he was hopping from one foot to the other as he usually did when he was excited about something, or was in the middle of some important project. He was a man of medium height whose head seemed too large for his body; his red frizzy hair was always out of control, flowing out in every direction lending him the air of an Einstein, a genius, which in fact he was. He was dressed in dirty blue jeans, an old T-shirt with the logo of the KGB on the breast, and unlaced tennis shoes. Even a successful marriage hadn't made him clean up his act, which every boss he'd ever work for thought was an act designed to irritate them, which it wasn't. He was just Otto, and had been this way since McGarvey had first met him years ago.

"Oh, wow, that was something not in the playbook," he said, giving McGarvey a massive hug. "Louise wants to know if you can you come over for dinner tonight. You haven't seen Audie in a long time."

"Not until this business is over," McGarvey said.

Otto gave him a sharp look, but said nothing until they were passed through security and headed down the busy first-floor corridor filled with displays from the early days of American intelligence efforts beginning with the OSS during World War II. The entire corridor served as the CIA's museum of its own artifacts.

"Eric Yablonski clued me in with what you guys are up to. We've been sharing files. He doesn't think Hutchinson Island was an isolated incident."

"Neither do I."

"What'd you find out about the schoolteacher in San Francisco?"

"His neck was broken, and his body wrapped in a plastic sheet and stuffed in a closet. Means our guy was in the apartment."

"Did you have someone dust the place?"

"The Bureau sent over a couple of people, but they came up with nothing, which is about what I expected," McGarvey said. "Points to this guy being a pro, which means he got his training from somewhere, and for now I'm betting South African intelligence, or maybe a paramilitary unit. A SSP&L clerk who talked to him said he had some kind of a British accent."

"Buffalo Battalion?" Rencke asked.

"It would fit. He lost his job and instead of letting all of his training go to waste he turned freelance."

"But why San Francisco?" Rencke wanted to know. "And why that particular schoolteacher? I'm coming up blank and so is Eric."

That had puzzled McGarvey as well, and it was one of the reasons he'd taken the time to go out to California to see if he could find any answers. And he had. "Benson was a homosexual, and he lived alone."

Rencke got it immediately. "Lots of gay men in San Francisco, lots of gay bars, meat factories. He might have started with any database, but he ended up with single males working for the school system who had the same general build. Sooner or later he was bound to get lucky, and he did with Benson, and picked up the poor bastard at a bar and went home with him."

"It gives up a couple of facts," McGarvey said. "Our man's smart, and we have a fair idea that he's slightly built, which matches what the parking lot camera picked up."

They got off the elevator on the third floor, and went down the hall to Rencke's suite of offices, which was a cluttered mess: maps, books, atlases, magazines, and newspapers in a half-dozen languages, scattered on tables, on the floor, on chairs. Most of the world's knowledge still wasn't digitized, and sometimes information had to be found the old-fashioned way. A long table in the shape of a big letter C was filled with computer monitors, all of them large, some of them touch screens. Images showed on all of the screens, a couple of them with lavender backgrounds, which was one of Rencke's coded systems that warned of some sort of trouble possibly heading our way.

There was room for a secretary and a couple of assistants, but he'd never felt the need to have someone work with him. "We all have our little secrets, ya know," he'd once confided to McGarvey. "And I don't want anyone prying into mine."

"What's coming up lavender, Hutchinson Island?" McGarvey asked.

"Nothing important yet, but I expect the threat level to rise, especially once we find out who the contractor was, because it looks like he was working for al-Quaeda. These are chewing on the Lorraine Fritch situation."

"She was one of ours."

"Yeah, COS Caracas. She and her number two were putting something together on Miguel Octavio and his connection with the UAE International Bank of Commerce, and she must have come up with something important. She called Ma   Bambridge and said she was coming here with something too big t   rust to the Internet or even encrypted phones. Had to be done in person Anyway a couple of guys dressed as cops took her out along with her driver and bodyguard within sight of the airport."

"No briefcase or computer disk?"

"Nada. Whoever made the hit took whatever she was carrying with her."

"What about her number two?"

"Don Morton. One of the good ones, sharp as they come. But he didn't have a clue what she'd found. He didn't even know she was heading out of the country. The only one she told besides Marty was the ambassador."

"Do you know Eve Larsen?"

Rencke grinned. "Everybody does. She's a bright lady. Just won the Nobel Peace Prize, though I figured her for physics in ten or twenty years."

"She was at Hutchinson Island talking to some SSP and L bigwigs when the attack occurred. And she thinks that Lorraine's assassination and Hutchinson Island are related."

Rencke was intrigued; it showed on his face. "That's a stretch."

"That's what I told her. But she had a pretty convincing argument that Lorraine was taken down by people who want to topple the Chávez government and take over oil production, so that they could eventually shut it down."

"Never happen," Rencke said.

"No. And I don't think this anti-oil group killed her. It was probably Octavio because of something Lorraine dug up. And the timing is the thing that Dr. Larsen picked up on, the assassination coming on the heels of the Hutchinson Island attack."

"None of the oil companies would be crazy enough to pull off stunts like those," Rencke said. "That just won't wash, Mac. You might argue that most of them didn't give a damn about anything except profits and the hell with the environment. But the same can be said of a lot of countries—China among them. Us. We're building coal-fired plants that pollute a hell of a lot more than nukes or natural gas, or even cars on the road."

"I'm just fishing here. But you just said that Don Morton and Lorraine had come up with a connection that linked Octavio to the UAE bank. Those people are probably just as dirty as the guys who ran the BCCI were."

"Whoa, wait a minute, kemo sabe," Rencke said, suddenly very excited. "Shit, it's al-Quaeda, supported by the UAE IBC." He dropped into a chair in front of one of the touch screen monitors and brought up Forcier's image data to the right. "This is your suicide bomber. Real name Achmed bin Helbawi, from Sadda, a little town on the Afghan border south of Peshawar. Al-Quaeda recruited him when he was just a kid, and sent him to Saudi Arabia to study nuclear engineering. We found out that he was a standout at King Abdul Aziz University, and then he suddenly disappeared for about a year, until he turned up at a couple of French nuclear power training facilities in Saclay and Montigny under a Saudi passport. Then last year sometime he shows up on the doorstep of a headhunter in New York who got him the Hutchinson Island job under the name Thomas Forcier with a legitimate French passport."

"Did the same bank that Octavio is connected with fund Helbawi's education?"

"I don't know that yet," Rencke admitted. "But it's an interesting thought. Maybe Dr. Larsen wasn't making much of a stretch after all."

"If we can make that connection it would be a common point between Lorraine and Hutchinson Island."

"And your pro," Rencke said. "An operation like that had to have a tight plan. Helbawi on the inside pumping info back out. I assume the Bureau has tossed his apartment. Have you been told anything?"

"Not yet."

"I'll put it on my shopping list," Rencke said. "But for now, job one is finding out who the contractor is."

"And where he's gone to ground. I'd like to have a chat with him."

Rencke laughed. "I bet you would."

And McGarvey was brought back to his conversation with Eve at the Watergate, and her speculations and fear that someone might be coming after her next. "The IBC has to be getting some of its money from the Saudis and some other oil interests," he said. "Octavio, for one. Who'd have the most to lose if Venezuela's oil production were to be interrupted?"

"Well, not Exxon, or BP or any of the others. But it might play havoc with some of the hedge fund guys and derivatives people."

"And who would have the most to gain, if the American public began to believe that nuclear energy was too risky, maybe deny any new permits or licenses?"

"The same people," Rencke said. And he'd gotten McGarvey's point. "Eve Larsen and her project could be on the firing line, especially now that she's won the Nobel Prize, because it's a safe bet she'll get the funding, and probably from some company like BP. Would be great publicity for them. Investing in alternative energy."

"Have you heard anything?"

Rencke started to shake his head, but then turned to one of his computer monitors connected to a keyboard and pulled up a media search engine. "I remember something on Fox News maybe a year or two ago. An accident."

A minute later he found the program with George Szucs and Eve Larsen aboard the *Gordon Gunther* in the Gulf Stream offshore from the Hutchinson Island nuclear power plant, and fast-forwarded the interview to where she took off her clothes and dove into the water, and then to the point where the cable had been brought aboard, and the question, an accident or sabotage was left hanging.

"If it was sabotage, someone was after her more than a year ago," Rencke said.

Left unsaid, because it wasn't necessary, was that the Nobel Prize had just made Eve Larsen the biggest target on the block. Coal, gas, nukes, oil, and everyone connected with the big four would be gunning for her.

"See what you can dredge up," McGarvey said. "But the contractor's identity is still primary."

"I'm on it," Rencke said.

TWENTY-SIX

InterOil's new international headquarters was housed in an impressively modernistic skyscraper rising as a narrow glass and steel pyramid twenty-six stories above the Mississippi River on Business 61 in front of Capitol Lake in Baton Rouge, Louisiana. InterOil had made fabulous profits when oil had hit $150 per barrel, and even at less than one half that, the company, rivaled only by ExxonMobil, was raking in good money.

Much of the company's profits were being invested in oil exploration along Florida's gulf coast, in Iraq's new green fields, and in partnership with Octavio Oil, drilling had begun in the Golfo de Venezuela. Permitting applications with the Canadian government for preliminary exploration in the Arctic's Parry Channel near Cornwallis Island with its settlement and airstrip at Resolute had been going ahead slowly for the past eighteen months, and the Parliament at Ottawa just last week had given its tentative approval, even over massive protests. Oil and oil dollars had become more important than the environment, even after the BP Gulf spill, even in sensitive places like the Arctic wilderness and Florida's beaches.

But InterOil had not given up its investments, though meager by comparison with exploration and development, in alternative energy sources, mostly solar power in Arizona and New Mexico, but in some wind farms along the Oregon and Washington coasts.

Joseph Caldwell over at Commerce had been as good as his word, and had personally telephoned Eve yesterday that he'd arranged an appointment with InterOil's Erik Tyrell, vice president of worldwide marketing.

"Can't promise you anything, Doctor, but Erik will at least hear you out," Caldwell had told her. "He's a careful man, and he'll almost certainly have someone else sitting in on your meeting. My guess would be Jane Petersen, their chief U.S. counsel, who is even more careful and tightfisted than he is."

"Can you suggest an approach that might work?" Eve had asked, swallowing her stubborn streak, because this stuff was every bit as important as the science. Without the backing, there would be no science.

"May I speak frankly?"

"Of course."

"You have a chip on your shoulder, Doctor, that is unattractive."

Eve bridled, and she wanted to protest. Who the hell did he think he was? Nothing other than a bureaucrat, while she was a scientist and had just won the . . . Nobel Prize. It made her smile, just a little, to realize the bastard was right. And so was Don, who'd tried to warn her to "play nice." She could blame her attitude on her upbringing in England, something she'd been doing for most of her life, but even when she'd been a kid she'd had the same "screw you" attitude. And now she didn't know if she liked looking in that sort of a mirror, though maybe it was time she finally did.

"You're right," she admitted.

"I'm a politician, which means I know when to push and when to back off, and when to show up at a meeting that's vitally important with my hat in hand. Every once in a while something like that actually works."

And this time Eve really did laugh a little, because Caldwell was not only a politician, he was an important man with a little bit of self-deprecating humor. "Thanks, Mr. Secretary. It's something new for me, but I'll try."

"Good luck."

At noon Eve got out of the cab in front of InterOil, and with her laptop containing a PowerPoint presentation of what she hoped to achieve, and how she wanted to get there, she squared her narrow shoulders and marched across the broad plaza and fountains to the vast, doorless entrance, the inside coolness separated from the sultry heat outside by a sheet of gently blowing air.

People were seated on benches and on the rims of the several fountains eating their lunches, and inside the lobby that soared upward for the entire twenty-six stories, more people were coming and going. InterOil's headquarters was a busy place. Prosperous, even booming, and bustling 24/7 because the company operated worldwide on Greenwich mean time so that office hours everywhere could be coordinated.

She had been told by Tyrell's secretary that noon local would be the only time open for her brief presentation. If it had been set for two in the morning she would have agreed without hesitation, though she'd been a little put off by the secretary's emphasis on brief. She'd had time on the flight from Washington to pare down the forty-minute fund-raising presentation she'd been giving.

"Bright, cheerful, but businesslike." She'd laughed when she told Don. "And brief."

He'd laughed with her. "Just remember to stay out of your lecture mode and you'll be fine."

"That'll be the toughest part."

The receptionist at the circular counter in the center of the lobby directed Eve to the southwest elevators. "Mr. Tyrell's office is on the twenty-fifth floor."

She was the only one in the car so she indulged herself by examining her image in the mirrored back wall. She was dressed in a khaki skirt, a plain white blouse, and a blue blazer, no earrings or necklace, and only a touch of makeup, even that much rare for her. She looked neat, freshly scrubbed, but as if she'd just stepped out of the pages of some outdoor adventure magazine. Queen of the High Seas come ashore to ask for a handout. She'd never thought much about her looks until now, and she felt a little shabby in this setting.

Tyrell's suite of offices was behind glass doors directly across from the elevator, and his secretary, a stunning blond woman with movie star teeth and a devastating smile, got up from behind her glass desk. "Mr. Tyrell is waiting in the boardroom for you, Doctor," she said, and she led Eve, who was really feeling shabby now, down a connecting corridor to a smallish room with a long table big enough to seat ten or twelve people.

Photographs of what appeared to be oil-drilling rigs in settings from deserts to frozen tundra and offshore platforms, some of them huge, and in one photograph a gigantic wave had risen as high as the main deck, were arranged on the walls.

Tyrell, seated at the head of the table, didn't bother to get up. "So good of you to be prompt, Doctor Larsen," he said. He was a short-torsoed, fat man with thick white hair that framed his perfectly round face like a halo. Except for an extremely stern set to his narrow lips and a harshness in his voice and eyes, he could have easily fit the role of a department store Santa Claus, and Eve's spirits took a little sag.

"Thank you for agreeing to meet with me," Eve said. She sat down at the opposite end of the table and laid her laptop in front of her.

"I noticed when you came in that your eyes were drawn to our photo gallery, especially the North Sea rig."

"Impressive."

"Carlton Explorer II, quite large, in size and in dollars. Built in Norway and dragged out to her present position by six oceangoing tugs, before her legs were extended to the seabed, and work could actually be done. We'll have invested nearly one billion dollars by the time we ever pump so much as a single barrel of oil."

Eve had no idea what he was trying to tell her. "It's good that InterOil has been successful enough to be able to spend that kind of money for exploration."

"It's a part of our business, Doctor," Tyrell said. "Do you know the size of that wave washing over our rig?"

"Probably seventy feet, perhaps higher if it was a rogue. I would assume the rig had been evacuated by then."

"Actually it hadn't, and it was a rogue wave measured at slightly higher than one hundred feet."

"Impressive."

"Yes, Carlton Explorer II is impressive in every respect," Tyrell said.

Eve started to open her laptop but Tyrell motioned for her to stop.

"Unfortunately our time is not sufficient to hear your full presentation." He looked past her. "I'm glad you could make it," he said.

Eve turned as a handsome woman with short dark hair and a slender, almost boyish frame, dressed in what was obviously an expensive dark blue skirt, silk blouse, and matching blazer, a gold-colored scarf artfully tied around her neck, walked in.

"Jane Petersen," she told Eve, not bothering to offer her hand. "I'm the company's general counsel for North America." She sat down next to Tyrell. "Congratulations on your Nobel Prize. You must feel vindicated."

Eve decided that she didn't like the woman, though she wasn't exactly sure why, except she'd detected insincerity in the remark. Jane Petersen didn't give a damn about the Nobel Prize, Eve's or anyone else's, unless it had a directly positive bearing on InterOil's continued profitability.

"Actually it's why I'm here today," Eve said.

Neither InterOil executive said a thing, and possibly for the first time in her adult life Eve felt out of her depth.

"May I assume that you know of my World Energy Needs project, and its possible significance?" she began.

"We know what you're trying to do," Tyrell said.

"I'm here to ask for funding."

"How much?" Tyrell asked directly.

Eve glanced up at the photographs on the wall. "The cost of an off-

shore exploration rig," she said. "Or at least a stripped-down version because we won't be doing any drilling."

"Why?" Jane Petersen asked, no curiosity whatsoever in her voice or
manner.

And in Eve's estimation the woman wasn't even being polite, but she
sucked it up. Hat in hand, Caldwell had recommended. "Because InterOil not only has the money, it has the expertise in offshore rigs. And
because alternative energy sources are the future for corporations such
as yours. Perhaps the only future, unless you believe that you'll forever
continue to find new oil pools."

"For the next one hundred years," Tyrell suggested.

"But the world's reserves are finite, everyone agrees with at least that
much. So why burn oil for power or transportation, when for the fore-
seeable future we'll continue to need it for lubrication, for pharmaceuti-
cals, plastics, and host of other manufacturing derivatives?"

"While I may tend to agree with you, Doctor, you're discounting a
fair bit of scientific work that actually stretches how we use oil, especially for transportation. You have to agree that the internal combustion
engine is probably in its last days. We'll go all electric, that's a foregone
conclusion."

"Exactly my point," Eve said. She didn't want to get excited, but
maybe they were getting it after all.

"Yes, but you need to see our point as well," Jane Petersen said. "We
have a business to run as profitably as we possibly can make it for the sake
of our investors. And InterOil's primary concern is finding oil reserves
and pumping them out of the ground."

Eve could feel her temper slipping. "That's so shortsighted."

"Is it?" Tyrell asked. "Tell us, please, if you were suddenly handed a
check for whatever sum you needed, let's say the one billion dollars
we've spent to date on Carlton Explorer II and the work she is doing for
us, how long before your project would begin to produce energy?"

Within a year, Eve started to say, but Tyrell held her off.

"The same amount of equivalent energy that Carlton Explorer II, which
will begin producing next month?"

"Years," Eve conceded. "But never unless we start now."

"But you're still in the experimental stage of your work, isn't that so?" Jane Petersen asked.

"Yes," Eve said, and she knew where the discussion was going, and knew that this trip had been a waste of time

"By which you mean to say that you cannot guarantee a steady production of energy—a significant amount of energy—until your experiments are completed."

"That's correct. In the meantime you're running out of places to find oil."

"That's not quite true," Tyrell said. "What we're finding and pumping now are mostly light sweet crudes—that is oil which has a low API density, which we call light, and oil which has a low sulfur content which we call sweet. These are the oils that are the simplest to distill. And you are perfectly correct when you argue that we are rapidly running out of those benchmark oils. But they represent something less than thirty percent of the known worldwide reserves. We still have Canada's crude bitumen and Venezuela's extra-heavy crude, mostly in the form of oil sands. Plus there are oil shales, which actually contain kerogen that can be converted into crude oil. Did you know that the largest reserves occur here in the U.S.?"

"Yes, but producing gasoline, diesel, jet fuel, or heating oil from those sources would be expensive," Eve countered.

"Fabulously expensive, which is why we are investing considerable sums each year to find new methods of refining those products."

And it was over. Eve knew it and she could see in the expressions of the two oil executives that they also knew it.

"Coming here asking for help is fine, Doctor," Jane Petersen said coolly. "But don't try to tell us our business. We know what we are doing, and contrary to what you apparently think of us, we are keeping our eyes on the future."

"Shortsighted," Eve mumbled, but she managed a slight smile as she gathered her laptop and got to her feet. "Thank you for hearing me out."

The door opened and an older man in a three-piece business suit, a pleasant expression on his square-jawed craggy face, walked in and tossed a thick manila envelope on the table in front of Eve.

"Lawrence Dailey," the man told Eve. "I'm chairman of the board.

Just happened to be in town when I found out you were coming down to ask for our help. Joe Caldwell asked if I could see what could be done."

"Yes, sir," Eve said for want of anything else. Tyrell and Jane Petersen had gotten to their feet, but were just about as dumbstruck as she was.

"That's the deed and specifications for one of our platforms in the Gulf of Mexico, just offshore from Pass Christian, Mississippi. Vanessa Explorer, she's called. We're in the process of shutting her down and scrapping her. Just a security detail and small maintenance crew left aboard. I think she should do nicely for your project."

Hat in hand, indeed, Eve thought. Yet she wasn't so naïve as to believe that something else hadn't been going on behind the scenes. Something that in all likelihood she would never know. But it didn't matter. The damned thing works. She would worry about the quid pro quo, if there was to be one, later.

"Thank you," she said. "We'll make good use of her."

Dailey shook her hand. "Congratulations on your prize, and have a safe trip home."

Peter Tolifson, an InterOil security officer, manning the security suite, watched the closed-circuit image from one of the cameras that monitored the plaza as Eve Larsen exited the building, crossed to the driveway, and got into a cab that had just pulled up.

Using his personal cell phone he called an international number, and when it was answered, he said, "She just left."

After a moment he nodded. "She was carrying a manila envelope that she did not have when she arrived."

After another moment he broke the connection and pocketed his phone, wondering why the hell someone in Dubai would want that information.

TWENTY-SEVEN

□

DeCamp, dressed in faded jeans, a plain T shirt and sandals, and a large, floppy straw hat, was on his hands and knees tending his flower garden behind his seventeenth-century Italianate villa in the hills above Nice, in the area known as Cimiez. The late morning was lovely, and he was at peace with himself, in a place he loved, with a woman he loved, who was in the rustic kitchen preparing their lunch, and he was on the heels of a reasonably satisfying assignment.

He stopped for a moment to look past his tiny, disorganized grove of orange and lemon trees framed by tall slender cedars of Lebanon and mimosa down into the city, and beyond the hazy blue Mediterranean that disappeared into the horizon, when he spotted a dark blue Mercedes slowly making its way up the hill on the Boulevard de Cimiez.

He watched the car for a couple of minutes until it turned up the Rue de Rivoli that wound its way to the villa, put down his small weeding rake, got up, and went into the house.

Martine looked up from the side board where she was slicing a loaf of her bread, and the smile on her pretty, always expressive, French Algerian face faded. "What is it?"

"Someone is coming here, I think," he told her.

They spoke in French, which he'd always thought was one of the greatest gifts Colonel Frazier had given him. "It's a far more civil and civilized language than English," the colonel had lectured. "The language of poetry, and of love."

"For lunch?" Martine asked hopefully. She was in love with DeCamp as he was with her; her only two complaints ever were his absences from time to time, and their lack of friends.

"It's possible," he told her, and he went into the front vestibule where he got his front-of-the-house pistol, a 9 mm Steyr GB, and stuffed it in the waistband of his jeans, beneath his shirt. When he turned, Martine was there at the end of the hall at the kitchen door.

She was slender with small breasts, a boyish bottom, and straight legs with knobby knees that he'd always liked, and that sometimes he kidded her about. She in return would give him one of her large, goofy smiles and mention his thinning hair: "I live with a bald man. *Mon Dieu*."

Only now she was serious, and a little angry and perhaps frightened, too. "*Q'est-ce que c'est, Brian?*" she asked. "Are we in trouble?"

"Go back into the kitchen, please."

"Why have you armed yourself? I demand to know."

"In case we are in trouble," he told her. "Now, please, Martine, return to the kitchen and remain there until I call for you."

She wanted to argue, he could see that from her expression, but it was the one part of their lives together that he'd made perfectly clear to her at the beginning. "There are certain aspects of my business that we will never discuss, that you will never ask me about, that you will never try to discover. It is just this one thing, *ma chérie*, that I ask you do for me."

She hesitated, but then nodded with a sad, weary expression and went back into the kitchen.

DeCamp felt sorry for her, but right now he had something more important to deal with. No one in the business, none of his contacts, no one he'd ever worked with, spoken to, or dealt with knew this place. Whenever he returned from a contract, he took great care to make absolutely certain that he hadn't been followed. Here he lived with Martine as Brian Palma, an ex-pat originally from Australia with the identification to prove it. Not even Martine knew or suspected anything different.

But now someone was on the way here, because no other houses existed on the Rue de Rivoli, a dirt track actually, this far up into the hills. And he didn't think that someone showing up here was a coincidence so soon after Florida.

He went outside and positioned himself at the end of the long covered veranda, the roof supported by Romanesque columns that he'd added a few years ago. The shade was nice in the mornings and sometimes he and Martine had their coffee and croissants out here, and watched the birds play in the thermals above them along the hilltops and ridges.

Pleasant, but when the Mercedes topped the last rise and came around the tight curve, his gut tightened a little and he could think only of what was about to happen, rather than what had happened.

The German car pulled up, and Gunther Wolfhardt got out, coatless, his long-sleeved white shirt tucked in the waistband of his dress slacks, the sleeves rolled up. He spotted DeCamp in the shade, and slowly turned completely around. Next he lifted both pant legs one at a time and let them drop. He'd come here unarmed, and he wanted that bit of business on the table from the beginning.

"You may have compromised me by coming here," DeCamp said.

"You'll have to trust my tradecraft."

"Or kill you and dispose of your body," DeCamp said. "Not so difficult."

Wolfhardt shrugged indifferently. "I've come with another assignment," he said. "And time is a critical factor, which is why I came here today instead of arranging our usual meeting in Paris. I brought everything for you to look at, including an advice of deposit for one million euros."

DeCamp's curiosity was piqued, he supposed because at some point he'd unconsciously made a sort of Faustian bargain, only instead of his soul for knowledge, he'd traded his future for money and for the almost sexual rush of battle that had been a part of him since he was a kid on the streets of Durban and then the glory days of the Buffalo Battalion. But now, no matter what happened, he had the melancholy feeling that he would have to give up this haven, give up Martine and their pastoral lives together.

And in the end, no matter what happened, he would kill Wolfhardt and then go to ground.

"Let's go for a walk," he said, stepping down from the porch. "And you can tell me about this new assignment. I'm guessing it will somehow relate to Florida."

"As a direct result, partly because you took so long with it."

"Couldn't be helped. It was the nature of the thing. Nothing more."

The dirt road narrowed to what once might have been a goat path that wound its way farther up into the stony hills, and DeCamp and Wolfhardt headed up away from the house.

"Have you heard the name Eve Larsen?" Wolfhardt asked.

The name was familiar. "In what context?"

"She's a scientist working on alternative means of producing electricity."

DeCamp had seen something about her on CNN. "She's just won the Nobel Peace Prize. Do you want me to assassinate her?"

"Yes," Wolfhardt said. "She's just been given an old oil-drilling platform in the Gulf of Mexico, somewhere down around Mississippi. Are you familiar with the geography?"

"Not intimately, but I have a working knowledge."

"Dr. Larsen's plan is to refurbish the platform and have it towed to the Atlantic side of the Florida peninsula where it would be anchored in the Gulf Stream about forty kilometers directly opposite the Hutchinson Island nuclear station. She means to start generating electricity from the ocean currents and plug it into the U.S. grid, the Eastern Interconnect. And it looks as if she has more than a fair chance of doing just that."

All of it suddenly came to DeCamp in one piece, and he suppressed a smile. "What happened to the facility is already beginning to attract a certain type of negative attention, which I think is exactly what your people wanted to happen. Sway public sentiment away from nuclear energy. And if, as you say you want to stop Dr. Larsen from achieving her goal, it must mean that you're working for one of the major oil corporations, or perhaps OPEC, or even Saudi Arabia, or Venezuela whose interests would be most hurt by more nuclear plants and by Dr. Larsen's project."

Wolfhardt did not smile, nor did he rise to the bait.

"You, or whoever you work for, arranged to give Dr.Larsen the platform, and probably money for her experiment, which you've come to hire me to stop," DeCamp said, nearly everything clear to him to that point. And suddenly he knew, or could guess the rest, and he thought it was ingenious, risky, and expensive.

"Go on," Wolfhardt prompted, not at all pleased.

"You think that her science is sound, that she has a chance of succeeding, but the blame must never hit your oil interest principals."

They walked a little farther up the hill in silence, until Wolfhardt stopped. "You're a very capable man. Bright. Perhaps too bright. But what you have guessed is precisely why we're commissioning you to kill her, the blame going to the Reverend Schlagel. Have you heard this name as well?"

DeCamp got no satisfaction from being right. But he took a few moments to work out at least some of the broad strokes of such an operation. He smiled. "I know the name. Question is do you have any direct influence over him? Enough, say, to get him involved in a public campaign against her?"

"It's already begun, in part because of the incident at Hutchinson Island, but in part because he means to use Dr. Larsen's project as his cause célèbre. He means to run for president."

DeCamp had deduced as much. "All eyes will be on both of them, which makes the hit all the more problematic."

"There's more. Schlagel's followers will be in Oslo for the Nobel ceremony. Kill her there, the blame will be easy to assign to them."

"It may ruin his chances."

"No," Wolfhardt said, but did not explain.

And DeCamp did not care, but with the world's attention focused on Oslo, the assignment had less than a fifty-fifty chance of succeeding in such a way that he could take her out and then manage to get away. "I'll take your one million euros as an opening bid, but I'll need a further one million when it is done."

"No."

"Then go home, Herr Wolfhardt," DeCamp said, satisfied by the quick expression of surprise and dismay in the German's eyes. They'd never given each other their real names, and DeCamp didn't know exactly who the ex-German spy worked for after Prague, but he knew at least some of the man's prior history. A friend in South African intelligence had gotten the information for him a couple of years ago. "Be careful of this bastard, mate, he could turn around and bite you on the arse."

Wolfhardt nodded. "I'll go now and present your proposal to my principals. I'm sure some accommodations can be made." He held out the manila envelope. "May I leave this with you?"

"Of course," DeCamp said, taking it.

"The material is quite sensitive, and included is the name and background of an ally who is almost always with her."

"Is this person to be trusted?"

"Implicitly," Wolfhardt replied.

After a quiet lunch in the garden, during which the appearance of the man in the dark Mercedes wasn't brought up, DeCamp led Martine into the high-ceilinged bedroom where they made slow, passionate love. It was something they always did before he left on one of his assignments, and as always this afternoon their lovemaking was bittersweet, for Martine because it signaled another period of being alone, and for DeCamp because he could see the end of his life here with her.

"Must you leave?" she whispered afterwards. She was lying in his arms, and she looked at him, her dark eyes wide and already filled with loneliness.

"This will be the last time," he told her.

And she smiled, not knowing the entire meaning of what he had promised. "Then bon," she said.

That evening Wolfhardt telephoned with the news that the one million would be paid within twenty-four hours, and an additional million when the assignment was successfully completed. DeCamp had expected his offer would be accepted.

TWENTY-EIGHT

Director of Central Intelligence Walter Page had a lot on his mind, most of it troubling, as his armored Cadillac limo was admitted through the West Gate onto the White House grounds, where it pulled up under the portico a few minutes before one in the afternoon. He was a man of medium build, totally undistinguished looking, with a pleasant face and calm demeanor who'd been president of IBM before being tapped to head the CIA.

Don Morton, the assistant chief of Caracas station, had flown up and together with Marty Bambridge, the Deputy Director of Operations, had gone over everything that he and his boss Lorraine Fritch had put together about Miguel Octavio and his connection with the Marinaccio woman and their shared business ventures, including ties to the UAE International Bank of Commerce.

On the surface none of that should have risen to the level of ordering the assassination of a high-ranking embassy officer, especially not the CIA's chief of station, nor was her death some random act of robbery, or even a hit by one of the terrorist groups down there.

Morton and Bambridge, but especially Morton, were convinced that whatever Ms. Fritch had learned at the end, which caused her to charter a private jet to bring her to Langley to speak with her boss, was the reason she was killed.

"She sounded excited on the phone," Bambridge said. "What she was bringing was too important to trust, even to one of our encrypted Internet circuits." He was a narrow-shouldered man with a perpetual look of surprise on his dark features, as if he could never quite believe what he'd just heard.

But neither he nor Morton had the slightest idea what it might be except that it probably had something to do with Octavio and the rest of what they had dug up.

"But there had to be a catalyst of some sort to send her running for headquarters," Morton had suggested.

And Page had sent him back to Caracas to do a full court press on the problem. After he walked out Page had ordered word be sent to as many of their field agents working under nonofficial cover as they could reach without causing a stir. But Bambridge was doubtful much would be turned up.

"It could come down to a matter of burning some serious assets we've been cultivating over the long haul."

"Do it," Page had ordered.

And the question that hung in the air, that still hung in Page's mind and perhaps the reason for the president's call, was a possible connection between Octavio, Marinaccio, the UAE IBC, and Hutchinson Island. It had to do with the timing; Ms. Fritch dropping everything to fly up to Langley immediately after the nuclear power plant attack was simply too coincidental for Page not to speculate.

He was met at the door by one of the president's security detail who led him down the West Wing corridor to the Oval Office where Lord's secretary told him that the president and his National Security Adviser Eduardo Estevez were expecting him. No one smiled when he walked in. The president, seated behind his desk, motioned for the door to be closed, picked up the phone, told his secretary that he was not to be disturbed, and then gave Page a hard look.

"Thanks for coming over, Walter. You have your hands full."

Estevez, seated on one of the couches, was watching a newscast on a laptop about the aftermath of the Hutchinson Island disaster. He looked up, the same hard expression in his eyes as the president's.

"I assumed you wanted an update on the situation in Caracas, Mr. President," Page said. He sat down on one of the chairs in front of the president's desk. "No one has come forward claiming responsibility for her assassination, but we think her death may have been a result of an investigation she was conducting on Miguel Octavio, and his connections with the IBC in Dubai."

Estevez looked up and laughed, but without humor. "That's not possible," he said, coolly. "In the first place he'd have no need to involve himself with those people, and neither would the Saudis. We've covered that ground already."

Page shrugged. He was getting boxed in just like every other DCI had when they tried to tell a president something the administration simply did not want to hear. Anything involving the Saudis, and now especially the Venezuelans, was tricky. The oil-producing nations had us by the short hairs, and policy planners and threat assessors over at the Department of Defense had been warning for years that our dependence on oil posed a real national security problem.

No administration, including this one, had cared to listen to that warning. The problem with facing the issue head-on was one of interims. Switching to alternative sources of energy, or even talking about going that way—if such talk were at the diplomatic level—could create a terrible ripple effect. Especially from the Saudis who had threatened to severely restrict OPEC's output, putting a squeeze on the economy like had happened in the seventies that would all but drive the U.S. into bankruptcy. We wouldn't have the money in the interim to wean ourselves from fossil fuels.

No president wanted to risk that happening, and people like Octavio were off-limits. Only this time it wasn't going to be so easy.

"Ms. Fritch was a highly thought of station chief," Page said, careful to keep any hint of confrontation out of his tone. He was reporting facts. "Bright, steady, experienced. She would not have wasted the agency's time on something that wasn't worthwhile."

"She was wrong," Estevez said. "Goddamnit, Walter, you know where this could lead if we're not careful."

Page remembered his swearing in ceremony in the Rose Garden behind the Oval Office. Afterwards the president had leaned in close so that his words would not be heard by anyone else, or picked up by the microphones. "I want the truth, Walter. It's why I hired you, because I think you can handle it, even if the truth is not what we want to hear."

"Yes, I know where this could lead," he said. "The truth, even if it's something none of us wants to hear."

If the president remembered his own words coming back at him, it didn't show in his expression. "The truth is one thing, but manipulating a delicate situation is something else altogether. And I want to make myself clear, none of this speculation will appear in the media. Not so much of a hint of it."

"I'm not sure I understand, Mr. President," Page said, though he understood perfectly. But he wanted the administration's position stated plainly so that months or years from now the president, and especially Estevez, a man Page had never liked, would not be able to deny what had been said.

"Do you have any reason to believe that Mr. Octavio, or better yet, Venezuelan intelligence, has any idea what Ms. Fritch was up to?" Estevez asked. "She wasn't under deep cover, everyone down there knew who she was. So, how careful was she?"

"She knew what she was doing," Page said tightly. He'd served on a number of boards and he had learned to spot the CEO or an adviser who was running scared. He could almost smell it, then as now. But this was different, this was the Oval Office and he was dealing with the president of the United States.

"I think the Chávez government would not have taken kindly to the CIA prying into the life of one of their most prominent citizens," Estevez said.

"He's almost certainly a crook, and it's possible that Ms. Fritch may have uncovered a connection to Hutchinson Island."

The president was suddenly angry, and it showed. "That's nuts, Walter," he snapped. "And you damn well know it."

Page spread his hands. "The Agency is doing what it's mandated to do, protect U.S. interests. But if you're telling me now to back off and look elsewhere, that's exactly the course I'll take."

"Is there any proof of this connection?"

"We're assuming that Ms. Fritch was bringing just that when she was assassinated."

"Assuming," Estevez said.

Page ignored him. "We can prove that Octavio is connected with the IBC. And we have high confidence that the bank is being used to funnel money from the Saudis and other oil-producing nations, especially Iran, to a number of terrorist cells, among them al-Quaeda."

"Bin Laden is old news," Estevez snapped. "You reported six months ago that you also had high confidence that he was dead."

"Al-Quaeda in the Islamic Maghred," Page said, keeping his cool, which had been his hallmark for his entire career. No one had ever witnessed his anger, it was one emotion he would never let show. His was the demeanor of the ideal public servant, calm, cool, and above all competent—a man in charge. "The group was formed originally to create an Islamic state in Algeria, but we're sure that they're taking part in al-Quaeda's broader jihad. And there are others receiving IBC money. The Hizbul Mujahideen and Jaish-e-Mohammed in Pakistan and to some extent in Kashmir. Not to mention Hamas, Hizballah, and a dozen other groups—some operating locally, some globally."

"And according to you, Octavio is somehow involved?" Estevez asked.

"Yes, by association."

"Good God, man, what would he have to gain?"

"We don't know that yet," Page admitted. "But the accident will have an effect on the thirty permit applications for new nuclear plants."

"Thirty-four," Estevez corrected. "And Hutchinson Island was no accident, that cat is out of the bag, which'll have a devastating effect on the permitting process. Especially with the Reverend Schlagel weighing in."

CNN had covered one of Schlagel's incendiary speeches about the evils of nuclear energy, and although Page had only caught a tail end of the report, the FBI had sent its file over to Dick Hanson, the Company's deputy director of intelligence as an FYI, considering the likelihood that the attack on Hutchinson Island had been planned and conducted by non-Americans. Page had seen the DDI's précis of the document, and just now the intriguing thought came into his head that if Schlagel were somehow connected with the IBC—no matter how far-fetched that idea might be—the Hutchinson Island attack might seem inevitable.

"Can't do anything but help fossil fuel interests," he said.

"Coal and natural gas."

"Oil, too."

"What is it that you want to do?" the president asked.

And Page sighed inwardly. He'd achieved what he'd wanted to achieve today: convince the president to let him pursue whatever Lorraine Fritch had begun. "Follow the leads we've already established."

"And?"

"Take them wherever they go."

Estevez started to object, but the president held his NSA off. "Do you think it's possible we may be attacked again?"

"Yes, sir."

The president nodded, a bleak expression in his eyes, in the set of his mouth. He suddenly seemed old beyond his years. But then at some point every president seemed to suddenly age overnight. "After you were sworn in I told you I wanted the truth, and I thought that you were the man to handle it. Do you remember?"

"Yes, Mr. President. I remember."

"Then find us the truth, Walter. But with care."

TWENTY-NINE

In the eight days after Louisiana, Eve never seemed to manage a full night's sleep, she was so filled with the possibilities open to her now. The Nobel Prize actually meant something concrete, and when she got back to her lab at Princeton to put together the reconfiguration project for the oil rig—her oil rig—Don had told her just that. And there'd been another celebration that even Bob Krantz had shown up for via video on someone's laptop to offer his congratulations and four million in NOAA funds. GE had promised to match that amount because the four impellers the company was building—if the thing worked—would only be the beginning of what could lead to contracts totaling in the trillions over several decades. Her project, if it ever fully developed, would be the largest single engineering job in history—larger than the Panama Canal and every nation's space programs and military budgets combined.

And the floodgates had opened even wider when, in a second dramatic turnaround, InterOil had agreed to not only pick up the entire tab for refurbishing Vanessa Explorer to Eve's specifications, but to supply the crew for the job, as well as the crew and offshore tug to tow the rig the southern length of the Gulf, thence up into the Straits of Florida all the way to a position offshore from Hutchinson Island—a distance of nearly nine hundred nautical miles.

It had been the oil giant's U.S. counsel, Jane Petersen, who'd made the call, and she'd sounded friendly, even cheerful to Eve. "I want you to know that InterOil is committed to this stage of your project. Anything we can do, aside from further funding, just ask."

"I'm overwhelmed," Eve had told the corporate lawyer and she'd meant it.

"Believe me, Dr. Larsen, this is not about altruism. InterOil is in the business of making money, and we believe we'll do just that with your project. We want it to succeed as much as you do."

"For different reasons," Eve had been unable to stop herself from taking the shot, and Don, seated across the desk from her, had been listening in and winced. But the woman had been so condescending in Baton Rouge that Eve had felt belittled.

"Of course," the lawyer said. "But to the same ends, and I hope that you can see that. InterOil is not your enemy, Doctor."

She hadn't seen it, of course, unless InterOil's executives were a lot broader minded, with their focus more tightly on the future than just about everyone else she'd talked to—lectured—in the past year and a half. It was all about public relations, because for a long time big oil had been leaving a sour taste in the public's mouth.

But Don's homily had been not to look a gift horse in the mouth. "The money and the rig have landed in our laps. So now let's do it."

She'd hugged him that morning in her office, felt his warmth and strength, and knew that she could count on him as she needed to count on him, and also knew in her heart of hearts that he would be there for her.

And he'd been there for her, literally, on the flight down from Trenton-Mercer Airport through Atlanta, talking about the probable state of the oil rig, and how much had to be done in how little time—because she'd set impossible timetables, something she'd done all of her life. He was just as excited as she was, and a little intimidated too, because if there was any sort of accident at this stage of the game the project would be all but over. The money would dry up, and certainly any further cooperation from InterOil would go away.

"So we make sure that there are no accidents," Don told her as the small Delta regional jet touched down at Gulfport-Biloxi International Airport.

"Or sabotage," Eve had said darkly.

"This time we check everything twice. We take nothing for granted."

Then why did she feel so nervous? Eve had to ask herself. Her ex had told her that she wasn't happy unless she was putting out fires—his euphemism for problem solving. "When everything's going fine your default mode is to think that the axe is going to drop any second."

But something was just over the horizon, something had always been just over the horizon for her, and the sabotage at Hutchinson Island on the very day she was giving her presentation struck her as an unlikely coincidence. She'd never been able to count on anything or anyone her entire life; not her parents, not her few friends at school, certainly not the headmistress, not her husband, and yet here she was with a man, younger than her, but just as smart, handsome, steady, reliable, and she had come to trust him, rely on him, and that frightened her the most. It was a weakness.

They had been so absorbed that they were the last off the airplane, carrying only small shoulder bags with notes, drawings, and specification lists, plus small video cameras, because their visit to the rig would only be for a couple of hours. Afterwards they were flying directly back to Princeton to gather and brief the same eleven techs who'd been with them on the Big G, and who would be installing and testing their scientific gear on the way down the Gulf.

A very large man, even taller and huskier than Bob Krantz, was waiting for them in the baggage claim and car rentals hall. Dressed in khaki slacks, a light blue business shirt, and a dark blue windbreaker with InterOil's logo, a four-pointed star on the breast, he was the most serious-looking man Eve had ever seen. And he did not seem pleased to see them.

"Doctor Larsen, Doctor Price, welcome to Biloxi," he said, his voice deep-pitched and southern. They shook hands. "I'm Justin Defloria, Vanessa Explorer's OIM—offshore installation manager. I'll be running the rig for you across the Gulf."

"We're happy to be here," Eve said. "Can you take us out there now, or do we need to be briefed first?"

"I have a helicopter standing by over at the general aviation terminal. Vanessa is about twenty-five miles offshore, so the flight out takes about twenty minutes, plenty of time for me to go over a couple of things. We've pulled most of the exploration and pumping equipment off, and we've already started work on getting her ready for your people and their gear, plus the tow. But a lot is going on, and a rig in this kind of transition can be a dangerous environment."

"Have there been any accidents?" Don asked.

"Not yet," Defloria said tersely. "As I understand it you have a flight to catch this evening, so if you'll follow me we'll get started."

Outside they got into a big Cadillac Escalade SUV and Defloria drove them around to the general aviation terminal where a very large Sikorsky S-61N helicopter capable of carrying thirty passengers plus two pilots was warming up on the tarmac. The machine looked old and banged up, the paint on its fuselage deeply pitted and the interior shabby, most of the upholstered seats worn and dirty. But Defloria didn't seem to notice, nor did the pilot who lifted off as soon as the hatch was closed and everyone was buckled in.

The chopper swung around to the west as it gained altitude, and once over Highway 49, it headed south over the port of Gulfport, across the Mississippi Sound and the barrier islands, and they were out over the open Gulf of Mexico, nothing but water dotted with ships and farther out to the horizon what looked like the edge of a forest of oil rigs.

It was noisy in the helicopter, but once the pilot throttled back to cruising speed of 120 knots, they were able to talk.

"Do you have a timetable?" Eve asked Defloria.

"That depends somewhat on you, Doctor," he said. "And the tolerance level of your people."

"Tolerance for what?"

"Discomfort," the rig manager replied, baiting her as so many men did.

"We'll manage as long as we have something to eat, a place to sleep, bathroom facilities, and space to install our monitoring equipment as well as the cable heads for the four impellers." She smiled. "Hopefully you won't have us camped out on deck in tents."

"No, but we'd ask that your scientists and technicians remain below decks as much of the time as feasible. There'll be a lot of welding and cutting, mostly getting rid of the last of the oil exploration systems and structures, and even a hard hat wouldn't be much protection if a fifty-pound piece of steel girder fell on someone's head."

"We'll keep that in mind," Eve said. "Besides Dr. Price and myself, I'm bringing a crew of eleven people, all of them accustomed to working while at sea."

"Will you need separate dormitories?"

And Eve smiled inwardly. The man was old-school southern, maybe even a gentleman ordered to do a disagreeable job, but he was concerned that he could provide propriety and decorum aboard the rig. "That won't be necessary, though separate showers would be nice."

"I think if you can give me until you return from Oslo, the rig will be ready for your people to come aboard and we can start the tow."

That was more than a month out and Eve was brought up against the simple fact that she would have to actually travel to Norway to pick up the Prize, which meant more dealing with the media, rounds of cocktails parties and dinners, that just about every Nobel laureate before her had detested. She'd gone online and looked up something of the frenetic ceremonies that led up to the presentation at Oslo's city hall, and then had put all of that out of her mind until this moment. To her the Prize had become a separate thing from the ceremony. And although she'd endured the half-dozen news conferences in Washington and Princeton, she hadn't enjoyed them. They'd interfered with her work. And Oslo would be the biggest intrusion of all.

She'd tried to explain something of her discomfort to Don, but he'd laughed at her.

"You know what you're doing, of course," he'd said.

They were in the computer lab on a CAD program with Vanessa Explorer's blueprints up on the big tabletop monitor. "What do you mean?"

He was exasperated with her. "For Christ's sake, Eve, you've won the goddamned Nobel Prize and it sounds like you're feeling sorry for yourself."

She wanted to smile just then, she wanted to laugh but she shook her head. "I'm frightened," she admitted.

"Of what?" Don had practically shouted.

They were alone in the lab, otherwise she wouldn't have said anything. "I might be wrong."

For a moment Don had been struck dumb. But he too shook his head. "Trust the data, isn't that what you've been telling us all along, drumming it into our heads? But look for the anomalies, the errors will show up in the odd bits. But we've seen nothing like that."

Just after three, Defloria pointed out the rig standing by itself, its nearest neighbor at least ten miles away. Two barges were tied up alongside, and as they approached from the southeast a crane on the platform's main deck swung out over one of the barges and lowered a section of steel as big around as an oil barrel and perhaps twenty feet long. As they got closer Eve could pick out workmen on deck dressed in dark coveralls with white hard hats. She counted at least a dozen, and at various other parts on the rig, above and below the main deck, points of light from cutting torches were bright even in the daylight.

From a quarter mile out the rig looked like nothing more than a pile of rusted-out junk in someone's backyard pond, nothing like the blueprints, and especially not the photographs InterOil had sent her to study, and her heart sunk a little. Discomfort, indeed.

"She's a semisubmersible rig, which means when she's in position her four legs are lowed to a depth of fifty meters and partially filled with ballast water to keep her stable," Defloria said. "If the sea gets up we can pump out some of the ballast water to raise the level of the main deck above the highest waves."

"Wouldn't that make it less stable?" Eve asked.

"If it gets too bad we evacuate the rig," Defloria conceded "But understand that this isn't the same as a North Sea platform where it's always rough. And its primary use was for exploration, not product extraction."

"What about hurricanes?"

"Every rig—no matter how large—is evacuated. Most survive, tattered but afloat; still we lost two during Katrina. Expensive hardware."

"Once we get to the other coast how do we keep her in place?"

"For the short term we can use dynamic positioning, a lot like bow and stern thrusters on a ship. For the long term she'll be anchored to the seabed."

Don had taken out his video camera and was recording images as the helicopter pilot came in just above the level of the main deck and slowly circled the platform until he flared and touched down on the landing pad at the opposite corner from the crane.

Now that they were actually aboard, and seeing the rig up close, not from a quarter mile out, Eve was even more disappointed in its condition, but excited too. Some rust and trash wouldn't detract from the real technology that was going to happen from this piece of equipment.

And the real science of actually modifying the planet's weather for the good.

"We'll make this work," she said, mostly for her own benefit.

"Is the Ping-Pong table still aboard?" Don asked.

"It's still here, along with the pool table and a pretty good library—mostly of video games," Defloria said.

"Princeton cafeteria food is horrible, any chance of hiring your chef?"

"One of our catering staffs will come aboard, and we'll even stock the pantry. At some point we'll contract your project manager to find out if any of your people have any special dietary needs."

Eve was surprised again and it showed.

"This will be a turnkey operation for your people until we get you settled off Hutchinson Island," Defloria said. "At that point you'll need to hire an OIM and a half-dozen other platform crew plus your own stewards, and I'm assuming electrical engineers. Once there InterOil will turn the operation over to you."

"We may need help finding the right people," Don said.

"In this job climate the word will spread. You'll have no problem."

Defloria handed Eve and Don hard hats before the chopper's hatch was opened and they stepped out onto the deck, and instantly Eve was struck by the sheer volume of noise—whining cutting tools, heavy pieces of metal clanging against each other, other tools that sounded like jackhammers and buzz saws and drills, plus the waves against the four buoyancy control legs, the wind that had gotten up to at least twenty-five knots, and men shouting, and here and there the sounds of music, mostly country and western, blaring from boom boxes.

Another impression that struck her the moment her feet hit the deck was the size of the platform. This was no 225-foot research ship; the platform measured more than 600 feet from the bases of the fully extended legs to the helicopter deck, and during drilling or exploration operations the drilling towers, which had already been partially dismantled and barged to shore, might rise another 200 feet. Bigger than a football field, the platform's three decks were crammed with living and working structures, stacked like some fantastic building blocks at one end of the platform, while gigantic tanks and hundreds of miles of color-coded piping and electrical cables snaked in and around an incomprehensible maze of individual pedestals, rising sometimes from the main deck and in other places from one of the lower decks, which held pieces of machinery, some that looked like pumps, others that looked like electrical generators and still others whose purpose Eve could only guess.

And everywhere, it seemed, rough-looking men were working at what seemed at first to Eve to be a measured, even indolently slow pace, until she realized that they were simply being careful. This indeed was a dangerous place.

"By the time your people come aboard we'll be finished with all the heavy lifting," Defloria said, and he had to shout. He led them down steep metal stairs and through a hatch into a corridor that seemed to run the width of the platform. Suddenly they were out of most of the noise, though the clatter of metal on metal rang out as if they were inside a giant bell.

"Is it always this noisy?" Eve asked.

"Sometimes worse during a drilling operation. But it shouldn't be as bad when your crew are aboard, though I don't know what noise level your impellers and gensets will transmit up the cables."

"There wasn't much noise aboard the *Gordon Gunther.*"

"Those were small impellers by comparison to the ones you'll be testing from this platform. You might want to ask GE's chief project engineer to study the issue. Probably come up with some damping mechanism."

Eve hadn't thought of it, and she admitted as much to Defloria, who nodded.

"Engineering and science aren't always on the same page."

"We learned that on the *Big G,*" Don said.

"Yes, I expect you did," Defloria said.

At the far end of the pipe- and cable-lined corridor, Defloria led them through another hatch and up five flights of stairs to a large space with wraparound windows and consoles and empty racks that had once contained the electronic equipment for oil exploration activities. They were at the highest point on the rig, not counting the drilling derricks, and the view was spectacular. From here they could see just about everything happening on the main deck, and out to sea other platforms on the horizon as well as ship traffic.

"This was the chief geologist's work space," Defloria explained. "He and his people directed operations from here, and I think it will suit your purposes."

"During the research phase," Eve said, the rig in not as bad a shape in her mind as before. This would work.

"What about the housekeeping infrastructure?" Don asked.

"Everything will be up and running by the time your people come aboard. Right now one of the electrical generators is online, while the second unit is being overhauled. The desalination system, which provides fresh water, is just about on its last legs, but it'll be as good as new within the week. We're waiting for some spare parts from the mainland."

"From the mainland?" Eve asked.

"You live and work on these things long enough you get to think of them as islands, versus the mainland where you get your supplies and take your vacations."

"What about waste disposal?" Don asked, and Eve was glad he was being the practical thinker just now.

"Normally these rigs have sewage processing plants, but we've dismantled the system on this platform, too much wrong with it. For now we're storing our wastewater in tanks that normally would be used for oil storage. Lot of capacity. Once a week it's pumped into a small tanker and sent ashore. It's something you'll have to consider once you get to Florida, though with only a dozen people aboard you won't generate very much."

"How about bunks, linens, towels, stuff like that?"

"Your people will have to bring their personal items, of course, but InterOil will supply everything else—as we do aboard all of our platforms."

"Where will you go afterwards?" Eve asked, suddenly curious about the man who would be in charge of getting her rig to Florida.

"An exploration platform in the Arctic, once we get permission from Canada."

"You'd rather be there now."

Defloria laughed humorlessly. "I'm an InterOil employee, Dr. Larsen. I do what the company tells me to do."

"Fair enough," Eve said.

"Would you like to see the rest of the rig?"

"Just our living quarters and then you can take us back to the airport."

THIRTY

The day after the Reverend Schlagel's fire-and-brimstone speech about Eve Larsen and her God Project and her Nobel Prize, Billy Jenkins, thirty-four, and Terrence Langsdorf, thirty-two, had gathered a few things from their bungalow in McPherson and headed east. Driving nonstop, except to gas up, grab sandwiches and coffee, and make pit stops, they made it to Princeton's Forrestal campus at eleven the next evening in a high state of excitement and agitation.

"God's meth formula," the reverend had said once, referring to his sermons. "A natural high for the work of the just."

Terry had downloaded a map that pinpointed the GFDL building and Dr. Larsen's office and lab. And they hoped with all their might that the bitch would be there, working late, so that they would have the blessed opportunity to teach her the real meaning of finding Jesus in your heart; the real meaning of salvation.

McPherson was simply not proactive enough for Billy or Terry, especially not for Billy who'd done three years as an Indiana Army National Guard at Abu Ghraib prison in Iraq. The reverend's sermons were exciting, no doubt about it, but that wasn't enough for either man who'd worked the antiabortion Christian circuit for three years, blowing up abortion clinics, and coming within inches of killing one of the hateful, baby-killing doctors, at which time they had to go deep. Upper Peninsula Michigan at first, then Montana, and finally McPherson.

God had been talking to Billy since he was eight years old in Indianapolis. He supposed it was a defense mechanism against his drunken father who started physically and sexually abusing him about that time, and his mother who cared more about the soap operas on television and gin and tonics then her son's well-being. But talking with God made him feel good about himself. If Jesus had been able to stand His betrayal and mock trial and torture and the horrible march up Calvary Hill hauling that terrible heavy cross and the crown of thorns and the crucifixion and even the wound in His side not to mention the nails— spikes actually—in His hands and feet, then Billy Jenkins could put up with a little abuse. Because, like Jesus, he figured that one day he too would be resurrected and take his rightful place at the right hand of God Almighty, though sometimes he got a little confused in which order and just where those blessed events might take place.

Terry was just about of the same mind, because he'd come from a very similar background, except that his drunken abusive fathers were the ones he'd encountered on his journey through the Georgia foster home system, and his military service was with the regular army in Afghanistan. He'd received an other than honorable discharge for the use of excessive force against civilian targets. Even his gung ho platoon sergeant compared it to what his old man had told him about a place in Nam called Mai Lai. He'd met Billy on the antiabortion circuit and the two had gone to ground together. Billy was called Bo Peep because wherever he went Terry was sure to follow.

Billy backed into a slot in the rear of the lab, only a few lights showing in the three-story building, and only a handful of cars in the lot. They'd spotted no campus security or local pigs and the ten-year-old Volvo they were driving fit right in.

"In and out in five," Billy said. "Ten at the most. We're just sending a message tonight."

"Yessir, just a righteous message," Terry agreed.

And sometimes Billy thought that his friend was just a few bricks short of a load. But he was loyal.

They took a crowbar and a five-pound sledgehammer from the trunk, and moving silently went to the glass door which luck would have it was not locked, something that surprised them. But then scientists had the reputation of being absentminded.

Dr. Larsen's office was in the west corner of the ground floor, but her lab and wave tank, where they figured they could cause the most damage in the shortest amount of time, took up most of the basement. Places like this were always controlled by a computer or computers, easy targets.

The main hall was deserted, all the office doors closed, only the corridor lights showing. They'd brought balaclavas just in case they ran into someone, and they pulled them on as they started down the stairs. Terry was a short, but stocky ordinary-looking guy, but Billy looked like a linebacker, with broad shoulders and a thick, beefy neck, and a full head of thick blond hair that since the service he'd kept long as a source of pride. But it was dead giveaway in operations like these, so whenever possible he went in with at least a lid.

A long unadorned corridor, dimly lit, ran the length of the basement. Doors with frosted glass panels lined the hall, some marked only with numbers, but near the end, one was marked DR. EVELYN LARSEN, NOAA.

They stopped and Billy put his ear to the door to listen. Some machinery was running inside, barely audible, but he couldn't hear anyone talking or moving around and he looked over his shoulder and gave Terry a nod.

"In and out in five."

"Righteous."

For just an instant Billy wanted to stop and ask his friend what he thought God was all about, at least in terms of what they'd been doing with the abortion clinics and now this. But he let it go and tried the door, which was unlocked. Stupid, the fleeting thought crossed his mind, but then he pushed the door open and went inside.

The lab was large, at least big enough for a dozen or more people to work at what were computer stations each at the heads of or in the middle of benches on which sat a myriad of strange-looking equipment, some of it mechanical, but most of it electrical or electronic, or in three cases on small tables in the middle of the tiled floor in front of large pieces of complicated equipment that rose to the ceiling. At the far end of the room, which measured at least one hundred feet in length, a large plate-glass window looked out on the wave pool.

"The computers first," Billy said, and he started forward, when a young woman seated at one of the terminals halfway across the room suddenly jumped up. He'd completely missed her.

"Who are you?" the woman said, a girl actually in Billy's estimation. Early twenties at the most.

"We're here to set things right, in the Lord's name, darlin'," Billy said, striding directly toward her.

But she stood there, rooted like a deer in the middle of a highway, caught in the headlights of an oncoming car, until at the last moment she shrieked something, turned on her heel, and sprinted to the end of the room and out a door Billy hadn't noticed into the wave pool room.

His military career and later his abortion clinic operations had taught him to beware of loose ends that could unravel the most carefully laid plan. The young woman surely fit that bill, but she stopped at the edge of the wave pool and looked through the window at him. Stared at him, and he had to sort of admire her courage, stupid or not.

He took a step forward, raising the sledgehammer, but she didn't budge. It was as if she was taking pictures of him, and he was of a mind to say the hell with the lab and go after her. Girls like that needed lessons in humility; it's what his dad had tried to teach his mother.

But something crashed behind him, and he turned in time to see Terry swing his crowbar into a computer CPU sitting on the floor beneath its station, then giggle like a girl. When he turned back, the young woman at the side of the wave pool was gone.

Terry smashed another computer, and Billy turned to his part of the work. "In and out in five," he said.

"Righteous," Terry agreed.

But in Billy's mind it surely could have been more than righteous, it would have been fine to lay his hands on the young woman.

◻

THIRTY-ONE

McGarvey accompanied Gail back down to Hutchinson Island for the simple fact that there was little else he could do in Washington until Otto and Yablonski came up with an ID on the contractor. But so far both men had drawn blanks.

"If we can get back inside the South Service Building, I want to take a look at the rest of the recordings for that day," she'd said. "Larry told me that the feeds from some of the cameras came up blank, on some sort of a loop that just showed the same frame over and over again."

"Maybe he missed one," McGarvey suggested.

"That's what I'm hoping."

They rented a car at the Fort Lauderdale-Hollywood International Airport and as they came to the south bridge over to Hutchinson Island, a few miles from the power plant, they encountered the first of the media trucks with satellite dishes on the roofs. "Like hyenas to a fresh kill," Gail said.

"They're doing their jobs," McGarvey said, though he'd never had any particular fondness for newspeople, especially not after he'd faced the Senate when he'd been nominated as director of the CIA.

"They did a number on my father when he was killed," Gail said bitterly. "Called him a misplaced cop with a hero complex and a pathological need for recognition that could have got some innocent people hurt."

"I know. I read the stories."

Gail glanced at him, a hurt look on her face. "They were damned unfair. And I'm next, only I don't understand why."

"For the most part they're just trying to figure out whatever it is they're covering, so that they can explain it to their audience."

"In an ideal world I might believe you, Kirk. But a lot of these people are less interested in the truth than they are about increasing their fame, so they can demand bigger salaries."

But McGarvey had wanted to believe differently after the storm of media coverage when his wife and daughter had been slaughtered by an IED at Arlington Cemetery, because he didn't want to vent his rage on the press. They had been insensitive, but they had not pulled the trigger. The deaths were not their fault. It was like apologizing for being Americans after 9/11. No, the cause had been radical terrorist hatreds under the guise of the Islamic jihad, which was supposed to spread the true faith. And in turn it was really about power; who had it and who wanted to take it from them.

"Sensationalism," McGarvey said, seeing her point.

"Voyeurism," she said. "People driving past a bad accident and slowing down so they can see the blood and gore. There but for the grace of God, go I."

"Worrying about it isn't going to help our investigation," McGarvey said, and he felt like a hypocrite, because that's exactly how he had operated throughout his career. When he was in the field he worried about everything; in the end it was oftentimes the minor, overlooked detail that cost the agent his or her life.

And across the bridge and onto the island when they were stopped by the first Army National Guard checkpoint, beyond which they could see the fringes of the crowd lining A1A the last five miles to the power plant, his gut reaction was that the media was being manipulated by the Reverend Jerry Schlagel. Many of the people streaming past the checkpoint carried signs with the theme: LEAVE GOD'S WORK TO GOD!

McGarvey powered down the window and he and Gail held up their NNSA identity cards for the armed solider. "What's that all about?"

"I don't know, sir," the soldier said. "They started showing up around midnight, and we were ordered to let them through."

A National Guard lieutenant dressed in BDUs came over and glanced at the ID cards. "Can you tell us what happened?" he asked. He looked a little green.

"We're working on it," McGarvey said.

"Any TV people up there?" Gail asked.

"Yes, ma'am. From all over the place. England, Germany, even Japan. It's like a rock concert."

There was no need in McGarvey's mind to ask who the star would be. "How far out is the perimeter?"

"Post One is five hundred meters, sir. But you'll want to drive up to the staging area just outside the main gate. The on-site commander is up there along with a first aid station and decontamination tent."

"How about A1A north?"

"It's closed."

"Can we get inside the South Service Building?" McGarvey asked.

"I don't know, sir. But they've already started evaluation work, and some cleanup. We've been told that it's nowhere near as bad as it could have been."

"Call ahead and let them know we're on the way," McGarvey said

"Yes, sir," the lieutenant said and he waved them through.

Driving the five miles north they passed a nearly continuous mob heading toward the power plant. Most of the people were dressed plainly in jeans or shorts, some with baseball caps, others with straw hats; men and women of all ages, children, some in their mothers' arms, some in strollers, even buggies, and tiny carriages that were towed by bicycles. None of them drove, except for the few bikes, all of them were on foot, and nearly everyone carried backpacks or big shoulder bags, as if they planned on staying at least overnight, and many of them carried the God signs.

"There has to be twenty thousand people here," McGarvey said.

"Probably more," Gail said. "But look at their faces. They're happy."

"These have to be Schlagel's people. Looks like they're going to a tent revival meeting."

"Yeah, but why, Kirk?" Gail asked. "What's the point of calling his flock to a sabotaged nuclear power plant?"

A pair of National Guard Humvees came up the highway and McGarvey had to move over to let them pass. The crowds were spilling out on to the roadway and he had to be careful not to run over anyone, until finally the highway was completely blocked and he had to slow to a crawl, the mob parting in front and surging back behind. It was like being in the middle of a low fog, nothing visible except overhead, until in the distance, finally, the plant's containment domes came into sight.

Gail sat forward. "They've already started to cap the north dome," she said.

A wall of what at this distance looked like large concrete panels rose nearly halfway to the top of the damaged containment dome. At least three large cranes surrounded the perimeter and as they continued north one of the cranes slowly lowered another concrete slab in place. They could see scaffolding, but they were still too far to see the workmen.

The outer perimeter of Post One was a hundred yards farther, and here the big crowd was spreading out on both sides of the road, some of the people all the way down on the beach, others on the fringes of a swampy area to the west. A pair of National Guard trucks was set up as a negotiable barrier, the first one parked halfway across the road from the right, and the other a few yards away parked halfway across the road from the left. In order to pass the barrier it was necessary to drive around the first truck, then make a sharp turn to the right to get past the second truck. None of the mob was being allowed beyond the barrier. National Guard troops formed a line from the water's edge to the swamp. And for now, at least, it seemed as if the people were content to come this far and stop, as if they were waiting for something to happen.

McGarvey pulled up at the barrier and he and Gail showed their IDs to a nervous first lieutenant.

"Colonel Scofield is expecting you," he said. "The CP is in the first trailer."

A lot of television vans had been allowed through and they were parked on either side of the road, nearly all the way up to the main gate area, where the command post trailer was parked. Several tents had been set up on either side of the highway, and just now there seemed to be a lot of activity inside the main gate. Even from here McGarvey could see that people coming out of the South Service Building were wearing bright silver hazmat suits, bulky hoods covering their heads. The building was evidently still hot.

"Where do we park?" McGarvey asked.

"This side of the CP," the lieutenant said. "You'll need to be briefed before you'll be allowed to go any farther." He stepped aside and waved McGarvey through.

A number of people in the crowd were watching them. They were not smiling.

McGarvey drove slowly through the barrier. "They're probably blaming us for all this."

"Haven't you seen Schlagel on TV?" Gail asked. "He's telling his flock that nuclear power plants are like having atomic bombs in your backyards. According to him it's just a matter of time before something will happen at every nuclear facility. We're playing with something that belongs only to God."

"Looks like they're buying the message."

"Not only his congregation is buying it, lots of other people are coming around to his message, pointing at Three Mile Island and Chernobyl. No one wants something like that in their backyard, and there's a hundred-plus nuclear plants in the U.S. with plans for maybe three dozen more."

McGarvey had a sudden, vicious thought. "Does Schlagel have any money? Serious money?"

Gail gave him an odd look. "He's raking in plenty from his ministry and television and radio stations. He's at least a multimillionaire. Why?"

"He wants to run for president."

"Yes, so?"

"He needs a cause, and what better than playing into the people's fear of nukes?"

"Are you serious?"

"I think it's worth looking into," McGarvey said.

THIRTY-TWO

The assignments had finally begun to lose their luster for Brian DeCamp. Wolfhardt showing up in Nice had been a stark reminder of how fragile his life was—had always been. In general, assassins did not live to retirement age, a fact that loomed large in his mind as he sat sipping an aquavit with a very good espresso at the sidewalk café in front of the Grand Hotel.

Oslo's fall weather was mild, though on the cool side compared to southern France, and the long-range forecast for the December Nobel Prize week was for continued moderate temperatures. It would make for an easier hit, though a heavy snowstorm, just like an overcast night or a fogbound morning, would help mask an escape.

But this was the situation he would have to deal with, and on reflection he remembered worse conditions from which he'd walked away, and coming here to spend a couple of days in Oslo as an ordinary tourist under false papers was the first step of four: the plan, the equipment, the hit, and the following ninety minutes, which always were the most crucial. If you weren't out of the immediate detection and arrest zone by then, it meant that the authorities probably had the upper hand and the odds against escape began to rise exponentially.

As he saw it now after touring the downtown area, there were three possibilities. The first was here at the Grand Hotel where he had booked a standard room. The Nobel Prize recipients and their guests and most of the attending dignitaries always stayed here, which opened a host of possibilities, all of them involving either the import of a silenced weapon to Norway, or a purchase here. The former, he'd concluded from the start, would present the smallest risk of detection. Unlike the U.S. and most of Europe, especially Great Britain, the Scandinavian countries had reacted the least to the attacks of 9/11, so getting a disassembled pistol, suppressor, and ammunition disguised in some way in his checked on luggage would be fairly straightforward. It was obvious that he wasn't a Muslim, and beyond that consideration the Swedes, Danes, and Norwegians had little interest.

So finding what suite she was staying in, arranging for a room key, slipping inside in the middle of the night and killing her, was the first and simplest plan, especially if any of Schlagel's people were staying at the Grand.

The second would be a long-range shot either just before or immediately following the ceremony at the Radhuset, city hall, a few blocks from the harbor. The crowds would be large, though not very noisy according to what he'd read and learned from talking to people yesterday and today. But again Schlagel's people would be on site, making their noises. Walking through the hall and across the broad boulevard to the harbor, he'd found no suitable shooting position from which blame could be directed toward the reverend's crazies. So again he considered the possibilities of loading only two rounds into an untraceable silenced pistol, taking his shots from inside the crowd, immediately dropping the weapon in the middle of Schlagel's group, and then melting away as the crowd began to react.

And the third, and in many respects the least problematic, would be making the hit while she took a horse-driven carriage tour of Oslo's old town. It would take the importation of a silenced long gun, something only slightly more difficult than a pistol, and finding the right spot from a rooftop, hotel room, or apartment somewhere along the route of her tour.

The next consideration was his appearance. His disguise at Hutchinson Island had been slight, consisting mostly of a change in hairstyle and color, tinted contact lenses, lifts in his shoes, and a studied shift in his demeanor—a different walk, a different tilt of his head, downcast eyes, compressed lips. But on the off chance that photographs had been taken from the power plant's security cameras, or a computer-assisted likeness of his face had been distributed to bodyguards assigned to Dr. Larsen, or to the Norwegian federal security police, he would need to do more this time. A wig, different clothing, a different eye color, different complexion, possibly even some minor plastic surgery, though he wasn't sure that would be necessary because when he came back here he certainly wouldn't be announcing his presence. He would remain in the background, anonymous in the polite Norwegian crowds.

And for some reason just now he thought about Martine's flat bottom and knobby knees, and he looked away momentarily to watch the orderly traffic moving along the broad, cobblestoned Karl Johansgate, and the people on foot. The Norwegians were an orderly people. But hardy for all of that because of the northern climate, and a very long history of war, mostly with Sweden against the Russians. And he was inestimably sad for just that moment, thinking that he might never see her again, because of Gunther Wolfhardt and the German's principal. And that led to an instant of intense hate, so that when the waiter came to ask if he would like another espresso or aquavit, DeCamp had to make a conscious effort of will to force a pleasant smile and look up.

"No, thank you. Just the check, please."

The waiter handed him the bill, and DeCamp laid an American twenty dollar bill on the table, and got up, and headed the few blocks past the parliament building and city park back to the Radhuset for a final look before he returned to his pied-à-terre in Paris to make his final preparations and wait until it was time to strike.

That early evening, his work done, DeCamp was sitting at the bar drinking a dark Martini & Rossi with an orange peel when he happened to glance up at the television tuned to CNN, in Norwegian but with an English crawl at the bottom of the screen. The Princeton laboratory of Nobel Prize winner Dr. Evelyn Larsen had been vandalized in the early morning hours. There were no injuries, though one of the laboratory assistants had witnessed the attack by two men armed with metal bars and sledgehammers.

And he came to the same conclusion that the news reader suggested: The attack must have been inspired by the Reverend Jerimiah Schlagel's recent sermons against what he called, "Dr. Larsen's God Project—an abomination against the Almighty's plan for us all."

Schlagel's denial came from his pulpit in McPherson, but DeCamp had to smile inwardly. Gunther Wolfhardt knew what he was doing.

THIRTY-THREE

Everything was the same and yet eerily different as McGarvey parked at the end of a row of military and civilian vehicles, and as he and Gail got out of the rental car she said so. They had driven into a war zone, and across the street and through the main gates the damaged containment dome loomed up like a mushroom cloud after an atomic explosion. The operators in the cabs of the three giant cranes lifting concrete slabs in place wore hazmat suits, as did the workmen on the scaffolding, who were careful to keep the rising concrete wall between them and the dome as they troweled mortar into the joints.

Other people dressed in hazmat suits came and went from the South Service Building, which just now seemed to be a beehive of activity. The thickness of the building's north wall had apparently taken the brunt of the radioactive steam, but most of the outflow had blown directly out to sea.

Bob Townsend and Chris Strasser, dressed in spotless white coveralls, came out of the decontamination tent and walked over to the Command Post trailer, their hair wet and their faces red. Neither of them looked happy, but when they spotted McGarvey and Gail coming along the road they held up.

"What are you two doing here?" the plant manager asked, his mood and manner brusque. He had a lot on his mind; it was his power station on his watch that had been damaged. And it was obvious that he was placing a lot of the blame on Gail's shoulders.

"We'd like to get up to security and pull out the digital records from the surveillance cameras," she said.

"You can look at them, but nothing's coming out of there until we've finished the decontamination process," Strasser said. "We'll have to tear down every piece of equipment, strip the ceilings and walls and floors, everything, before we can start to put the place back together and get reactor one online."

"That'll take at least a year," Townsend said.

"How about the damaged reactor?" McGarvey asked.

"It'll never come online," Townsend said. "But it could have been a hell of a lot worse if you and your people hadn't shown up. They were heroes. You were."

"We were doing our jobs," McGarvey said, his gut tightening. "But this scenario wasn't in the playbook, so instead of beating up on anybody, we'll find out who did it and why, so just maybe we'll have a shot at preventing a next time."

"Any ideas?"

"A few."

"Is there electricity in the building?" Gail asked. "We'll need it to power up one of the computers and send whatever images we come up with back to Washington."

"Portable generators," Strasser said disgustedly. "But the hard disks may have been fried, and even if they weren't it's possible that the digital records were corrupted."

"How bad is it?"

"Better than we expected, less than one hundredth of a sievert per hour," Strasser said. "Less inside the suits, of course, but we're limiting exposure to four hours per shift just to be on the safe side. There was a pretty strong electromagnetic pulse—that was the blue tinge we saw from the air—which may have caused some damage to the data circuits. We just don't know yet. Right now our primary concern is to clean up so that we can put our crews in there to rebuild everything."

"Do we need to be briefed before we go inside?" McGarvey asked.

"Essentially it's don't take your suit off for any reason, don't eat or drink anything inside the building, no souvenirs, stay no more than four hours, and if you tear a hole in your suit, no matter how small, get the hell out of there on the double. There's a pretty good team of National Guard people helping ours in the tent, so just do what they tell you. Suits are inside."

"What about the bodies?" Gail asked.

"They've been buried," Townsend said, his jaw tight.

"Where?"

"Nevada."

The hazmat suits were bright reflective silver, large clear Lexan faceplates giving them nearly unrestricted vision straight forward and ninety degrees to either side, but they were hot and the bottled air was so dry it parched their mouths and throats after the first five minutes.

They walked across the street through the main gate and into the parking lot. Several cars had been left behind, including, McGarvey presumed, the rental car Eve Larsen had used. He'd promised her that if it wasn't glowing in the dark she could come back and get it, but all the cars here would be transported out and buried with the other nuclear waste.

Gail pointed to a Volvo convertible. "If I stop payments do you suppose the repo man will take it?" she shouted.

"Yours?"

"Yeah, I bought it two months ago. Hell of a waste."

Two large semis were backed up to the front entrance, and workmen were trundling out irradiated material from inside the building: desks, chairs, lockers from the break area, coveralls and hardhats, doors, windows, light fixtures, and acoustical ceiling tiles, plus the monitors and panel electronics from the control room.

The cleanup crews hadn't started on the second floor yet, but when they did the entire place would be stripped bare so the reconstruction could begin if the basic structure was radiation free. Otherwise the entire building would have to be razed.

Just inside the entry hall they stopped at the foot of the stairs, and Gail shook her head. "They'll never put this place back together."

"They're trying to save money," McGarvey told her.

"Shutting down has put a huge strain on the state's energy needs."

"It could have been worse."

"You've already said so, but it shouldn't have happened in the first place," Gail said. "When they start to pass out the blame, a ton of it will come my way, which I don't give a damn about. But what frosts me is that they'll stay so shortsighted they won't beef up security the way they know they should."

And she was right, of course, McGarvey thought. Nothing much had been done so far to harden security procedures at the other 103 nuclear plants, except to temporarily cancel public tours. Homeland Security was still looking for attacks from the sky. Airliners were not allowed to fly through exclusion zones around any nuclear facility.

But increased security measures were expensive. And in these troubled times money was tight.

Upstairs they went down the corridor to the blasted-out observation window. The glass had been swept up and the blood cleaned from the floor and wall, nevertheless they walked with care lest they step on a stray shard and cut a hole in their booties.

The bodies had been removed from the corridor as well as from the control room below where workers were busy disassembling the control panels for both reactors and carting them away. The supervisor's desk and the two control consoles had already been removed and Gail shivered.

"It doesn't make sense," she said.

"It never does from the outside looking in," McGarvey told her, and she turned to look at him.

"It makes sense to someone?"

McGarvey nodded, the gesture mostly lost inside the hood. "It's up to us to find out who," he shouted.

"Does it always work that way for you?"

McGarvey felt a short, sharp stab of pain for what he had lost and how he had lost it. But in the end he had found the who and the why. "Yes," he told her.

She read something of that from the expression on his face. "Let's get on with it," she said. She glanced down at the work being done in what was left of the control room and then headed back down the corridor to the security suite.

Nothing seemed to have been disturbed in Gail's or Wager's offices, her purse was where she had left it behind her desk and Wager's jacket was still draped over his chair. Everything here would eventually wind up in a nuclear waste dump somewhere.

The light switches worked, and she powered up the computer in the monitoring room, but it wouldn't boot up, and neither would any of the monitors that had displayed the closed-circuit television images from around the power plant.

"Your engineer was right, the computers are fried," McGarvey said.

"It means even if the DVDs stayed intact we have no way of accessing any of them, unless we come back with a laptop," Gail said bitterly. "This was a wasted effort."

"It was worth the try," McGarvey said, just as disappointed as she was.

Gail walked back out to her office and took a photograph out of the wallet in her purse.

"No souvenirs," McGarvey warned her.

"This is my favorite picture of my father," Gail said. "I just wanted a last look." She put the photo and wallet back in her purse and went back downstairs and outside with McGarvey.

The noise of the angry crowd that was pressing its way past the barricades hit them at once. People were chanting, "God's work is for God."

At least a dozen TV broadcast trucks had moved up as well, nearly to the command post trailer, and the cameras and microphones were trained on Reverend Schlagel, who stood in the bed of a pickup truck, preaching to the crowd with a bullhorn.

"Nuclear energy is death!" he shouted. "God's work. He created the sun and the stars—nuclear furnaces—and men whose only faith is technology have presumed to duplicate His work."

"No! No! No!" the crowd screamed.

"What will happen at the one hundred and three remaining nuclear hellholes in operation in this country alone? More accidents? More disasters? More death and destruction? People displaced from their homes by rude beasts slinking out of Bethlehem?"

In just a few minutes he had whipped the crowd into a frenzy.

He pointed over his shoulder at the heavily damaged containment dome. "The devil's handiwork. Is this what you want in your backyard? The sure and certain sign of the evil that walks the earth?"

"No! No! No!"

He gestured toward the National Guard troops standing by at the fringes of the crowd. "They couldn't even protect this one hellish installation. Should the idolaters of technology, the shortsighted men and women in our nation's capital, the fat cats at companies like Westinghouse and Mitsubishi whose only interest is that profits be allowed to build even more insults to God Almighty's mysterious purpose for us? Construction of more than thirty of them will start this year unless we stop them. Will we allow this to happen?"

"No! No! No!" The crowd chanted. "God's work is for God!"

"Do you think they'll try to get inside the plant?" Gail asked. None of Schilling's security people had come back to work yet, and even with the National Guard standing by she felt vulnerable.

"Schlagel's not that stupid," McGarvey said, leaning closer so that she could hear him over the roar of the crowd. "He's here to make his point."

"And he's doing a fine job of it."

.   .   .

Otto called McGarvey's cell phone. "Oh, wow, Mac, they hit Dr. Larsen's Princeton lab in the middle of the night. Trashed the place."

Listening to the crowd it came as no surprise. "Anyone hurt?"

"No. Two guys, in and out in under ten minutes. Wiped out a bunch of computers and other equipment. One of the techies was there but she managed to stay out of their way."

"Descriptions?"

"Nada."

"What about Eve?"

"She and Dr. Price went out to take a look at their oil platform."

"Has she been informed?"

"Presumably," Otto said. "When are you coming back?"

"Tonight."

"Talk to you in the morning."

THIRTY-FOUR

Eve arrived with Don Price on campus that evening after missing their connection in Atlanta where they'd spent an anxious few hours in the terminal on the phone with Lisa and the rest of the team. The FBI had sent a couple of agents to the airport to ask a few questions, and provide a little security until she got on the plane, though no one was suggesting that Eve's safety was in any doubt.

They'd cabbed it in from the airport, and standing in the doorway to her laboratory, surrounded by campus security, Princeton cops and the FBI, and her techies, Lisa on one side and Don on the other, Eve was all but overwhelmed at first by the destruction. Someone had invaded her personal space with violence and she felt physically ill, almost the same as when one of her first papers for publication had failed a peer review—for being too fringe, in the words of one of the docs who thought she was a little nutso, in addition to being a female in a man's profession.

Lisa was physically okay, but she'd been traumatized witnessing the attack. "It made no sense," she'd said first thing. "I mean why smash up some computers? We'll pull the hard drives and retrieve the data. Maybe lose a half day, tops. Were they dumb, or what?"

But she'd been shaking and Eve had held her for a long moment. "Dumb."

Aldo Bertonelli, the FBI special agent in charge from the Bureau's Trenton office, was pleasant enough except he wanted only to ask questions but not give any answers. "I'd like you to take an inventory, if you would, Doctor."

Eve wasn't sure that she understood him. "Nothing's going to be missing," she said. "They weren't here to steal anything from us. Hell, they could have asked and we would have shared any of the data they wanted." She looked at the mess. "They came here to send us—send me—a message."

"And what message would that be?"

"They call this the God Project."

"Who are they?"

"Schlagel," Eve said.

Bertonelli shrugged. "It's a theory, but have you received any threatening phone calls, e-mails, or text messages that would lead you to believe such thing?"

"Bloody hell," Eve said half under her breath. "Do you watch television at all, Agent Bertonelli? The son of a bitch is gunning for me, and he's all but ordered his crazies to pull the trigger."

"He's denied any involvement, Doctor."

"Of course he has," Eve said, disgusted, and she was finished with the authorities, who in her estimation spent more of their time covering their own asses than actually doing real investigative work when sensitive issues were involved.

When Bertonelli and the others had gone, she shared her opinion with Don, who disagreed. "They're doing their jobs, and you have to cut them some slack."

"Like you did with Defloria about Vanessa?" she shot back, knowing they were two different things, not related to each other, and she immediately apologized. "It doesn't make any sense."

Now that the police had finished their investigation, taking photographs, presumably looking for fingerprints or DNA evidence, Lisa and the others had started the data retrieval and cleanup work, which would be finished by morning.

"From their standpoint it might," Don said, meaning, of course, Schlagel and his people.

But Eve had been looking at her techies, especially Lisa, and she was startled, almost as if she'd seen a vision of all of them lying in bloody heaps, smashed like their equipment. Only humans had no hard drives to retrieve, and she was frightened.

"I feel like we're in the Dark Ages," she said. "The Inquisition."

"It'll pass," he said.

"Promise?"

Don nodded and smiled. "You bet," he said, and he hugged her.

THIRTY-FIVE

It was late by the time they got back to Washington and cabbed it to McGarvey's small third-floor apartment in Georgetown. The front bowed windows of the brownstone looked down on Rock Creek, and last fall the changing leaves had been restful for his nerves, which at that point had still been shattered.

"Nice view," Gail said putting down her bag.

"When you have the time to look," he said. "Take the bedroom, I'll sleep out here."

She looked at him. "Wouldn't it be better if I got a hotel room after tonight?"

"No," McGarvey said, although it was difficult for him to let anyone inside his circle of comfort. But just now it was necessary. "I don't know how long this will take, so for now we'll work out of here. At some point we'll probably go in separate directions. And this place is reasonably safe. My lease, phone, and computer accounts are all under different work names. So just keep your eyes open."

"Are you expecting someone?"

He shrugged. Not a day had gone by for the last twenty years plus when he hadn't expected someone to show up. It had been one of the overriding facts of his existence. "It depends on what we turn up and how close we get. They weren't afraid to attack Hutchinson Island, so it'd be no stretch for them to come after us, especially if we hit a nerve."

"What's next?"

"I'm going to talk to some friends about Schlagel. In the meantime, you can get Eric and Otto pointed that way."

Gail was skeptical. "Do you really think he's somehow connected?"

"After the attack on Eve's lab?" he asked rhetorically. "I don't know. It's just a feeling. But he was quick off the mark to take advantage of the Hutchinson Island, and now this. And I don't think it's going to end there."

"More to come?"

McGarvey had been giving that idea a lot of thought. Hutchinson Island could have been much more spectacular than 9/11, and vandalism at the lab was little more than a pinprick, maybe a warning. But if another strike of some sort had been planned it would almost certainly be much stronger. After the trade towers and the Pentagon, al-Quaeda's next target had most likely been the White House; one-two-three hammer blows at the purveyors of free trade, the planners of war and the leadership of the satan government. If Hutchinson Island and Princeton were indeed just the opening shots, whatever was coming next would depend entirely on who was behind it. "The contractor who walked away, and the engineer inside the control room were first-rate, and that sort of expertise does not come cheap."

"It wasn't just another terrorist bombing, nor was Princeton unrelated."

"No," McGarvey said. "They have a larger plan. Had it all along."

"That's a cheery thought to end the day on," Gail said. "I'm going to get some sleep." She picked up her bag and headed to the bedroom, but hesitated, suddenly shy for just a moment. "You don't have to sleep out here, you know."

A lot of old wounds—though not all—came back at McGarvey, and he too hesitated for a moment. "No."

"As in not tonight, not yet, not ever?"

"Not tonight."

"Okay," Gail said. "I'll let you know when I'm out of the shower and it's safe to come in." And she went into the bedroom and shut the door.

Gail made breakfast in the morning, and it was just after nine before they were finished and went downstairs to grab separate cabs. Schlagel's diatribe on Hutchinson Island was getting a lot of airtime on all the major networks, especially *Good Morning America*, whose news anchor called it "the Sermon on the Isle." But Schlagel had planned on the publicity. Whatever could be said of the man did not include incompetence; he was the consummate showman, though so far there'd been no mention of the attack on the lab. And from what little McGarvey had noticed of the preacher's rise to national prominence, his visits to the White House stood out like beacons. Fox News had dubbed him the spiritual adviser to the president—and the two before Howard Lord.

"I expect you'll be at it all day," Gail said. "How about dinner somewhere tonight?"

"I'll let you know," McGarvey said, and she pecked him on the cheek and then ran out to a cab that had pulled over, leaving him to wonder if it had been such a good idea after all to have her stay with him, knowing how she still felt.

On the way into town McGarvey called Otto on his cell phone and asked him to set up a meeting with Walter Page sometime later this morning, and fending off his friend's questions, telephoned William Callahan, who right after 9/11 had been appointed as the FBI's deputy assistant director for counterterrorism. They'd known each other briefly a couple of years ago when McGarvey had been working the operation in Mexico City. The Bureau had helped search for the missing Polonium

210 that had supposedly been smuggled into the U.S. Nothing to date had come of the investigation, but McGarvey had been impressed by Callahan's intelligence and professionalism. He wasn't simply a desk jockey, he was the real deal, coming up the ranks as a special agent.

"Mac, it's good to hear from you," Callahan said, after his secretary had put the call through. And he sounded genuinely pleased.

"Do you have a few minutes to spare this morning?"

"Absolutely," Callahan said without an instant's hesitation "You're with the NNSA, so I'm assuming this has something to do with Hutchinson Island."

"Actually Reverend Schlagel."

This time Callahan did hesitate. "I see," he said. "How soon can you be here?"

"Twenty minutes," McGarvey said, and he told the cabbie to take him to FBI headquarters.

It was a weekday and downtown Washington was as busy as usual. The receptionist in the lobby checked his identification and telephoned Callahan's office. "Your guest is here, sir," she said, and she directed McGarvey to wait in the visitors' lounge. "Mr. Callahan will be with you shortly."

McGarvey was the only one in the nicely furnished lounge this morning, aware that he was being watched, as all visitors were, by agents behind a two-way mirror. Guests of assistant directors and above were not required to sign in nor were they subjected to the normal security checks.

Callahan, a large, fit-looking man in his midforties with salt-and-pepper hair and broad shoulders, showed up a couple of minutes later. He'd played tight end for the Green Bay Packers for two years right out of college, but had been sidelined with a torn rotator cuff and had gone back to school to get his MA in criminal justice, and from there had been hired by the Bureau. He was a seriously steady man, with a wife and a couple of kids, who nevertheless liked to crack jokes. This morning he wasn't smiling, though his greeting and handshake were friendly.

"Joan and I were very sad about your loss. I can't imagine how bad it must have been," he said.

"It wasn't a good year."

Even though Callahan was only in charge of one section of the Bureau's Division of Counter Terrorism, and technically was only a deputy assistant director, he was senior in line for that promotion when the current division assistant director was bumped farther up the ladder, therefore his ID pass had the gold background of an associate director with all the privileges.

When they were settled in Callahan's unimpressive office on the ninth floor in the rear part of the building McGarvey came straight to the point about his suspicions.

"I see your point," Callahan said. "But so far we've come up with nothing that would make a possible link between him and Hutchinson Island or Princeton."

"He's using Hutchinson Island as his soapbox."

"I'll give you that much, but I think it'd be a stretch to believe that he would have funded something like that merely to create an issue that he could use. The man wants to be president, and he's smart enough to understand that if he did run he would be subject to more scrutiny than anyone could imagine. Every eye in the world would be looking his way. Every investigative reporter worth his or her salt would be taking his background apart. Every move he ever made since childhood would be gone over with a fine-toothed comb. And a lot of that would happen even before he got the nomination. And he certainly wouldn't have directed an attack on Dr. Larsen's lab."

"It got her attention."

"It accomplished nothing."

Callahan was right, of course. Yet McGarvey couldn't shake the premonition that Schlagel was somehow involved. "I assume that you've seen the material that we've come up with," he said.

"On the contractor who walked away?" Callahan asked. "We don't have him in any of our files, nor do I think you have any solid evidence he was involved."

"He killed the teacher in San Francisco to use his identity to take a tour of the facility."

"Sorry, but any defense lawyer would throw that out as circumstantial evidence. He'd be stuck with a suspicion of murder, but not an act of terrorism."

"I agree," McGarvey said. "But assuming the man who walked away from the tour was the pro who was hired along with the control room engineer, you'd have to admit that he's damned good. You have no record of him, and neither does the Company. Hell, even Rencke is having a tough time finding anything."

"Could mean he's innocent," Callahan suggested. He was playing devil's advocate; disprove all the possibilities you could, until you were left with one ironclad lead.

"Innocent men leave tracks. Passports, driver's licenses, bank accounts, things like that. But we're all coming up with blanks. This guy simply doesn't exist. Add his behavior at the power plant and that makes him my prime suspect."

"I'll give you that," Callahan said. "We've certainly begun investigations on slimmer leads. But where does it lead if you can't find him, can't even learn who he is?"

"If he was the contractor, we at least know that he's a pro. He'd have to be to leave absolutely no trace."

"Interpol, MI5, MI6, BND, anybody?"

"All blanks so far."

Callahan spread his hands. "Okay, you're here, Mac, and you put the reverend's name on the table. Where are you going with this? You certainly don't think he'd be involved in the Princeton thing?"

"No, that's a separate issue. Almost certainly Schlagel's crazies. For an operation like Hutchinson Island a pro, like our contractor, would not come cheap. Whoever hired him had deep pockets."

"According to your people al-Quaeda was behind educating the engineer."

"But we think it's possible that someone else got the engineer into contact with the contractor who then managed to get him to the States and inside the plant," McGarvey said. "More money. A lot more."

"And you don't think the New al-Quaeda is that well-heeled these days?"

"We have to ask who's got that kind of money—millions—to spend on an act of terrorism, and who has the reason for it—something to gain, something worth the money and the risk?"

Callahan sat back and shook his head. "Schlagel has the motive, and we think he probably has the means, but going after him could be dicey. He has a lot of powerful friends, including some in the White House, he has a very large and at times fanatical following, he has a media empire three times the size of Pat Robertson's, and he has some top-notch lawyers, and I mean first-class lawyers, who've managed to create a wall of nearly impenetrable interlocking organizations, a lot of them supposed charities, plus at least three dozen corporations, most of them offshore."

"So he has the means and the motive," McGarvey said. "And a lot of guys like that think that they're invincible, above the law, nobody's smart enough to catch them. Makes him a suspect. And he sure came out of the chute in big hurry with his antinuclear movement."

Callahan hesitated for just a second, and he shook his head again. "Knowing what you're capable of doing, I'm not sure if I should tell you the rest of it."

"We won't catch these guys keeping shit from each other," McGarvey said. "Those are the old days. No interagency rivalry now. Won't do us any good."

"It'd be nice if that were actually the truth, but nothing much has changed," Callahan said. "Look, it's possible that Schlagel may have some connection with Anne Marie Marinaccio and her financial group out of Dubai. We've had her under investigation ever since the dot-com boom days, but we couldn't prove a thing that would hold up in a court of law. She's damned good, and at that time she had a half-dozen senators in her pocket one way or another. When she got out of the technology stocks she wound up in real estate, mostly Florida and California, and when she walked she took several billions of dollars with her and set up in the UAE, which took her in with open arms."

"Has she been indicted?"

"No, but we've classified her as a person of interest who we'd very much like to talk to. And there's more."

"There always is," McGarvey said. He'd been down this path many times before, gathering information, gearing up for the opening moves. He sometimes thought of his work as an elaborate dance, in which very often one or more of the partners ended up dead.

"Marinnacio may have a connection to the United Arab Emirates International Bank of Commerce, which is almost certainly involved in the funding of a number of terrorist organizations, funneling money from dozens if not hundreds of charities around the world, including here in the States."

"Don't tell me that Schlagel is connected?"

"We don't know about any ties with IBC, but he's almost certainly done business with the Marinaccio Group."

"Put it to a grand jury," McGarvey said, but Callahan shook his head.

"Wouldn't fly, Mac. We don't have the proof."

"Maybe I can help," McGarvey said. "I've been given a free hand to take a closer look, see where this all leads."

"For God's sake don't shoot the man."

McGarvey had to smile despite himself. "Leastways not immediately. But I think there's more coming."

Callahan escorted him back downstairs to the lobby. "Keep me posted," he said before they parted.

McGarvey nodded. "It's a two-way street."

THIRTY-SIX

McGarvey had turned off his cell phone at the FBI, and outside he switched it back on to find that Otto had sent him a message. He called back. "What do you have?"

"Page will see you anytime you want," Otto said. "The sooner the better. He's got something on his mind."

"I'll bet he does."

"You get anything from Callahan?"

Switching off the cell phone hadn't disabled the GPS memory, but all the sensitive areas in the J. Edgar Hoover Building were shielded from any kind of electronic transmissions. Callahan was just a guess on Rencke's part, typical of his genius at figuring things out.

"The Bureau's going to help."

"That's a comfort," Rencke said with a touch of sarcasm.

"Looking a little closer at the Reverend Schlagel and his possible ties to the UAEIBC."

"Yeah, Eric called a little while ago. We both got a strong tie between Schlagel and the bank, and possibly to a derivative fund's manager setup in Dubai."

"The Marinaccio Group."

"Callahan give that to you?"

"Yes, he did, but he thinks it's a stretch that Schlagel had anything to do with Hutchinson Island. Maybe his people at Princeton, but not Florida."

"Run it by Page," Otto said. "We'll talk afterwards."

Word had been left at the front gate that McGarvey was coming in, and the cabbie was given a dashboard pass that allowed him to drive up to the Old Headquarters Building and drop off his passenger. But he had to return immediately and hand in the pass, which was date and time stamped.

Each time McGarvey came back like this, he was sharply reminded of his history there, some of it extremely painful, but most of what he had done in the name of his country had been necessary. Or at least it'd always been so in his mind. And now he was in the middle of it again, something he'd been expecting for months. He'd been getting the old sensations at the nape of his neck and somewhere deep in his head that something was heading his way. Something out of the darkness, something that he would have to deal with. And it was at times like these over the past few years when he'd become a little tired of the game. Yet that's who he was; it's who he'd always been.

Marty Bambridge met McGarvey in the main hall to escort him up to the director's office on the seventh floor. He was an odd-looking man with a hawk nose that hung over a large mouth, and thinning black hair that he combed straight back, held in place by a lot of hair spray. He was dressed in a sloppy suit and tie, and although he didn't seem to take any care with his appearance he was reputed to be an outstanding DDO with a lot of imagination and a great deal of empathy for his people, both on campus and out in the field, including his NOCs.

"Welcome back, Mr. Director," he said, giving McGarvey a VIP visitor's pass. "Mr. Page is expecting you." They shook hands.

"My friends call me Mac."

"Yes, sir," Bambridge said.

Page was waiting for them in his office along with Carleton Patterson, now in his early seventies, who had been the Company's general counsel during McGarvey's days, a post he still held. Where Page seemed nondescript, Patterson was tall, slender, and patrician-looking. Before he'd taken the temporary post with the CIA, he'd been a top-flight corporate attorney in New York.

They all shook hands and sat down on the couch and a couple of easy chairs grouped around a large coffee table. The room hadn't changed much since McGarvey had sat behind the desk.

"Thanks for seeing me on such short notice," McGarvey said.

"I was going to ask you to come over in any event," Page said. "And may I assume you want to discuss the Hutchinson Island event? I'm told that Mr. Rencke has been providing you with some assistance, and I approve."

McGarvey couldn't decide if he liked or trusted the man. But according to Otto, morale at the Agency had picked up since his appointment; among the reasons were Page's ability to handle Congress, where he'd developed some real bipartisan support. He'd built a reputation as a straight shooter by freely admitting, when it was necessary, that certain of the CIA's operations had to be withheld from the public for security reasons, delicately sidestepping the fact that Congress, especially the House, sometimes ran a little fast and loose with classified information that had some political benefit.

"Ultimately yes," McGarvey said. "The DOE has asked me to help find out who was behind the attack."

A look of satisfaction passed between Page and Bambridge. "The president ordered me to do exactly the same thing, and I promised that I would have someone in the field who'd be our point man."

"Me?"

"Sounds as if you're already in the middle of it," Bambridge said. "I'm assuming that you'll share product with us?"

"Through Rencke."

Bambridge wanted to object but Page held him off. "Fair enough," the DCI said. "But you asked for this meeting. What do you have on your mind?"

"What was Lorraine Fritch working on in Caracas that got her killed?"

"She was investigating a connection between Miguel Octavio and a derivative fund manager in Dubai."

"The Marinaccio Group."

Page showed no surprise. "Yes."

"Not enough motivation for her assassination," McGarvey said. "There had to be something else."

Bambridge spread his hands. "She was on her way up with something she told me was too important to trust even through encrypted channels. Had to be done in person."

"Hutchinson Island," McGarvey said, dropping the bombshell, and he saw by a quickening expression on Page's face that he had hit the mark. "You had the same thought?"

"The timing was coincidental," the DCI said. "She'd been working on this connection between Octavio and Marinaccio for some time, but within hours after she'd gotten word through the usual channels about the attack, she called and said she was on her way here."

"My dear boy, what makes you think a connection exists?" Patterson asked.

"Too many leads go back to Marinaccio, including the Reverend Schlagel, who's using the attack to lash out at nuclear power plants."

"He's looking for a campaign issue," Patterson said.

"That's right," McGarvey said. "But doesn't it strike you that Marinaccio's prime interest is in oil derivatives?"

"If that's his motivation then he'll be against a hell of a lot more than just nukes," Bambridge said.

"Something like that," McGarvey said. "I think that Hutchinson Island was just the opening move. There's more to come. Coal-fired plants—and we have some big ones—for a start. Schlagel could just as well go on his soapbox about carbon dioxide emissions killing us."

"But oil—diesel, gasoline, or jet fuel—is bad too," Bambridge pointed out.

"People will give up nuclear and coal-produced electricity, but not their cars," Patterson suggested.

"If you're right, and I think you are, they'll go after whatever would hurt us the most," Page said. "Coal, because it won't be wind farms or solar centers. At least not yet."

McGarvey had come to the same conclusion. A big coal-fired plant would be a likely target. A lot of environmental damage could be done depending on how sophisticated the attack was. But he'd been thinking about something else. "I expect that you've all heard of Eve Larsen. If what she's trying to do actually works she could be a prime target."

"Some people in Oslo think she's on the right track," Patterson said. "And her laboratory in Princeton was vandalized last night. Did you hear about it?"

"Yes."

Page sat back, a sudden thoughtful expression on his face, and he and Bambridge exchanged a look. "Do you know the woman?"

"She was at Hutchinson Island when the plant was evacuated. I helped get her out."

"Erling Hansen telephoned me yesterday afternoon," Page said. Hansen was the director of the Norwegian Intelligence Service. "Asked for a back-channel favor."

"The Nobel ceremony?"

"The NIS got an anonymous tip that something might happen to her either on the way to Norway or sometime shortly after she arrives in Oslo."

"Anything specific?" McGarvey asked.

"No," Page replied. "But he said the way the warning was stated struck one of their analysts as religious in nature."

"Schlagel," McGarvey said.

"Since you brought it up, yes, the thought has crossed my mind."

"What'd you tell Hansen?"

"That we'd look into it. But I don't think it would be politically wise to send someone over with her. She can hire her own bodyguards if she—or you—think it's necessary."

"I'll ask her," McGarvey said.

. . .

Bambridge called down to Rencke's office for McGarvey, but a recorded message merely stated that he was out of the building for a couple of hours.

"He doesn't punch a time clock," Bambridge said. "But he spends a lot of nights here when he's on to something."

"Has that been happening lately?"

"Yes."

"Before Hutchinson Island?"

Bambridge hesitated for a moment. "I don't know what he's been working on. Nobody here does. But he's been at it for a couple of months now. Just before Hutchinson Island one of his computers showed a lavender background, which I'm told means some sort of trouble is coming our way. But he wouldn't talk about it."

It had struck McGarvey as odd at the time that Otto had not confided in him, and again he felt slightly depressed.

THIRTY-SEVEN

□

DeCamp carried no photographs of Martine in his wallet, relying instead on his almost photographic memory to see her. But pulling on his jacket and getting set to leave his tiny apartment in the working-class Twentieth Arrondissement in the late afternoon, he stopped for a moment to remember her face in his mind's eye, and he couldn't. As often was the case when he was on assignment, his concentration was elsewhere.

"It's not the stray bullet that kills you or your lads," his sergeant instructor had taught in his officers combat training course. "It's the stray thought. Keep your heads out of your arses, gentlemen."

The early afternoon was mellow as he headed downstairs and south through the Menilmontant neighborhood with its nightclubs, strip joints, and occasional whorehouse, not yet alive for the evening, and before he got ten meters he'd already forgotten about his vexation over Martine. Thinking about her would come later, because he'd made the decision that when he went to ground—very soon—he would take her with him.

She would understand the necessity. He would make her understand.

He carried a dark blue ripstop nylon duffle bag over his shoulder, his head up, his step confident; to do otherwise was to invite attack. This was a tough neighborhood where the strong preyed on the weak. Even the Paris metro police presence here was minimal; it had always been a perfect place for DeCamp's needs.

The streets were heavy with traffic, as were the mostly narrow sidewalks, and although he was noticed he remained anonymous. The trouble was that although he operated best on his own, he never fancied himself a loner—at least not in his heart of hearts. When his father had been killed and his mother had abandoned him he'd felt an almost overwhelming crushing sense not only of loneliness, but of defeat. To this day, this moment, he remembered his feelings very clearly, and they were just about akin to what he was feeling now.

But first things first, he told himself, allowing a slight smile to show at the corners of his mouth. And for a moment he could see Martine clearly in his mind's eye, before he clamped off that line of thought. Business.

The Père-Lachaise Cemetery, a couple of blocks down the hill from his apartment, established by Napoleon in 1804, was actually the largest cemetery in all of Paris. Other than the nightclubs and strip joints, it was the most popular tourist attraction in the arrondissement. Chopin was buried here, as were Sarah Bernhardt, Edith Piaf, Bizet, Proust, Balzac, and most curiously, to DeCamp, the American rock star Jim Morrison of The Doors.

DeCamp entered through the gate in the tall white stone wall and made his way slowly up a series of winding paths and lanes to the upper end of the cemetery near Oscar Wilde's grave. At this hour, just before early cocktails, the place was nowhere near as busy as it was in the early morning openings just after nine on Sundays and holidays. But still it was anonymous; he was just one visitor among many.

He stopped at the grave of some Frenchman and waited a minute or so until a party of middle-aged men passed him. He stepped off the path and made his way to a small mausoleum a few meters away with a centopath of a winged warrior outside an ornate bronze door.

Bowing his head for a second, and looking back to make sure he was not being observed, DeCamp opened the door, slipped inside, and closed it after him.

He had a clear line of sight through the filigreed panel at eye height, and so far as he could tell no one had taken notice.

The chamber was divided into two sections: the first was a small chapel designed for six or eight people to kneel and pray at one time, and the second was a smaller, innerchamber that held niches for the cremated remains of the French-Catholic family, beginning in 1898, with two niches remaining.

Putting his nylon bag down, DeCamp went to the small altar at the front of the chapel and muscled the one-meter-long stone countertop aside to reveal a dusty space a half-meter square by one-and-a-half meters deep. It contained two canvas rucksacks that he pulled out. From the first he removed a plastic-wrapped package that held an Austrian-made 9 mm Steyr GB semiautomatic pistol with two eighteen-round box magazines, a suppressor, and a cleaning kit.

Next he took out a package containing several passports, from which he selected one of Canadian and one of U.S. issue, with matching American Express platinum credit cards and supporting credentials including valid driver's licenses, social security and national IDs, health insurance cards and photos of wives and families, along with several thousand in euros and Canadian dollars.

He'd decided that importing a long rifle and associated equipment to Norway was not worth the risk. Whichever scenario he selected in the end—a hit in the hotel, a hit while Eve was taking a buggy tour of the old city, or a hit just before or just after the Nobel ceremony—the Steyr, which was a favorite of his, would be adequate.

He loaded his choices into his nylon bag, replaced the two rucksacks into the space beneath the altar top, and slid the stone back into place.

He remained at the door for a full ten minutes before a family of four lingering at one of the graves across the lane finally moved off then slipped outside, and shouldering the nylon duffle bag reached the street and headed back to his apartment.

He would remain in Paris for a few more days before shipping a parcel to himself at the Grand Hotel in Oslo and then flying there to arrive the day before the package arrived. The cargo-sniffing dogs would not detect the odor of gunpowder in the bullets because they would be packed in two containers of mentholated spirits—Vicks VapoRub.

The TGV could get him to Nice in a few hours where he could rent a car and do a drive by on the corniche highway above his house. Just to see if all was well. To reassure himself that because Wolfhardt had found him nothing had happened.

But not yet. There would be time later.

THIRTY-EIGHT

In a cab on the way back into town, McGarvey left a message on Otto's cell to call him, and then phoned Gail who had been working with Yablonski all morning, but she had no news for him. Everyone was coming up short, and they were all frustrated. It was like knowing the sword of Damocles was about to fall but not when it would happen or from what direction it would be falling, except that the thread holding it above their heads was getting thinner by the minute.

There'd been no arrests yet over the Princeton attack, and one of Eve's techies who was the only witness hadn't been of much help except to describe their approximate build and the clothing they wore—including the balaclavas.

"Are you coming into the office?" Gail asked.

"No," McGarvey told her. "But if something turns up, anything, call me."

"Okay," Gail said, and she sounded a little hurt. "I'll see you back at your apartment this evening. Maybe we'll go someplace for a bite to eat."

"Maybe," McGarvey said, and he broke the connection and telephoned Eve Larsen's cell, and she answered after three rings.

"Speaking of déjà vu all over again," she said. "I was just thinking about calling you. Are you here in town?"

"If you mean Washington, yes, I am."

"How about dinner tonight after the show," she said. "I could use an escort. Someone who knows his way around."

"Sorry, Doc, but I don't have any idea what you're talking about," McGarvey said. "What show?"

"I thought you knew. Fox News is doing a special on my energy program tonight at seven. They did some of the taping last year aboard the ship I was using for the first in-water experiment, and more aboard the oil rig and up at GE's Stamford facility where they're building my impeller-generator sets. Anyway they want me live at their studio on North Capitol Street. I'll be out of there by seven thirty."

Then he knew what she was talking about, and he could hear a little bit of concern in her voice. "Are you expecting trouble?"

"After last night, sure. But you should watch TV sometime," she said. "Reverend Schlagel and his bunch are planning a demonstration in front of the studio. I'm told that the police will be there, and the network's own security people won't let any of them into the building." She hesitated.

"Where are you staying?"

"I have a small apartment at Watergate East."

"I'll pick you up at six."

And he could hear her relief now. "Thanks. I'll be waiting in the lobby. And if we're going to dinner tonight, you'd better start calling me Eve. My friends do."

McGarvey was back at his apartment around noon where he had a quick sandwich and bottle of beer before he changed into sweats and Nikes and headed across the street into the park for his run.

Five miles used to be his daily routine, and when he was in Florida on the beach, he would swim that far in the Gulf. But since Katy's death and the deaths of his daughter and son-in-law he'd slacked off a little. Training NNSA field officers hadn't been much of a strain.

But running now, alternating his pace from easy to occasionally flat out, he felt as if he needed to get in good shape as quickly as possible. And after the first couple of miles, his shirt soaked, he was gratified that he hadn't lost as much of his edge as he thought he had, and getting past the first burn when his body finally started to process the energy demands being placed on it, he felt good. At least physically good.

He'd lost a good man at Hutchinson Island, and at Lundgren's funeral he'd met his wife who'd wanted assurance that Alan's death hadn't been in vain. What he gave his life for was worth something. Her two teen-aged sons, who were totally devastated by their father's death, hung on every word.

"What he did down there saved a lot of lives," McGarvey told them. "And he wouldn't have had it any other way."

"Other people were killed trying to help out. Did they know my husband?"

"One of them did. Her name was Marsha Littlejohn and she was sitting next to him trying to defuse the explosives the same as he was."

Lundgren's wife was a sturdy, no-nonsense woman from somewhere in the Midwest, and she looked up into McGarvey's eyes. "No lies?"

"No," McGarvey told her.

Before she walked away, she touched McGarvey's arm, and managed a tiny smile. "Thank you," she said. "Alan said that you were the best man he'd ever worked with."

The boys shook his hand, and mumbled their thanks, and went with their mother back to the limousine.

And it was Arlington and the same kind of limo that Katy and Liz had driven away in, and running now along Rock Creek he'd remembered that he'd almost lost it at that point. But he'd taken a deep breath and sucked it up as he'd been told to do when he was training at the Farm.

The afternoon was pleasantly cool, and a lot of people were out jogging or biking, and though lost in thought McGarvey was completely aware of his surroundings, of the people on both sides of the narrow, winding creek, others seated at park benches or picnic tables, cars and the occasional taxi passing on the road, the rooflines of the buildings in the distance, even the woods where a lone man with a silenced sniper rifle could be concealed. That too was a part of who he was.

A call to arms, he thought. At last. And he welcomed it.

Most of the time when McGarvey was in Washington in the past year and a half he'd found no need to drive his own car, but this evening was different. If there was trouble, he didn't want to rely on getting out of there in a cab. He kept his metallic blue-gray Porsche Cayenne SUV in a concierge garage a block and a half from his apartment. It was always kept washed and gassed, and once a week the service took it up the GW Memorial Parkway past the CIA, and before turning back the driver looked for incipient problems that would immediately be tended to.

At three he called to ask that the car be delivered and parked as close to the apartment as possible. The concierge rep, an older man in a dark blue blazer, showed up fifteen minutes later with the key, and had McGarvey sign for the car. "We managed to get you a spot right outside the front door."

"That's lucky for this neighborhood."

"Yes, sir. Will you be needing your vehicle picked up later this evening?"

"Not till first thing in the morning," McGarvey said. "I'll call first."

Gail got back to the apartment shortly after five just as McGarvey finished cleaning and loading his pistol at the kitchen counter and she pulled up short, dropping her purse on the chair, a quizzical expression on her face.

"Are we expecting some trouble that you haven't mentioned?" she said.

"Schlagel's in town."

"Did he follow us here from Hutchinson Island?"

McGarvey shook his head. "I don't think he knows we exist yet. He's evidently got a permit to stage a demonstration outside the Fox News television studio downtown, and I was asked to provide a little backup security."

It suddenly dawned on Gail what McGarvey was talking about. "Dr. Larsen asked," she said, an odd set to her mouth.

"I think that she and her project could be the next target. Norwegian intelligence asked the CIA to watch out for her. Apparently there've been threats against her safety, maybe from a religious group or groups who might show up in Oslo for the Nobel ceremony."

Gail was intrigued. "Schlagel?"

McGarvey shrugged. "Unknown. But if he was somehow connected with Hutchinson Island and Princeton he might be taking another step tonight."

"He's not going to be that open about it," Gail said. "I mean if he makes himself so visible like this, and then something happens to the lady scientist it'd be all over for him."

"Not if he didn't strike the blow himself. It's like the crazies who bomb abortion clinics and kill the doctors and nurses because they're whipped up by the rhetoric. When it happens, which is inevitable, the same people who ranted and raved about the baby killers deny any knowledge or responsibility. They make a big public show of deploring the bombings and killings."

"I see what you mean. But what's your part?"

"I got her off Hutchinson Island before the meltdown, and she thought she'd like to have me around after the TV show, just to get her past the crowd."

Gail started to say something, but then shook her head. She went into the kitchen and poured a glass of Merlot. "Do you want some?" she asked.

"No."

She came back to the counter and sipped the wine, an intensely thoughtful expression in her eyes. "What about Oslo? Are you going with her?"

"I'm thinking about it," McGarvey said, knowing that's exactly what he was going to do, because Eve Larsen was the key.

"You're going to use her as bait," Gail said in wonder. "And you're going to put yourself directly on the firing line."

McGarvey got up and holstered his pistol at the small of his back. "It's the only game in town until we find out who the contractor is."

"Rain check on dinner?" Gail asked.

"Yes."

THIRTY-NINE

□

McGarvey's cell phone rang as he was passing the Kennedy Center on his way over to pick up Eve Larsen at the Watergate. It was Otto. "How'd it go with Page?"

"He wants me to be the unofficial point man on the investigation," McGarvey said. "They said you'd left the building. Anything I need to know?"

"Sorry, Mac, but we didn't want to worry you until we were sure. It's about Audie. We took her to the doctor this afternoon."

Something so cold, so alien, so completely beyond understanding flashed through McGarvey's body, nearly causing him to run off the street. But then he got hold of himself. "What's wrong with her?"

"Nothing, honest injun. It's just an ear infection. The doc gave her some antibiotics and eardrops and said she'll be fine." Rencke was talking in a rush. "But she had a fever last night so Louise stayed home with her, and she called me this morning. Anyway, it's okay now."

"Jesus."

"Yeah," Otto said. "Raising a kid isn't as easy as Louise and I thought it would be. But I'm not complaining. We love her, and there's nothing we wouldn't do for her. And not a day goes by when I don't think about Todd and Liz who should be here with her."

McGarvey settled down and it was like starting to hear again after being temporarily deafened by a sudden loud noise, and things seemed to be just slightly out of focus. "I'm on my way over to pick up Eve Larsen and take her to the Fox studio on North Capitol. Get into the D.C. police system and see if Reverend Schlagel has a permit to stage a demonstration on the street."

"Just a sec," Otto said.

McGarvey turned off New Hampshire Avenue at the parking entrance for the Watergate Mall and the East and South buildings, and drove around to the lobby of Eve's building.

Otto came back. "Yup. Leonard Sackman, who's the Soldiers of Salvation Ministry special events coordinator, if you can believe that, arranged for the permit. It's been limited to one thousand people, for ninety minutes from six thirty to eight. So if you're on the way you'll definitely run into them. But there'll be plenty of cops, and none of those people will be allowed inside."

"Have you tried to get anything from the computers in Schlagel's organization?"

"Yeah, and it was easy, but nothing important's there. It looks like all the major decisions are made face-to-face. Probably paper records at their McPherson headquarters. I suppose we could find someone willing to break in and give it a try."

McGarvey had been born and raised on a ranch in western Kansas and he knew the state well. Most of the towns out on the plains, well away from Kansas City and Wichita, were small. Just about everybody knew just about everybody else. Strangers tended to stand out. It was one of the reasons the FBI had such a tough time getting any in-depth information on the reverend. "Take a look at their security measures. If you can get inside the system without attracting any attention, do it. And find out about the local and county cops. See what sort of a relationship they have with the church."

"Or if any of them happen to be on the payroll."

"It's worth a shot," McGarvey said, pulling up under the sweeping portico of the East Watergate building. "I'm at the Watergate now, I'll talk to you later."

Eve, dressed in a stylish charcoal gray pin-striped suit and a white blouse with long collar points under a jacket with turned-up sleeves that showed off the white, came out of the lobby as McGarvey got out of his car and came around to her. She seemed tense, understandably so.

"Thanks for this," she said, and they shook hands. "Anyway, it's my treat for dinner."

"It's a deal," McGarvey said. He started to help her into the SUV but she looked at him as if she wondered what he was doing, and he just smiled. The message was clear: she was a capable, self-sufficient woman. Modern. A scientist, not fluff. She was accustomed to opening her own doors.

Heading down Virginia Avenue to Constitution, traffic reasonable at this hour, McGarvey decided to wait until after the program to bring up the security concerns for her at the Nobel ceremonies. And for her part she kept her silence, her thoughts elsewhere, probably a combination of how many of Schlagel's people would be in front of the studio and what their mood would be and how she would come across in the live segments of the program.

Fifteen minutes later, after turning left at Louisiana Avenue onto North Capitol Street, they got the answers to one of the questions: there were a great many more than one thousand people in the crowd, and Schlagel himself, standing in the bed of a pickup truck, was using a bull-horn to exhort his flock about the extreme danger of allowing someone, anyone, to play God.

Police were everywhere, many of them on horseback, others dressed in riot gear with shields, batons, and helmets with Lexan facemasks, trying to keep the mob to one side of the street. But Schlagel's people completely ignored them, their attention totally riveted on their reverend.

A half-dozen television vans had gathered at the fringes covering what was turning out to be a major media event, three helicopters circled overhead, and cameramen were shooting the scene from the roof of the building that Fox shared with NBC and C-SPAN.

McGarvey pulled up short. "We're not getting through this way," he said.

Eve's cell phone rang. It was Jeff Meyers, the Fox producer for the special, who told her to stay away from the main entrance and use the E Street doors.

"Someone will meet us there," she told McGarvey, who made a U-turn onto D Street, up to New Jersey Avenue, and then went east on E Street where he found a parking spot not too far from the side entrance.

Traffic was nearly normal here, but some of the mob had spilled out beyond the intersection a half a block away, and as they hurried up the street they could hear Schlagel's amplified voice, loud but distorted, echoing and reechoing off the buildings.

A tall, muscular man in a dark blue blazer unlocked the door for them, as a slender man in his late twenties came down the corridor, and introduced himself as the show's producer.

He and Eve shook hands after she'd stepped through the security arch.

McGarvey held back. He pulled out his NNSA identification wallet and held it up. "I'm carrying a weapon."

The guard in the blazer stiffened. "You can't come in here armed."

"Do you know what's going on in front of this building?"

"The police are handling it."

"Mr. McGarvey is providing security for me," Eve told Meyers.

"He'll have to leave his gun down here," the security guard said. "No need for it past this point."

"Do you know who he is?" Eve said, her voice rising a little in anger.

"Ma'am, I know who he is and I have a great deal of respect for him. But he's not coming any farther carrying a weapon,"

"Do your interview," McGarvey told Eve. "I'll be here when you're finished."

"I'd like you to see it," she said, and from what McGarvey already knew of her, he figured it had to have been tough for her to ask.

"I'll give you a couple of disks of the program," Meyers said.

"Fair enough," McGarvey said, and he gave Eve a smile. "Break a leg, this is the easy part."

She gave him an odd look as if she didn't understand what he'd meant, yet she thought she should have, but then she nodded, and headed down the corridor with the producer.

"Sorry, Mr. McGarvey, but I don't know of any television studio anywhere that allows armed men," the security guard said.

McGarvey shrugged, because it didn't matter. He wouldn't be needed upstairs, not until later when Eve was finished. "No exceptions?"

"No, sir."

"Not even for the president's Secret Service detail?" McGarvey asked, and the guard, caught out, was suddenly angry.

"Either surrender your weapon or leave the building."

Or what? McGarvey wondered irascibly. But it was not worth the effort to find out. Instead he went outside and walked to the end of the block to where a couple of plainclothes cops were leaning against a beat-up Chevy Impala across the street from the outer edges of the crowd, which had grown considerably in the past couple of minutes.

McGarvey pulled out his NNSA identification and held it up for them to see, and when they realized the full import of who he worked for and what it might mean right now, he had their attention.

"I hope you're not here to tell us something bad," one cop said nervously.

Schlagel had just said something and the crowd roared its approval.

"No," McGarvey said. "I thought they had a permit for only a thousand people."

"Nobody's counting. What are you doing here?"

"I'm riding shotgun for the woman they're here to protest," McGarvey said.

The cop glanced back the way McGarvey had come. "She inside already?"

McGarvey nodded. "If they have a television monitor they'll know she made it, and it won't take long for them to figure out she came in through the rear door. Can your people keep the crowd back?"

"Not a chance in hell. It's a peaceful demonstration and they have a permit. Where's your car?"

"Around the corner on E Street."

"When is she coming out?"

"The program ends at seven thirty," McGarvey said. "I'm assuming she'll be at the door a few minutes after that."

"Okay, bring your car up to the door and we'll make a path for her. It's the best we can do."

"Good enough," McGarvey said. He glanced at his watch. It was coming up on seven, and Schlagel's mob was about to find out that Eve had gotten past them.

He walked back to the side entrance and pressed the buzzer beside the keypad. The security guard looked up from behind his desk, and shook his head.

"I can't let you in unless you're willing to give up your weapon," the man's voice came from the speaker grille.

"When Dr. Larsen comes downstairs, some of the crowd will probably be just outside," McGarvey said. "I'll be parked on the street, and the police will provide her with an escort. Tell her that it'll be okay."

The guard looked a little worried. "Do I need to call for backup in case they try to get inside?"

"No," McGarvey told the man. "They're just here to make their point."

A half-dozen uniformed cops came around the corner just ahead of the first of mob, and hustled to where McGarvey stood waiting. The Fox special had started.

"You McGarvey?" one of them demanded.

McGarvey nodded.

"Bring your car up now."

McGarvey went to where he'd parked, and drove back to the Fox building and pulled up in front of the door as Schlagel's pickup truck rounded the corner and slowly eased its way through the growing crowd, the reverend not missing a beat.

"Leave God's business to God," Schlagel's amplified voice boomed.

And the crowd responded, "Amen!"

"First it's nuclear reactors that will poison the earth for a million years, now this work by a godless woman who proposes to change the very air we breathe! We're not ready! More work needs to be done before it's too late. Close nuclear power across the country. And put an immediate stop to Larsen's God Project."

"Amen! Amen!" the crowd chanted.

"Now," Schlagel shouted. "Now, before it's too late!"

"Amen! Amen!"

Some of the television remote broadcast trucks had managed to make their way closer, even as more people filled the streets, and within minutes McGarvey was parked in the middle of a sea of humanity, the six uniformed cops just holding a path open from the door across the sidewalk to the curb.

By the time Eve showed up, E Street was completely jammed with people, and McGarvey had to push his way around to the passenger side of his SUV and open the door.

"The high priestess of evil is among us!" Schlagel shouted, his amplified voice hammering off the side of the building. He was about thirty feet away and he pointed a biblical finger at her. "God's word is writ in all things in heaven and on earth! Stop your meddling! Stop your God Project now, before you doom humanity!"

"Amen! Amen!" the crowd was chanting.

Sheltering Eve among them, four of the cops hustled her across the sidewalk as a large blond man in jeans and a Midwest Christian College sweatshirt standing between her and curb suddenly lunged at her, his right arm cocked as if he was getting ready to punch her.

McGarvey stepped forward, brought the man's arm back, breaking it at the wrist, and slammed a quick jab into the man's throat just below his Adam's apple, sending him to his knees.

Before anyone could react, McGarvey hustled Eve into the SUV, made his way back to the driver's side, and eased his way slowly through the crowd that reluctantly parted.

"I didn't expect it would be this bad," Eve said.

"I don't think the reverend and his people like you," McGarvey said.

FORTY

Eve picked the 1789 Restaurant on Thirty-sixth Street just off the Georgetown University campus—one of her favorites, she told him. Driving over past Mount Vernon Square and taking K Street, McGarvey could see that she was still shook up. "Would they really have tried to hurt me?" she asked.

"I think some of them would," McGarvey said. "And I have an idea that the number will grow as long as Schlagel keeps pushing his message."

"The God Project," she said in genuine wonder. "It makes no sense. I'm offering them cheap, renewable energy and the possibility of making the weather a little better. And he's fighting it."

"They don't give a damn about your work, most of them probably don't even understand what you're doing. They're just following the reverend."

"And what about him? He was down at Hutchinson Island making trouble, and now this. What does he want?"

"The White House," McGarvey said. "He wants to be president, and he thinks that you and Hutchinson Island are causes that will get him there."

"You can't be serious," Eve said. "And he's actually willing to have his people hurt me?"

In her world, scientists didn't usually get physical with each other or with their critics. Some of them might shout or bluster, but mostly they'd go to their offices and fire off a critical letter to *Nature* or *Scientific American* or *Smithsonian* or some other scientific journal. In her world that and being right were striking the blows.

"That's exactly what he wants."

Eve was trying to understand. "The media would be all over him if something happened to me."

"He'd be the first one to stand up at your funeral and praise your pioneering spirit, and damn the people who brought you down. He's coming after you, Eve, and he believes that he'll come out on top no matter what happens."

She sat back. "I think I need a drink," she said. Then she looked at him and smiled. "You're a pretty good man to have around in a pinch. This is the second time you were there when I needed you."

They used the restaurant's valet service, and when they were seated Eve ordered a martini straight up with a twist and McGarvey a cognac. And now that she was calming down, he told her the rest of it. "The Norwegian authorities think that you may be in some danger during the Nobel ceremonies, and they asked for our help with security. I'm coming to Oslo with you."

Her eyes were large. "My God, he'd actually try to get to me over there? That's more than crazy."

"Not him specifically, but one or more of his followers."

She thought about that for a long moment. "To do what?"

"Kill you," McGarvey told her. He didn't think there was any use sugarcoating the possibility that someone might want to more than just hurt her because of her project. And if she knew what could be coming at her, she would take her personal safety a little more seriously, at the very least until Schlagel was neutralized, if ever.

"Are you telling me that I need to hire bodyguards for the rest of my life?" she demanded. She was even more shook up than she had been leaving the television studio and encountering the mob and the man who'd tried to reach her. "Goddamnit, that's not the way science works. You pose questions and then search for answers that make sense. Free and open exchanges. Not billy clubs and knives and guns and bombs."

"You need to think about it, at least until your project is in place and you can prove that it works."

She looked away. "Galileo and Giordano Bruno should have had bodyguards to save them from the church. I thought we were past that."

"It's not just religion, like the antiabortion activists claim it is, or the Islamic fundamentalists who're waging war against the rest of us, or even Schlagel. It's about power. And for the moment you're a means to Schalgel's end."

Eve shook her head. "It's so unfair."

McGarvey felt sorry for her. Living in an ivory tower had apparently blinded her to the realities of the present-day world, just as Bruno had been blinded into believing that teaching the truth about astronomy as it was known in the sixteenth century would protect him from the Inquisition. But it hadn't and he'd been burned at the stake in Rome. "Yes, it is," he told her.

"Do you want the job?" Eve asked.

McGarvey nodded. "At least as far as Oslo, and we'll see what happens. In the meantime, try to keep a low profile."

"Winning a Nobel Prize tends to make that difficult," she said pensively.

· · ·

It was ten when McGarvey finally made it back to his apartment after dropping Eve off at the Watergate. She'd asked him to come up and have a drink, but he'd declined, telling her that he had a full day tomorrow. She'd handed him a copy of the disk. "This will explain what I'm trying to do," she'd said. And before she'd walked away she'd given him an odd, thoughtful look, as if she knew something and wanted to say it but then decided against it.

Gail was in bed reading. "I caught your lady scientist's special on Fox. She's an impressive woman."

"She's in trouble and she didn't see it coming," McGarvey said, hanging up his jacket and removing his holster and pistol.

"All the networks covered Schlagel's little circus word-for-word, move-for-move. The guy is good."

"Was my name mentioned?"

"Front and center. Former director of the CIA squiring the lady scientist, protecting her from the zealots who the reverend blasted for trying to take the situation too far. It'll make the front pages by morning."

"Exactly what he wanted," McGarvey said.

"And it puts you in the crosshairs, exactly what you wanted," Gail said, and she smiled wistfully. "I suppose it would be dumb of me to tell you to take care."

McGarvey stopped and looked at her, really looked at her. She was an attractive woman, always had been in his estimation, though with her dark eyes and hair she was almost the complete opposite of his wife Kathleen. And she was young, fourteen years younger than he was, and he felt a little guilty about feeling something for her.

"What?" she asked after a moment.

He shook his head. "Nothing. It's just been a long day and I'm tired."

"Are you still planning on going to Oslo?" Gail asked.

"I'm pretty sure that they're going to come after her."

"From what I saw on Fox there's no doubt about it. And I can even see a little of why Schlagel might be genuinely frightened. If her project develops on the scale she's talking about there just might be some unintended consequences. Something that even she can't see. Consequences that might affect us all."

"It's the oil people who want to stop her," McGarvey said.

"InterOil gave her a seagoing oil platform for the next step of her experiment, along with the money to fix it up and tow it to Florida's east coast."

"Good PR," McGarvey said. "Even if the rig doesn't get that far. But I think the same people who did Hutchinson Island will come after her for the same reasons. It's oil, but it has more to do with propping up the oil derivatives and hedge funds. From what I'm told if you added up all the oil derivatives you'd come up with a number that is seven—maybe even ten—times larger than all the actual oil in the ground. They're all betting on the same horse. The system is like a house of cards, one misstep and everything comes crashing down around us. And those consequences would be even worse than our mortgage meltdown or the Great Depression. Countries have gone to war for a lot less."

"Oil," Gail said. "In the end the hedge funds don't really matter as much as what's in the barrel and where it's shipped to."

"That's right," McGarvey said.

"And that kind of thinking puts your lady scientist right in the middle, and the rest of us could be just as well damned whatever happens; if her project is stopped we'll be at the mercy of OPEC, and if she succeeds we could be facing another depression and maybe a war for oil. With China?"

"We're not there yet," McGarvey said, and he went into the bathroom to take a shower, his thoughts alternating from Eve Larsen falling into the center of a growing storm, to Gail Newby and his relationship or lack thereof with her. And he couldn't sort out his feelings, which he decided was stupid. He was a decisive man, always had been. When Katy had given him the ultimatum early in their marriage, it had taken him less than a split second to turn around and run to Switzerland. But now he felt like an emotional cripple.

When he was done, he pulled on a pair of sweatpants and went back into the bedroom.

Gail had put her book aside, and had turned off the bedside lamp. "It's been two years since your wife was killed," she said. "It's time for you to rejoin the world, don't you think?"

And he thought about Katy and their life together. A photograph of the two of them standing on the Eiffel Tower was on the nightstand.

Lately he'd been having a little trouble seeing her face and every night that he was in the apartment he would stare at her picture, study it, remembering how the corners of her eyes would wrinkle when she was really happy and smiling or laughing. But when he was away on assignment those details were still in his memory, but not in his mind's eye. And even at this minute he couldn't remember her laugh, not exactly; he couldn't hear it in his ears, but he knew intellectually that she would chuckle at the back of her throat when all was right in her world.

"It's all right, Kirk," Gail said, her voice soothing, gentling, sensing something of what was going through his mind. "No commitments, not ever unless it's something you want. Just two people comforting each other. We need it. I need it."

McGarvey was about to say no, but the word died on his lips.

Gail tossed the covers aside. She was wearing one of his T-shirts, one leg bent at the knee. And she smiled shyly

He went to her finally, and for a long time they just held each other until in the end they made slow, gentle love. He didn't feel guilty because there was no reason for it, and he knew that Katy would approve.

December

Assassinating someone, even in the light of day when the subject is surrounded by a mob, guarded by security types, including the local and federal police, and whose every move is documented in real time by television cameras and for posterity by press photographers, is relatively simple. Get into the correct position with the correct weapon and pull the trigger.

Na'ef Radwan, a twenty-one-year-old kid from Lod, walked up behind Menachem Begin and put a bullet into the man's head. Easy. But the kid had been arrested on the spot.

The tough part about an assassination is the escape in the confusion immediately following. That takes planning. And luck.

DeCamp arrived in Oslo four days before the Nobel ceremony, checking into a small suite at the Grand Hotel on Karl Johans Gate just across the street from the Parliament at four on a cool overcast afternoon. He'd booked the room within the hour after Wolfhardt had left him in Nice, and even that far in advance he'd been lucky.

The hotel was full because of the ceremony, the lobby bustling with former Nobel laureates and VIPs from around the world. In many circles this was the biggest game of the year, anywhere. The world's best and brightest, honored and on display for their feats.

Dressed in faded jeans, a white shirt, and an expensive black blazer, DeCamp used the Canadian passport that identified him as Edward Grecinger, with an American Express card, which showed a billing address in Quebec. He'd changed his eye color to bright green with contact lenses, wore an expensive wig of salt-and-pepper hair, longish in the back, and with lifts in his shoes was nearly two inches taller than at Hutchinson Island.

His wallet open on the counter, the pretty young clerk glanced at the photo of his wife and two children and she smiled.

"You have a lovely family, sir," she said.

"I miss them already."

He signed the check-in card and upstairs declined the bellman's offer to help unpack his single suitcase, but tipped well.

A half hour later, satisfied that there were no bugs in the suite. De-Camp, still wearing the jeans and blazer, added a sweater to the outfit and a soft gray scarf around his neck, and went outside for a walk down to the town hall where the ceremony would be held. He would be remembered as the quiet Canadian with a lovely family who tipped well.

Eve Larsen would forever remember the three days in Oslo mostly as a blur of images: press conferences in the morning of the ninth, followed by lunch with dignitaries, followed by dinner with more dignitaries including former vice president Al Gore, himself a Nobel laureate, and finally her two bedroom suite at the Grand Hotel, her chastely in one room and McGarvey in the other. And the ceremony, of course, and the attack on her life.

That first night she'd come out of her room shortly after midnight, too keyed up about the next day's speech—lecture, as the Norwegians called it—to sleep and she found McGarvey staring out one of the balcony windows that looked down on Karl Johans Gate, Oslo's main drag. His back was slightly hunched, his head down, and looking at him from behind Eve thought he was a man with the weight of the world on his shoulders, yet the only trouble they'd encountered to that point had come from her postdoc Don Price, who'd been genuinely put out that McGarvey had not only accompanied them, but that it was McGarvey who stayed in the suite with her, while he had to accept a room of his own, two floors down.

"A penny for your thoughts," she said softly.

Startled, he turned around suddenly, and for just an instant his face was a mask of agony and maybe regret. But then the look was gone and he shrugged. "So far so good," he said. "Worried about tomorrow?"

"I hate giving speeches, but Don's read it and says it's good."

"He's in love with you," McGarvey said. "And a little jealous of me and of your work."

She smiled. "All of the above. And sometimes I think there might be something between us, but beyond that he's a damned good scientist, and I trust his judgment."

"That's a good thing."

He was still dressed though he'd taken off his jacket and she'd seen the pistol in its holster at the small of his back, and she was just a little thrilled as well as frightened by the danger and immense power the man radiated. "Do you ever sleep?"

"Just change the batteries now and then."

She'd wanted to ask him what he'd been thinking about, staring out the window, but she respected his space, as she wanted others to respect hers. Yet she was curious, in part because he'd rescued her twice, and because he'd come to Oslo with her, but mostly because he was a complicated man and she wanted to understand him, though she couldn't say why. The silence between them suddenly became awkward.

"You should try to get some sleep," he said. "Tomorrow will be even busier than today."

"I've looked at the itinerary. By the time we actually get around to the ceremony in the evening, I don't know if I'll have to energy to make my lecture."

"You'll do just fine," McGarvey said. "If you get some rest."

She was practically dead on her feet, but she'd managed the day because she was pumped up and felt a little fear. She nodded, and started to return to her bedroom, but then turned back. "If there's going to be trouble, when and where will it happen?"

"Maybe first thing in the morning in front of the hotel, or during one of your press conferences," McGarvey said. "But your afternoon is free, so you're going to stay put here."

"Don wanted to do some sightseeing, just the two of us," Eve said, but McGarvey shook his head.

"The cops here are good, but not that good."

"What about outside town hall just before the ceremony?"

"The royal family will be there, and security will be tight," McGarvey said. "So I'm guessing that if nothing has happened by then you'll be in the clear."

She had another thought, something she had pondered all afternoon and even during cocktails and dinner with Gore and a lot of the Nobel Prize committee members including its chairman Leif Jacobsen, a thoroughly enjoyable gentleman of the old school. And because she'd been so distracted she guessed that she must have seemed aloof to everyone at the table. "No one at the press conferences brought up Schlagel's name. Didn't you find that odd?"

"They were being polite," McGarvey said. "You've won the Nobel, which is a very big deal, and you'll get a lot of respect for it wherever you go, but no more so than here."

"But you think that it's going to happen," she said, more as a question than a statement.

"That's why I'm here," McGarvey said.

"Maybe we'll get lucky," Eve said and she went back to her bedroom. But still she couldn't sleep, nor could she concentrate on her written speech, so just like McGarvey had done she went to the window and stared out at the city. It had begun to snow again lightly, lending an almost heavenly air to the scene, complete with ice crystal halos around the streetlights. For the first time in years she thought about Birmingham when she was a child, before she realized that she was different than everyone else. There'd been one Christmas in particular that stuck in her mind. She could see the snow-covered Midland Plains the morning she'd ridden out into the countryside with her father and her brothers to find a tree. The weather was cold, her coat threadbare, and she was a little hungry, but she remembered being excited and happy. Happier, she thought just now staring out at the streets of Oslo, than she'd ever been except for maybe at this moment.

"The damned thing works," Don had told her, and she was here because of it.

When sleep finally came she dreamed about Schlagel racing after her in the middle of the night, a horrible grimace on his face, his mouth filled with fangs that dripped with blood. He meant to kill her and her happiness was gone, replaced by fear.

The package with DeCamp's pistol, the ammunition, silencer, and cleaning kit arrived the day after he'd checked in to the hotel. None of his telltales had been tampered with; neither the customs authorities nor FedEx had bothered to look inside to make sure that the small international air box from Paris actually contained a notebook computer, battery charger, and external hard drive.

He'd signed for it at the desk and back in his suite had loaded the Steyr and put everything into the wall safe. No need to run the risk of carrying it around the city until he needed it.

That night, seated at the lobby bar, he'd spotted Eve Larsen dressed in evening wear emerging from the elevator with a man and crossing to the street door. He'd only got a fleeting glimpse but he was sure the man was Kirk McGarvey, the former director of the CIA. And he'd sat back in his bar stool to consider his options with this new piece of information.

Every intelligence officer on the planet, every contractor who'd ever been in the business for the past twenty years, knew or at least had heard of McGarvey. The man was a legend, and legitimately a legend if only half of what was said about him was only half true.

Formidable, the thought crossed DeCamp's mind. A professional who would be bound by his training and experience to follow certain procedures—modi operandi that had worked in the past. It was a weakness that DeCamp thought would work to his advantage. And a plan had begun to form in his mind that by morning had solidified so strongly that he had walked back to the town hall to watch the preparations for the ceremony.

The hall was closed for now, but a small crowd of curious Norwegians had gathered outside and he had mingled with them, looking for sight lines, judging angles. He dropped his wallet and turned and made his way through the crowd to the street where he stopped and looked back to see what would happen.

No one had paid him any attention, their eyes focused on the workmen and media coming and going. After the ceremony, when Dr. Larsen and the others came outside, the people waiting would be even more mesmerized.

He walked back to retrieve his wallet that had lain undisturbed where he'd dropped it, made something of a small show finding it and picking it up, even excusing himself twice, and still no one really noticed him.

Just before lunch, strolling in the city park across the street from the Grand, he'd used his Nokia encrypted cell phone to place a call to Wolfhardt in Dubai. When he got through he explained how he meant to carry out the kill.

And the German had understood at once. "You need a plausible diversion," he'd said.

"One of Schlagel's admirers."

"Yes, of course."

"Someone with a history," DeCamp said. "A police history."

"I have just the man. In fact he is already there in Oslo. I'll overnight his dossier to you."

"At the Grand, under the name Edward Grecinger."

"Yes," Wolfhardt said. "Suite four-oh-seven."

And DeCamp held his anger and vulnerability with the German in check. For now. "I'll look for it."

.   .   .

Eve's fear, which had turned into a vague sense of unease, stayed with her through breakfast and the last of the news conferences before the ceremony, these mostly with Norwegian and Swedish television and radio stations. Halfway through one of them the reporter motioned for her cameraman to interrupt filming for a moment.

"Are you feeling well, Doctor?" the reporter asked, obviously concerned.

Eve knew what the woman meant and she shook her head. "Just a little tired," she said. "The past few weeks have been chaotic, and I think maybe I'm feeling a little jet-lagged. Sorry."

The woman reporter smiled. "No need to apologize, Doctor. Nearly every Nobel laureate I've interviewed on the day of the ceremony was in the same shape. Except, of course, for Mr. Gore. But then he was a politician and quite used to the pace. May we continue?"

"Yes." Eve had nodded, and she concentrated not only on what she was saying, but how she was speaking.

The worst part so far, she'd confided to McGarvey, was the constant stream of people wanting to meet with her, and fellow environmental scientists were even worse than the politicians and businessmen because they insisted on talking shop, mostly about new carbon dioxide capture technologies. She wanted to tell them that when her water turbines began to come online, carbon dioxide would cease to be an issue. Any trends toward global warming would come mostly from naturally occurring cyclical events. But scientists were specialists and had trouble seeing beyond their own disciplines.

The ballroom on the mezzanine had been partitioned for the last three news conferences, and Don had remained at the rear of the ornate hall during all of them, avoiding any contact with McGarvey who stood to one side where he could watch not only Eve but the closed door and, she supposed, the faces of the reporters and technicians. He was dressed in a light-colored sport coat and knowing that he carried a gun in a holster beneath the jacket didn't help her uneasy mood. The mere fact that he needed to be here with her was bothersome. And some of that mood, she guessed, had shown on her face

An older man in a leather jacket raised his hand. Eve pointed at him and he got to his feet, his cameraman focusing on him at first.

"Thank you, Doctor Larsen. I'm Arvid Morkum, TV 2, and I would like to add my congratulations."

Eve nodded. "Thank you," she said. She had been introduced by Jacobsen, who'd withdrawn to the side leaving her seated alone at a small table, a single microphone in front of her.

"As I'm sure many of my colleagues were, I was impressed watching the special program on the Fox network for its succinct explanation of exactly how your World Energy Needs project will not only produce electricity but, according to your work, reduce the number and severity of tropical cyclones around the globe, as well as have a decisive effect on global warming."

Eve forced a smile even though she suspected what was coming next. "Is there a question in there, Mr. Morkum?"

A few of the reporters twittered.

"The televangelist Jeremiah Schlagel led a demonstration outside of the television studio even while you were inside, claiming that what you are trying to accomplish goes against—the reverend's words—God's will. How do you feel about his crusade?"

"His is a point of view apparently not shared by the Nobel Prize committee."

Several of the people in the audience laughed out loud, but Morkum was not amused. "Aren't you taking the man and his message seriously?"

"Not at all."

"Then can you explain why you have hired a former director of the Central Intelligence Agency to act as your personal bodyguard? And my follow-up question is, are we to see a repeat of the strong-arm tactics used by Mr. McGarvey at the Fox studios in Washington?"

Jacobsen, who'd been standing to one side, spoke up. "Pardon me, Mr. Morkum, but I do not believe that is a relevant question at this news conference."

The TV 2 camera swung toward him, and then panned to McGarvey.

"I believe it is," Morkum said. "Outside the hotel at this very moment, a small group of the Reverend Schlagel's followers are preparing to wage a demonstration against Dr. Larsen the moment she steps out the door." He turned to McGarvey. "Would you care to comment, sir?"

McGarvey shook his head. "No."

"Is it true that you entered Norway on a diplomatic passport and that you carry a firearm?"

McGarvey held his silence. Everyone's attention was on him now, and Eve had to admire his control.

"Isn't it also true, Mr. McGarvey, that you and Dr. Larsen were together during the attack on the Hutchinson Island nuclear facility in Florida? And can you explain your presence there? Certainly it was not a coincidence."

Jacobsen stepped forward. "This concludes today's final news conference. I'm sure that you will all understand Dr. Larsen's need to prepare for this evening's ceremonies and her lecture. Press kits have been provided for your information. You will find them on a table just outside of this room. Thank you, ladies and gentlemen."

Morkum was protesting, but the doors were opening and most of the other reporters, rather out of politeness or not, were getting to their feet and heading away.

"I'm terribly sorry, Dr. Larsen," Jacobsen said.

Eve looked up as McGarvey came over. "I didn't expect anything like that," she said.

"There will be no further trouble, I would hope," Jacobsen said to McGarvey.

"More protest demonstrations probably," McGarvey assured him. "But your police will keep the peace."

"Dreadful."

As the newspeople, including Morkum and his cameraman, were clearing out, Don came forward, scowling. "That was good," he said.

"Dr. Larsen will remain in her suite until it's time to leave for city hall," McGarvey told the Nobel committee chairman. "I assume a car will pick her up."

"Yes, of course," Jacobsen said. He turned back to Eve. "Again, my sincerest apologies, Dr. Larsen. If there is anything else that I or the committee or the staff of this hotel can do for you, please don't hesitate to ask."

"Thank you," Eve said, and she felt a little sorry for the man.

"Until this evening then," Jacobsen said with a half bow and he left.

Don was agitated, all the muscles in his face tense. "You coming here has ruined everything," he told McGarvey.

"That's not true, Don," Eve said. She'd seen him like this before, not often, but when he got like this it usually ended up with him stalking off and staying away until she could find him and talk him down. Sometimes he was like a spoiled kid.

"Yes, it is. This afternoon was supposed to be ours to enjoy. But now this incident will be all over Norwegian television, and will probably be picked up by CNN or someone like that. All the networks are here." He turned back to McGarvey. "Are you really carrying a gun?"

Eve put a hand on Don's sleeve. "I asked him to come here with me."

Don gave her a bleak look. "Christ," he said, and he stalked off.

"He'll get over it," Eve said.

McGarvey nodded. "Will you?"

The afternoon had turned chilly, especially for DeCamp who had spent most of his life in the southern portions of the African continent or Mediterranean France, so in the afternoon of the ceremony he'd purchased a warm, fur-lined jacket from the upscale department store Bertoni Byportenshopping.

He'd returned to his suite where he'd had a light snack of pickled herring, small toasts, and two bottles of Ringnes beer, and had watched the Nobel news conferences, especially the one on TV 2. Dr. Larsen had come across as a tired woman who'd rather be in her lab, or soon aboard the oil exploration platform en route to Florida's Atlantic coast. The TV journalist had been an ass, but he'd focused on McGarvey with a couple of pointed questions, giving DeCamp at least a small measure of the man. Impressive, the thought came to mind. In control.

Afterwards he'd taken a shower, got dressed and cleaned, and loaded his Steyr and attached the suppressor. When he was finished he packed his single suitcase, for his early morning departure on the six fifteen flight to Berlin, and packed the second magazine of 9mm ammunition and cleaning kit in a FedEx package and addressed it to William Jenkins, SOS Ministries, McPherson, Kansas, USA.

Downstairs at the desk, he settled his bill, arranged for the package to be sent out in the morning, and asked for a wake-up call.

"Early flight, sir?" the clerk asked.

"Unfortunately business in Berlin first thing in the morning. You know how that can be."

"Yes, sir." She smiled.

By the time the first dignitaries began showing up at city hall, and along with them the growing crowd, DeCamp took a quick pass once through the hundred or so onlookers satisfying himself that Billy Jenkins, the abortion clinic bomber, whose dossier, including photographs, that Wolfhardt had sent him, had not shown up yet. The man was blond and had the physique of a rugby player, hard to miss. But best of all the FBI considered him a man of interest who'd shown a propensity for religious intolerance and violence.

Wolfhardt had written a note on a second dossier, that of Terrance Langdorf, warning that the two men often worked together. Almost certainly both of them had been involved in the act of vandalism against Dr. Larsen's Princeton lab, and they'd both been in front of the Fox television studio the evening she'd been interviewed. In fact it had been Jenkins whose arm McGarvey had broken.

The ceremony was held at Oslo's city hall a short distance from the Grand Hotel. Eve rode over in the back of a Mercedes limousine with McGarvey and Jacobsen, Don in the front with the driver. Already a big crowd of onlookers lined the street outside the north doors that led to the ornate central hall where the medallion, certificate, and a document that confirmed the prize amount set since 2001 at more than one million U.S. would be presented in the presence of Norway's King Harald V. The Prize was a point of great national pride for the Norwegians. Jacobsen had explained on the way over that when Alfred Nobel bequeathed his fortune to fund the Nobel Prizes in 1895, Norway and Sweden were a confederation. Since Sweden was responsible for all the foreign policies of the two countries, it awarded the prizes in the sciences and economics, but left the Peace Prize to Norway to avoid any hint of political corruption.

Police had kept a path from where the limousines were pulling in to the entry doors up two broad ramps that flanked a fountain and cascading waterfall. McGarvey, wearing a tuxedo, handed Eve out of the car, his attention on the people waving Norwegian and American flags. None of the religious demonstrators were evident.

Jacobsen and Don, also dressed in tuxedoes, got out of the car, and followed behind McGarvey and Eve, who was wearing a long, flowing white gown beneath a borrowed mink wrap, elbow-length gloves, her short hair done up that afternoon in her room by a stylist the Nobel committee had arranged for, and a diamond tiara, looked stunning. She was a completely different woman, in McGarvey's estimation, from the one yesterday and this morning at the news conference. She finally had confidence.

"I think I belong here," she said to McGarvey, her voice low enough so that no one else could hear her. "Is that too vain of me?"

McGarvey smiled for her. "Like you told that television reporter, the Nobel Prize committee thinks that you've earned this. Enjoy."

"Not until I'm aboard Vanessa Explorer," she said.

But then they were inside the fabulous Grand Hall that had been decked out for the ceremony with a stage and podium at one end and rows of chairs facing it. The hall soared three stories, the walls covered with elaborate frescoes, a line of windows at the ceiling level, which during the short northern days would practically flood the space with the oddly slanting natural light.

Already most of the seats were filled with dignitaries, everyone here strictly by invitation, and almost all the seats on the stage were occupied by members of the royal family, along with the prize selection committee. Eve handed her mink wrap to Don, and Jacobsen led her and McGarvey to their places. Don had been assigned a seat at the rear of the hall.

People got to their feet and applauded politely, and on stage Eve shook everyone's hand, smiling and nodding.

When everyone was finally settled, Jacobsen went to the podium. "Ladies and gentlemen, His Majesty Harald V, king of Norway, and his consort, Her Majesty Sonja Haraldsen."

Everyone rose, and moments later the king and queen in formal state dress entered from a rear door and came onto the stage. Everyone in the hall applauded.

Harald was a tall man, thin white hair at the sides of his head, his face long, his eyes kind. He'd been a chain-smoker but after a bout with cancer had quit. Jacobsen introduced him to Eve, who curtsied, which seemed to take the king by surprise and he smiled.

"I'm so pleased to finally meet you, Dr. Larsen," he said, still smiling. "I've followed your work with great interest." And he winked. "Perhaps this evening's affairs will help quiet your critics."

"I hope you're right, Your Majesty," Eve said.

The king turned to McGarvey. "We've never met, but I've heard a great deal about you, and your service to your country. We're most pleased that you're here with Dr. Larsen."

They shook hands. "Thank you, sir, but I hope that my being here remains totally unnecessary."

"But you don't think so," the king said. "Not here and not later after she leaves."

"No, sir," McGarvey said.

"No," the king said, and he and the queen moved down the line, and when they had finally taken their seats and everyone else in the Grand Hall were seated, Jacobsen began the ceremony, introducing the honored guests on stage, including McGarvey, giving a short history of Alfred Nobel and the prizes, and finally the citation detailing Eve's work to solve the world's energy needs and calm violent weather around the world for which reasons she had been selected to receive this year's Nobel Peace Prize.

On cue the king got up and Eve remained in her seat until he reached the podium, then got up and went to where he and Jacobsen and an aide, who'd spent an hour coaching her on the etiquette and choreography of the awards ceremony, waited.

The hall was silent, and Eve would remember this solemn moment for the rest of her life. Every Nobel laureate did.

"On behalf of the Nobel Foundation, and of a grateful Norway for your contributions, I am happy to present you with a this year's Nobel Prize for Peace," Jacobsen said. He took an open velvet box containing the Peace Prize medal cast in eighteen-carat green gold and plated with twenty-four-carat gold the aide handed him, and presented it to Eve. The medal was heavy, nearly a half a pound, and she hadn't expected that. Nobel's profile was cast on both sides.

Jacobsen took the ornately decorated diploma in a leather folder, embossed with Nobel's profile, and handed it to Eve along with the document confirming the prize amount.

The audience got to its feet and applause rolled through the hall, and Eve fought a nearly overwhelming urge to cry. She found Don on his feet at the back, applauding, and she nodded. The damn thing works, he'd told her that morning on the *Big G* in the Gulf Stream, and now nothing would stop her, stop them actually because he'd worked just as hard as she had, in some ways even harder. She would make this up to him, because at this moment she felt in her heart of hearts that he should be up here with her as a corecipient.

Television cameras were, according to Jacobsen, broadcasting the ceremony around the world to 450 million households in 150 countries, and Eve was allowed to savor the thing for only a few moments before she handed the medal, diploma, and document to the aide. Jacobsen and the king stepped aside for Eve to come to the podium where her speech, leather-bound, had been placed for her, and then they withdrew and took their seats.

She took a moment until everyone was seated and silence returned before she opened the leather folder. And she waited for another beat, the words on the first page suddenly meaningless to her, as if they'd been written in Chinese characters or Arabic script and she panicked. But just for an instant. She could only think for that moment of the banquet immediately following her speech, and tomorrow night's concert hosted by Harrison Ford and Oprah Winfrey, and starring among others Andrea Bocelli. She wanted this and all of the rest to be done so that she could return to her work.

But then she began in much the same way Al Gore had begun in 2007. "Your Majesties, Your Royal Highnesses, honorable members of the Norwegian Nobel Committee, excellencies, ladies and gentlemen.

"More than thirty years ago a young scientist by the name of Amory Lovins raised the important argument that the United States had reached a critical crossroads. Down the path we were taking guaranteed an ever-increasing demand for and a reliance on nuclear fission and dirty fossil fuels.

"He warned that burning coal to produce electricity would double the atmospheric carbon dioxide concentrations early in the next century. This century. Unless something was done soon we were headed for a possible change in global climate that could become irreversible."

Eve looked up and paused for a moment.

"Lovins called this road the 'hard path,' but he proposed an alternative. His 'soft path.' He called for renewable energy sources from the sun and the wind that along with conservation and new efficient technologies would bring about a cleaner, healthier environment in which the energy wars of the near future could be eliminated.

"An important article that appeared in 1977 in the magazine *The Atlantic* outlined Lovins's ideas and warnings, and went on to explore other emerging technologies. The message was very clear, yet we continued on the hard path."

Again Eve paused. The damn thing works.

A woman in formal dress seated at the rear of the hall suddenly jumped up. "Stop this evil before it is too late!" she screeched at the top of her lungs.

The king's two bodyguards suddenly appeared at the side of the stage, and McGarvey got to his feet.

"You are an affront to our Holy Father's plan for us!" the woman screamed.

A pair of metro policemen reached the woman and bodily dragged her to the doors as she shouted, "Repent now, apostate, before it is too late for your mortal soul!" And then she was outside, and as the doors opened and closed Eve could hear people on the street actually cheering.

Jacobsen was on his feet and he started for the podium, but Eve waved him back and turned to the audience and smiled. "Actually I'm quite glad to see that Norway honors freedom of speech as well as America does."

The king behind her applauded and then so did everyone in the hall, and it took a long time to die down before she could continue.

"In actuality, Lovins was speaking not merely for the U.S., but for the entire world, which is why I'm here today to tell you about my vision for taking the soft path."

.   .   .

The streetlights switched on about the same time Jenkins and Langsdorf came sauntering up the street from the direction of the harbor. They were dressed almost identically in jeans, leather bomber jackets, and dark blue knit watch caps, Jenkins's right arm was in a cloth sling that fit over his jacket. They both wore gloves.

DeCamp had positioned himself a few feet back from the front of the crowd that pressed the walkway from the main doors to the hall. Oslo police had erected barriers and held people back. But Eve's speech had been piped outside to loudspeakers and the crowd, probably more than three-quarters of them Schlagel's people, in his estimation, had become restive, and the cops nervous.

The two men passed within a few feet of DeCamp, stopping nearly at the barriers, and he gently shouldered his way through the crowd until he was within touching distance directly behind them. He had a very good sight line on the walkway from the hall out to where the limos had pulled up, the chauffeurs waiting at the rear passenger doors.

A burst of applause came from the loudspeakers and minutes later the city hall doors opened and the first of the dignitaries who'd been up on stage began coming out, all of them stopping on either side of the walk, forming a tunnel of well-wishers that Eve Larsen, and presumably Kirk McGarvey, would have to pass through.

The problem as he saw it was twofold. First he had to get a clear shot, preferably two. If he hit the woman center mass, the explosive bullets he'd loaded would be fatal. There was little doubt of it. The second was convincing the onlookers that it was Jenkins or Langsdorf who'd fired the shots in such a way that the crowd would become hysterical, leaving the police no option but to return fire.

To solve both problems, DeCamp had removed the suppressor. In the first place shooting without the silencer vastly improved the pistol's accuracy. And in the second, the noise would startle the crowd, and like a flock of birds they would almost immediately spread out.

He'd put a little Vaseline on his fingertips and the pad of his thumb on his right hand, and he reached for the Steyr inside his jacket pocket, cocking the hammer so that it would take only a light pull to fire.

More people were streaming out of the hall, taking up their places in the reception line, until finally Eve Larsen, flanked by McGarvey on her right, and Leif Jacobsen on her left, came out and began moving slowly through the line. More applause began from the people on the walkway and some in the crowd, but most began booing and chanting something about going against God's will. The Oslo police stiffened up and McGarvey's head was on a swivel, but his attention was directed toward the people nearest to Eve, those in the reception line.

DeCamp moved closer to a position directly between Jenkins and Langsdorf, almost touching them, from where he had a clear sight line and their bodies would effectively shield his gun hand from the people on either side.

Eve would pass within twenty feet of him and as she shook hands with a woman dressed in furs, DeCamp pulled out his pistol, holding it in front of his chest.

She leaned over and said something, then moved closer. DeCamp raised his pistol and fired one shot at the same moment Jacobsen moved in front of Eve to speak to McGarvey. The bullet caught the Nobel Prize committee chairman in his shoulder, slamming him backwards off his feet into the line of people.

McGarvey shoved Eve to her knees as he pulled out his own weapon, and the crowd reacted, going wild, women screaming, everyone trying to get away.

Jenkins was turning toward DeCamp, who thrust the pistol into his hands.

"My God, my God!" DeCamp cried. "The reverend knows!" He backed off.

Jenkins took a step toward him.

But DeCamp melded with the crowd. "He's got a gun! He's got a gun!"

Both Jenkins and Langsdorf, confused, turned back toward the police. Suddenly they were out in the open, all alone, the people moving away from them.

One of the cops shouted something, and Jenkins tried to answer back, raising the pistol over his head.

DeCamp turned and watched from the fringes of the still-moving crowd as the police opened fire, Jenkins and Langsdorf falling back to the pavement, each hit more than a half-dozen times.

Back in Paris, DeCamp waited at noon for the first two days since Oslo just within the entrance to the Saint-Germain-de-Près church where he had a straight line view of the Deux Maggots café across the boulevard. He was armed. Although he was certain that Wolfhardt would come to him, he wasn't sure of the reception because the second half of his payment for assassinating Eve Larsen had been deposited into his account.

It was a mixed message the German and his employer had sent him; the woman had not been hurt and the assignment had been a failure except that the blame had gone to the two men shot to death by the Oslo police. They were wanted by the FBI for questioning about a series of abortion clinic bombings a few years ago, and their names were being linked to the Reverend Schlagel's ministry.

Schlagel had gone on his SOS television network the morning of the very next day and on Fox News that evening, saying in effect that although he vehemently disagreed with what Dr. Larsen had set out to do, he would defend to his death her right to practice science as she saw it. He would fight her godless research with everything in his body and mind, including his hourly prayers to Jesus Christ his Savior, but he would also thank God for her miraculous escape, and for the souls of his poor lost sheep, shot to death in Oslo.

A priest in a cassock and wide-brimmed hat, head lowered so that his eyes were not visible, came out of the nave. "You failed," he said. "Again."

DeCamp turned suddenly, reaching for his pistol, but then stayed his hand. "The vagaries of these sorts of assignments," he said. He willed himself to remain calm. This meeting was expected. "Yet you paid my fee. Why? Do you want me to try again?"

"Yes, but in a different fashion. This time the assignment will be much larger, more complex, and it will require additional personnel."

"I work alone."

"Not this time."

"If I refuse?" DeCamp asked.

"That's not an option, something you know, otherwise you would not have waited for me to show up here."

"I will need additional funds."

"Under ordinary circumstances I would have told you to pay for this one out of the profits you've earned from the monies you have already received for two failed assignments. But my employer is generous. An additional two million euros will be deposited to your Prague account within twenty-four hours."

On the surface of it the offer was more than fair, it was generous. Afterwards, no matter the outcome, DeCamp would fetch Martine and they would disappear. Perhaps to Australia. An outback sheep station. Anonymous, safe, where a man could see for miles if an enemy were to approach.

"Am I to be told the details?" he asked.

Wolfhardt reached beneath his cassock for something, and DeCamp almost pulled out his pistol, but it was a thick manila envelope.

"Here are the details. And I sincerely wish you luck, for all of our sakes, including yours, of course."

"Of course," DeCamp said, and he turned and walked away.

Two Days Later

Wolfhardt had come back from France with assurances that DeCamp would accept the new assignment, and Anne Marie busied herself talking to investors, reassuring them actually, telling them that their hundreds of millions were safe in the dozen MG funds. "We make money on the way down as well as on the way up," she explained. Though no one asked how, because they all knew that making profits from a declining market meant only that the MG was essentially stealing money from investors in other funds. And she'd always made sure, in those cases, that she never raided any fund in which some of her investors held positions.

The American Securities and Exchange Commission, which in Anne Marie's estimation had always been run by idiots who had risen to their levels of incompetence, were working to put a stop to what was called high-frequency trading, which amounted to nothing more than letting computers buy stocks and a millisecond later, before the results showed up on the big board, and before mere humans on the floor could make their orders, the machines would automatically make a sale. In those brief millisecond bursts, profits that totaled in the billions each year were made. Of course the SEC thought it gave the high-frequency traders an unfair advantage, which was why the practice was under fire. Supposedly. But she had her own cadre of highly paid computer friends working out of Amsterdam who'd managed over the past several months to do some trading on the side, so far without detection.

Making money was so easy this way that sometimes Anne Marie felt a stab of guilt, or even boredom, because she agreed with her father's original philosophy that systematic macro trading, which was what this amounted to, was only for idiots and cowards. But then no profit held any shame. Nor could it ever, by definition.

Even though it was winter and a series of cold fronts had marched across the Mediterranean since November, Anne Marie had gone back to her yacht to get away for a few days or weeks, however long it took to refresh her batteries. And everything seemed to be on track. Her investors were content, al-Naimi was off her back for the moment, DeCamp was presumably in the process of bringing the next operation together, and Schlagel's God Project campaign was in full swing, especially now that Eve Larsen had been presented with the Nobel Prize and had survived an assassination attempt. The woman was blessed, and she was in the clear for the moment.

And it was more grist for Schlagel's well-oiled mill. People in the U.S. were already putting a lot of pressure on Congress to rethink the permitting process for new nuclear power stations, along with a growing call for immediate inspections of every nuclear plant. The inspections would probably result in closures, or in repair orders that would be so expensive to complete that the utility companies would be forced to take the matter to their boards. The conservative ones, faced with gigantic repair bills and the growing tide of fear and distrust among the general public, would likely decide on even further shutdowns.

People in the southeast, especially in places like rural Kentucky, Tennessee, Georgia, and Alabama were actually knocking down power lines by shooting out the insulators because they were convinced the electricity coming from nuclear power plants was itself radioactive and using electrical appliances inside their homes would give them radiation poisoning. It was Schlagel's doing, of course, and in Anne Marie's estimation the man was nothing short of brilliant, and in a Machiavellian sort of way he might make an interesting president after all.

Her thoughts had been flitting around like that ever since Hutchinson Island, and even out here in the Med she hadn't been able to settle down. Her mood, like the weather, had varied from cold and damp, during which she was too depressed to work or even think, or to cold and blustery, during which she had sudden bursts of energy even though she felt somehow scattered, not together. And all of it was disconcerting.

Yesterday they'd been slowly cruising east to Athens to pick up a few people she'd considered inviting aboard because she'd started out with just her crew and two bodyguards and she'd thought that some of her depression might be plain loneliness, but she'd been spooked for no good reason she could think of, and she'd ordered the captain to turn south toward the African coast where the weather might be a little warmer. She was more tired of the cold than of her loneliness.

She sat at the bar in the main saloon drinking a glass of champagne. Dinner had been tasteless, and now that it was fully dark outside, no lights on any horizon, not even those of a passing ship, no moon, no stars under an overcast sky, the thought of going to bed alone was so dreary at this moment, she was almost frightened. So frightened that when her encrypted sat phone buzzed, the caller ID showing al-Naimi's number, she was almost relieved, even though his call probably meant trouble of some kind.

"Mr. al-Naimi, good evening," she said.

"Are you alone at this moment?" the Saudi intelligence officer asked.

Anne Marie felt a slight tingle of fear. "Yes."

"You are doing a good job with the antinuclear power movement in the United States. We're pleased—the royal family, unofficially, of course—but if the next phase of your operation goes as well as the first we will allow even more money to be placed in your fund."

"Thank you. But you must understand that the timing is critical. We cannot make a move until the oil platform is in the middle of the Gulf."

"Yes, I understand everything," al-Naimi said impatiently. "Tell me, where you are at this moment, exactly."

Anne Marie was puzzled. "If you want the exact latitude and longitude, I'll have to get that from Captain Panagiotopolous. But I think we're about one hundred kilometers off the Libyan coast, running parallel."

"Who are your guests aboard?"

"No guests. Just my crew and bodyguards."

"Where is Wolfhardt?"

"In Dubai," Anne Marie said, truly alarmed now. Al-Naimi never called to simply chat. "What's this all about?"

"You have a crew member by the name of Walter Glass."

It was a statement, not a question, and Anne Marie had to think for a moment if such a man were indeed aboard, but then she remembered. "He's an engineer's mate. We took him on sometime this summer. Gunther vetted him, and he came up clean."

"I've learned otherwise," al-Naimi said. "In fact his real name is Dieter Schey and he works for the Frankfurt Stock Exchange. The security division. He's aboard your ship to spy on you."

"Good heavens why," she said, but then she knew not only why he'd been sent to spy on her, but why al-Naimi had called.

"There've been some tax dealings with a number of your German investors that have raised a red flag."

He was talking about what were called partnership flip structures and inverted pass-through leases, in which the MG had helped fund a couple of infrastructure deals in Germany—one for the rebuilding of ten bridges along the autobahn, and the other the construction of a water treatment plant outside Munich. The construction companies were given healthy tax credits, which they used in return to shelter income gained by investing money back into the MG. Technically it meant that the German government was investing with Anne Marie, and someone smart in Frankfurt had sat up and taken notice.

"It's not a problem," Anne Marie said. "He couldn't have learned anything aboard ship. And soon as we dock I'll get rid of him."

"There's more to it," al-Naimi said.

Anne Marie girded herself. "I'm listening."

"Herr Schey is a clever man, but he'd have to be because of his excellent training with the KGB in Moscow. He is ex-Stasi."

Stasi had been the old East German secret police, and what al-Naimi had left unsaid, the most disturbing message he'd given to her, was that Gunther, himself ex-Stasi, should have caught it. He'd dropped the ball. If it had been unintentional his worth to her was diminished. But if he'd vetted Schey on purpose, for whatever purpose, something would have to be done.

All of that passed through her thoughts in a beat. "Thank you for the information," she said. "I'll take care of it."

"All of it."

"Yes," Anne Marie said.

She poured more champagne and sat at the bar for twenty minutes thinking about her chief of security; thinking that it was nearly impossible to know someone so completely that trust was inviolable. Something like a mother's unconditional love for her child, even if the child turned out to be a mass murderer. She'd never trusted anyone to that extent. It was another lesson she'd learned from her father. Yet she'd allowed Gunther inside her very inner circle, to such an extent that in some ways he knew more about her business dealings and associates than she did. Where the skeletons were buried.

She didn't know whether to curse or cry, but finally she reined in her emotions and called her bodyguard, Carlos Ramirez, on the ship's phone. "We have a crewman by the name of Walter Glass."

"He's an engineering mate."

"Bring him to the main salon in ten minutes," Anne Marie said. "And bring a flashlight, a pair of kitchen shears, and your pistol. With your silencer, I don't necessarily want to alert the crew."

"Will we need Willy?" Ramirez asked. William Harcourt was Anne Marie's other bodyguard.

"No. This won't amount to much."

"Ten minutes."

She finished her champagne then went forward to her stateroom where she changed into an old pair of blue jeans and a Harvard sweatshirt she wore when she worked out in the fitness room. Barefoot, she went back to the salon, and was just finishing another glass of champagne when Ramirez showed up with a wary engineer's mate.

"Good evening, Mr. Glass," she said.

"Ma'am," the man said. He was of medium build with a solid square face, thinning light hair, and just a hint of worry at the corners of his mouth and in his eyes.

"Actually your name is Dieter Schey, you once worked for the Stasi, and now work for the Frankfurt Stock Exchange. What are you doing aboard my ship?"

Schey hesitated for just a second, but then he shrugged. "Investigating your business practices. It's believed that you may have broken some German financial laws. I was asked to gather evidence."

"Have you?" Anne Marie asked. "Gathered evidence."

"Not yet."

"Have you ever heard the name Gunther Wolfhardt?" she asked, watching the investigator's eyes.

He shook his head. "No."

So far as she could tell he'd told the truth. "Let's go out to the after deck," she told Ramirez.

"What are you going to do?"

"What we do with all of our trash. We throw it overboard."

Schey started to back away, but Ramirez pulled his Glock 17. "Outside," he said.

They went out the sliding doors from the salon and all the way to the aftermost deck from where swimmers could reach the water down a half-dozen broad stairs to the rear platform at the water's edge.

"Take off your clothes," Anne Marie said dispassionately. She was not in a hurry, nor did she have much of any emotion for what was about to be done to the spy. It was simply a job that needed attending to.

"The water is damned cold," Schey protested. "And no matter what happens, as soon as my body is found it will get back to you."

"Do as you're told," Ramirez said.

It was bitterly cold, a sharp wind blowing across the deck as Schey slowly removed his clothes. His body was solid with very little fat. A long scar on his right leg just above his knee looked old, as did what was probably a bullet wound in his left shoulder.

"Now you want me to jump?" Schey asked.

Anne Marie took the pistol from her bodyguard. "No," she said. "I want you to die."

She fired one shot into the middle of the man's face, killing him instantly, and driving his body backward against the rail, a spray of blood going overboard and lost in the wind.

"Hold him up," Anne Marie told Ramirez. "Head above the top of the rail. I don't want to damage the deck."

Ramirez did as he was told, and Anne Marie methodically fired several more shots at close range into the man's face, destroying his features and his dental work.

"Fingertips?" Ramirez asked. This was the kind of work he understood, and he wasn't squeamish about it. He'd never been squeamish about anything he'd been asked to do.

He eased the body on to the deck and using the kitchen shears snipped off the ends of Schey's fingers and thumbs and tossed them overboard, making it nearly impossible for a quick identification if and when the body was ever found.

When Ramierz was finished, he lifted the body up over the rail and let it fall into the sea. "He'll be missed by morning."

"Have the ship searched. You saw him drunk on deck around three in the morning, and the dumb bastard probably fell overboard."

"Very well."

"Get rid of his clothes, and clean the blood off the deck, please," Anne Marie said, and she went back into the salon where she poured another glass of Krug. She was no longer bored.

In the morning she would call Lt. Col. Mustapha Amrusi, chief of Libya's External Security Organization and ask if she would be welcome in Tripoli first thing in the morning, merely in transit for a flight to Dubai, which considering the amount of money Amrusi and others had made from the MG, would not pose a problem. She would call for her private jet to pick her up and the ship would return to Monaco. For the moment she felt that it would be best to stay away from Europe.

But then her mood darkened as her thoughts turned to Wolfhardt. She would miss him.

PART
THREE

The Following Weeks

FORTY-ONE

Three days after Oslo, Eve went back to her office at Princeton to make the final preparations for moving out to Vanessa Explorer, and McGarvey cabbed from Dulles to his apartment in Georgetown.

None of Schlagel's crowd had been there at the airport, which had not been a surprise to McGarvey after the assassination attempt, but it had been a momentary relief for Eve.

"How's Mr. Jacobsen, have you heard anything?" she'd asked McGarvey at the airport.

"Tore up his right shoulder pretty badly, but he's a hero for saving your life," McGarvey told her.

"I'm glad. He's a genuinely nice man."

"What's next?" he'd asked her before they parted.

"Depends on when the next shot will come."

"I think you'll be okay for now," McGarvey told her, and yet he was having a hard time accepting that the situation was all that simple. The assassination attempt and the shooting of the two assassins had ended it all a little too neatly for him. He just wasn't sure that it was over with yet. Some intuition, some voice, niggled at the back of his head.

She shrugged. "In any case Princeton first, then back here to Washington for a couple of days, and then out to my rig. The extra million-plus will be a big help, because Commerce doesn't want to give me any funding, and NOAA's strapped." She'd smiled uncertainly. "What about you?"

"We're still looking for the guy at Hutchinson Island, but we're coming up empty-handed." Which was a puzzlement to McGarvey, because Yablonski was damned good and Otto was even better. Whoever the contractor was, he'd left absolutely no track. Almost as if he were a street person, homeless with no background, no driver's license, no passport, no traceable bank accounts, no criminal record, nor any record tying him to any military service in the world, including the South African Defense Force.

Eve got serious. They were standing outside in the queue for a cab, and the place was noisy. "Do you think he'll be the next to come after me?"

"Not just you personally. He'll want to sabotage the oil rig somewhere out in the middle of the Gulf. Send it to the bottom."

"With me and everyone else aboard."

"Whomever he's working for definitely wants to see you fail."

"InterOil gave me the rig."

"To prove your project can't work."

Eve had turned away, a sudden look of anguish and incomprehension coming over her, as if after finally reaching this point, the Nobel Prize, the rig, the vindication of her science, she still had enemies who not only wanted to see her fail, but were willing to do horrible things to make that happen. "I always figured that I knew what rationality was. Rational thoughts, rational arguments, which would result in logical outcomes. But I'm not so sure anymore, you know?"

McGarvey felt sorry for her. "How rational are two professors fighting for the same tenured position?"

She looked startled, as if it were a new concept, but then she smiled and nodded. "You're right, of course. You should see the fights. No holds barred. Common sense out the door. Pitiful, actually, because it's all about professional jealousy. But this isn't the same, is it? It's not that simple."

"No," McGarvey admitted. "But what they're doing is rational from their perspective because they're protecting what amounts to several trillions of dollars over the next fifty to one hundred years. And all that's not just for the rich guys. It includes the oil field workers from the geologists all the way down to the grunts, most of them with families to support, mortgages, braces for their kids' teeth, college funds, eventually retirement, and you're the one who wants take all that away from them. And Schlagel is an opportunist, and from his pulpit what he is doing is rational. He wants to be president, he needs a cause, and you're it. Do you think any of them would hesitate to pull the trigger if they thought it would make their lives a little better, a little safer?"

Eve's lips compressed, but she nodded. "I see your point," she said. Her cab came and she kissed McGarvey on the cheek. "Dinner in town when I get back?"

"Sure thing," McGarvey said.

After he'd shaved, taken a shower, and dressed in a pair of jeans, a white shirt, and a dark blue blazer he found the note from Gail on the kitchen counter, welcoming him home. The Air France flight had landed around one, and now it was a little past three, and she'd written that she would be at the office when he got back. He found the note slightly disconcerting. It was the message from a wife to her husband, possessive, expectant, confining just now.

Staying in his apartment, cooking, making love, was giving her a sense of ownership. It was a natural feminine emotion to make sure that the nest was safe from predators that his wife Katy had found early on didn't work with McGarvey. Couldn't work. Same as his career with the Company. They wanted ownership. Some years ago a deputy director of operations had called him an anachronism, a throwback to the Wild West, a cowboy. And the man had argued that the CIA no longer had need of his kind. Yet they'd kept calling him back to figure out the mess of the day that couldn't be addressed by any governmental agency on any sort of an official basis.

Sitting in the backseat of a cab heading out to Tysons Corner, he wondered, as he had wondered before—often—if it wasn't finally time to get out. But it was a meaningless question, especially now that he had the bit in his teeth.

Otto called on his sat phone. "Oh, wow, Mac, she really looked good on stage. Especially the freedom of speech thing. Have you watched CNN's take on the assassination attempt?"

"No, what's happening?"

"Oslo took the wind out of Schlagel's sails, and he's backed way off."

"Just for now," McGarvey said. He was beginning to have a grudging respect for the reverend, who was no tent revival preacher, no simple circus performer. The man knew when to strike, and when to lay back. His timing was that of a national level politician, of a serious presidential contender. Though he would never directly attack Eve, he was capable of inciting it—that was already proven—and he had the motivation.

"That's for sure, but it gives you some breathing room."

"Anything new on our contractor?"

"Nada, but I have a couple of ideas that we can talk about over dinner tonight. Bring Gail with you, because she's part of this thing, too."

McGarvey was feeling cornered again, the same anger he'd carried around for more than a year still simmering just beneath the surface, but Otto was an old friend—his only friend. "Don't play matchmaker," he warned.

"I'm not, honest injun. But you haven't seen Audie for a long time."

"Not tonight."

"Why not?" Otto insisted, and it was unlike him. His wife, Louise, had probably made the suggestion. Strongly.

"Because I'm not ready to expose my granddaughter to another woman. Another relationship."

Otto hesitated for a long time, and when he spoke he sounded resigned. "It'll have to happen sooner or later, kemo sabe, and maybe everybody knows it except for you."

McGarvey was on the verge of lashing back, but a wave of sadness nearly overpowered him. "Later," he said quietly.

"La Traviatta around the corner from your apartment. We'll get a babysitter. Eight?"

"Eight," McGarvey said and he broke the connection.

When he looked up a minute or two later he realized they were just getting on the Beltway outside Falls Church, less than ten minutes from the office, and he also realized that he had nothing to say to Admiral French that made any sense at this point. He told the cabbie that he'd changed his mind and to turn around and take him back to Georgetown.

Gail hadn't tried to call the apartment to find out what was keeping him, which McGarvey appreciated. It gave him a little time alone to get his thoughts and emotions in order, and to get back into focus. Sitting by the bow windows that looked over at Rock Creek Park, an oasis of calmness and serenity in a city that had always kept a frenetic pace, he tried to balance his need to work alone with the realities of the situation they would be faced with out in the Gulf. The Coast Guard could escort them all the way to Florida's east coast. A SEAL team could be stationed aboard the rig, or stand off in a submarine that would shadow the platform. Short of that, the rig could be put under constant satellite surveillance and at the first hint of trouble a rapid response team could be deployed from McDill Air Force Base in Tampa or, when the rig was farther south, from Homestead Air Force Base in Miami.

But all of that would do nothing more than delay the attack on the rig, which might not even take place until after it was anchored, and the Pax impellers installed. If a cable on one of the huge water augers were to part, serious damage would be done to the platform, and certainly there would be casualties, including deaths.

When the attack did come, McGarvey preferred that it would be out in the Gulf, where he had a better chance of dealing with it. In tight quarters aboard the rig he figured that he could more easily handle a strike force that probably wouldn't involve more than a half-dozen men. Professionals, which would be their one exploitable weakness: pros were predictable. It was their training.

McGarvey looked up suddenly as someone came to the door, and he reached for his pistol and glanced at the wall clock at the same time Gail walked in. It was a few minutes after seven already, and he hadn't noticed the fading light outside until just now.

She started to smile when she saw him by the window, but then spotted the pistol in his hand, and her expression dropped. "Is something wrong?"

"No." He'd been lost in operational details, and reaching for the gun was merely a reflex move. Like most professionals he too was predictable, something the contractor who had done Hutchinson Island had not been. It was the one troubling aspect left to consider.

She came across and kissed him lightly on the check. "I watched her acceptance speech. Bright lady. But she doesn't look like the type who suffers fools gladly."

"I think she's a little overwhelmed," McGarvey said, and he didn't catch the odd set to Gail's lips, because she'd turned away to put her coat over the back of the couch.

"And the shooting afterwards was nothing less than stunning. How is she doing?"

"She's tough. But I don't really know what she's thinking. She holds in just about everything."

"I figured you'd come out to the office this afternoon. The admiral wants an update."

"It was a long trip, and I had some stuff to figure out."

"If you're tired I can fix us something to eat here."

"I'm meeting Otto and his wife at La Traviatta around the block at eight," McGarvey said. "And I want you to come with me because this concerns the operation."

"Has he come up with something?" Gail asked, suddenly bright.

"He has some ideas he wanted to talk about, and so do I because I want you with me on the oil rig, just you and I."

Gail saw the logic. "A Coast Guard escort would scare them off, and you *want* them to attack. Risky, isn't it? They could drop a couple dozen men on top of us before anyone knew what was happening."

"Not if it's the same guy from Hutchinson Island. He'll have help, but it won't be squad size."

"Why not?" Gail asked.

"Because he's too arrogant, too sure of himself," McGarvey said. "Anyway it's a moot point. We're getting no help because no one believes Eve is in any danger now. The bad guys were taken out in Oslo. And it would be politically incorrect to interfere in a civilian operation."

After a moment she nodded. "I'm in," she said.

It was a Sunday evening and the Italian restaurant was only half full. Otto and Louise were sitting at a booth near the rear of the dining room, and when McGarvey and Gail walked in Otto waved them back. He jumped up. "Oh, wow, you're Gail, and you're prettier than Mac said you were, honest injun."

Gail smiled. "Thanks." She and Otto shook hands, and Otto introduced his wife, Louise.

"Welcome to the club," she said, her smile warm, as she and Gail shook hands.

They all sat down, and for the first minutes busied themselves with Chianti and breadsticks and ordering their food. And McGarvey watched the naturalness between Otto and Louise and Gail, which compounded his feelings of being painted into a corner. But it was warm, and despite the bit of resentment nagging at the back of his head, he relaxed and went with the flow, because they were no nearer to any answers that made sense than they had been from the beginning and he was with friends.

"I think the assassination attempt on our lady scientist is a dead end now—no pun intended—but Kirk told me that you might have some ideas about our contractor," Gail said. "Eric didn't say anything to me, but have you guys worked out something?"

Otto shrugged. His usually out-of-control frizzy red hair was brushed back and tied into a ponytail, and although he had no tie, his shirt was clean and his dove gray sport coat was new, all due to Louise. "We're getting nowhere trying to trace his background by any conventional routes. He's a total blank, as if he doesn't exist."

"But he does," Gail said, and McGarvey just listened.

"We saw the back of his head in the video, we have the record of his renting the car, and we have the murder of a gay schoolteacher in San Francisco. But he left no physical evidence behind, not at Hutchinson Island or anywhere else. He even wiped down the hard hat and visitor pass he used on the tour."

"Makes him a professional," Gail said.

"Maybe the best since Carlos."

"Methodology," McGarvey said, knowing exactly where Otto was taking it.

"That and his connections and the motivation. He's good, which means he's been well trained, though we've come up blank down that path. But it also means that he's well paid. Somebody with big bucks hired him."

"Schlagel's got the money," Gail suggested.

"Too obvious," Otto said. "He couldn't afford to have such an immediate tie to his organization. And he's distanced himself from the two guys in Oslo."

"Oil," McGarvey said. "Marinaccio in Dubai with help from the Saudis, and Octavio with help from his pals in Caracas."

"It would fit," Otto said. "But those people are all but unapproachable unless we have rock-solid proof. And even then it'd be next to impossible to dig her out of Dubai and especially not him out of Venezuela."

"They have to travel," Gail suggested.

"With bodyguards," McGarvey said. "And most governments don't look kindly on the FBI snatching people and hauling them across national borders—especially not people with that sort of money." He smiled slightly. "But there are ways."

"Proof?" Gail asked.

"A few years ago, just after Marinaccio showed up in Dubai, a Frankfurt Stock Exchange minister and his mistress were shot to death in his lake house outside the city. Assassin or assassins unknown. But the Marinaccio Group was under investigation by the FSE, and the driving force behind the investigation was the minister—Rolph Wittgen."

"What else?"

"Two years ago, Charles Atkenson was shot to death in his Washington apartment. Assassin or assassins unknown, but whoever did it was good. There was tight security on the apartment building, and even tighter security on his penthouse apartment, but absolutely nothing showed up. And the man's wife was asleep in the next room and she hadn't heard a thing."

McGarvey remembered the still unsolved murder because it had hit all the newspapers, especially The Wall Street Journal. Atkenson was an assistant director at the Securities and Exchange Commission. "Another Marinaccio connection?"

"He'd been head of the team investigating her since before she bolted," Otto said.

Gail looked from Otto to McGarvey. "Okay, so what's next? Can we give it to the Bureau?"

"They already have it," McGarvey said. "Both the woman and

Octavio are multibillionaires, and they have connections just about everywhere, so nothing will be done."

Otto was suddenly alarmed. "We don't have enough for something
like that."

Gail sat up. "Something like what?"

"If we can't get to either of them officially, Mac could go in alone and
take care of each of them," Otto said.

"Isn't that how your mysterious contractor operates?" Louise asked
quietly.

McGarvey shrugged.

"But to different ends," Gail suggested. "Doesn't that make this different?"

"Sure," Otto said, looking at McGarvey. "But not until we have the
proof."

Which might never happen, McGarvey thought but didn't say. "I
think that they'll want to try to take Eve and her oil platform down.
Probably in the middle of the Gulf."

"That'd suit Marinaccio and Octavio as well as Schlagel," Otto said.
"Which is the other idea I'm working on. Schlagel has to be connected
to them, and I just gotta find out how."

"What about Eric?" Gail asked.

"That one was his idea, and he's already on it," Otto said. "In the meantime what about you two?"

"We're going to take a ride on Eve's oil rig," McGarvey said, and there
was nothing else left to be said because Louise and Gail, and especially
Otto, understood the idea of Eve Larsen as a lightning rod, inviting the
strike.

None of them were happy, but none of them could see any other
viable means to a solution. And especially McGarvey, because he meant
to put some innocent people in harm's way, which made him every bit
as arrogant, at least in his own mind, as their contractor. "Doesn't it ever
bother you to put people's lives on the line?" his wife Katy had asked
him just before she'd given him the ultimatum—the CIA or her—that
had caused him to run to Switzerland. He should have stayed and tried
to make her understand the only answer he could have given her. Did it
ever bother him? All the time.

FORTY-TWO

A few of Eve's techs from the GFDL's lab at Princeton had already gone down to Louisiana to ferry crates of equipment out to Vanessa Explorer, but the others were waiting in the small lecture hall on the Forrestal campus, and when she walked in with Don Price everyone got on their feet and applauded and cheered loudly enough for her to blush.

There were other Nobel laureates on campus, but as the Atmospheric and Oceanic Sciences Director Brian Landsberg had told her just before she'd left for Oslo, none of them had faced such an uphill battle for recognition as she had. "And it has sometimes been public and ugly." Nor had either of them thought it was really possible that someone would actually try to kill her.

"At least no one's pushing for me to recant like Galileo," she'd told him, but she'd been pleased that he had taken the time to see her off and to reassure her that she had his, and therefore the university's, approval and full support.

It had meant a lot to her, just as this outpouring now did.

"On the backs of the poor serfs who serve her!" Lisa, one of the young postdocs, shouted, and everyone laughed even harder than the comment deserved because they were so happy, so proud and even awed to be working elbow-to-elbow with a Nobel doc, especially one who'd survived a pair of gunmen. It was almost like the Wild West, or at the very least a television series. Exciting stuff.

But it struck her that Landsberg had no appreciation for the real threat that her project faced, just as her techs here today had no idea. Their heads were buried in the sand, as hers had been, she supposed, before Kirk McGarvey had shown up on her horizon. She'd done a little research on him, but beyond the fact of his employment with the CIA, and the murders of his wife, daughter, and son-in-law, which had caused him to drop out until he'd shown up with the NNSA, she'd found little of anything substantial. Except that he was a man who commanded a great deal of respect on both sides of the Beltway. And being inside his circle she'd felt power radiating from him, like heat from a furnace. She didn't know if she liked the sensation, or was simply being a moth diving toward the flame. Whatever it was that he had—charisma, self-confidence, or arrogance—he was a seductive man.

"Thank you for that, Lisa," Eve said, walking down to the head of the hall where on Mondays she laid out the coming week's work with her group, and they all shared the previous week's progress of lack thereof. The meetings were almost never lectures, and they were always free-wheeling. A bunch of very bright people exchanging ideas. Arguing, debating, endlessly debating, but never disparagingly. Everyone respected everyone else, and it was one of the prerequisites Eve insisted on before hiring someone new. No idea, however far fetched it might be, would ever be dismissed out of hand.

Prove it right or prove it wrong. It was a team mantra, chiseled in stone.

They all laughed again. Something was up.

"We have a lot of work to do before the Gulf, and this is not a Monday so will someone explain what this is all about?"

A lot of scientists were like children, eager and excited. It was on all their faces now, including Don's. He pulled a stool out in front of the lectern and motioned for her to have a seat.

"What?" she demanded, which nearly brought down the house.

"Please," Don said.

"This better be goddamned good," she groused, but good-naturedly because this was the same way Don had acted when he'd brought the news that she'd won the Nobel Prize, and she felt a little tickle of nervous apprehension. But a good tickle.

Don took a piece of paper out of his pocket. "This is a fax that came in overnight, and I caught it first thing this morning before you got to your office."

"From who?" Eve asked.

"Let me read it," Don said, and he grinned. "A drumroll is appropriate at this time." He paused for a moment. "This is a letter from Mr. Ahmad bin Mubashir al Mustapha, president and CEO of the United Arab Emirates

International Bank of Commerce in Dubai, UAE. Addressed to, and I quote, 'The Honorable Dr. Evelyn Larsen,' here at your office in the lab." He looked up for a beat. "Short and to the point. 'May I, on behalf of the bank and its officers, offer our heartiest congratulations on your Nobel Peace Prize. In recognition not only of this great honor that has been bestowed upon you, but of your continuing work with the World Energy Needs project, and your recent breakthroughs in the production of energy with the possible additional benefit of someday controlling adverse weather conditions, we would like to offer you a conditional grant in the sum of one billion dollars U.S.' "

Eve was rocked to the bottom of her soul, and it took a seeming eternity before she could breathe again, and realize that her people were watching her, waiting for a reaction, just like people watched television when the sweepstakes winner opened the door and was told they'd just won ten million dollars. Only here and now, they were a part of the sweepstakes pot, not just voyeurs.

Then it came to her, what the message said. "Conditional on what?" she asked. Where's the catch? Banks—oil banks—did not hand out that kind of money to the Queen of the High Seas without a lot of serious strings, maybe unacceptable strings, attached.

" 'When electricity flows from Vanessa Explorer to the U.S Eastern Interconnect, thus proving that your project is a practical reality,' and I quote again, 'the full amount of the grant will be made available to you to use any way you see fit.' "

Eve's people held their breath, practically on the verge of exploding.

"And the last line is sweet and to the point," Don said. " 'Details to follow. Again, our heartiest congratulations.' "

"What else?" she asked.

Don shook his head. "Lots of other verbiage, about your visionary thinking for the future of the planet, service to mankind despite numerous obstacles and even setbacks." He looked up. "And brilliance."

"That's a gross understatement!" one of her techs shouted, and again everyone laughed harder and longer than the comment deserved.

They were keyed up to the max, and Eve figured today was either going to be a bust, production wise, or set some kind of a record for manic frenzy.

"Speech!" someone shouted.

"No," Eve said. "We leave for the rig in two days, and I've given all the speeches I'm going to give this year."

"Champagne?" Don asked.

"Work," Eve said, standing up.

"Boo."

"Slave driver," Lisa said, but everyone was getting up, huge smiles on their faces, and heading out the door, chattering like excited schoolchildren. They couldn't help but look over their shoulders at her, and she couldn't help but smile back.

Don handed her the fax. "With this kind of money on the table, along with InterOil's rig, Schlagel becomes practically a nonissue. Oil and money equals power."

But she didn't agree and he saw it on her face.

"What are you worried about now?" he asked.

"We're still facing the same trouble. Only now the stakes are higher."

Don was vexed. "Landsberg said practically the same thing when I showed him the fax. He wants to see you as soon as we were done here."

And Eve softened; she couldn't help it because of Don's obvious disappointment. He'd gotten over his snit from Oslo, in part because of the shooting, and he refused to understand why she wasn't over-the-moon happy, why she was still nervous. It's what all of her team, and especially him, wanted for her. "Did you actually bring champagne?" she asked.

"In the lab. Only four bottles."

She grinned. "What the hell. Let me talk to Landsberg first."

Eve walked across campus from the GFDL lab building to Sayre Hall where the AOS program director and staff had offices. Forrestal was also home to the Princeton plasma physics department. A lot of bright people here, she thought, watching the foot and bicycle traffic, most of them dressed in standard scientific uniforms—jeans, sneakers, sweatshirts, and sometimes photographer's vests with lots of pockets for pencils, pens, markers, scientific calculators, iPods, BlackBerries, and for the older faculty, endless scraps of paper with world-shattering notes, observations, or calculations.

Home. She carried the thought further, places like this were the only homes she'd ever known. She felt comfortable here. Safe. Cocooned—there was something to the ivory tower notion after all—and mostly accepted.

Landsberg's secretary, an older woman with gray hair up in a bun, scurried around from behind her desk and gave Eve a warm embrace. "My goodness, we're so proud of you."

This now was exactly what she'd been thinking about on the way over. "Thanks, Doris, but my team had a lot to do with it."

"Of course, we know, but, my goodness, what an achievement. Not many lady laureates you know."

"Well, we're changing that statistic," Eve said. "Is the director in?"

"He's expecting you."

Landsberg was a tall, lanky man, all arms and legs and angles, who never seemed to sit or stand still. Common campus wisdom was that if he ever did pull up short it would mean that his extremely fertile mind had shut down; his movements were a physical manifestation of his thoughts.

He was seated behind his desk, his fingers flying over his keyboard, and he looked up and smiled. "Quite a surprise, I'll bet," he said, without interrupting his typing.

"The money or the assassination attempt? "Eve asked, sitting down.

"Both, but I wanted to talk to you about the money."

"Do you want to finish what you're doing first?"

"Nope, just answering a few e-mails," Landsberg said. "I have a friend on Wall Street who has advised me on how best to manage the occasional big grant we receive. I talked to him this morning and mentioned your good fortune."

"Might be a bit premature. We haven't got the rig over to Florida, let alone up and running."

Landsberg glanced at the screen for just a second then looked back at Eve as he continued typing. "I don't think there's any question that you're on the right track, and you'll get the money. Problem is handling a billion dollars is complicated. You'll need help."

"I don't know if I trust the guys on Wall Street," Eve said. "Not after all the crap we've gone through over the past few years. A lot of them didn't seem so smart."

"His name is James McClelland, manages a couple of successful hedge funds, one of them that includes InterOil who gave you the rig. And he's done fine by this institution. All I'm suggesting is that you sit down and talk to him."

"When the experiment is a success," Eve said, and she knew that she was being stubborn. She supposed it was her British parsimony because of her upbringing, but the grant was hers.

Landsberg read something of that from her posture, because he stopped typing. "You're a brilliant scientist, but I read your monthly financials and department budget and expenditure reports. If I didn't know better I would have to assume that you flunked fifth grade arithmetic."

Eve was startled for just a moment, but then she laughed out loud, all the way from her gut. "You're right," she sputtered, spreading her hands. "Damned if you're not right."

"Manage your own prize money, but a million or so dollars is a drop in the bucket compared to what the bank has offered you."

"When the time comes I'll talk to your friend."

"Good," Landsberg said, and went back to answering his e-mails. "If I don't see you before you head to the Gulf, bon voyage."

"I'm going to Washington first," Eve said. "But thanks."

FORTY-THREE

William Callahan, the FBI's assistant deputy director for counterterrorism, had never been to the White House except once about five years ago on a public tour with his wife. He'd been impressed then, but he was even more impressed this afternoon as he was escorted by a White

House staffer to the West Wing office of Eduardo Estevez, because the president's adviser on national security affairs had called this morning to ask him over for a chat.

"To get all of our cards on the table," Estevez had said mysteriously, and Callahan had absolutely no idea what the man was talking about, and he said so. "The Hutchinson Island attack. The president wanted me to kick around a few ideas with you."

The incident concerned the Bureau's domestic intelligence and criminal investigation divisions, but Estevez said he wanted to start with counterterrorism. "Around two o'clock?"

It was that time now, and Estevez, who was seated on a chair facing two men on the couch, waved Callahan in. "Bill, glad you could make it."

"Yes, sir," Callahan said.

A desk and credenza were set in front of a window at one end of the pleasantly furnished office. A small conference table on one side of the room faced the couch and easy chairs.

"I don't know if you've met Marty Bambridge, he runs the directorate of operations over at the CIA."

Bambridge stood up, reached across the coffee table, and shook hands. "Heard good things about you," he said.

"Of course I think you must know Joe Caldwell. He's deputy secretary over at the Department of Energy."

"You were on *Meet the Press* a few weeks ago," Callahan said, shaking hands, and Estevez motioned for him to have a seat in a chair drawn up from the small oval conference table.

"I'm sorry, Mr. Estevez, but I'm at a total loss why I'm here," Callahan said, and he looked at the others to see if they were wondering the same thing. But if they were it wasn't obvious.

"Hutchinson Island, as I told you on the phone this morning," Estevez said. "And what it could mean for us. Future ramifications."

"I understand that Kirk McGarvey came over to have a talk with you," Bambridge said, almost too casually, and Callahan caught a glimmer as to why he'd been called.

"A couple of months ago. Right after Hutchinson Island."

"Care to share with us the general substance of your meeting?" Estevez said. "It wasn't a privileged conversation was it?"

"No, not at all," Callahan said. He didn't like the position he had been put in, but at this point he could see no way out, nor had McGarvey asked that their meeting be kept confidential. "The NNSA asked him to investigate the incident and he wanted to know what, if anything, the Bureau had found."

"It's only natural," Caldwell said. "He was there when it happened, after all, and he helped limit the damage. Lost his partner."

"Did he share any early conclusions with you?" Estevez asked.

"He mentioned the Reverend Schlagel who's been capitalizing on the incident to further his political career. Then, of course, there was the incident at Oslo."

"The reverend's people. Both dead."

"Yes, sir. Anyway McGarvey was suspicious even two months ago about the coincidental nature."

Estevez exchanged a glance with the others. "He's a bright man. What else?"

"We discussed Schlagel's possible connection with a hedge fund manager in Dubai and the UAE International Bank of Commerce. The Bureau has had them under investigation."

"Anne Marie Marinaccio," Estevez said. "We know all about her."

"And that's about it," Callahan said. "We agreed that there wasn't enough evidence to link Marinaccio or Schlagel to a professional who apparently pulled off the Hutchinson Island attack with only one man inside helping out."

"Yes, we know about that, too," Bambdrige said.

"Any contact with McGarvey since then?" Estevez asked.

"No."

"Where are you at with your division's investigation? Any progress you could share with us?"

"I'm sorry, sir, but we don't have a thing other than the probability that the hired gun is someone at the top of his game. Likely international, with a lot of experience and enough intelligence and professionalism that he's left no tracks which we could use to trace him."

"We're running into the same problem," Bambridge said. "Even Otto Rencke is drawing blanks."

"What are the chances McGarvey will come up with something useful?" Estevez asked the CIA officer.

"He's never failed before. Walt Page has a lot of confidence in him."

"You're aware that he's become something of an attachment to Eve Larsen. Almost her personal bodyguard," the Energy Department's deputy secretary said.

"He thought that whoever was behind the Hutchinson Island attack would go after her again," Bambridge said. "Seems he was right. Just maybe he's using her as a lightning rod."

What they were saying made a certain chilling sense to Callahan. "The Marinnacio Group deals mostly in oil derivatives," he said. "And it would be in her best interest, and in the best interest of the major oil-producing nations to limit the development of alternate energy sources."

The three men looked at him, but said nothing.

"That would include nuclear energy. There's a rising public sentiment against the thirty or so permits for new construction, a lot of it engineered by Schalgel. So I see where McGarvey is taking it. And it would also include an opposition to Eve Larsen's project—especially now that she's received the Nobel Prize."

"Your point, Bill?" Estevez asked.

"We need to help out. We need to protect her. And Homeland Security and the NNSA need to up the threat level and increase security on all of our existing nuclear facilities."

"And there is the crux of the problem the president is faced with," Estevez said. "Besides the fact the guys who tried to take her out in Oslo have been bagged we have to deal with the interim, and we need to provide the solution."

"I'm not following."

"In November the President met with Salman bin Talal—he's the the new Saudi oil minister—here in the White House, mostly about continuing basing privileges for our Air Force, and the Iranian nuclear issue."

"It was in the news," Callahan said.

"They were very cooperative," Estevez said. "The president scored a couple of points. But what wasn't in the news was Talal's warning that we not rush so quickly into unproven alternate sources of energy. Americans, he said, aren't willing to give up their SUVs yet. Coal is unsustainable in terms of carbon dioxide, and it will take a viable oil industry to meet demands. First, he said, switch to all electric transportation—for which oil will be the primary resource alongside nuclear energy. Then on a small scale, investigate alternate energy, because such resources may be as far off as the next century."

"Nonsense," Callahan said.

"Of course. But the implied threat was that if we put national resources behind projects like Dr. Larsen's water wheels, the Saudis and other OPEC nations would began to decrease outputs by substantial percentages. It would place the U.S. in an untenable position."

"Worse than the gas lines in the seventies," Caldwell said. "Strangely at Interior agrees." Strangely Blumenthal was the Secretary of the Department of Interior, which regulated oil drilling.

"Blackmail," Callahan said.

"Real-world politics," Estevez said. "We can't afford to drag our heels on alternate energy research, but we've been forced into that position. So unless people like Dr. Larsen can come up with a solution, and I mean a plug-and-play fix, we'll have to keep hands off."

"Or appear to," Bambridge said. "Which is where McGarvey has already been useful, and it's up to us to keep him in the middle."

"We can't give him any overt assistance," Estevez said. "As I understand it, he may ride Dr. Larsen's oil rig all the way to Florida, and we won't stand in his way. He's doing this on his own."

"We can let it leak that there may be a romantic interest there," Caldwell said. "He lost his wife eighteen months ago."

Callahan thought the suggestion was pure sleaze, but he said nothing.

"It would be a good fit," Estevez said. "Plausible."

Callahan wanted to ask if this was what the national security adviser had meant by real-world politics, but he thought he knew what the answer would be

"It also helps that she got the Peace Prize," Caldwell said. "Trivializes her work to some extent. She's making a noble effort and all that—no pun intended—but her science wasn't sound enough to get the physics prize."

Estevez was nodding. "I see your point, and it helps," he said, and he looked at Callahan. "Don't be confused by what you think you're hearing. All of us here have the utmost respect for Dr. Larsen and her project. What we're actually trying to do is protect her."

"I'm sorry, sir, but I don't see how unless you're willing to have the rig accompanied by the Coast Guard or Navy, perhaps have a SEAL team standing by."

"That's exactly what we can't do," Estevez said. "Let me explain something. We know about Schlagel's connection with Marinaccio and probably with the bank in Dubai. And do you know how that information came to us?"

"Not from the Bureau," Callahan said.

"And not from the CIA. It came to me directly from Abdullah al-Naimi, right here in this office in November. And if the name's not familiar, al-Naimi is the deputy director of the GIP, which is the Saudi's chief intelligence agency."

"We're keeping an eye on Marinaccio and Schlagel," Bambridge said. "There's no proof that either of them were connected in any way with Hutchinson Island, or the incident in Oslo, but we think it's a fair assumption that the bank might have provided some or all of the financing."

"We're helping Dr. Larsen by monitoring the probable source of the money that would be used to harm her, while complying with the Saudi's warning to go easy on alternate energy for now," Estevez said. "Al-Naimi gave us a quid pro quo."

Real-world politics, indeed. "You do understand that if this thing goes bad, and McGarvey is in the middle of it, a lot of bodies will probably pile up. Worse than Hutchinson Island."

"We won't allow piracy," Estevez promised. "We'll get a message to him that if he needs help, we'll back him up."

But Callahan wondered if he believed the president's national security adviser.

□

FORTY-FOUR

McGarvey went into the office, bringing Admiral French up to speed, including what had happened in Oslo, and his plan for him and Gail to ride the oil platform to Florida with Eve Larsen and her techs. "Wouldn't it be smarter to have some backup? A Coast Guard escort?"

"I don't want to scare them off," McGarvey said.

"You're expecting an incident?"

"I think it's possible."

French just stared at him for a few beats, then shook his head. "It's why I hired you," he said. "Doesn't mean I have to like your methods or even approve of them. When do you leave?"

"A couple of days, I think. Whenever Dr. Larsen has her equipment and people aboard."

He spent the afternoon working with Gail and Eric in the computer center, connected through several programs with Otto over at the CIA, and all of them were frustrated by the total lack of progress. McGarvey especially so because he'd wanted some lead, even the barest of hints about what might be coming their way, before he flew down to Mississippi and joined Eve and her crew aboard the oil platform.

During a break when he'd stepped outside to get a breath of fresh air, Gail joined him and they sat at one of the picnic benches in the park across the street without saying a word to each other for at least ten minutes. Until Gail broke the silence.

"Do you still want me on the rig with you?" she asked, not looking at him.

He'd felt her tension over the past few days. "Can't order you to come with me."

"Not what I asked, Kirk."

"What then?" he said, refusing to get sucked into the discussion he knew was coming.

"Us."

He turned to face her. "There is no us," he said, and he held off her objection. "Not until after we're finished with the situation and it's time to get back to our jobs."

She'd searched his eyes. "I don't think you're coming back. You're not NEST team trainer material."

"A lot of them need it. Gruen needs it."

"I can handle that part," Gail said. "Teach them what I learned from my mistakes. What I'm still learning. From you."

McGarvey didn't have the answers she wanted. Maybe having her at the apartment had been a mistake, and thinking about it now he didn't know why he'd made the decision. Fear for her safety? Loneliness? Maybe more of the latter. But he didn't want being lonely to drive his decisions. Especially not in the field when his life and the lives of a lot of other people were on the line.

"Yes, I'd like you to come out to the rig with me," he said. "You're a good cop, and everyone else aboard will either be scientists and technicians, or InterOil's delivery crew. I can't cover everything twenty-four/seven."

She smiled. "If you knew how much I hated shift work you'd really appreciate my telling you I'll be happy to help out. When do we leave?"

"I don't know," McGarvey said. "I'll find out in the next day or two. I'm supposed to have dinner with her at some point."

"Since this concerns me, shouldn't I tag along?"

And it was exactly what he hoped she wouldn't say, but knew she would, and why. "There's no need for you to be jealous," he said, and she reacted as if she'd been slapped, but before she could say something, he finished the thought. "Nothing is going on between us."

She looked at him, her eyes squinty whenever she was frustrated. "I'm anything but jealous. And even if there was something between you it'd be none of my business."

McGarvey shrugged, not wanting to provoke an argument.

"You and I have a working relationship. You've already made that very clear and I'm going along with it."

"On the rig we're partners not lovers," McGarvey said, and the instant he did he regretted it, because he saw that Gail had been stung and she was angry. Having her stay with him at the apartment *had* been a mistake, and making love to her had been an even more colossal error. He hadn't been thinking straight; he'd been thinking through his loneliness, not considering the kind of hurt she would feel afterwards—like right now—when he had all but told her that there would never be anything between them.

It had been the same last year during her training, when they'd fallen into bed together. Both of them had been lost, hungry, needy. And he'd handled that aftermath just as badly as he was handling the situation now.

But he refused to lower his eyes. "I'm sorry, Gail. That came out badly. What I meant to say is that we have to keep an eye on what we're doing twenty-four/seven, no distractions. Once we make it to Florida we can decide which way we're going."

But she already knew what the outcome would be and it showed on her face, her anger gone, replaced by sadness. "Then I should start packing."

"I'm going to fly down to take a quick look at the platform first. I want to see if it's going to be the kind of security nightmare I think it'll be. In the meantime I want you here to work with Eric and Otto."

"I need to go down to St. Lucie and pick up some things from my apartment."

"It could get rough, so pack accordingly."

She nodded. "What about weapons?"

If there was more to say, and McGarvey suspected there should be, he didn't know what it was. "I'll get what we need from the CIA."

She got up to leave, and managed a slight smile. "No pressure, Kirk."

"None felt," McGarvey said, and they knew that both of them were lying.

Later that afternoon, even more frustrated with their continued lack of progress, McGarvey cabbed it back to Georgetown and on the way his cell phone chimed. It was Eve, and she sounded out of breath. She was in Washington up to her eyeballs with last-minute work before heading down to the rig the day after tomorrow, and she wanted to have dinner with him tonight. Five thirty at the restaurant in the Watergate. Her apartment was just across the parking lot, and she needed to make an early night of it because she still had a ton of work to do.

McGarvey found that he was glad to hear from her, in part because he finally had a timetable. And she was waiting for him in a booth at 600 at the Watergate, a reasonably priced restaurant, she said, with a reasonable menu and reasonably decent food. They had a view of the Potomac, and the place was less than half full because of the early hour.

When their drinks came, and they had both ordered filets, Eve came straight to the point, and McGarvey thought that she seemed a little more intimidated than she had been outside the Fox studio after her interview and again when they'd first arrived in Oslo.

"Up in Princeton in my lab, I pretty well run the show. I'm my own boss, but down here in Washington it's a different story, because technically my project comes under NOAA's umbrella, and sometimes they can get pretty heavy-handed."

McGarvey shrugged. "I've worked with and for the government for most of my adult life, so I know what you mean. But they're the ones with the big bucks."

Eve brightened a little. "You haven't heard about my good news."

"No."

"If we get the rig to Hutchinson Island, and set up the impellers so that we're delivering electricity to the grid, I'll be given a nonconditional grant for one billion dollars."

Alarm bells immediately began to ring, but McGarvey just smiled at her. "NOAA?"

She laughed. "Not a chance. This comes from Dubai, from the International Bank of Commerce. The fax came to my office two days ago, but we've decided to keep it quiet until Florida."

But it was an empty gesture meant to lull her into a sense of complacency, make her believe that with that kind of money no one would try to stop her. But that's exactly what the offer meant. No money would ever be paid to her, because the rig would never reach the Gulf Stream and the UAEIBC would make sure of it.

"That's a bank funded primarily with oil and oil derivatives money," he said.

She was taken by surprise, and she shook her head. "That's what Bob Krantz told me yesterday. Almost word for word. He's head of special projects for NOAA, which makes him my boss. He suggested I turn it down."

"Wouldn't matter," McGarvey said.

"I don't know what you're talking about. Do you realize what that kind of money will do for my project? How many impeller-generators we can anchor out in the Gulf Stream? It'll give me a five year head start."

"If you get to Hutchinson Island."

Suddenly Eve was alarmed. "Bob tried to get a Coast Guard escort for us, but they turned him down flat. No evidence that we would come under attack, especially now that the guys who tried to kill me in Oslo are no longer a threat."

That wasn't surprising to McGarvey, considering the tensions between the U.S. and Saudi Arabia, and just about every OPEC country. The U.S. government had made enough mistakes in Iraq, and combined with its unwavering support of Israel against the Palestinians, U.S. popularity in the region was nil. The administration had to be walking a fine line, because it needed OPEC more than they needed the U.S. Any oil not sold to the U.S. would be snapped up by the Chinese; it was becoming a worldwide sellers' market.

"I'm coming with you," MacGarvey said.

She laughed nervously. "Do you actually think someone will try to stop me?" she asked. "Try to sabotage the rig? The same people who hit Hutchinson Island?"

"I thought it was a possibility. Now I'm sure of it."

"Because of the grant offer?"

He nodded. "Yes."

Her eyes were round. She looked a little overwhelmed, as if she'd been given a problem that had no solution or set of solutions that made any sense. "I can't accept it."

"We've already gone over their reasons, and nothing has changed. You represent a serious threat to a lot of people."

"Explain this to the Coast Guard, or the CIA, you have the connections."

"Won't help. The government will not get involved, unless an actual attack takes place."

"By then it would be too late."

"It's why I'll be aboard the platform, and I don't want you telling anybody who I am. As far as your people are concerned, I'll just be a part of the delivery crew."

"Don will know."

"Ask him to keep it quiet, your lives might depend on it," McGarvey said.

She wanted to argue, he could see it in the set of her jaw, in her eyes. "One man against however many they—whoever the hell they are—send against us?"

"I'll bring one other person with me."

"And you'll be armed. You'll have weapons."

"Yes."

Again she was nearly overwhelmed by what he was telling her. "What if they just drop a bomb on the rig, or fire a missile at us?"

"I think it'd take more than that to destroy something that large," McGarvey said.

"Okay, so they plant bombs," Eve argued, her voice rising.

"I'm going to fly down to the rig and take a look, see how I would do it if I wanted to stop you."

"All right, what about a suicide bomber?"

"They'll be professionals, which means they'll want to get away. It's their one weakness."

She laughed humorlessly. "Some weakness. And I suppose I can't refuse your help. I don't want to put my people in harm's way, most of them are just kids. But, goddamnit I'm not going to let the bastards beat me. This experiment is too important."

"I agree."

"But what about afterwards? I mean if my experiment is a success, and we begin delivering power to the SSP and L connection with the grid, what then? Armed guards forever?"

"Maybe, at first," McGarvey said. "Until you go to the next phase and anchor your impellers to the ocean floor. And sooner or later, if I understand what you're trying to do, there'll be hundreds of them."

"Tens of thousands," Eve said absently.

"By then the project will be far too large to sabotage."

She focused on him. "I just have to survive long enough for that to happen," she said, and smiled wanly. "Welcome to the team."

FORTY-FIVE

☐

Brian DeCamp, dressed in desert camos, lay in a hollow, studying the fantastic-looking structure nearly the size of a soccer field that a squad of Libyan Army engineers had knocked together over the past thirty days. It was the middle of the night in the deep desert more than six hundred kilometers southeast of Tripoli, the only time the construction crews worked, and the only time DeCamp and his three operators came out of their tents, or moved from under the camouflage netting that covered just about everything.

One of the engineers came to the rail of the partial mock-up of Vanessa Explorer, and pissed over the side. It was an insult to the four nonbelievers he knew were preparing for another assault exercise. But an insult that meant absolutely nothing to DeCamp and his team.

"Lead, team two set," Nikolai Kabatov radioed in DeCamp's earpiece. A former KGB senior lieutenant who'd killed a pair of prostitutes in Lengingrad, and had resigned his commission for the good of the agency, lay in the sand fifty meters to the east, with his teammate Boris Gurov, a former Spetsnaz captain who'd been kicked out of the service for driving a squad of men to such depths of exhaustion during a winter exercise above the Arctic Circle that four men had died.

"Go in thirty," DeCamp replied.

"Copy."

The two men in addition to DeCamp's teammate, Joseph Wyner, who'd been a helicopter pilot with the Australian Special Air Service Regiment, were all that he figured would be needed for the initial stage aboard the rig, which would be manned only by the scientists and technicians, plus the delivery crew. A total of thirty people, none of them with any combat experience.

Finding the three operators had been a simple matter of logging on to the Web site of Contractor Services Unlimited, which like the old *Soldier of Fortune* magazine was practically an employment agency for contractors and military officers and enlisted personnel, who for one reason or another had either resigned or been forced to resign, and were looking for work. Actually, as Gurov had explained, when DeCamp had interviewed him in London, guys like him wanted to get back into the game, wanted the thrill of combat, wanted to blow up something, kill someone.

"The bigger the bang the better," he'd said. "And I don't give a *pizdec's* asshole who the target is."

Out of nearly one hundred résumés online, DeCamp had picked three men to meet face-to-face, and he'd hired all of them, because they were perfect: they were well trained, they had combat experience— Chechnya for Gurov and Kabatov, and Afghanistan for Wyner—they were hungry, and they were expendable.

He'd arrived in Tripoli two months ago, where he met with his Libyan military contact, the assistant chief of staff, Lt. Col. Salaam Thaqib, set up a financial presence with the Libyan Arab Foreign Bank in the amount of two million euros, one hundred thousand of which was transferred into Thaqib's Swiss bank account, and rented four adjoining suites in the Corinthia Bab Africa, the country's leading hotel.

Three days later blueprints of the reworked oil platform had been delivered by a messenger from the Czech Republic embassy on behalf of the ABN Commerce Bank in Prague where DeCamp maintained an account. The drawings had originated from his contact aboard the rig via InterOil and spreading them out on a conference table he'd ordered be brought up, it had taken him less than ten minutes to find the rig's weakness and devise a number of plans to send it to the bottom of the Gulf of Mexico. Included with the blueprints was a list of everyone who would be aboard, all of whom would go down with the platform. There would be no survivors.

That afternoon he'd had two copies made of the blueprints, sending them by courier over to the colonel's office, one to be used to construct the mock-up in the desert and the second to build a scale model of the rig that had been brought over to the hotel and set up in his suite ten days later, making at least one of his plans perfectly clear. In some ways, he'd thought, toppling the platform would be easier than the assault on Hutchinson Island had been.

During his off hours in those weeks, DeCamp kept in shape by running five miles each day, swimming in the Med, and working out for hours at a time in the hotel's spa. His meals were nearly all protein, and he drank no alcohol, a regimen he'd learned in the Buffalo squadron before any tough field assignment. The protein built lean muscle mass, and the lack of carbohydrates toned him down, sending him into a form of ketosis, almost like a diabetic whose hypoglycemic index was altered, only in this case giving him a lot of extra energy. Almost like floating an inch off the ground after the first week. Almost like being on uppers.

Thirty seconds later Wyner raised his left fist and pumped it once and DeCamp nodded.

"Now," DeCamp said into his comms unit, and he and Wyner headed up out of the hollow, crawling on their hands and knees toward the plywood and canvas full-scale mock-up of one of Vanessa Explorer's four semisubmersible legs.

Waiting for his three operators to show up at the Corinthia, DeCamp had worked out two possible scenarios; one of which was dropping two scuba-equipped teams from different directions one mile out from the rig. The insertion boat would be a low-slung cigarette, showing no lights, capable of speeds in excess of sixty knots, and perfectly capable of crossing the Gulf to reach the platform.

They would set explosive charges well beneath the waterline on two of the legs, then swim back to the boat. When the charges went off, the two legs would rapidly fill with water, and the unstable rig would suddenly list sharply to one side, so suddenly that nothing aboard could be done to stop a capsize.

Twenty feet away from the leg, DeCamp could see why it would not work, and he stood up. "Abort," he said softly into his comms unit.

Wyner saw it, too. "Shit," he said, and he got to his feet. "Unless the

seas are flat calm we won't get anywhere near the leg. Too much movement. Barnacles would cut us to shreds."

"I didn't see it from the blueprints or the model," DeCamp said without
rancor. Mistakes in the field could get you killed. Mistakes in a training
mission were usually only embarrassing. He'd learned a part of that lesson the hard way from Colonel Frazer on the streets in Durban, and the
rest of it in the field with the Buffalo Battalion when he helped carry
casualties out of the hot zone; the blokes who made the mistakes, the
ones who'd not paid enough attention in the training missions, were the
ones who returned to base in body bags.

Wyner was tall and slender, like a greyhound, and he stood relaxed,
most of his weight on one foot. He'd taken ballet lessons as a teenager, not
because he'd wanted to go on stage, but because he wanted to develop his
agility so that he could become a better fencer. He was deadly in a knife
fight, which was all about footwork; DeCamp had never seen a better man
with a blade.

"We could use magnetic attachers," he suggested. "With whisker poles
we wouldn't have to get all that close."

"No," DeCamp said.

Kabatov and Gurov came out of the darkness from the east side of the
rig, both of them short, sturdy men with broad Slavic features and
sometimes sly smiles that made it impossible to guess what they were
thinking. They looked like oil roustabouts, roughnecks who'd done
manual labor all of their lives; they looked like men who'd grown up on
the wharves of busy seaports, or in coal or uranium mines in Siberia, on
the high seas aboard container ships—the men who would be sent forward in a storm to replace the chains on a stack of containers about to
topple overboard, because they were just so much cannon fodder in the
minds of the captains and the owners. And it was exactly the reason
DeCamp had hired them, because they fit perfectly, especially for the
only option left open. Something he'd thought might be difficult but not
impossible for the right men.

The three of them had filtered separately into Tripoli over a five-day
period, Wyner first, Gurov, with his rough humor, three days later, and
Kabatov the day after that. They were put on DeCamp's regimen without
grousing because they'd been promised one million euros each; the catch,

making the payday a big one, was that the chances one or all of them might end up dead was better than fifty-fifty.

"I'm the paymaster, which makes me the squad leader," DeCamp told them when they were all together in his suite. "You guys are good, which means I want to hear what you have to say. My door is open twenty-four/ seven to any idea, any complaint, any suggestion, any comment, starting now right through the end of the op."

They'd nodded, but said nothing.

"Refuse a direct order, hesitate for one second, drink alcohol, smoke, or try to communicate with anyone in the real world other than the four of us in this room, and I will kill you," DeCamp said. "Questions?"

"No, sir," Wyner said. "What's the mission and how do we get there?"

DeCamp removed the bedsheet covering the oil rig model. "Vanessa Explorer," he said. "She's an out of commission oil exploration platform anchored right now in the Gulf of Mexico a few miles off the Mississippi coast. Sometime in the next thirty days her anchors will be pulled up, and an oceangoing tug will tow her out into the Gulf and around the tip of Florida where she's to be positioned on the Atlantic coast north of Miami. We're going to sink her with all hands before she gets there."

The three operators gathered closer to the model, none of them showing any signs that they were surprised or skeptical. Missions with million euro paydays were always interesting, but never easy.

"What about the crew?" Gurov asked.

"Fourteen scientists and technicians from the National Oceanic and Atmospheric Administration, plus seventeen delivery crew and deck-hands, give or take, including electricians, pipe fitters, and welders who'll be doing work on the rig while en route."

"I didn't know oil exploration was going on in that part of the Atlantic," Wyner said.

"It's a scientific experiment, but that part is irrelevant. I was hired to send the rig to the bottom."

"That's thirty-one people versus the four of us," Gurov said. "Any of them with security or military backgrounds?"

"To this point no, and we will have the help of one person aboard who'll provide us with real-time intel."

"Military background or not, the crew will not simply jump overboard when we show up. Some of them will resist," Kabatov said. "What equipment will we have to use?"

"That will depend on which option we go with," DeCamp told them. "At this point there are two, and I'll want your input."

"It'll take a hell of a lot of explosives to do any real damage to something that large," Wyner said. "I did a year of contract security work aboard one of them in the Persian Gulf, during the first American war. The Saudis were a little nervous with all the ordnance flying around, and the money was good."

"I didn't see that in your résumé," DeCamp said, vexed.

Wyner shrugged. "I didn't put down every job I'd ever had."

"Anyone else with oil rig experience?"

The Russians said no.

Patience was another of the virtues that the colonel had taught him in Durban. "The angry man is the out-of-control soldier, usually the first to die in battle. Remember it."

"The delivery crew and deckhands have shore leave days on a rotating schedule. Option one is to arrange for an accident that would take out four of them, and then apply for jobs aboard the rig."

"Doesn't wash," Wyner said. "Why would they hire the four of us and not someone else?"

"InterOil does the hiring, and we have help there. But you're right, might be a bit of a stretch. The alternative would be for us to take out only two."

"Assuming it would be two of us, and not you, how would you and whoever else get aboard?"

"They'll have a media event, which I would attend, for starts, to legitimize myself. And then when the rig is well offshore, we'd return aboard a helicopter with four more operators and take over. If we go with that option it would be your job to disable whatever communications gear you could get to, including sat phones."

"And number two," Wyner asked.

"We scuba to the rig, and plant explosives in a pair of the legs."

Gurov suddenly grinned, seeing everything. "Only one problem with that scenario. The rig will capsize and sink, but there will be survivors. The only way we're going to get rid of them all is to kill them first and lock their bodies in one of the compartments, so there'd be no floaters."

"Why kill them?" Kabatov asked. "Just herd them into the crew's mess and lock the door."

DeCamp had wanted to try the scuba approach first, mainly because it had been drummed into his head to plan for every possibility and to train for each one and find the unknown variables, the overlooked problem that could ruin everything. Like this tonight.

"So, what's the problem?" Gurov asked.

"Won't work this way," Wyner said, and he explained.

From the moment DeCamp had realized the scuba approach wasn't going to work, he'd decided on the other simpler plan, more elegant, less chance of failure. He would make a call to his contact aboard the oil platform to arrange for two of the least skilled men on the construction crew, roustabouts, to be fired for whatever reason he could find, and replace them with Kabatov and Gurov. The contact's name had been supplied by Wolfhardt, who'd apparently had something on the man. Money, De-Camp had suspected, which was one of the great motivators, and he didn't expect any difficulties. And it would give them additional inside information, the only danger if either Kabatov or Gurov—especially Gurov—got into it with one of the legitimate crewmen or scientists aboard the rig. They would have to keep their mouths shut, and do their work until the attack. Perhaps one week, or a little less.

"We're flying back to Tripoli tonight," he told them. "We're done here."

"What's next?" Wyner asked.

"Nikolai and Boris are going to make their way to Biloxi, Mississippi, where they'll be hired as replacements for a pair of deckhands aboard the rig."

Gurov brightened. "How will we know which guys you want us to take down?"

"Won't be necessary. Just show up at the union hall and you'll get the jobs."

"Too bad."

"You'll have plenty of chance to spill blood," DeCamp said. "A lot of blood."

"What about me?" Wyner asked.

"You're coming to London with me to hire four more operators, familiarize them with the rig, and from there move the ops to New Orleans, where we'll pick up our equipment."

"How will we communicate?" Kabatov asked. "In case something changes or goes wrong."

"I have a Nokia encrypted sat phone for you."

"How do we get out of there when it's over?"

"By helicopter out to a ship heading to the Panama Canal."

"A lot could go wrong," Wyncr commented.

"And probably will," DeCamp said.

Gurov laughed. "I say fuck it! I'm in."

And the others nodded.

FORTY-SIX

They didn't notice the stiff breeze when the 737 touched down at the Biloxi Airport, because it was right on the nose, but when the big passenger jet left the runway and trundled slowly to the terminal it almost felt as if the airplane would tip over on a wing. Then they came into the lee of the big building and it seemed as if they'd come indoors out of a gale.

"I hope the helicopter pilot knows what he's doing," Eve said. "Vanessa is twenty-five miles out in the Gulf, and it's going to be a lot worse out there."

"Oil rig ferry pilots have to be good enough to pull guys off the platforms in all kinds of weather," McGarvey said, trying a little to soothe her.

She'd been preoccupied all the way down from Washington, not about a possible attack but about the two tons of equipment that had been trucked from Princeton. As of eight this morning when she'd talked to Don, who'd come down two days ago, the truck hadn't shown up yet. Which was just as well. Keeping her focused on the logistics and then the science of her project would make his job all the easier.

"You're right," she said. "And I'm acting like an idiot."

McGarvey laughed. "At least a smart idiot."

And she laughed, too. "It's not that I'll be glad when it's over, I'll be glad when it starts at Hutchinson Island. Because that's really the beginning, to actually see if the damned thing works."

"Doubts?"

"Yeah, plenty of them," Eve said. "Don calls it healthy skepticism."

Most of Eve's clothing and personal things she would need for the twelve-day trip and afterwards when the experiment began had been packed aboard the truck with the scientific equipment, which was just one more minor irritant she'd been facing. One among a million, she'd confided in him at one point.

"Scientists are absolute nitpickers," she'd said. "Detail people, patient, persistent, persevering, unremitting, and usually unhurried. But almost always worried that they're overlooking something, not seeing the forest for the trees, missing the obvious." She'd smiled. "The best of them have the capability to step back at just the right moment and see the whole picture. Einstein lost in some calculations, suddenly daydreams about a man riding up in a glass elevator that's accelerating with the same force as earth's gravity. Someone outside watches the guy in the elevator let go of a tennis ball, and the elevator floor rises up to meet it. But every experiment inside the elevator convinces the guy that the tennis ball fell to the floor because of gravity. And voilà, he saw the big picture and gave us relativity."

"And he got the Nobel Prize."

"Yeah, but not for relativity, special or general. He got it for showing how the photoelectric effect works. You know, the device that opens the door for you at the supermarket."

She was bitter all of a sudden, and in some ways McGarvey understood her Angst. Eve Larsen was a complicated woman, filled with a lot of self-doubts and insecurities that even a Nobel Prize had been unable to unravel. He'd known people like her at the CIA, especially in the Directorate of Intelligence, who were geniuses at what they did, but who needed constant approval, constant pats on the back, constant reinforcement, or else they would fall into depressions sometimes so deep that they would commit suicide.

"You won the Nobel Prize."

"Not for physics," she practically shouted, and several people getting off the plane with them gave her an anxious look. "Only two women ever got that prize—Madam Curie and Maria Mayer, and they had to share their prizes with men."

When they reached the gate area inside the terminal McGarvey took her aside. "You're betting just about everything on this experiment working, I understand that. But you've gotten yourself so wound up that it might just happen that you won't be able to step back and see the whole picture."

She was angry. "How can I help it?" she asked, her voice crisp. "You've tagged along as my bodyguard, once again, because you think my rig will never make it to Florida."

"Concentrate on the science, and let me deal with security," he said just as tightly.

She wanted to argue, but she compressed her lips and nodded, visibly coming down. But it took a few seconds. "My ex never figured out how to do that," she said. "Get me to take a deep breath." She touched his arm. "I'll worry about my part and let you take care of the rest. Deal?"

"Deal," McGarvey said, figuring that it would take an extraordinary man to be married to her. She was as high-strung as she was brilliant and she was carrying a very large feminist chip on her shoulder, probably something from a long time ago.

They carried just their overnight bags, Eve because her things were being trucked down, and McGarvey because he was planning to stay aboard the platform just long enough to meet the delivery crew and figure out in practical terms what it would take to send the rig to the bottom.

Don Price, dressed in jeans and a Princeton sweatshirt, was waiting downstairs in front of the baggage claim area, and when he spotted McGarvey he scowled and turned away as if he were going to walk off. But then he stopped and turned back.

"Thanks for coming to pick us up," Eve said pleasantly, trying to ignore his show of displeasure. "How's everything going on Vanessa?"

"I was hoping that you would change your mind," Don said, glaring at McGarvey.

"He's going to provide security for us."

"With any luck I'll just be along for the ride," McGarvey said.

"Stay the fuck out of our way."

Price was posturing for Eve, and it struck McGarvey as almost funny, even a little pathetic. But there was something else in the man's manner. Something in his attitude, how he held himself, the words he was saying that wasn't adding up. It was as if he were hiding something, as if he were afraid of something. Losing her to another man?

McGarvey shrugged. "Sure thing."

Price held on for a moment or two longer, as if he wanted to push it, but then nodded tightly, took Eve's arm, and headed out to where he had parked an InterOil van, leaving McGarvey to trail behind.

"The truck got here an hour after you called, and we've managed to get most of the stuff out to Vanessa."

"Good," Eve said. "Computers?"

"Most of them are up and running, and we've already got a good start on stringing the cabling for the monitors to all four pods."

"How about housekeeping?"

"It's not the Ritz but we managed to help get the water treatment plant up and running, so we have plenty of hot water for showers. Separate showers at that. And the food isn't any worse than we get on campus."

"Problems?" Eve asked.

"The biggest are the deck mounts for the impeller cabling and restraints," Don said and she protested but he held her off. "Defloria is working the construction crews practically around the clock. But they're so goddamned stupid and inefficient it's a miracle that anything gets done. Anyway he promises that the mounts will be in place by the time we get to Florida. Before, if the weather cooperates."

"What about the wind today?"

"It's a little hairy on deck, but inside you can't feel a thing, except it's damned noisy, drives you nuts sometimes, especially at night."

They got in the van, McGarvey in the backseat for the short drive over to the InterOil hangar. "Who's managing the rig for you?" he asked.

Eve turned around. "Justin Defloria. He and the construction crew and delivery people are on loan from the company."

"I want you to set up a meeting with him and the delivery captain as soon as we touch down. I'd like to make an inspection of the entire rig with them, and share some of my concerns."

"No problem."

"Then I'll want to meet with your scientists and technicians for about ten minutes."

"Not a chance in hell," Don said. "You're staying out of our way."

McGarvey ignored him. "I'll let you know when I'm ready to talk to your people."

"We'll all be up in the control room," Eve said, and she said something to Don that McGarvey didn't catch, but whatever it was it seemed to work because Price shut his mouth and concentrated on his driving.

From five miles out Vanessa Explorer looked impressive, the whitecaps below the helicopter little more than harmless patterns on the water. But as they got nearer it became obvious that no matter how large the oil platform was it couldn't compare to the Gulf of Mexico. Every fifth wave that slammed into the two windward legs parted and rose monstrously almost to the main deck level more than fifty feet above the water, the spindrift rising even higher.

"Don't worry, it looks worse than it is!" Don shouted to Eve.

The chopper pilot was good, but the big machine shuddered with each gust, and coming around into the wind he kept well clear of the upper levels of the superstructure, approaching the landing pad slowly, and easing down, dumping the lift five feet above the center mark. Immediately two deck hands scrambled up on to the pad and lashed the helicopter's landing struts to the deck. As soon as they gave the thumbs-up, the pilot cut the power, and the engines began to spool down.

Most of the tube-framed web seats in the helicopter's main bay were folded up against the hull, and the space was filled with sturdy cardboard boxes, a few wooden crates, and a large number of aluminum cases, all marked with numbers and other abbreviations.

"This is the bulk of it," Don said. "Maybe one more load this afternoon." He slid the hatch open and instantly the helicopter was filled with a howling wind that was cold and damp and smelled of a combination of oil, diesel fumes, presumably from the electrical generators aboard, and the sea.

"I want this unloaded as quickly as possible," Eve said. "No telling when this weather will deteriorate, and I want everything aboard before dark."

"I'll send Tommy and some of the others up," Don said, and he and Eve jumped down to the pad, without bothering to thank the pilot.

"I need a ride back in a couple of hours," McGarvey told him. "Can you hold that long?"

"No sweat," the pilot, a fussy-looking man with thinning black hair and a ruddy complexion, said. His name tag read Dyer. "I'll probably be in the crew's mess, give me a ten-minute heads-up if you would."

"Sure thing," McGarvey said and he patted the pilot on the shoulder. "Good flying."

The pilot grinned. "Nobody lost their lunch."

Before Eve headed up to the control room she sought out Defloria, who was in the construction foreman's space two levels up from the main deck where he and another man were busy on a CAD display of the impeller cabling mounts. They looked up. "You might want to take a look at this, Doctor," Defloria said.

"Don told me that you might be having a few problems," Eve said, glancing at the display. "But it doesn't matter as long as the work is done by the time we get to Hutchinson Island and the impellers are barged down to us."

"It's the stress loads they'll put on the deck. We think they'll be greater than the specs that the GE engineers gave us, so we're going to reinforce the underlying structure before we begin welding the restraint tripods."

"The extra weight won't matter?"

Defloria shook his head. "Negligible," he said. "We don't want to have a repeat of what happened to you at Hutchinson Island."

"No," Eve said. "Costs?"

"The company's picking it up."

"I'll go along with whatever you recommend," Eve said. "Would have in any event."

Defloria and Eve looked up as McGarvey came in. "I'm surprised to see someone like you here."

"Do you know each other?" Eve asked.

"I doubt Mr. McGarvey knows me, but he was in the news when he was the CIA director. Are you here to sightsee, or here to tell us something?"

"A little of both," McGarvey said, immediately liking the man's straightforward nature.

"Justin Defloria," the OIM said, shaking his hand. And he looked a little wary, as if he knew he was about to hear something he didn't want to hear, but could find no way out of it.

"I'll be topsides with my people whenever you're ready," Eve told McGarvey. "Anyone can direct you."

"What can I do for you, Mr. McGarvey?" Defloria asked when Eve was gone.

"Who's your delivery captain?"

"Al Lapides."

"Is he aboard?"

"Yes."

"I'd like to talk to the two of you, and just the two of you right now, if it's possible."

"Shit," Defloria said, but he took a walkie-talkie out of his jacket pocket and made a call.

FORTY-SEVEN

They met in Defloria's personal quarters, a nicely furnished space about the size of a luxury hotel suite with a bedroom, sitting room, and large bathroom, and broad views of the platform, alive at this moment with workmen despite the nearly gale force winds. A framed photograph of a pleasant-looking woman and two teenaged girls sat on a desk strewn with papers and blueprints.

Lapides, in his midfifties, was a short, very slender man with a large nose and ears, salt-and-pepper hair, and the deeply lined outdoors complexion of a man who'd spent a lifetime on the sea.

Defloria made the introductions and they sat on the couch and chairs in front of the desk.

"Assuming you're not here merely to continue as Dr. Larsen's body-guard, what do you want?"

"If I wanted to send this rig to the bottom of the Gulf, with everybody aboard, how would I go about doing it?"

"Good Lord almighty," Lapides said.

"You think that someone will try to do something like that?" Defloria asked. "Schlagel and his group of fanatics?"

"They might try to pull a Greenpeace against you, try to stop you from reaching Florida, but there'd be no violence."

"I've dealt with that group before," Lapides said. "In the North Sea. They're a pain in the ass, but mostly just a danger to themselves."

"Who then?" Defloria asked. "And why?"

"This is merely speculation to this point," McGarvey said. "There've been no warnings and we have no solid evidence that anything is going to happen. But I'm going to come along for the ride and mostly keep my eyes and ears open."

Defloria was angry. "I'm not going to place my people in harm's way," he said, his voice tight. "If you think we're facing a problem call the goddamned Coast Guard for an escort."

"They've refused."

"I'm pulling my people off," Defloria said. "Al?"

"Whatever the company wants," Lapides said.

Defloria got a sat phone from his desk and speed-dialed a number as he walked out into the corridor.

"How do we destroy this rig?" McGarvey asked the delivery skipper.

"Not my area of expertise, I'm just a pilot. Maybe if you had a couple of fighter aircraft, drop some bombs, but even something like that might not do much of anything but superficial damage unless the bombs were very big. Of course, if we were pumping oil a stick or two of dynamite would start a fire. Still might not sink the rig. But why would anyone want to do such a thing? Where's the gain for them?"

"Some people might want to stop Dr. Larsen's project," McGarvey said, and he watched the light turn on in Lapides's eyes.

"You're talking about oil people," he said. "Could make some sense if InterOil hadn't donated this platform, and wasn't paying for its conversion and delivery. But the company has made a sizeable investment here, and they're going to want something in return. At least that's the way I always thought business was supposed to work."

"It could be nothing."

Lapides was troubled. "But you wouldn't have come out here to warn us if you didn't think so." He shrugged. "Justin's right, we're not going to put our people at risk. It's not our project. Maybe you should hire private contractors to come aboard if the Coast Guard won't help. With a few guns on board it would be pretty tough to hijack something this large."

"I thought about it," McGarvey said. "But I don't want to call attention to what might happen. I just want to make sure that the platform ends up offshore from Hutchinson Island and that no one gets hurt. I'm here for your protection."

"One man?"

"I'll have some help."

Defloria came back, looking a little angry and perplexed, and even more troubled than Lapides. He stood for a moment in deep thought, before he pocketed his sat phone and sat down. "The company thinks that it's a possibility some of Jerry Schlagel's people might stage a protest, but we're not in any real danger. At least not of the sort that Mr. McGarvey's talking about."

"So we stay," Lapides said.

"Spencer said the company spoke with people at the DOE, Commerce and the Coast Guard who gave us the green light," Defloria told him. He turned to McGarvey. "They were frankly surprised that you were here."

Those instructions had probably come either from Page or from the White House, who were willing to go along with the suggestion that if an attack on the rig were planned by the same contractor who'd hit Hutchinson Island he wouldn't go ahead in the face of a show of force. Eve's worst-case scenario that she would have to hire contractors 24/7 to secure her experiment might become fact. But if he was lured into hitting Vanessa while she was en route to Florida, the danger—at least from that source—could be eliminated within the next week to ten days, maybe sooner.

And if that were to happen, Mac figured he would have a real shot at finding out who'd hired the operator and why.

"We're back to square one," he said. "How do we destroy this rig?"

"A half ton of dynamite, I suppose," Defloria said. "Hurt it so badly that there'd be nothing left that was worth rebuilding. And I doubt if the company would be willing to supply Dr. Larsen with another platform."

"I don't mean hurt it," McGarvey said. "I mean how do we send it to the bottom of the Gulf with all hands aboard?"

Defloria spread his hands, and shook his head. "I've never thought about it."

"What's the most vulnerable structure aboard? The legs?"

"If you released the high-pressure air and punched holes below the waterline, they'd flood, and the platform would settle to the surface. If a big sea was running, the waves would do a lot of damage, but the platform would probably still float."

"At least long enough for us to get everybody into the lifeboats," Lapides said.

They weren't thinking like terrorists bent on destroying the rig, they were engineers working out how to save it. But McGarvey saw it. "What if we destroyed any two adjacent legs?"

Defloria was thinking about it now, really thinking, and the conclusions he was drawing were extremely disturbing. He looked like a man who was lost, and was just beginning to realize it. "And you're here to protect us?" he mumbled.

"You have to think like them."

"Like who?" Defloria asked. He was angry but intimidated.

"Would it sink?"

"The platform would capsize. But it might not sink right away, not until the compartments in the superstructure flooded out. And even then there might be enough reserve buoyancy in the empty oil storage tanks and tool lockers to keep us afloat. But what would you do with the crew? Some of them would probably survive. Or would they be murdered?"

"Is there a space that could be sealed that's big enough to hold everybody?" McGarvey asked.

"The crew's mess," Lapides said.

"More reserve buoyancy," Defloria said, but he looked sick.

"Could it be flooded?"

Defloria took a moment before he answered. "What kind of people are you talking about? Islamic terrorists? Nine/eleven fanatics, willing to die for the cause? I mean, this is nuts, isn't it? Completely crazy?"

Both he and Lapides were trying not to understand what McGarvey was asking for, it was perfectly clear from how they looked at him, and yet they knew. And it was obvious that they knew.

"Two hatches, one from the main corridor and the other through the kitchen to the loading area at the rail," Lapides said. "They could be spot-welded in place. And when Vanessa turned turtle the ventilation shafts would be underwater."

"Could someone swim out?"

"Too far," Defloria said. "And besides, the water would be rushing in. It would be like trying to swim against the stream of a fire hose." He shook his head again. "They'd all die in there."

"Anything else?" McGarvey asked.

"It would have to be done from aboard the platform. Unless they had a sub and fired a couple of torpedoes, it would be just about impossible to get close enough to plant explosives if there was even a small sea running."

"When do you get under way?" McGarvey asked.

"We're about done here, everything else we can finish en route," Defloria said. "The tug will be heading out to us tomorrow, and Dr. Larsen has her news conference on Thursday. When that's done we can get under way."

McGarvey hadn't been told, but it was about what he should have expected. Eve and her people couldn't think like a terrorist any more than Defloria or Lapides could. "I didn't know about the media being here," he said.

"It was the company's idea. Is there a problem?"

McGarvey shook his head. "No." On the contrary, he thought, because it was possible that his contractor would come aboard to look things over, and he had to suppress a little smile. Maybe the bastard would make a mistake after all.

Defloria gave McGarvey a hard hat and walked with him through the main pipe and cable corridor along the back of the platform directly beneath the superstructure. The sound of the wind was muted, but each time a wave broke against the windward legs the entire rig shuddered a little, and the racket of metal crashing on metal, of welding torches and cutting tools and the two large lifting cranes was practically deafening, so they had to shout to be heard.

"You don't paint a pretty picture."

"It's just a precaution," McGarvey said.

Defloria was angry. "The thing I don't get is why everyone is willing to risk our lives? It makes no sense. Are we being used as bait?"

McGarvey wanted to tell him that there were bigger issues at stake, that the attack on Hutchinson Island, the assassination attempt in Oslo, and possibly one against this rig, were only three parts of something much larger. As long as oil was being pumped out of the ground and used as a major source of the world's energy, experiments like Eve Larsen's had to be stopped. Trillions of dollars were at stake.

But Defloria's questions had been rhetorical, and he pointed out a hatch at the end of the corridor. "Five flights up."

"You're not in this alone," McGarvey said.

Defloria's eyes were hard. "Somehow that doesn't give me much comfort. And what do I tell my crew?"

"Nothing for the moment."

When McGarvey reached Eve's lab on the fifth level the expansive space with wraparound windows was a beehive of frenetic activity. Most of the techs and postdocs were dressed in jeans and GFDL or NOAA sweatshirts, a few in khakis, and Don Price in white coveralls, and they were unpacking electronic equipment from the boxes and crates and aluminum cases and installing all of it in racks, or on four computer consoles that formed a broad U. Don was the first to spot him at the doorway. "He's here," he said.

Eve, who'd been on her hands and knees behind one of the consoles got to her feet, the look of happiness, total joy, and contentment, maybe even a little excitement, dying a little when she saw him. She too was dressed in white coveralls, the knees dirty from crawling around on the deck.

Some of the others had stopped what they were doing to look at the former CIA director who had twice been there to protect their scientist, most of them with curiosity, but a few of them, Don Price included, with resentment and perhaps fear.

"Okay, listen up," Eve said, coming around the console and laying down a screwdriver. "And that includes you, Lisa."

A few of her techs chuckled, but they stopped what they were doing.

"For those of you who don't know this gentleman, his name is Kirk McGarvey, the former director of the Central Intelligence Agency, who has been of some service to me. He's here to help with security and I'd like you to listen to what he has to say."

"You're busy, so I'll only take a couple of minutes," McGarvey said. "It's likely that the Reverend Schlagel and some of his followers will stage some sort of a Greenpeace-type demonstration against your project."

"The hell with them," someone said.

"They might even try to get in our way, somehow stop us from reaching Florida. But I don't think they'll be very effective. This platform is just too big."

"Will they try to board us?" a young woman who'd been working at one of the computer consoles asked. "Like the Somali pirates?"

"Not them," McGarvey said, and it took several beats for the real meaning of what he'd just told them and its implications to sink in.

Don Price started to protest, but Eve touched his sleeve. "Continue," she said.

"We believe that there are people other than some religious fanatics who don't want this platform to reach Florida. They want to see your experiment fail."

"What people?" Don demanded, his anger spilling over.

"We don't know for sure," McGarvey said. "But it's possible they're the same ones who attacked the Hutchinson Island reactor."

"Speculation," Don fumed, and Eve didn't stop him from voicing his opinion. "What proof do you have?"

"None," McGarvey admitted. "But I'm hitching a ride with you across the Gulf just in case something does develop. I wanted you to know who I was and why I'm here."

"So now we know," Don said. "Just get the hell out of here, we have a lot of work to do."

"Could I have a word with you?" McGarvey asked Eve.

And before Don could object, she nodded and went with McGarvey out into the narrow space at the head of the steel stairs.

"Sorry about Don. He can be overbearing sometimes."

"Don't worry about it," McGarvey said. "I'm interested in your news conference the day after tomorrow."

"Interested or concerned?"

"Interested. Do you have list of the media people coming out?"

"No. InterOil set it up, and it was an offer I couldn't refuse," Eve said. "Should I be worried?"

And what was the answer? McGarvey wondered. By his nature he was, if not a worrier, a man who paid very strong attention to the details. Especially the ones he had no direct control over.

He smiled. "No, that's my job, remember?"

Her smile was a little less certain, but she nodded. "You're leaving now?"

"Yes. But I'll be back in time for your news conference."

FORTY-EIGHT

McGarvey went back to Washington, calling Rencke on his sat phone before boarding the commercial flight at Biloxi-Gulfport Airport to find out the latest in the search for the contractor. "This guy doesn't exist," Otto said, and he sounded frustrated.

"But we know he does."

"Yeah," Rencke had said. "Maybe I'm getting too old for this shit."

"He's had years to devise his cover, but you've only had a couple of months to break it," McGarvey said.

He'd spent a good deal of time over those same weeks trying to think like their contractor, trying to get inside the man's head, trying to figure out what motivated him, trying to work out his background, and the direction he was headed—had likely always headed. And he had come to a few conclusions, actually just probabilities, based on the notion: If I were in his business, what would I do? Where would I live? How would my life be structured?

"He probably doesn't live in the States," he said.

"Eric thinks so too, but we don't have any indicators," Rencke said.

"Just bear with me. If he lived here he might have made mistakes. He'd likely to be in some database somewhere. City taxes, car registration, something. The only reason I think that he doesn't live here is because he killed a teacher in San Francisco for an identity to get into the power plant."

"He wouldn't crap in his own nest."

"Something like that. So where does he live?" McGarvey asked. "Not in some Third World country. He's doing this work for what's probably a great deal of money, which means he likes his comforts."

"I'm working Switzerland, the Channel Islands, the Caymans, honest injun."

"Let's forget the money trail for a moment. Gail said the clerk at the

Southern Power reception desk told her that the man had an English accent, but not Australian. Right now South Africa seems the most likely."

"I've come up with nothing from SADF records."

"Computer records," McGarvey said. "I'm betting that this guy got out of the service *before* the South African military went digital."

"Shit," Rencke said. "Good point, Mac. I wasn't thinking."

"So where would a guy like that go to ground? Someplace civilized."

"Europe," Rencke said. "With the immigrant problem, a Westerner with culture and money would get no hassles from the local authorities. Long as he kept his nose clean no one would give him a second look. Switzerland, Germany, France."

"Maybe France," McGarvey said. "It'd be easy to get lost in Paris."

"It's a start," Rencke said. "But there'd have to be more."

"A woman. He wouldn't live alone."

"She'd leave no traces."

"She might if she were bored," McGarvey said.

And Rencke saw it all at once, his frustration giving way to excitement. "Oh, wow, kemo sabe, you're right. When this guy is at home, he's really at home. With his lady twenty-four/seven. But when he gets an assignment he'd have to drop out of sight for a week or two, maybe for months at a time, and she would get bored. She'd want to do something to keep from going crazy."

"He would have warned her against getting too friendly, so whatever it is she does for pleasure will have to be very low-key. Maybe a garden club, maybe a tour guide or museum docent. If it's Paris there'd have to be hundreds, probably thousands of such women."

"Who don't socialize."

"It's a start."

"I'm on it," Rencke said. "In the meantime have you found anything useful down there?"

"I think I know how he means to sabotage the rig, but he'll have to get aboard to do it, and he'll need some help."

"When are they heading out?"

"Probably by the weekend, but they're holding a news conference the day after tomorrow, on InterOil's suggestion. See if you can come up with a list of who'll be there."

And Rencke saw that, too. "You think that he's going to try to get aboard. Reconnoiter?"

"It's something I might try."

"Do you think it'd be worth the risk?"

McGarvey had thought about that too on the way back from the oil rig. There'd be only one reason for the man to take such a gamble, and that would in part depend on inside knowledge. "If the company plans on giving the media a guided tour he'd have to try it."

"That'd mean someone at InterOil was feeding him information."

"Find out what you can, but especially the names of everyone invited. And I want them vetted, all of them, including the cameramen and anyone else in the group."

"I'm on it," Rencke said.

McGarvey found that it was impossible to relax on the flight up to Washington. He couldn't get out of his mind how vulnerable even something so large as an oil exploration platform was. A few kilos of well-placed Semtex as shaped charges on two legs would do the job, and once they exploded nothing could stop the platform from capsizing and ending up on the bottom of the Gulf.

A couple of operators could easily handle that task in fifteen minutes or less. In the meantime three or four others would round up the crew and technicians and herd them into the mess. But the biggest problem would be finding and destroying the oil rig's single sideband radio used for communications with the company before a Mayday could be transmitted. Sat phones would present another problem, as would the crew and communications equipment aboard the tug.

And it came to him that he'd missed something obvious, something beyond the possibility that the contractor would be coming aboard with the media; in fact the man might have no need to take such a risk, not if he'd already managed to place one of his operators aboard. Probably as a deckhand. Someone who had worked on an oil rig at some point in his career.

It was late by the time he got back to Washington and cabbed it to his apartment in Georgetown, and he would forever remember that at this point he'd become a man in a hurry, and in some ways a man worried that he had been forgetting something important that could get a lot of people killed.

Gail was in bed, but not asleep when he let himself in, and she got up, a shy expression in her eyes on her face, as if she was worried that he'd brought her bad news. She was wearing one of his shirts. "How'd it go?" she asked.

"I found out how they're going to sink the platform, but we might have caught a break," McGarvey said, putting down his bag. And he knew just by looking at her what she was thinking and why, but he didn't want to go there, not yet. "We're flying down tomorrow afternoon. Can you be ready by then?"

"I'm packed," she said, and she seemed to relax a little. "Why don't you take a shower while I fix you something to eat, and we can talk."

And McGarvey hesitated, wondering for just that moment what he felt about her, or if in fact he'd redeveloped the ability to feel something about anyone after his wife's assassination. Too soon, he wanted to say, and he wanted to turn around and walk out. But in the end he couldn't.

He went to her and took her in his arms. "After tonight we're going to become a couple of professionals with a job to do. Nothing more. Understood?"

Gail nodded.

"I'll take a shower, but forget the kitchen. Deal?"

"Deal," she said happily.

"We can talk in the morning on the way down to the Farm."

John Nowak, the new commandant of the CIA's training facility at Camp Peary on the York River near Williamsburg, Virginia, was expecting McGarvey and had an escort at the main gate waiting to bring him and Gail down to the office. His was a new face to McGarvey, but according to Otto, morale at the Farm, which had taken a dive when Todd Van Buren and his wife Elizabeth were assassinated, was recovering.

He was a short, rotund man in his late forties or early fifties, with a red jowly face and a broad smile; he was a man who obviously enjoyed what he was doing, and when McGarvey and Gail got out of the Porsche

SUV he came out and dismissed the young officer in training escort, and shook their hands.

"This is a great pleasure finally getting to meet you, Mr. Director," he said effusively. He was dressed in camos, his boots bloused, a Beretta holstered across his chest. And his boots looked scuffed, well worn. Otto had said that appearances to the contrary Nowak could easily keep up with the youngest trainees; he'd been a top sergeant with the army's Delta Force. "Mr. Rencke told me what you folks were in need of and we have everything ready for you. It just wants your approval before we pack."

"Transportation?" McGarvey asked. He wanted to like the man, but it was difficult. The only reason the Farm had a new commandant was because Todd and Liz were dead.

"One of our Gulfstreams is standing by to get you and your gear down to Biloxi. We'll keep your car here for the duration, if that's okay with you. Or I can have someone take it wherever you'd like."

"Here is fine," McGarvey said.

He and Gail followed Nowak across the commons to a low brick building that served as the Farm's armory and primary inspection center for new weapons sent down from Langley for field evals as well as a repair depot for everything the recruits misused or destroyed. Everything from Knight Armament Company personal defense weapons to Wilson and Rohrbaugh sidearms, to Colt Commandos, Sterling silenced submachineguns, MAC-10s, Steyr AUG 9mm paras, and especially AK-47s in a variety of configurations, plus at any given time a number of exotic weapons, most of which didn't stand up to field trials.

"Mr. Rencke was quite specific that you wanted only the simplest, most tested equipment, including a variety of flash-bang grenades—we'll give you a half-dozen Haley and Weller E182s, old but proven—along with a few small bricks of Semtex with a variety of fuses, night-vision oculars for each of you, our new body armor—a lot lighter and more flexible than the standard Kevlar vests, yet capable of stopping most armor-penetrating projectiles fired from handheld weapons—a pair of thermal imagers, plus our new EQ high-frequency comms units, which should work well in the environment you'll be operating in."

"What about weapons?" Gail asked.

"We'll leave that up to you, but for reliability I don't think you can get too far off the mark with the standard Beretta 92F for a sidearm, and for a close-in balls-to-the-wall firefight, the Franchi SPAS-12 automatic shotgun."

"Weight will be an issue," Gail said.

"Can't help with the ammunition, but we've managed to shave a considerable amount of weight from any weapon you might chose," Nowak said. "But if you'll pardon me saying, ma'am, I believe you can handle yourself. I know about your father. He was a good man in a bad situation."

Gail asked how he knew.

"I do my research. Like to know something about the people I'm sending into the field."

Jeane Davis, a petite woman with large brown eyes and long chestnut hair up in a bun, worked as the chief armorer for the camp, and she was ready for them. Like Nowak she was new since Todd and Liz, and like Nowak she had a ready smile and pleasant demeanor.

"I'm told that you've switched back to your Walther, in the nine millimeter version," she told McGarvey. "Not much stopping power, but then I've learned that you prefer the head shot, so caliber isn't so important. Will you be sticking with that weapon for this op?"

"Unless you have another suggestion."

"No," she said. "Ms. Newby, what's your preference?"

"I'll take the SIG P226," Gail said. "I've used it before."

"Not my choice, but it's a fine weapon," Jeane said. "All your equipment will be completely untraceable, so if the need arises you may safely drop your gear in place and run."

"Sounds good."

"Questions?"

"No," McGarvey said, and his cell phone rang. It was Otto, and he stepped outside to take the call. "What do you have for me?"

"Twenty-one people in all for the news conference—four networks including Fox, their cameramen, actually one woman, *Time, Scientific American, Smithsonian,* plus three photographers and five newspapers, including *The New York Times, The Washington Post, The Los Angeles Times,* and five foreign papers, two from the UK, one German, one Japanese, one French, and the Mexican wire service Notimex."

"Have you had time to check them out?"

"They're all clean, Mac. I'm sending your sat phone a précis of their jackets along with photographs. A couple of them, especially Marcel Allain from *Le Figaro*, could be a fair match with our contractor, as far as size and general build go, but all of them have rock-solid backgrounds. I shit you not, it doesn't look like our guy is on the list."

FORTY-NINE

By noon they were flying southwest toward Mississippi aboard one of the CIA's Gulfstream G550s, with a crew of three including a young attendant named Melissa who served them Bloody Marys before a lunch of lobster salad with French bread and a good Pinot Grigio. Afterwards she left them alone, seated across a cocktail table from each other looking at the information and photos Rencke had sent to McGarvey's sat phone.

Had the information come to them from anyone other than Otto, McGarvey would have questioned the validity of the material. And as it was, Otto had sent the list of names to Eric Yablonski who'd independently come up with the same background information and the same photos

"Only two real possibilities," Gail said. "The French guy from *Le Figaro*, and the Mexican from Notimex. Same general build, but darker skin."

"That could be fixed," McGarvey said distantly. Even if their contractor had managed to place one or more of his operators aboard Vanessa he'd still want to take a look for himself. At the very least his ego would demand it. He was a man who paid attention to details, which was why he'd never been caught. And the more McGarvey thought about him, the more respect he had.

Gail looked up from the images on the sat phone screen. "What?"

"He's coming."

"Are you sure?"

McGarvey nodded. "Yeah, one way or the other he'll be in this group. Or maybe as a last-minute addition. But he'll need to see the rig with his own eyes."

"He could have people aboard," Gail suggested. It was a technique he'd drummed into the heads of everyone he'd trained for NNSA field-work. Anytime an idea was floated it was the duty of everyone to try to shoot it down. Find the weak points, find the flaws, find the improbables, come up with what in the aircraft design and construction industry had always been called the *unk-unks*, the unknown unknowns. The problems that no one had foreseen, the ones that unexpectedly cropped up out of nowhere to blindside everyone involved.

McGarvey picked up the intercom phone and called the flight deck. "I need to make a sat phone call."

"Go right ahead, Mr. Director," the pilot told him.

Otto answered on the first ring. "I was just about to send you tomorrow's schedule."

"Will they be taken on a guided tour of the rig?" McGarvey asked.

"Yup, just like you suspected, right after Eve Larsen briefs them on her project these guys will get to see everything."

"What else?" McGarvy asked. He was looking for something, an opening that he could use to get close to the media people. The point at which they would have gotten what they'd come for and would be the most relaxed.

"A champagne reception on the main deck for everyone, scientists and crew," Rencke said. "Sort of a send-off party. All the media should be gone no later than four, and the rig under tow first thing in the morning."

"Anything from Schalgel and his people?"

"I was going to call you about that, too. He'll be on *Fox and Friends* in the morning. They're calling it a major announcement in his war against the God Project."

"Good. As long as he stays out in the open we don't have to worry about him," McGarvey said.

"Wrong answer, Mac. He'll be making his speech live from Biloxi."

"Is he going to try to get aboard?" McGarvey demanded.

"He hasn't said. But I did some checking on marinas from New Orleans to Panama City, and just about anything that floats and is capable to crossing the Gulf has been chartered, starting tomorrow morning."

"Under the name of his church?"

"Individuals, some of them local charter boat and shrimp skippers. You'll have company."

It was about what McGarvey had expected. "It'll just be background noise. They can't stop the rig."

"What if our contractor and maybe some of his operators are aboard one of the boats?"

"He wouldn't risk making an attack out in the open among all those witnesses. He still has to get aboard the rig. And when he does we'll have him."

"Alive if possible, kemo sabe," Rencke said. "We need to know who hired him."

"We know who hired him," McGarvey said. "We just need the proof."

One of Defloria's crew met them with hard hats at the helicopter and brought them across to the main living quarters, which were on the opposite corner of the platform from where Eve had set up her lab and monitoring station. Rising five levels above the main deck the superstructure looked more like an afterthought than a planned part of the overall structure, more like a series of Lego models stacked in an array that staggered outward over the edge with iron balconies, catwalks, and stairs. The wind wasn't as strong today, and much of the main deck had been cleared of its oil exploration equipment and workmen, but any offshore oil platform was an inherently dangerous environment. Accidents could and did happen nearly every day, and deaths were not unkown.

They'd been given separate but connecting suites each large enough to accommodate a queen-sized bed, a sitting area with a small couch, a pair of chairs and a coffee table, plus a desk with a computer connection routed to a satellite dish. The view from their large windows was out across the Gulf, dozens of oil platforms dotting the horizon. Each of them had their own tiny bathroom, fully equipped with soaps, sham-poos, shaving gear, towels, even a hair dryer and toothpaste and tooth-brush.

Three pairs of white coveralls had been laid out along with a pair of sneakers and a pair of steel-toed work shoes, all in the correct sizes.

When they'd stowed their gear, Gail knocked on the connecting door and McGarvey let her in. She'd found a generalized floor plan of the en-tire platform, and she spread it out on the coffee table. "This place is a nightmare," she said. "Hundreds of places to hide in ambush to pick us off one by one."

McGarvey had seen it the other day when he'd come aboard for the first time. But they only had to concentrate on the four legs, somewhere just beneath the lowest work deck and the waterline. And no matter what happened they had to remain alive and uncaptured. "Works both ways," he said.

And she glanced again at the floor plan and nodded. "I see your point, but there's only two of us, and no way of predicting how many they'll be."

"Maybe a half dozen. A couple to take care of the communications equipment, or at least the satelite dishes. A couple to kill or round up the crew and Eve's people, and a couple more to set the explosives on two of the legs."

"What about the tug?"

"I think that once he has everything in hand here, he'll send a boat across and kill the crew. When the rig capsizes and goes down, it might take the tug with it."

"Will he spread himself that thin?" Gail asked. "The man is a pro."

"Just him and one other at Hutchinson Island," McGarvey said.

"The bastard has a plan which he thinks is foolproof," Gail said bit-terly. She still felt responsible for the attack.

"Indeed he does," McGarvey said.

Someone knocked at McGarvey's door, and it was Defloria. "I was told that you were aboard," he said, eyeing the several aluminum cases stacked by the closet door. It was the CIA equipment, weapons, and ammunition from the Farm. "I brought you the personnel list and files you asked for. Three new ones came aboard this morning. Company hires."

McGarvey took the file, and introduced Gail. "Additional crew or replacements?"

Defloria seemed uncomfortable. "Replacements, actually. Three of my people supposedly got into it with a couple of the scientists yesterday, over what I don't know, but my guys denied getting into any trouble. Didn't matter, this is Dr. Larsen's rig. I'm just the OIM and I do whatever the company tells me to do."

"What about their employment histories?" Gail asked.

"Solid."

"Who did they have trouble with?"

"I'm not sure," Defloria said. "But from the way I get it, they apparently screwed up something with a pair of sensors that Dr. Price had been working on." He shrugged. "That doesn't matter either. We have three new people, and it's going to be up to me and Al to keep the peace around here."

"I know Don Price, and I'll see what I can do," McGarvey promised. "Are we listed on the rig's complement?"

"Security hired by the company," Defloria said. "None of my people know any differently, so you won't get any static."

"Will any of them recognize me?"

"These guys watch television, but mostly sports and the Playboy channel."

"What about communications equipment?" Gail asked. "What's aboard and where is it?"

"If you mean internally, there're the platform's interphones, and walkie-talkies. For rig to shore, our primary link is via satellite—works with the phones as well as the computers—plus we have a dedicated data system that automatically transmits information back to Baton Rouge."

"How many satellite dishes?"

"Just the one, plus the dish Dr. Larsen's people set up. They're both atop the control room."

"Sat phones?" Gail asked.

"Al and I share one," Defloria said.

"Where is it kept most of the time?"

"On Al's belt, unless it's in the charger in his quarters," Defloria said tightly. "What're you trying to tell me? That we're definitely going to get attacked and the first thing they'll try to knock out are our links to shore?"

"Just taking inventory," McGarvey told him. "What about communications with the tug?"

"Normal VHF intership safety on channel six, or if that's busy we switch to eight. And there must be a half dozen or more handhelds aboard."

"Lifeboats?"

"Enough for sixty people, slide launched from A deck. All of them equipped with emergency locator beacons, rations for ten days, and portable water makers." Defloria shook his head. "I don't think I want to know about any of this, but I suppose I must. May I share it with Al?"

McGarvey nodded. "But no one else. Especially not Dr. Larsen or her people. We'll take care of that."

Defloria wanted to argue, McGarvey could see it in his impatience. Vanessa Explorer was his rig until Florida, but he'd been told that he was no longer in charge—by the company two days ago and again here and now. "What else?" he asked instead.

"We're probably going to have an escort," McGarvey said. "Schlagel's people. And from what we're seeing they'll probably be an impressive flotilla."

"Should I be worried?"

"Not very," McGarvey said. "And not yet."

"How many crew aboard the tug?" Gail asked.

"Captain Andresen, his first and second officers—who split the watch—and two deckhands."

"Have you worked with them before?"

"No, but Andresen has a good reputation in the business. His last job was towing one of our rigs across the North Sea in some pretty bad weather. He knows what he's doing. Should he be warned that something might be coming our way?"

"Tell him about Jerry Schlagel," McGarvey said.

Clearly unhappy, Defloria nodded tightly and turned to leave, but at the door he hesitated. "Who the hell would want to hurt us? Environmentalists afraid that we're going to wreck Florida's beaches? We're not going to drill for oil, don't they understand?"

"It's not the rig, they're afraid of. It's Dr. Larsen's project."

Defloria nodded again and left.

McGarvey scanned the personnel files Defloria had given him and sent them to Rencke, who came back in less than ten minutes. "All of them old hands in the business. A couple of troublemakers—the get drunk and brawl sort—but no real badasses, Mac."

"At least one of them belongs to our contractor," McGarvey said.

"Eric and I will keep checking," Rencke promised. "But honest injun, Mac, I feel really bad about this. It's like I've dropped back into the Stone Age."

"You haven't and that's the problem. Our contractor is very careful how he uses the Internet, and so do the people who hired him. They share most of their information face-to-face, something that's just about impossible to hack into unless you're right there when they meet."

"No one can live without a computer," Rencke said. "He's left a trace somewhere, and I'll find it."

"Still nothing?" Gail asked.

"No," McGarvey said. "But someone's aboard who works for our contractor, so from this point on neither of us goes anywhere unarmed or without our comms units."

"What's our first move?"

"I want to take a look at the satellite dishes, see just how vulnerable they are, and then the legs, figure out what it would take to destroy them."

"What about Dr. Larsen and her merry band?"

"We'll jump that hurdle in the morning, because I think that before the media people arrive at noon, Schalgel's flotilla will be out here and I think that when her people, especially Price, sees what we're up against, they might have second thoughts about ignoring us."

Gail went to her room to get her pistol and comms unit, leaving McGarvey to stare out the window at the oil rigs in the distance. The last century had really been all about oil, the technologies that used it, the countries that had become superdependent on it and the people and governments who'd made trillions of dollars, and wanted very much to guard the status quo. The problem was that the list of everyone who had a finger in the pie, everyone who had a stake in the game, everyone who had something to lose, some terrible price to pay was, if not endless, nearly so. And therein lay the problem. The enemy base was so broad, so far-reaching that there was no practical way of defending places like Hutchinson Island, or experiments like Eve's aboard Vanessa Explorer.

Right after 9/11, Seceretary of Defense Don Rumsfeld told a group of journalists, who wanted to know how such a thing could have happened, that our entire nuclear arsenal had been of no use to us. This was a different sort of war and different ways of defense were needed. Problem was, no one had figured that out yet.

FIFTY

McGarvey and Gail spent a couple of hours poking around the rig, checking the two satellite dishes on the roof of the control center, access to which was ridiculously easy, either through a pair of corridors and up one flight of stairs or outside up stairs attached to the side of the super-structure like fire escapes. And getting to the legs beneath the lowest deck was nearly as simple. The platform was just too big and too compli-cated to easily defend, nor had it been designed to withstand an attack.

Standing at the south edge of the main deck, looking at the massive oceangoing tug, *Tony Ryan,* Gail brought up her earlier point. "What about the tug's crew? At the first sign of trouble up here, her skipper is going to call for help. And it's going to get hell of lot more complicated when Schlagel's people show up in force."

"There'll be a lot of confusion," McGarvey said. The huge cable har-ness connecting the tug to Vanessa was slack. But when the platform was actually under tow a tremendous strain would be taken up and any small boat that happened to stray anywhere near would be in serious trouble. If something like that were to happen, especially late at night, or very early in the morning before dawn, it wouldn't matter what was going on aboard the rig, the tug's crew would be engaged in a rescue operation.

"Do you think Schlagel is a part of this?"

McGarvey had considered it, and there were plenty of reasons for such an alliance to be possible, chief among them the reverend's bid for the Democratic Party's presidential nomination in two years. He was, in his own words: "The architect of the new back-to-fundamentals program that made this country great in the first place."

"I don't think he or his people would be so stupid to be a part of the attack, but they'd make great witnesses. When this platform went to the bottom he'd be able to say 'I told you so.'"

Gail looked at him, a wry expression on her lips. "You don't watch enough television to know how popular Schlagel has become since Hutchinson Island. People are frightened that things are going to be taken away from them by a power or powers they can't understand. Everyone's afraid of nuclear war and yet rich corporations want to keep building nuclear power plants. It's tough enough as it is to make a decent living, yet the same corporations give their CEOs multimillion-dollar bonuses. It's obscene. Gas prices keep going up, health care costs are bankrupting the country, but nothing is being done. Essentially it's the lobbyists who're running everything. And we're selling our souls to the Saudis for oil and sending all of our manufacturing jobs to China."

"It's the world we live in," McGarvey said, not meaning to sound as callous as that. But it was the truth.

"Yes, and it's a world that we made," Gail said passionately. "We're either a part of the problem or a part of the solution, and our hands aren't clean, Kirk."

"Mine especially," McGarvey said, a flood of dark memories overtaking him. He looked at her. "But we're not going to turn away from this. The Coast Guard's not along for the ride because no one wants to piss off big oil, especially the Saudis and the rest of OPEC, and no one wants to get in the way of the handful of heavy hitters making big money with derivative funds and credit default swaps."

"They buy the lobbyists."

"That's only a part of it. These people fund armies, insurgents, soldiers for God, al-Quaeda, Hamas, the Muslim Brotherhood, Hizballah, al Muhajiroun, Jamat e-Islami. The list goes on. Nuclear research in Iran, North Korea, and Pakistan. We're in a war, and have been since the eighties, and certainly since Nine/eleven. Not about religious freedom, not about territory, but about oil and money and power. And the jury's still out."

"We'll end up a second-class country," Gail said bleakly.

"It's certainly possible, unless we can give the Eve Larsens of the world the time to change the tide."

They had dinner in the practically deserted mess hall one level up from the main deck. Oil rigs were usually worked around the clock, and the kitchen was always open. Oil men in general had large appetites, and when they were hungry they expected to be fed. None of Eve's people were there. "It's not just the Eve Larsens, it's the nuclear people, too," Gail said. "There're thirty applications for new generating stations, and even if every one of them were to be approved today not one kilowatt of power would be produced for at least ten years, and probably longer."

"We can't wait that long."

"I worked at Hutchinson Island long enough to understand that we're facing a crisis right now, and no one knows exactly what to do about it. Everything's so fabulously expensive that it's almost impossible to make any sort of a decision for fear of losing billions of dollars."

"If Schlagel gets his way, and it looks like he might, nukes will be out. Which brings us back to Eve Larsen's project."

"We can't let it fail," Gail said with some passion. She did not want to be on the losing end of an operation twice in a row. "But it makes you wonder about Washington, and what sort of collusions are going on."

Have always been going on, McGarvey wanted to say, but he didn't.

Schlagel's God's Flotilla, as Fox News was dubbing it, started arriving at the platform just after dawn. At first only a pair of shrimp boats, but by eight in the morning dozens of boats, some of them as large as the 120-foot ex-Japanese fish factory ship now named the *Pascagoula Trader*, refitted three years ago, according to Rencke, as a private yacht belonging to the Reverend Wilfred Sampson, head of the Mississippi-Alabama Baptist Alliance. A small Bell Jet Ranger helicopter was tied down on an afterdeck.

The media was scheduled to arrive aboard an InterOil chopper from Biloxi at noon, something apparently whoever was in charge of the flotilla knew, because the boats merely circled the platform and its tug, giving both a wide berth, making no attempt to interfere or create a problem. That wouldn't happen until the cameras were pointed in their direction. Schlagel's machine was slick and professional.

McGarvey and Gail had walked over to the superstructure that housed Eve Larsen's lab and operations center and stood outside on one of the lower-level balconies just above the main deck to watch the gathering fleet, still more boats showing up on the northern horizon.

"Your lady scientist knew this was going to happen, but seeing it now like this can't make her very happy," Gail said. "She won't be able to ignore us."

"It's not so much her, she came to me for help in the first place. It's her assistant, Don Price. He's in love with her."

"Oh, Jesus," Gail said. "And you're her Sir Galahad who's come to rain on his parade."

"Might be more than that," McGarvey said. Rencke had vetted Eve's people too, and they'd all cleared with flying colors, including Price who held two Ph.D.s, one from M.I.T. in ocean science and engineering and the other from Princeton in oceanography. His paper on the origins of the Gulf Stream and how it controlled climate was, according to Otto, nothing short of stunning, groundbreaking.

"The guy's probably an asshole," Rencke had reported after Oslo. "But he's a smart asshole and from what I can tell one hundred percent devoted to Larsen and her project, even though he could have had his own lab and funding by now."

"What does he want?" McGarvey had asked. He'd been fishing, because he had nothing solid to go on, only intuition.

"Reflected glory," Rencke was quick to suggest. "His boss got the Nobel Prize and he was the number two man on her team. Part of the credit goes to him. Pretty good paragraph on a résumé."

McGarvey still wasn't sure about Price, but it was nothing he could put his finger on. No solid reason for mistrust, only mutual dislike.

"Let's go up and introduce you and let them know how we're going to handle today and the rest of the trip," McGarvey said, and he started to turn toward the door, but Gail put a hand on his arm.

"I just had a thought," she said. "All these media types, unless they're just kids, are going to know your face, and they're going to want to know why you're aboard, right?"

"So what?"

"No use advertising why you're here. You went up against Schlagel's people in New York, and you were there in Oslo, so if your name pops up again he'll probably think you've targeted him. But our contractor will know better. So why don't we keep you in reserve, as a sort of a nasty surprise?"

"I want to see exactly what the media people are shown, and I want to know if any of them takes a particular interest in anything, especially the communications equipment and the legs."

"I can do that," Gail said. "Otherwise why did you bring me along? Let me earn my pay."

It was penance for her self-perceived failure at Hutchinson Island. But she had a point, and McGarvey conceded it. "You'll stay in the rear, but use the EQ, I want to know everything."

"I'll save you some champagne," she said, and she glanced toward the door to the corridor and the stairs up to the control room. "Do you want to introduce me now, or should it wait until we're under way?"

But it was difficult for him. He'd lost some good people in the past, Lundgren at Hutchinson Island, and his family, so that it was hard to let go, hard not to be in the middle of things, in charge, calling the shots. And a part of him, because of his age he supposed and his upbringing by strict fundamentalist parents on the western Kansas plain, made him chauvinistic at times. His first instinct was almost always to open the door for a woman, take her coat, hold her chair, pick up the dinner check. Go into harm's way first.

"Later," he told her. "There won't be any trouble this soon. When it comes it'll be farther out in the Gulf and it'll be late at night or early in the morning before dawn. But watch yourself."

Gail glanced at her watch. "We have a couple of hours, what do you want to do?"

"I want you to find Defloria and tell him that you're going to tag along on the tour, and in the meantime I'm going to check on something."

"Anything I should see, too?"

"I'll let you know," McGarvey said, and he turned and headed back along the corridor to the stairs that led to the lower levels of the platform.

FIFTY-ONE

Kirk McGarvey was cut from a different material than any other man Eve Larsen had ever met, and yet there'd been the brief moment in New York and again in Oslo, where she thought that she'd known him all of her life. In several ways she'd been reminded of her father's strength and unshakable self-assurance that what he was doing, that the direction his life was leading, was correct. And yet, like her father who'd understood his place as a low-paid mill worker, and had accepted his lot in life, even though he didn't like it, there was a sadness in McGarvey's eyes that Eve was familiar and even comfortable with.

Standing at one of the large plate-glass windows looking down at the flotilla—Schlagel's flotilla—that had started gathering three hours ago, she thought about him, and wondered where he was and why he hadn't warned her. He'd come aboard yesterday but she'd been too busy, too excited, even a little overwhelmed by the progress they were making to take much notice until this very moment.

"They're buffoons," Don said at her side.

She looked at him. "Enough of them to easily take over this platform. Even Kirk and whomever he brought with him wouldn't be able to stop them."

Don glared at her. "Those fools out there don't intend to hurt us.

They're making their stupid mumbojumbo fundamentalist points by calling us names. And the only reason they came out here this morning is because of the news conference. I wouldn't be surprised if one of the networks tipped them off. The bastard is gathering sound bites, and once the TV guys are gone, the mob will head home, and we can finally get underway."

She wanted to believe it was that simple. But the incident in Oslo had deeply shaken her, and made her wonder how the situation might have turned out if McGarvey hadn't been there. Jacobsen, who would recover, had taken the bullet for her, but it was McGarvey's fast action, pushing her down to the walkway and covering her body with his, that may have saved her life.

"The man's a magnet for trouble," Don said as if he'd read her mind. "I looked him up online, what little there is that makes any sense involves him in at least a half-dozen incidents in which there was a shooting, and in one case the car bomb a few years ago in Georgetown. Yet he was actually picked to head the CIA—which proved what I've always said about Washington—and we had Nine/eleven."

"There were larger issues than just one man," Eve argued. She was no politician, though it was something she would have to become if her project really did blossom after the Vanessa Explorer experiment, because she was going to need funding—government funding on a very large scale. And neither was Don, politically savvy, even if he believed otherwise. But she felt a surge of affection for him, because he was just trying to be worldly for her sake. An arm around her shoulder to assure her that everything would turn out all right.

The rig's interphone buzzed, and Josh Taylor, a gangly grad-school tech from the U.P. Michigan, picked it up. He was working on his doctoral thesis, under Eve's supervision, on saline variations in the Gulf Stream and their effects on energy distribution among eddy currents compared with industrial- and farm-produced dust concentrations in the atmosphere and their effects on low-pressure systems in the prevailing westerlies across the North American continent. He held up the phone. "For you, Eve."

"Anyway, he's been a help to me," Eve told Don. "So try to be at least civil to him, okay?"

He managed a brief smile. "You're the boss," he said. But it looked like he was angry or maybe just as frightened as she wanted to be, but trying to hide it.

Defloria was on the phone. "The helicopter is twenty minutes out."

"Any last-minute no-shows?" Eve asked.

"No such luck, Doctor. And you can bet that the first questions they're going to ask won't be about your work, but about the circus outside."

"I'm starting to get used to it, but I'll depend on you to answer their questions about the platform."

"No problem," Defloria said. "The reception area has been set up on the main deck in front of the housing superstructure. The wind shifted, so we had to switch sides. We can start and end there, if that's okay with you."

"Just fine," Eve said. "I'll need about ten or fifteen minutes for my opening remarks and initial questions and then we can either come directly up here, or head below."

"We'll start at the top and work our way down," Defloria said. "See you on deck in about fifteen minutes?"

"Yes," Eve said. "Have you seen Mr. McGarvey this morning?"

"No. Would you like me to find him for you?"

"Not necessary," Eve said a little too quickly, and when she hung up she saw Don looking at her.

Defloria's people had set up two dozen folding chairs facing a small podium equipped with a portable PA system out of the wind in the lee of housing. All work aboard the rig, except for normal maintenance, had been suspended for the afternoon, and the platform was eerily quiet so that when Eve came out on deck she heard the heavy chop of the incoming InterOil helicopter from Gulfport.

She had decided to change into clean white coveralls rather than a blazer and the khaki slacks she'd worn for her presentations despite Don's objections.

"You're a good-looking woman. People appreciate it."

"I'm a scientist, not a Rockette," she'd countered, and now glancing up at the control-room windows, she saw her techs watching her, but Don wasn't with them, and she was a little disappointed.

Defloria came out of a hatch with a slightly built and attractive woman and they walked over to where Eve was standing next to the podium. "Don't think you've met," he said, introducing her as Kirk McGarvey's partner at the NNSA. "Ms. Newby will be tagging along for the tour."

They shook hands and Eve got the distinct impression that the woman was carrying a chip on her shoulder; she seemed to be angry about something, but was keeping it just beneath the surface. Her smile was forced.

"I don't think we have," Gail said. "But Kirk has certainly told me a lot about you."

"All of it good, I hope," Eve said in an effort to keep it light. "Will he be joining us?"

"No, Doctor, it'll just be me. And as far as the media is concerned I'm just one of Mr. Defloria's gofers."

"Are you expecting trouble?" Eve asked, but instead of letting her off the hook Gail merely shrugged.

And approaching the platform from the northwest, the InterOil helicopter flared above the landing pad, and they watched as it touched down. Several of Defloria's people were up there to meet the media people, hand them hard hats, and then guide them down to the corridor that led across the rear of the platform.

"Do you want me to introduce you?" Defloria asked.

"No need," Eve said, and although she'd done dozens of these things she was still nervous, her Nobel and the UAEIBC funding notwithstanding. Thankfully this would be her last media event until the Hutchinson Island experiment either succeeded or failed. "The damn thing works," Don's comment aboard the *Big G* had become the team's mantra, and a comfort just now because she felt a little unbalanced that Kirk wouldn't be here. She needed him, and although she knew that she was being irrational about it, she was vexed that he hadn't felt it, hadn't read her mind.

The media people came through the hatch onto the main deck, and Defloria went over to help them around the maze of piping, cabling, and pumps to the reception area out of the wind. At first some of them looked and acted like tourists in white hard hats, rubbernecking the seemingly haphazard superstructures, spindly cranes, and the remnants of the drilling tower. Gail had moved to one side, well away from the podium, trying to be as inconspicuous as possible, just another deckhand or roustabout, and Eve had to smile, because the woman wasn't so bright after all. She stuck out like a sore thumb. Kirk's picking her as his partner was a mystery, and oddly it made her relax a little.

She went to the podium as the television people took light readings, while a couple of the reporters looked at her as if they were examining a bug under a microscope, the same sort of reaction she'd gotten for the past year and a half, maybe more intense now because of the Nobel Prize and because of where they were and why they'd come. The Fox cameraman was panning from left to right across the main deck and then out at Schlagel's flotilla, before turning back in a complete three-sixty until he focused on Eve.

"Anytime you're ready," she said as the reporters settled down.

Lloyd Adams, from ABC, glanced over his shoulder at his cameraman who nodded, and he in turn inclined his head for Eve to begin.

"Thank you for coming out here today for what I think is the first step toward America's energy independence," she began. "An important step. A necessary step."

She and Don had worked on her presentation last night in his cabin, and she felt as if she'd begun on the right note, and she paused for effect—important, he'd assured her—and a deep basso boat horn close by to the west suddenly cut the silence.

Everyone looked up, and other boat horns joined in, a few at first, but then tens and dozens of them, surrounding the platform, the volume rising and falling like a chorus on the wind.

Don had told her to expect this. "Don't let it fluster you," he'd told her. "You're the Nobel doc in charge. You're trying to do something positive. The freaks don't stand for anything, they'll be here only to destroy what they can't understand."

"Shall we continue this inside, where it's a little less noisy?" she shouted.

"No," one of the newspaper reporters shouted, getting to his feet. "We understand what you're trying to do and why. And we understand what's at stake—not just the money, but the climate control issue you've talked about for the last year or two." He swept his hand toward the edge of the platform over his shoulder. "Were you expecting this demonstration, and what do you say to the Reverend Schlagel's charges that you're playing God?"

"If the reverend is right, maybe I should just wave my hand and make them all miraculously disappear," she said, and she regretted the remark the instant it popped out of her mouth.

"Is that what you want?" the Fox reporter asked.

It was exactly what she wanted, but she shook her head. "Of course not, as long as they don't try to interfere with my work."

"Like now?" the network reporter relentlessly followed up, and the other media people were curious enough to let him continue.

"A little humility every now and then wouldn't hurt," Don had warned her.

Gail had moved to the rear, behind the cameramen, and she shrugged, only this time the gesture wasn't indifferent, it was sympathetic. Eve nodded.

"I have a big mouth that tends to get me in trouble," she said. "What I mean to say is that I welcome scientific criticism, not attacks based purely on emotion or popular opinion that has been manipulated."

"Is that why you were given the Nobel Peace Prize and not physics?" the *Time* magazine reporter asked.

The cacophony of boat horns seemed to be closing in on the rig, making it nearly impossible to hear or be heard on deck, and Eve wanted to shout back at the smug bastard. At the top of her lungs. This was the twenty-first century, goddamnit, not the Dark Ages. Yet a paleobiologist friend of hers told her recently that more than half of all Americans did not believe in evolution—they thought Darwin was a crock. Talk about Dark Ages. Sometimes it seemed to her as if the country was slipping backwards, the lights were really starting to go out. The age of exploration and discovery had given way to the new age of religious intolerance and war. Worldwide jihad.

She couldn't help herself. "Why are you here?" she shouted.

"You're front-page news, Doc," one of the reporters said. "You and your God Project."

. . .

The news conference, more like a circus with her as the chief clown, ended shortly after that remark. Most of the reporters were only mildly curious about the equipment in the control room, and the work that would be done as soon as the GE-built impellers were barged down to Hutchinson Island and attached to the platform. The depths and exact positions of the generator augers in relationship to the continuous micro-changes in the speed and angle of axis of the Gulf Stream at each particular location, which could affect the electrical output and any given moment, would be monitored. It was unknown at this point if a mechanism to change the depth and angle of incidence for each impeller would have to be designed and installed. Also unknown were the effects of salinity and temperature, or especially the opacity of the water, which might change the parts per million of biological organisms present at any given depth. With an intake diameter of twenty-five feet, a density differential could exist between the tops and bottoms of the impellers, which could affect efficiency.

Hundreds of other measurements would be taken from more than one thousand sensors, in the impeller blades themselves, on the internal bearings and gears inside the generators, on the electrical output—not only the amperage developed, but the consistency. How steady an output could be expected on a 24/7 basis for an entire year? Would this project act like solar cells, which produced energy that was subject to extreme fluctuations depending on how much dust landed on the solar panels, how many clouds were in the sky and how fast they moved, and at what latitudes the panels were located?

"There are a lot of variables," Eve told them. "It's what this stage of my experiment is all about."

"What precautions have you taken to avoid another accident like the one last year in which a man was killed?" the French newspaper reporter asked.

"Better seals and redesigned fail-safes," Eve answered matter-of-factly, though she was bitter. It was no accident, and everyone in her lab knew it, but there was no proof. No way ever of discovering the proof unless they could find the impeller that had fried its cable and now lay somewhere at the bottom of the ocean. But no one was looking, nor were there plans or money for such a search. So it was an accident.

"What comes next?" Tomi Nelson, who wrote for *Scientific American*, asked. She and the reporter from the *Smithsonian* had been the only two really more interested in the science and technology than the men in Schlagel's opposition. But then they weren't as interested in spot news as the others.

Don, who'd been missing for the briefing, had come in just as the question was asked. "If all goes well, and nothing bites us in the butt, we'll hook up to the grid ashore and start giving Sunshine State Power and Light free electricity," he said, coming around to where Eve stood facing the media people. "Sorry I'm late, Dr. Larsen."

Press kits, including the bios of Eve and Don and everyone on the team, along with the science including diagrams, a little bit of math, some economic projections, and the long-range weather effects they were aiming for, had been sent ahead of time, so introductions weren't necessary.

"I meant beyond that, Dr. Price," Nelson asked. "What's the next stage, or are you planning on going directly into production?"

"How many oil platforms do you expect it will take?" the Japanese reporter interrupted impolitely. "Excuse me, but do you think your environmentalists will object?"

"Let me answer both questions," Eve said. "No more oil platforms, this one is just a tool for us to generate needed data. After we're finished here, we'll anchor the four impellers and their gen sets fifty feet beneath the surface and continue sending electrical power ashore. There will be no rig, and therefore no environmental issues."

"And before anyone asks, because of the design of the impellers we will not be making sushi in the Gulf Stream," Don said, and he got a few chuckles.

The boat horns had been blaring nonstop for about a half an hour, so that it had become mostly just background noise. But the *Washington Post* reporter nodded toward the windows. "Thad Schlagel promises to follow you all the away to Florida. What effect will that have on your work?"

"We brought earplugs," Don said. "Anyway the extra publicity when we start giving away free electrical power won't hurt."

"If it works," the *Post* reporter said.

Defloria and Gail came to the door. Eve introduced them as the tour guides, and although the reporters from *Scientific American* and *Smithsonian* wanted to stay and ask more questions, they also wanted to see the rest of the rig, and Eve promised to do follow-ups with them afterwards.

When they had cleared out, Eve took Don aside. "Where were you?" she demanded. She didn't like being deserted.

"I'm sorry but I had to get the hell out of the way, I didn't know what I'd say if I got started."

And Eve came down a little. "I don't blame you," she said. "But it wasn't nearly as bad as I thought it would be."

"Except for the noisemakers."

"Did you really pack earplugs?"

"I don't think we'll need them," Don said. "Those people will get tired and go home as soon as the media bails."

Vanessa's private catering service rose nicely to the occasion, providing a pleasant champagne brunch that afternoon for the media and for the scientific staff, and Eve spent most of the hour and a half answering questions about her project and whether some of Schlagel's objections might be valid.

"The creationists are still down on Darwin," she told Enrique Obar, a *L.A. Times* reporter. "The Flat Earth Society believes Magellan was a liar. There's proof that we never walked on the moon. Earth is only six thousand years old—and change. Airplanes can't really fly. Baseballs don't curve. An arrow can never reach its target. And four thousand seven hundred and fifty-eight angels, or some number like that, can dance on the head of a pin. Makes me one of the crazies."

"All that sounds good, Dr. Larsen," Obar said, smiling. "But in fact he's gained quite a following. What are you going to do about him?"

Gail had changed into jeans and a light pullover and she was standing nearby, drinking a glass of champagne and obviously eavesdropping.

"About the only thing I can do, I suppose," Eve said.

"What's that?"

"Prove that the world is round."

FIFTY-TWO

The flight back to InterOil's Gulfport-Biloxi VIP terminal went without incident, the weather calmer inshore than it had been out on Vanessa Explorer. A number of the reporters made calls on their cell phones as soon as they came within range of a tower, while a couple of them tilted their heads back and fell asleep, and others were making notes on their laptops or BlackBerries.

Twenty minutes out the Japanese journalist Kobo Itasaka turned to Brian DeCamp. "Tell me what you think."

DeCamp, who'd traveled as Joseph Bindle, special correspondent to the *Manchester, England Guardian*, had been busy working out the next steps based on what he had learned this afternoon. The rig was even more vulnerable than he'd first thought, but getting aboard without raising too much of an alarm—enough of an alarm that someone would call for help—remained a problem he'd yet to solve. He wasn't overly concerned, it would be seven days before it reached the 1,800 fathom mark about two hundred miles southwest of Tampa, but it was the one detail left. He glanced at the Japanese sitting next to him. "Think about what?"

"The chances the woman's experiment will succeed."

DeCamp shrugged. "Oh, I shouldn't think it will," he said, flattening his rounded vowels so that he sounded more like a Midland's Plains Brit than a South African. "The science isn't very sound, is it?"

"Then you agree with the religious right here?"

This or any other discussion that might draw attention to him wasn't what he'd wanted. But a couple of the other reporters had looked interested and he couldn't back away. "Heavens no. It's just that meddling with the weather could very likely have some unintended consequences, I suppose. She means to diminish anticyclones in the Atlantic, but mightn't that increase the intensity of storms sweeping west across North America?"

"Interesting possibility, something I'll look into," Itasaka said, and turned away.

But one of the other reporters was curious. "Who did you say you wrote for?" he asked.

"The *Guardian*," DeCamp said, and all of a sudden he realized his mistake, and he grinned. "I suppose I should have said hurricanes. It's the three years I did at our Canberra bureau. New habits die hardest."

"Have you been to Iraq yet?" the reporter asked. Something wasn't adding up for him, and it was plain by his questions.

"No, and I bloody well have no desire to witness the slaughter of a lot of fools, some of them my own countrymen, for an American ambition. Or for that matter put my arse on the line for the next IED to pop off while I'm on the way to the loo."

The reporter started to say something else, but DeCamp turned away and looked out the window, dozens of oil rigs in every direction, clouds sweeping in for what looked like a rainy evening to come, which suited his suddenly dark mood.

Using the Bindle identity to get out to the oil rig had carried a set of risks—one of which was running into someone who knew the real correspondent—and another of which was being drawn into a discussion about some subject only an actual journalist would know something about. And Iraq was one of them. He'd been to Baghdad on a number of occasions, once before the second Gulf War had begun, but as an assassin, not a newspaper reporter. He didn't know the language, or the places where the international press usually hung out, or the little problems and everyday irritations that came with being a newsman embedded with a military unit. He couldn't talk the talk that would convince a veteran reporter that he was an actual correspondent.

But it had been worth the gamble to inspect the oil platform first-hand. Now he had a much clearer picture of what problems his team would be faced with and the solutions to all but two—how to get aboard and how to deal with the tug's crew and communications equipment.

And it had been worth the price of fifty thousand euros to the real Bindle, living and working as a freelancer in Paris, to take a vacation in Rome and let DeCamp take his place on the tour. An assignment two years ago required that he be allowed access to the German Parliment building, the refurbished Reichstag in Berlin, but not as a tourist, as a member of the press, which would give him nearly unlimited access to the offices of a deputy on a hit list.

DeCamp had reasoned that an accredited journalist would have just the sort of access that he needed, so he went looking for the right man, who had his similar build and height, who was a freelancer, lived in Europe, and was down on his luck. And Bindle had been fairly easy to find. An afternoon spent on the Internet researching British freelance journalists came up with a list of a dozen men of approximately the right age, five of whom had published a decreasing number of stories over the past five years. Bios on each of them, though scant, led him to two men, one a former Australian yellow journalist who'd come to London nine years ago and had never really made his mark.

And Bindle, who had been a success until four years ago when his output dropped dramatically from twenty or more big freelance pieces per year to just a handful, had brought him to the top of the list. A little digging brought up a London newspaper article about the deaths of Bindle's wife and teenaged daughter in a car crash. Though Bindle had not tested positive for alcohol or drugs, he'd been driving, and had failed to yield the right of way. The accident had been his fault; he'd killed his wife and daughter.

DeCamp, in disguise, had found him drunk in a Paris bar, followed him home, sobered him up, and offered him the proposition.

"No real way out for me is there," Bindle had agreed. "Just let me write the actual pieces, and never tell me what you're really up to, you bugger. I don't want to know. I don't care even if you're a spy for the goddamned Chinese or somebody."

Which had led to Germany, and the deputy.

DeCamp had followed him into a bathroom on the third floor, killed him with a stiletto thrust to the heart, and placed the body in one of the stalls. He was long gone from the building before the man's body was discovered and the alarm was sounded.

DeCamp sent his notes and photos for the story to Bindle, via a blind IP address, the reporter obligingly wrote the piece, submitted it to the *Guardian*, and went back to his drinking.

No one connected Bindle's visit with the murder, because the next day the reporter's human-interest story on the differences in governing styles between Berlin and the old post–World War II capital in Bonn appeared in the newspaper. He was a reporter, not an assassin.

Biloxi's weather had thickened by the time the InterOil helicopter touched down, and the journalists dispersed, most of them aboard the courtesy VIP shuttle over to the airport's terminal for their flights out. A couple of them cabbed it to the Grand Biloxi Casino and Hotel, making DeCamp the last to leave, taking a cab rather than the shuttle over to the terminal because, he told the driver, he didn't like mobs.

He had a beer in the lounge, and lost a roll of quarters to a slot machine over a half-hour's period, then walked across to the baggage pickup area, and outside to get a cab to the Beau Rivage Casino and Hotel on the beach, where he'd stayed in a suite for the past three days.

No one at the desk recognized him as he entered the hotel, passed through the casino, and then made his way back to the elevators and up to his suite where he took out the contacts that made his eyes look bright green, makeup that aged him by ten years, and padding on his torso and hips that'd put twenty-five pounds on him

Afterwards, looking out at the deepening gloom over the Gulf, first making sure that none of the telltales on his laptop had been disturbed, DeCamp felt a bit of nostalgia for Martine and his soft life above Nice. And sadness. Listening to the woman scientist speak about her project, watching the expression on her pretty, outdoorsy face, seeing her enthusiasm for what she was doing, and sensing her fears—some of which probably had to do with the presence of the flotilla, but at least some of which had to hinge on the outcome of her experiment—he could imagine someone like him coming to kill Martine. For perhaps the first time in his life he wanted something different, and for just a moment he thought he could put words to what he wanted; it was a notion just outside his immediate grasp, at the back of his head, on the tip of his tongue.

But then it was gone, and he ordered a bottle of Krug from room service, and when it came he sat down at his computer to make his notes, and download the photographs from his digital camera, sending them to Bindle when he was done.

DeCamp's cover here was as Peter Bernstein, a businessman from Sydney, who was obviously wealthy, though not filthy rich by American standards, who was quiet and generally kept to himself, although each night he had a different woman up to his suite. He ate and drank well, tipped well, his credit was triple A, and although his losses at the tables—especially black-jack, a game he despised—were modest, they were steady. His initial reservation had been for three days, but he'd extended that indefinitely. "I'm on holiday, in absolutely no hurry," he'd told the front desk. "Besides, it's winter in Auz. No reason to go back till spring."

After a short nap, he took a shower and changed into a European-cut soft gray suit, open-collar silk shirt, and hand-sewn Brazilian loafers. He'd left the television on a local news channel and as he was putting on his jacket, ready to go down to the casino, something caught his eye and he turned up the sound. It was a Fox News report on Eve Larsen's oil rig and Schlagel's God's Flotilla. Schlagel himself had been asked by the Fox reporter, "What comes next?"

"Why, to stop this abomination against the righteous hand of God, of course."

"How are you going to do it?"

"Make all Americans aware of the danger Dr. Larsen represents," Schlagel said, his voice rising, and he started on his diatribe delivered in neatly scripted sound bites.

As he preached, Fox ran some of the footage of the flotilla taken from the main deck of Vanessa Explorer that morning. Although DeCamp's attention remained atuned to Schlagel's arguments—which he actually had to admire because of the man's sheer brilliance—he suddenly saw the solution to both of the remaining problems, and he smiled, something he hadn't done for a very long time.

Simplicity. The concept had been drummed into him from the day he'd come under Colonel Frazer's roof.

He went back into the bedroom and used the encrypted Nokia sat phone to call Boris Gurov aboard the rig. "There has been a change of plans. For the better."

"I'm listening," Gurov said. "But something's come up out here. Two new people have come aboard, and one of them is Kirk McGarvey."

"Do you know this name?" DeCamp asked.

"Yes, and you should, too. A few years ago he served as the director of the bloody CIA. And he's damned good. The best."

"Who's with him?"

"Some woman."

"That's it?"

"Yes, but McGarvey could be trouble," Gurov insisted.

DeCamp thought about it for a moment. "His presence changes nothing. We'll deal with him the same as the others. But listen, Boris, this is what's going to happen."

When he was finished the line was silent for a long beat, but when Gurov came back he sounded good. "It makes sense. Besides, if they keep up with all the racket, it'll provide good cover."

"What about the primary problem?" DeCamp askled.

"Nearly all communications to and from the rig go through a pair of satellite dishes on the roof of the control center. Taking them out will be a breeze. Presuming we do this outside cell phone range, it only leaves sat phones. This one, plus one the delivery captain carries in a holster on his belt, maybe one or more the scientists brought with them, and McGarvey might have brought one."

"Find them, job one," DeCamp said. "You have four days."

"We'll see you then," Gurov said.

Schlagel was still on the television when DeCamp walked back into the living room. The reverend stood on the back of a pickup truck in front of a large crowd, exhorting them to make their voices heard in Washington and everywhere across the country. "We must work together to stop this abomination against God's will."

DeCamp called the second encrypted phone, that he'd given to Joseph Wyner who'd been holed up in New Orleans for the past five days with a four-man team they'd hired in London. All of them were mercs,

Julius Helms and Edwin Burt, former British SAS demolitions experts, Paul Mitchell, a former U.S. Delta Force hand-to-hand instructor, and Bob Lehr, a German cop who'd grown up in the east zone, and whose KGB methods were too rough in the west.

Wyner answered. "You're early," he said.

"There's a change of plans," DeCamp said, and he told his team leader the same thing he'd told Gurov.

"Sounds good. When do you want us to join you?"

"As soon as possible. I want you to book three rooms at the Beau Rivage, for three nights, starting tomorrow. Absolutely no drinking and especially no gambling."

"I don't know if I can keep them under control for that long."

The Fox camera had pulled back to show a large building behind Schlagel. The marquee in front read MISSISSIPPI COAST COLISEUM & CONVENTION CENTER, and a crawl at the bottom of the screen announced that the Reverend Jeremiah Schlagel's God Project rally and revival meeting would begin at eight in the coliseum.

"It'll only be for one night," DeCamp said.

"We'll be there before noon," Wyner said. "What about a boat?"

"I'll leave that to you," DeCamp said. "A cabin cruiser in the forty- to fifty-foot range. Spare no expense. But use your work name."

"I'll call you with the details."

"Do," DeCamp said.

Five minutes later he reached navy captain Manuel Rodriguez at his home outside of Havana. He'd worked with the Cuban two years ago on an assignment in Miami for the government, for which he made an under-the-table kickback payment of fifty thousand dollars. Rodriguez was in his debt, and when DeCamp had called last month with his proposal and an offer of another fifty thousand, the man had been more than willing.

"I'll be needing my boat ride within seven days. Can this be managed?"

"Of course, señor. Can you supply me with the latitude and longitude at this time?"

"Only approximately," DeCamp said, and he gave him the numbers for an area in the Straits of Florida, well west of the Florida Keys. "Will this present a problem?"

"None whatsoever."

"Good. The payment will be made in the usual manner."

"I would expect nothing less," Rodriguez said.

DeCamp hit the End button, then went into the bedroom to change back into khaki slacks and a light pullover—more fitting attire than his suit for a religious revival meeting.

FIFTY-THREE

Since the news conference this morning McGarvey had become increasingly restless, and by midnight, unable to fall asleep, he'd gotten up and went across to the crew's mess where he bummed a cigarette from the cook. He got a cup of coffee and went out on deck, the evening thick, but almost no wind and only a slight sea running.

Schlagel's God's Flotilla was still out there, surrounding the rig, some of the boats still blowing their horns, but it had been going on for so long that the noise had just become an ignorable part of the background.

They'd gotten underway a couple of hours after the reporters had left aboard the InterOil helicopter, and he could still make out the glow on the bottoms of the clouds on the northern horizon from the taller condos and casino-hotels in Biloxi and Gulfport.

Their speed was barely two knots, so it would take a week to reach the deeper parts of the Gulf where he figured the attack would come. Time to relax, time to figure things out, time to prepare, and yet McGarvey felt that he was missing something vital. Like he was being outthought

He'd spent the morning more or less trailing the media group, and after they'd left, Gail had sought him out and they had a cup of coffee together in the mess, seated alone in a far corner. "The Englishman," she'd told him. "His accent was more or less right, but I got a pretty strong feeling."

"I saw the one you're talking about, but all I have to go on are the images from your surveillance camera at the power plant."

"He was in the tour group that walked right past me, and I got a good look at his eyes," Gail had said. "Different color this time, but they had same expression, or lack of it. Like he was sizing me up, working out how he was going to kill me."

"Otto vetted him," McGarvey said, but he too had the feeling that at least one of the reporters was in actuality their contractor.

"So did Eric," Gail said. "But I'll have them check again. At the very least see if this guy filed a story with his newspaper."

They'd spent the rest of the afternoon together, wandering around the rig, which was a gigantic, impossibly complex maze of rooms and corridors, piping and girders, electrical runs, and machinery bolted or welded in what seemed like an endless series of random placements. At least a dozen steep stairways connected all of the levels from the helicopter deck, control rooms, and living spaces down to just above the sea level, where water sloshed over the catwalks. The noise at this level, from the blasting horns and the heavy rumble of the tug's powerful diesels, rumbled around the struts and hammered off the surface of the water and the underside of the deck above, making it nearly impossible to be heard.

Work refurbishing the platform had gotten underway again, and at one point they'd run into Defloria who'd warned them they were out on deck at their own risk. "I can't be responsible for your safety unless you stay inside."

"Thanks, but we have a job to do, too," McGarvey had told him.

"Just watch yourself."

Dead tired, McGarvey had turned in right after dinner, seeing the brief look of disappointment on Gail's face but ignoring it. She was pumped up from the day and she didn't want to be alone.

But he needed to be.

For all of his career, first in the Air Force, then in the CIA as a black operations field officer, then as an administrator, and finally as a sometimes freelancer, he'd done best working alone. Or at least being alone in the sense that he was not emotionally involved with someone. When his wife had given him the ultimatum—the CIA or her—he'd chosen neither and instead had run to Switzerland, where for a while his life had seemed orderly to him. Until he'd become involved with Marta Fredricks, a Swiss cop assigned to watch him, which ultimately led to her murder. She'd fallen in love with him, and followed him to try to get him back. But she'd stumbled into the middle of an operation and had lost her life.

Because of him.

It had happened again in Georgetown where an explosive device meant for him had instead killed Jacqueline Belleau, a French intelligence officer who'd worked with him on an assignment in Moscow, and who'd followed him to the States.

And again outside Mexico City two years ago when Gloria Ibenez, a Cuban-born CIA field officer, had given her life to save his.

And still again eighteen months ago when his wife and daughter were killed in another attack meant for him.

So much carnage, so many lives wasted uselessly. The list wasn't exactly endless but sometimes it seemed like it was, and over the years he'd been rubbed so raw that he didn't know if he could care about anyone ever again. At the very least, he'd come to reason, his proximity to someone very often ended up as a death sentence for them.

"A penny," a woman said from behind him.

He turned as Eve Larsen appeared out of the darkness. She was dressed in jeans and a dark windbreaker against the damp, chilly night air, and she looked worn-out, almost haggard, her face even a little gaunt. "It'd take more than a penny," he said.

She inclined her head, and came next to him and leaned her elbows on the rail. "Do you think they have the stamina to keep up the racket all the way to Florida?"

"Probably not."

"You're still expecting an attack."

"I think it's possible."

"But no one else does."

It was more complicated than that, because even the White House thought that an attack on the rig was possible, though not by Schlagel's group. But there was no proof, not one shred of evidence, not one indication, not one warning, even a distant warning that something like that might happen. Everyone was going on McGarvey's instincts, while at the same time hedging their bets in case he was wrong. And he'd been in this position before. More than once.

"No."

She fell silent for a time, staring out at the dozens of boat lights—red, green, and white—surrounding them, while straight ahead the tug's array of lights stacked up in a vertical column indicating she was engaged in a tow presented an almost surreal image against the thick dark of the overcast night sky and no visible horizon. "I haven't seen you since you came aboard."

"I didn't want to get in your way," McGarvey said, and in the lights on the rig that lit up the superstructures like a forest of Christmas trees, he saw her expression harden. "Gail and I are here to provide security in case something goes wrong. And believe me, Doc, I sincerely hope this will be a wasted trip."

"Eve," she said. "My name is Eve." And she sounded very vulnerable.

"You have your work . . . Eve."

"Yes."

"What do you want?"

"Someone to put their arms around me, tell me that everything will work out, that there's really nothing to worry about."

"You have Don," McGarvey said. He wanted to run.

"No," she said. "You. Five minutes is all I'm asking."

He stared at her with absolutely no idea of what to say or do. She was younger than him, smarter than him, and driven so hard that she was almost shaking. It was in her eyes and on her lips, in their swift movements as if she were ready to argue her point or at the very least spring into some sort of a defensive posture. And he thought that her being here like this was the worst thing that could happen, especially with the sort of memories he'd been dredging up.

But then he supposed she really did need him, and he reached out for her and she came into his arms, shivering at first until she slowly began to come down, and he could feel her tears on the side of his face.

"I'm afraid," she said.

"This will work out," McGarvey told her. "You'll see."

FIFTY-FOUR

□

Late the next afternoon Eve and Don went down to the main deck to inspect the work Defloria's crew had completed on the first of the four massive steel tripods that would support the 150-millimeter titanium and carbon nanofiber cable holding the huge impeller in place. They were well out into the Gulf now, completely out of sight of land, and the weather had turned nasty with a light drizzle from low overhanging clouds that scudded to the east on an increasing wind, but the weather didn't seem to be slowing down the work.

"I've been in much worse conditions on the North Sea," Defloria told them, and he introduced his construction foreman, Herb Stefanato, a short, bulldog tough guy from Queens who'd paid his way through engineering school by working as a roustabout on oil rigs.

"We've engineered a safety factor of five above what you and the other eggheads at GE told us we'd need," Stefanato said. "No offense, Doc."

"None taken, I've been called worse," Eve said. Each tripod, standing nearly the height of a five-story building from base to apex with a spread of forty feet, was a geometric maze of intersecting girders of impressive proportions. The entire rig was bolted through the deck to what Stefanato explained were a series of two-inch-thick stainless-steel backing plates, that were in turn reinforced by a series of girders interlaced like a spiderweb with the platform's main beams.

The cable, attached to the impeller's pivot point located at the center of mass, would be led up and over roller bearings at the top of the pyramid, and back down to a winch powered by a donkey engine reeling out cable from a spool.

In addition to the structural purpose of the umbilical cord, the cable also contained the data links from the impeller to the measurement and control devices up in the science room. Once the impeller was up and spinning, and its generator switched on, the electrical energy the apparatus produced would be sent ashore via a heavily sheathed power line lying on the ocean floor.

All four of the impellers would be led from the down-current side of the platform, lowered to a depth of seventy-five feet at the central shaft, which would put the top edge of the blades a little more than sixty feet beneath the surface, plenty deep to avoid even the deepest draft commercial ships.

She'd thought of everything, they'd thought of everything and except for the accident aboard the *Big G,* the damned thing worked. The only difference now was the scale, and it worried her. But then Don had reminded her almost on a daily basis since Oslo to slow down, trust the data, trust her science.

"There'll be a considerable drag," Don said. "We can't get energy for nothing."

"This will handle the stress," Stefanato said.

"What about the stress on the platform with all four impellers on the same side? The rig's going to heel over."

"Seventeen degrees at full load," Stefanato said. "We'll pump water into the two up-current legs, which'll even things up a bit."

"Have you worked out the torsional loads something like that will put on the main deck?" Don pushed.

Eve realized that he had become just as big of a worrier as she was. She'd never noticed it before, maybe because she'd been so wrapped up in her own world, but now she could see that he was actually tense. Maybe even a little frightened that they had come so close, that so much was at stake, that if anything went wrong, the slightest thing, the entire project would go down the drain.

Stefanato smiled tightly. "Listen to me, son. You're a scientist and I'm an engineer. You stick to your lab upstairs and let me take care of the engineering on my rig down here, and it'll all work out."

Don took a shuffling step forward, his aggressive don't-give-me-any-shit expression on his face, but before Eve could put out a hand to stop him, Defloria broke in.

"Herb is one of the company's best construction engineers, and he knows oil platforms top to bottom. There's no one better. I'm trusting my life and the lives of my crew to his judgment."

"This is our rig now, and let's just say that I'm a skeptic," Don said.

"And let's just say that Vanessa is the company's rig until we reach Florida and turn it over to your team," Defloria said mildly. "But if you have a problem with that, Doctors, I suggest that you call the company."

Don started to say something else, he clearly wanted to press the argument—no simple mechanical engineer was going to tell a man who held two Ph.D.s anything—but this time Eve was able to hold him off.

"Accept my apologies Mr. Stefanato," she said. "We've been working on this project for a long time and there's a lot at stake for us, including the careers of everyone upstairs who've stuck with me despite the nearly universal criticisms we've gotten from just about every direction. We're all a little touchy."

And Stefanato came down and he nodded out toward the flotilla. "And that crap isn't helping anyone's nerves," he said. "But trust me, when we're finished Vanessa will hold up to the stresses—torsional as well as traverse, compressional, and repetitive. If you want to stop by my office I'll show you the CAD programs I used, and the communications I had with GE's chief engineer on your impeller project, plus with the guy who designed the things, and with my boss, the VP of the company's engineering division."

Don actually grinned. "I guess I can be a shit sometimes," he said. "Sorry."

Eve almost wanted to reach out and hug him. He had pressed his charm button, and even shook Stefanato's hand, and yet a little part of her was slightly disappointed because his charm was fake. She didn't think the engineer could see it, but Defloria had and he remained cool.

"Is there anything else?" he asked Eve.

"Will this be finished by the time we get to Hutchinson Island?" she asked.

"In plenty of time," Defloria said. "Actually the work is going faster than we thought it would. No accidents yet."

"Do you expect something like that?"

"This is an inherently dangerous environment. Things happen."

And all of a sudden Eve's remembrance of that day on the Big G when the cable parted was painted vividly in her mind's eye; the blood and gore all over the deck, the look of resignation in the drowning crewman's face, the hypoxic flashes of light in her head just before she surfaced, and the Fox news producer's reaction.

"We'll try to stay out of your way as much as possible," she said.

Defloria looked at her critically. "When's the last time you got any sleep?" he asked, not unkindly.

"Not much since we came aboard," Don answered for her.

"Accidents happen to tired people. Maybe you should get some rest. Our work will go at its own pace, and there's not much for you to do until we get to Hutchinson Island."

Eve wanted to protest, yet she knew that Defloria was right, and she finally nodded. "Let's take tonight off," she told Don.

"I'll let them know," he said. "Come on, I'll walk you back to your room."

And Eve was even more exhausted than she'd realized until this moment, so tired she couldn't object to what she knew was a chauvinistic gesture on Don's part, and she went with him, hand in hand almost as if they were schoolkids or lovers, almost meekly.

Back inside, out of the wind and noise from the flotilla, she shivered. Krantz and everyone else she'd ever worked for or with had told her that she was too intense for her own good. That she worked so fast—like a maniac sometimes—that she was bound to make mistakes. Science was supposed to be slow and steady. Her rejoinders from the beginning had been simple: Check my data. And it had shut most of them up most of the time.

But now she realized that she had been pushing herself too hard, since the accident aboard the Big G and especially since Kirk McGarvey had shown up at her side in Hutchinson Island and since Oslo. Her project had become more than a scientific experiment. Practically every eye in the world was turned her way. Academics, engineers, big oil, the media, and even the religious right, most of them either expecting her to fail or wanting her to fail. They'd given her enough rope with which to hang herself, and they were sitting back now waiting for her to drop.

Upstairs at the door to her room, she hesitated for a few moments, swaying on her feet, but then she was in Don's arms, and he was kissing her and she was kissing him back passionately, their hands all over each other. And she couldn't stop, she didn't want to stop, except that for a brief instant when she looked up into Don's face she saw Kirk McGarvey's green eyes, but it was just a fleeting feeling, like suddenly jerking awake in bed because you had the sensation of falling.

They went into her room, not bothering to lock the door, pulling their clothes off and falling into bed, their bodies intertwined tightly, and they made love. Fast and with more passion than love or any feeling of tenderness; just two people, hungry nearly to the point of starvation for a lifesaving connection, for the sexual release, with no expecations for any sort of a future.

Afterwards, Eve vaguely remembered Don leaving, getting out of bed, and until he covered her with the sheet and blanket, a sharp feeling of coldness, but she never saw him get dressed nor did she hear the door close when he left.

Don went over to the dining hall and had a couple of pieces of surprisingly good pizza and a couple of Cokes, then went up to the control room where he joked around with everyone with an easy smile that people always seemed to respond to. They worked for a couple of hours, mostly calibrating their monitoring equipment and setting up the data link between their onboard computers and the mainframe at the lab back in Princeton.

"Where's the boss lady?" someone asked at one point.

"She was dead on her feet, so I put her to bed," Don told them.

"She was practically asleep on her feet all afternoon," Lisa said.

And he glanced out one of the windows. It was getting late and although the drizzle had stopped, the wind across the deck was twenty-five knots with higher gusts, yet Defloria's crew had begun work on the second tripod, and by the looks of it they would be at it all night. Stupid bastards, he thought.

"Let's call it a night, guys," he said turning back. "I think we all need some R and R. Back up here at 0800."

"Slave driver," one of the techs said, but they laughed tiredly, switched off the equipment they'd been using, and trooped out laughing and talking, ready to party at least until midnight or later. They'd deal with 0800 at 0800. Science could be fun.

He checked his and Eve's e-mails one last time, but nothing pressing had come in, only a couple of bon voyages from fellow faculty members, and he switched off the lights and went back to the windows to watch the work on deck and Schlagel's flotilla still circling the rig and tug.

He'd been attracted to Eve from the moment he'd read the first paragraphs of her "Studies on the Problems of World Energy Needs in the Face of Finite Reserves of Fossil Fuels and the Predicted Lack of Commercially Viable CO_2 Capture and Sequestration Technologies." Like a moth to an open flame, he thought, with a lot of anger and resentment. Her project was his. He'd come up with the solution first, well before she'd published her first paper in *Nature* and later as a less technical popular science piece for *Scientific American*. But his had been much broader in scope; energy from the ocean currents, in his estimation, was only the first step. Energy would have to be produced wherever possible—inland from the winds, in a large measure because even the U.S. did not have a national power grid. Electricity produced off the East Coast could not be exported much beyond the Ohio River, and certainly not as far as California. And solar power would have to be produced in the Southwest desert, and in the Gobi and Sahara and Australia's Great Victoria, Chile's Atacama, and Antarctica's five and a half million miles of arid landscape—at least during the summer months when the sun was shining.

But Eve had NOAA's backing, while despite his superior education he'd become nothing more than another of her postdocs, and when the time came to hand out grants and recognition, it was Eve who'd received the Nobel, and it was she who'd been given Vanessa Explorer and the promise of one billion dollars from the bank in Dubai.

Christ, it rankled. Right now to the soles of his feet, gnawing, pulling, dissolving his gut, making him fuzz out so badly sometimes that his default mode had become a smile so broad it crinkled his face at the corners of his eyes, when all he really wanted to do was lash out. Pull out a pistol and shoot someone, or beat the bitch to death with a baseball bat.

"Doctor Price," someone said behind him.

Price, caught totally off guard, turned away from the window so fast he almost lost his balance and he forgot to smile. "Who the fuck are you and what are you doing up here?"

"My name is Boris Gurov, and I was sent here to become your new best friend. Can we talk?"

FIFTY-FIVE

Otto Rencke had been in a blue funk for the past four days, so totally wiped out that he'd made no progress in the search for the contractor, and so contrary because of it, that his wife Louise threatened to take Audie and go back to Wisconsin to visit her parents until he came to his senses. But a telephone call from Eric Yablonski at eight this morning just before he was about to leave for Langley had changed everything.

Afterwards he'd stared out the window for the longest time, until he became aware of his wife watching him, and he smiled and began hopping from one foot to the other. "Oh, boy," he said. "I just talked to a genius."

Louise was grinning, and the baby clapped her hands. "And what did he tell you?"

"How to find our contractor."

"Who's your genius?"

"Eric Yablonski from the NNSA," Otto said, and he tapped his fingers against his forehead in frustration. "And it was right there in front of my big nose all the time. But I was so wrapped up in letting the programs do the work that I forgot to do my own. Machines are incapable of thinking out of the box."

Louise was enjoying this. "Pun intended?"

And Otto looked at her for a moment until he got it. "Pun indeed," he said, and he went to get his jacket, then came back to the kitchen and explained what Yablonski had come up with.

"I'll make a couple of calls," Louise told him. Until last year when she'd taken an early retirement she had been chief of imagery analysis at the National Security Agency, and she still had a lot of contacts at Fort Meade.

"Send it to the Dome," Otto told her.

Eric was waiting for him at the visitors center around noon and they shook hands. "I've been wanting for a long time to meet you face-to-face. It's a rare honor, Mr. Rencke."

Otto was embarrassed, and he just nodded his head. "Anyway, my name is Otto, and you have a hell of a rep yourself."

"Nothing like yours."

"Well, I didn't come up with the solution," Otto practically shouted and the three security officers behind the bulletproof glass looked up.

"Everything okay, Mr. Rencke?" one of them asked.

"Nope, 'cause I just met a guy smarter than me. But I'll survive."

And it was Yablonski's turn to be embarrassed.

Otto got a visitor's pass and drove Yablonski up to the OHB where he parked in his underground slot, but instead of taking the elevator up to his third-floor office he led his guest through a couple of security check-points on the other side of the garage, then down a long tunnel that ran beneath the main entrance and the circular driveway.

"When did it finally hit you?" Otto asked.

"I was dreaming about the oil rig and how I would sabotage it, if that were my assignment," Eric said. "I mean that may be a big assumption, but it's something to start with."

"Not such a big assumption. Mac and I looked down that path but neither of us came up with what you did."

"I figured that our contractor was probably in some military somewhere—from what we know and guess, most likely South Africa—and standard operating procedure for those guys is planning and training. Either he got the use of an oil platform sitting out in the Persian Gulf—assuming he's been hired by someone with connections to OPEC, or at the very least someone in the oil markets—or he got the blueprints for Vanessa Explorer and had a mock-up, or at least a partial mock-up, built out of plywood and two-by-fours."

"That'd be a big construction project. Out in the desert somewhere."

"Saudi Arabia?" Yablonski asked.

"One of the Royals might be funding the op, but they wouldn't put something like that on Saudi soil. My guess was Syria or Libya. But if it's there, it would have to stick out like a sore thumb, even if it was camouflaged."

"Where are we going, by the way?" Yablonski asked.

"The Dome," Rencke said. "Have you heard of it?"

Yablonski was impressed. "Jesus," he said. "Only rumors."

"Well, you wanted to know if we'd spotted anything interesting in the past thirty days or so, and I think we've come up with something in the Libyan desert about six hundred klicks southeast of Tripoli."

Nearly a hundred yards down the bare concrete-walled tunnel they came to another security door, where Rencke had to submit to a retinal scan, and inside a small anteroom an armed security guard, who'd monitored their progress from the parking garage, looked up from where he was seated behind a small desk. Getting beyond this point required visual recognition; only people the security guard on duty personally knew could pass.

"Good morning, Mr. Rencke. Your operator arrived fifteen minutes ago."

Otto and Eric signed an electronic reader, and the security officer buzzed them through into a long corridor and then through another security door into a large dimly lit circular room with stadium seating for two dozen people under a domed ceiling much like the ones found in planetariums. A projection device with several lenses was built into a platform in the center of the room, computer-controlled by an operator in a booth in the rear. Each seat had its own monitor and keyboard to control the presentation if the material being displayed were too sensitive to be shared by an operator.

"Good morning, Mr. Rencke," the operator's voice came from speakers. "Are we ready to begin?"

"Yes, please," Otto said, and he and Yablonski sat down.

The room lights dimmed further, and overhead a 360-degree image of what appeared to be a training base of some sort in the middle of a desert appeared on the dome. The image was so startlingly clear, almost 3-D, that they felt as if they were actually there in person.

"It's a former Libyan army desert warfare training base at Al Fuqaha'," Otto said. "But Gadhafi rents it out from time to time to anyone whose cause he finds worthy, and whoever has the most Western currency."

"It looks deserted."

"You're seeing satellite images from sixty days ago," Otto said. "But watch." He touched an icon on the monitor.

The static daytime image began to move, shifting from sunlight into dusk and finally full night in which the view changed to an infrared mode in which anything mechanical like a car or truck engine or an animal that emitted heat would show up. But no heat blooms appeared anywhere.

Otto sped up the progression from day to night to day until ten days later when four trucks showed up in the middle of the night, and two dozen men began erecting what looked like circus tent poles over which, just before dawn, they draped a mesh fabric.

"Camouflage netting," Yablonski said. "But the size of it!"

Otto stopped the image just after the sun came up when nothing was visible to the satellite except what appeared to be an expanse of empty desert, fifty or sixty meters on each side.

"Plenty big to hide a mock-up," Yablonski said. He was excited.

"That's exactly what happens over the next thirty days," Otto said, and he moved the image forward. A steady stream of trucks and workmen arrived by night, unloaded what appeared to be construction materials that they placed beneath the netting, and were gone each morning an hour before dawn.

The trucks and workmen stopped coming after a month, and the camp remained deserted for nearly a week until a pair of small army trucks showed up one afternoon and disappeared from view beneath the netting. Otto slowed the image at nightfall, where the heat blooms of several people showed up, at least two of them brighter than the others.

"My guess is that they built the oil rig mock-up, and the two brighter images were standing on top of it closer to the netting," Otto said. "Now watch this."

Three nights later two brighter images showed atop the platform again, while four other heat blooms in two pairs approached from separate directions.

Yablonski sat forward. "That's a military operation if ever I saw one," he said.

Less than twenty minutes later, the four images on the ground stopped and then came together, and after a few minutes they walked away and disappeared, as did the two heat blooms on the platform.

"Where'd they go?"

"Watch," Otto said, and the two panel vans appeared from beneath the netting and headed to the northwest. The next day the camp was once again deserted, and it remained that way.

"Thank you, Don," Otto said. "That'll be all for today."

"Yes, sir. Would you like me to quit this program?"

"Yes, please," Otto said, and after the images on the Dome blanked out and the auditorium's lights came up, he turned in his seat and watched until the lights in the booth went out.

"I didn't realize that we had this capability," Yablonski said, impressed.

"And more," Otto said. "But what's more important is that I did some digging, and I found out that an ex-South African Buffalo Battalion officer by the name of Brian DeCamp used the training base about nine years ago. We have someone in Gadhafi's government who found out for me. It was risking an asset, but I leaned on him and he came through."

"It's a start. Where's he been since then?"

"He disappeared. No trace, not even a glimmer. And my source in Tripoli had no idea who used the base or why. But DeCamp fits our profile."

"Do we have a photograph of him?"

"No. Not even a decent physical description. Our asset never actually met him."

"Have you shared this with McGarvey?" Yablonski asked.

"I will this afternoon, I gotta check out something else first," Otto said, and he explained McGarvey's suspicion that one of the journalists who'd come aboard Vanessa for the news conference could have been DeCamp.

"Check their backgrounds. See if all of them actually filed stories, because it's a safe bet that DeCamp is a killer but not a journalist."

"I already have, and it's a dead end," Otto said. "But assuming our contractor is Brian DeCamp, the same guy who hit Hutchinson Island, and assuming he's going after the oil rig—who's paying him to do it and why?"

"Back to the money trail."

Otto nodded. "For now it's our best bet."

FIFTY-SIX

The accommodations level aboard Vanessa Explorer was always reasonably quiet because as shorthanded as they were, the roustabouts, welders, and construction crew worked twelve hours out of twenty-four on rotating shifts—six hours on, followed by eight off, and then another six on followed by four off—someone was always sleeping. This schedule also meant that each crewman got his own compartment, a luxury usually observed only for foremen and above.

It was around one in the afternoon and after making sure that no one was coming down the corridor, Gurov knocked lightly on Kabatov's door. Both their sleep times had coincided for the first time and early today they'd agreed to meet in secret. No one aboard knew that they were friends, and both of them had kept to themselves, so aloof and surly that no one bothered them. As long as they did their jobs, no one cared.

Kabatov let him in. "Any further word?"

"No," Gurov told him. "But it'll happen in six days, so I thought now would be a good time to go over everything."

"You're right. And I'm getting goddamned tired of actually working for a living."

Gurov had to laugh, even though both of them had done plenty of manual labor when they were kids growing up—Kabatov in Siberia working with his father and uncles in the coal mines, and Boris in a foundry in Noginsk, outside of Moscow. But when they'd met almost ten years ago on the mercenary circuit they found that they, and just about every other gun for hire, were kindred spirits "It's a hell of a lot easier blowing up shit and killing people than working in a factory."

Kabatov unfolded a floor plan of the platform and spread it out on the bed. "Between what information you've brought, plus what I've seen with my own eyes, I think we have all the comms units spotted."

"Except for sat phones."

"Well, we know that Al Lapides, the delivery skipper, has one, and Price told you that the bitch has her own phone, but it's usually stashed in her cabin."

"He promised to take care of it when the time comes," Gurov said.

Kabatov looked up. "Leaves us with two problems, the first of which is McGarvey and the broad he brought with him. I've seen both of them around the rig and neither one of them are carrying anything that looks like a sat phone. But both of them are armed."

"Naturally," Gurov said. "And the second problem is the tug?"

"Right. It'll be equipped with a SSB transceiver, maybe two, and the skipper will most likely have his own sat phone. Somebody will have to get aboard and take care of the crew before they can send a Mayday."

"I think he's got it covered," Gurov said. "I don't think much gets past the bastard."

"He was wrong about the first approach with scuba gear."

Gurov conceded the point and nodded. "But he was man enough to admit it, and listen to our advice."

"Have you ever heard of him before this job?"

"Rumors only. But he's got money and it showed up in my account on time."

Kabatov nodded. "And mine, too. So he's got deep pockets, but I'm wondering just how reliable he is in the field, and who the other guys are he's bringing along."

Gurov had had the same rising misgivings over the past few days. He and Nikolai had worked together before, and they knew and trusted each other's tradecraft and abilities. And in normal circumstances, if there was such a thing in this business, teams were assembled long before an operation and trained together until they got it right. This time was different, and it was worrisome.

"We'll take it as it's handed to us," he said. "Either that or quit right now while we're still within helicopter range of land."

But Kabatov shook his head. "No way I'm walking away from a payday like this. I'm just telling you that we need to cover our own arses, just in case something should go south at the last minute. Dead mercs can't collect on payday no matter how good a job they did."

"I agree," Gurov said.

The first principle wasn't the mission, it was personal survival, something definitely not taught in Spetsnaz training, which had been all about mission and teamwork. But the drill instructors hammered home one overriding skill that the good operator—the man who completed the mission and returned to base for debriefing—needed, which was the ability to improvise. Think on your feet, come up with the right solution in the field when you'd run into an ambush, or had no way out, or found yourself in an impossible situation.

After five years of basic training and advanced schooling, each officer candidate was given a one-man operation for his final examination. Most candidates didn't make it past this point, and reverted to the rank of sergeant. A great many ended up disabled and a few dead.

Gurov and four other officer candidates were airlifted as prisoners to the Kara-Kum military prison in the middle of Turkmenistan's desert of the same name, their status in Spetsnaz unknown to the prison guards. Their mission was to escape, singly, and make their way to the town of Kizyl Arvat, two hundred kilometers to the southwest. It was high summer with daily temperatures that could reach fifty degrees Celsius, and there was no water or food, except what they could carry from the prison.

Three of the candidates gave up before nightfall of the first day, so dehydrated and sunblinded they'd been unable to hide from capture.

But Gurov had improvised. He'd not only carried water, he'd brought one of the prisoners with him—a man accused of killing his family in a drunken rage while at home on leave from the army for which he was serving a life sentence with no hope of parole. They traveled by night and hid behind sand dunes during the day, their water running out less than thirty-six hours after they'd escaped. With thirty kilometers to go, both men nearly on their last legs, Gurov pulled out a knife, slit the prisoner's throat, and drank the man's blood. Survival at any price.

Four days later he was commissioned as a Spetsnaz lieutenant along with only a handful of graduates from a class of one hundred during ceremonies outside Moscow. And he'd spent the remainder of his relatively brief career improvising and surviving—priority one. Nothing had changed now.

"Did he tell you anything about the other four guys he hired?"

"No," Gurov said, and that too was slightly bothersome. "And you're right that we need to cover our arses, because I think in the end we could end up dead. We need a plan."

"Funny you should make the suggestion, Boris, because I've worked out a few things."

FIFTY-SEVEN

McGarvey awoke, automatically reaching for his pistol on the nightstand, not knowing what he'd heard. It was five in the afternoon, and he was still a little slow on the uptake. He'd spent the last few nights prowling around the rig, looking for the things he'd missed on his previous inspections, and wondering sometimes if he'd been too long away from the field and his tradecraft had become rusty. He took catnaps during the day, and although he and Gail were often together, they were just as often not. They mostly maintained separate schedules in an effort to keep an eye on things 24/7.

His sat phone rang a second time, and he laid his pistol down, got up, and went to the phone on his desk as it rang a third time. It was Otto.

"We think we know who our contractor might be. An ex-Buffalo Battalion light colonel by the name of Brian DeCamp. No photographs, of course, which means he was able to erase his records and change his identity, and in all the years since the Battalion was disbanded he only ever made one mistake. And he's done it again."

McGarvey was impressed and he said so.

"Eric actually came up with the idea that if our contractor wanted to hit the platform it stands to reason that he would have to train a team either on an oil rig in the Persian Gulf or somewhere like that, or on a mock-up. Maybe full scale of at least a part of the rig. Louise made a couple of calls, and I came up with a search engine for all of our surveillance satellite feeds over the past month and a half, and displayed it for Eric in the Dome."

"What'd you find?"

"A Libyan army desert warfare training base about six hundred Ks southeast of Tripoli. Been used off and on over the past few years by the Libyans and possibly by al-Quaeda, so we've keep an eye on the place. Just lately it's been deserted, but about seven weeks ago workmen came in and put up a lot of camouflage netting, and built something very large under it. Took them four and a half weeks working only at night."

"The mock-up?" McGarvey asked, and he could see the sense of it. And he could also understand why DeCamp, if he were their contractor, would have expected total anonymity out in the desert. As far as he was concerned no one would be looking for him in Libya. No reason for it.

"I think so, and Eric agrees," Otto said. "Anyway, six warm bodies showed up about a week after the work crew left—project apparently completed—and then it got interesting. Two of the infrared images seemed to be stronger than the others, and we're guessing it means they were at a higher elevation than the others. Closer to the underside of the netting."

"On top of the mock-up."

"Right. And then what had to be a practice run for a military operation, the other four approached the mock-up from two separate directions."

McGarvey saw that too, and he walked to the window and looked outside at the flotilla still circling Vanessa. "They'll be coming from the sea, from the protestors. I didn't think Schlagel would take the risk."

"Well, maybe not, Mac," Otto said. "The four only approached the rig, but then they stopped, moved together, and in the morning they left. Never came back."

"They built something in secret, something they didn't want satellites to see, used it once, and then left," McGarvey said. "Someone spent a lot of money for what? To try to reach the rig from the sea, but for some reason decided it wouldn't work?"

"My snap guess would be that they wanted to approach the rig underwater, attach explosive charges to the legs, and then back off. The rig would capsize and maybe sink to the bottom."

"But they cut off their training op," McGarvey said. "Because they realized that it wouldn't work. They couldn't guarantee that there'd be no survivors."

"Means they're coming aboard."

"How'd you come up with DeCamp's name?"

"Source Beta in Tripoli, works for Army Logistics. Name is Peter Abu-Junis Jabber, left over from the British SAS training missions. Anyway he's on his way out of badland, and I figured he was worth tapping. Told me that DeCamp had used the base about nine years ago for some sort of training mission. He wasn't sure, but he thinks it might have been De-Camp again this time."

It was more than circumstantial, it was thin, and yet McGarvey had a feeling that they'd found their contractor at last. "Find out who's paying him, and maybe we'll get the why."

"We're working on it," Otto said. "But if our guy is DeCamp, whoever's paying him has deeper pockets than Schlagel."

"Marinaccio and her friend in Venezuela?"

"That's what I'm thinking. Anyway, kemo sabe, watch your ass out there because he's coming your way, and if Schlagel is involved it'll be just as a smoke screen."

"I haven't watched much television lately. What's he been up to?"

"He held a send-off rally at the Coliseum in Biloxi for his flotilla. Standing room only in the fifteen-thousand seat arena, and they were stacked up out in the parking lot, and still coming even after it was over. Since then he's been holed up at his place in McPherson, spreading the message on his SOS network every night from seven till ten central. And the guy is good, he's generating a lot of buzz."

"Serious attention? Enough that we might not have only DeCamp to worry about?"

"If you mean some nutcase coming after you, I wouldn't be a bit surprised, though Schlagel makes it a point to tell everyone who'll listen that his is a ministry of peace and all that Lamb of God bullshit," Otto said. A long time ago he'd worked for the Jesuits and he still had bitter feelings about religion in general. "But if you're asking for help out there no one is going to lift a finger, he's become that powerful."

"Have you been able to hack into his system?"

"Yeah, and it was easy. Too easy. There was nothing there. If he has some sort of a secret agenda he's keeping it to himself, or maybe a trusted adviser or two, just word of mouth. But I did find out something interesting. His real name is Donald Deutsch, a poor kid from Milwaukee who did a stint in the army, got busted for selling tax-free cigarettes and liquor in Europe, and then disappeared in San Francisco about the time the reverend Jeremiah Thaddeus Schlagel showed up."

"If he really pushes for the presidency the media will nail him."

"Won't matter, Mac. In fact, if he's as smart as I think he is, he'll go public with his past. Had to reinvent himself, had to pull himself up from the gutter, up by the bootstraps. If the timing is right, he'll get a boost."

"And if it's wrong, maybe we'll get a boost."

Otto laughed. "I'm on it," he said.

"I want some options," McGarvey said.

"I hear you, but you lost one. Joseph Bindle, the *Guardian* reporter you thought might be our contractor, is a no-go. He filed his story on the platform, and the writing isn't half bad. DeCamp might be a trained killer, but he's probably not that good a writer. Bindle's a freelancer out of Paris."

Work on the second impeller cable frame was nearly completed, and when McGarvey walked out on deck, the crane was lifting the last of the steel girders into place, and two welders started working, sparks flying everywhere. Defloria was speaking with Herb Stefanato, his construction foreman, and he looked up, a little irritated.

"As you can see we're a little busy, Mr. McGarvey."

"I only have one question."

Defloria nodded, knowing that he had no choice.

"Would it be possible to get someone aboard by boat, maybe through a hatch in one of the legs, without anyone knowing about it?"

"No hatches in the legs are accessible from outside the rig, but I suppose someone could toss grappling hooks and climb up over the side. But we're a long ways off the water, and the seas would have to be calm. Wouldn't be like the Somali pirates boarding a cargo ship or supertanker."

Stefanato, who'd been closely watching the welding operation, looked over his shoulder. "Someone's on deck twenty-four/seven, and we're very well lit up. Are you saying something like that might happen?"

"Other than by helicopter, how do you get people and equipment aboard?"

"The crane lowers a basket to a resupply ship. And that can be a dicey operation if any sort of a sea is running. People have been hurt."

"One other thing," McGarvey said. "Has anyone from the flotilla tried to contact you in any way?"

DeFloria gave him a bleak look; he was obviously a man caught between a rock and a hard place, between wanting to get his men off the rig, out of harm's way, and needing to follow the company's orders if he wanted to keep his job. "They're on the radio to us constantly," he said. "The only channels they don't interfere with are six and eight that we use for intership communications with the *Tony Ryan*."

"What do they say?"

"They want us to turn around and go back to Biloxi, and they're willing to send someone over to negotiate with us."

"What do you tell them?" McGarvey asked.

"Al's given his crew strict orders not to respond under any circumstances," Defloria said.

"Even in an emergency?"

"They have enough boats to handle just about anything, including communications with the Coast Guard, and I was told by the company to keep out of it, no matter what. Our job is to see that Vanessa gets to Florida without delay."

"Very good," McGarvey said and he started to turn away but Defloria stopped him.

"Let me know if something should develop."

"If possible. But it'll be fast."

"Goddamnit, what the hell are we supposed to do if the bastards start shooting at us?" Stefanato demanded angrily.

"Keep out of sight, someplace where you can abandon ship if need be," McGarvey said.

"Christ," the construction engineer said.

Eve Larsen's techies generally avoided the construction crew and only four of Defloria's people were in the dining room when McGarvey came in and got his dinner, ordering his steak rare with French fries and a small salad. The food was very good around the clock, and although there was no alcohol aboard there was plenty of iced tea and soft drinks and the coffee was outstanding.

He was just sitting down when Gail showed up and joined him. "Buy a girl dinner?" she asked. She was smiling, which McGarvey had learned was usually a cover-up when something was bothering her.

"Sure, anything on the menu," he said. "What's the problem?"

"It's the waiting," she said, almost too quickly. "And the constant noise. And the feeling that we're overlooking something right in front of our noses." She was strung out. "It's like the cartoons where a ten-ton weight has been pushed over a cliff, and like a dummy you're standing at the bottom without a clue what's about to happen to you."

It was the lack of knowledge that was driving both of them crazy.

"We know the name of our contractor," he said, and she brightened.

"Jesus, you talked to Otto?"

"He's an ex-South African Buffalo Battalion lieutenant colonel by the name of Brian DeCamp," McGarvey said, and he told her everything that Otto and Eric had come up with, along with the likelihood that Joseph Bindle was a legitimate journalist.

"So it still leaves us with no clear description of the bastard, other than what my receptionist at Hutchinson Island gave me and what I saw in the corridor, and it's a safe bet he was in disguise."

"Otto's following the money trail. Somebody somewhere must have come in physical contact with him at some point. The real him."

"And lived," Gail said. "And in the meantime we sit it out waiting for the ten tons to drop."

"Five days," McGarvey said. "Maybe six."

"And what are we supposed to do in the meantime? Same old?"

"Something like that," McGarvey said.

Gail looked away for a moment, and when she turned back she wasn't smiling. "What about your lady scientist and her mob?"

What about them? McGarvey asked himself for the hundredth time, because something wasn't right. Call it a gut feeling, even paranoia, but he was convinced that not all was as it seemed in her shop. He knew enough about scientists, especially of Eve Larsen's and Don Price's caliber, to understand that professional jealousy was the norm—the supernorm. But everyone up there absolutely *loved* their doc, *loved* her work, *loved* the fact she'd won the Nobel Prize, even though it wasn't for physics.

What about them indeed.

"They're doing their thing, and we're going to stay out of the way for now."

"And wait?"

"And wait," McGarvey said.

She nodded a little grumpily. "How about that dinner you promised?"

FIFTY-EIGHT

□

Eve Larsen had not slept well for at least a week, even though she'd thrown herself into the work of getting the rig ready for Hutchinson Island and the impellers, and the work was going well, and everyone seemed to be having the time of their lives. Normally under circumstances like these she would have collapsed into bed at odd times for a few hours of deep sleep, then wake with a hundred new ideas bursting inside her head like shooting stars.

But instead of ideas, she'd been having *the* dream; not one in which monsters were chasing her down a long dark tunnel, not even the one in which she had to be someplace, and she knew where it was, but she just couldn't seem to get there, no matter how hard she tried, and no matter the urgency of the thing. This was the one where she was called back to Oslo in disgrace to give back the Nobel Prize. It was the same room at city hall, with the king and queen and the same people in the audience, only no one was applauding her; everyone, including the king, was booing. Shouting that she was a fraud, that she wasn't a real scientist, that she was a liar and user whose wish was fame, not discovery. Outside, the gunman's aim had been perfect and she could almost feel the bullet plowing into her brain.

And the most frightening part of the nightmare wasn't the shame, or the hostile reception she was getting, it was the certainty in her own mind that they were right. She *was* a fraud. And each night the dream got worse; she could see how the impellers in the Gulf Stream and the Humboldt Current and the Agulhas would never produce the electricity she'd predicted, and she'd developed the mathematics to prove it. She could see the partial differential equations marching in front of her mind's eye so clearly that when she would awake in a cold sweat she would try to write them down. But as close as they were in her head, she was unable to do it. And it was all the more frustrating, because when she was awake she knew that she could prove her dream equations wrong so that her self-confidence would return.

Last night the nightmare got even worse, much more intense. This time it was Bob Krantz in the audience in Oslo and he threw the copy of *Nature* in which she'd proposed her World Energy Needs project up on the stage.

"You know that this thing doesn't work!" he'd shouted. "It's impossible to do what you want. There will be unintended consequences that you're hiding from us. Catastrophic consequences. Change the weather indeed. Who do think you are, God?"

And in her dreams she knew that Bob was correct. She was able to see exactly why her experiment was bound to fail, and yet she knew that she could never admit it publically. The shame and humiliation would be too awful to bear. She would be alone and isolated, and just before she'd awakened this morning she'd dreamed that she was back home in England. It was winter, and no one was there at the train station to meet her, just like no one had come to see her off to America.

And when she awoke at dawn she was freezing cold, and during the day she'd had the chills so bad at times that Don had asked her if she was coming down with something and he'd put the back of his hand to her forehead.

He'd seemed nervous off and on all day, and his concern had touched her. Getting ready now to go down to the dining hall for dinner, she went over to where he was seated at one of the computer monitors working on his study of mid-Gulf eddy currents against temperature, salinity, and suspended particle gradients. It was a continuation of his own project that they all hoped might have some bearing on the placement of the impellers. Perhaps a little far-fetched, in Eve's estimation, but she'd never suppressed independent studies by anyone on her team so long as they did their primary work.

"Anything interesting showing up?" she asked.

He was startled and he looked up at her, his eyes a little wide as if he were a kid just caught with his hand in the cookie jar. But he recovered nicely and smiled. "Still collecting data, but my programs haven't turned up anything useful yet." His hypothesis was that the formation of some eddy currents might depend in part on a physical event or trigger presence, like raindrops forming around particles of dust.

"I'm going to get something to eat. Do you want to come along?"

"Might as well," he said. "Everyone else has already gone down."

And Eve had been so absorbed in her own work that she'd actually not noticed it was just her and Don up here, and that it was beginning to get dark outside. "I thought it was too quiet without Lisa's wisecracks," she said a little sheepishly.

Don got out of the program he was working in and they left the control room and headed downstairs. He'd brought a GFDL windbreaker with him and he gave it to her. "You might need this, it's a little chilly outside now that we're at forty-two-double-oh-three."

For just an instant she had no idea what he was talking about, and she could see that it made him nervous. But then she understood. "My God, I wasn't keeping track," she said.

Forty-two-double-oh-three was a navigation buoy out in the middle of the Gulf, anchored in nearly 1,800 fathoms of water, more than 10,000 feet. It essentially marked the halfway point between Biloxi and the westernmost end of the Florida Keys where they would make their turn to the east toward the Atlantic. Don and the others had planned a celebration, modeled after the kinds of initiations that sailors went through after crossing the equator.

And she also understood why he'd been on edge for the past couple of days. According to McGarvey, if trouble were coming their way it could happen any time now, something she'd practically, though not completely, forgotten in the press of her work.

"Everybody okay with this?" she asked. "I mean, considering the threat."

Don gave her an oddly bleak look. "I don't think we have any choice. It's either that or hide in our cabins. Anyway the religious freaks haven't done a thing except make noise, your gun-toting pals are keeping watch, and we need a break." He managed a thin smile. "Lisa's called you a slave driver from the beginning, and now everybody is starting to believe it."

And Eve had to smile, too. Maybe a celebration was exactly what they needed to break the tension. "Even you?" she asked.

"Especially me."

It was a little cool on deck, but the wind from the north had subsided to near zero so that their slow forward motion canceled the apparent wind to absolutely nothing. It was fully dark now, but because of the lights on the rig the stars were invisible as was the horizon, and even the lights on the flotilla were mostly hard to pick out. But the noise of the horns and boat whistles was constant as it had been for nearly one week, but now it was mostly background noise, almost below the level of notice unless you stopped to listen for it.

Eve and Don walked past two of the completed impeller tripods and a third one that was nearly finished. Everyone aboard had been given the evening off for the celebration, and when they came around the corner of one of the storage containers about the size of a semi-truck trailer, lashed to the deck, where a long table laden with drinks and food was laid out, music suddenly began. And it wasn't a recording, because it was, if not terrible, amateuristic and Eve had heard it before. A few of her techs had a little musical ability and they'd formed what they called the Test Tube Jug Band. Two out of tune guitars, an electronic keyboard Richard played hesitantly, missing a lot of notes, a set of drums that just about drowned out everyone else, and Lisa on vocals.

There she is,
Miss Queen of the Seas,
Come from Neptune's Locker,
Or maybe Mars,
We can't really tell.

All of it badly performed without rhymes, more or less to the tune of Bert Parks's "Here She Is, Miss America." And everyone was laughing, cheering, and singing, Lisa with tears in her eyes. An emotional group, tired, strung out, but they were on their way and they were one hundred and ten percent behind their doc, their Nobel Prize doc.

And when the song, which was embarrassing but wonderful in Eve's estimation, was finally over, and after everyone had hugged her and kissed her cheek, the champagne was poured.

"To the Queen of the High Seas," Lisa said into the microphone, her voice now louder than the drums, which caused even more laughter, and everyone raised their glasses.

Everybody drank the toast, and a couple of her techies called for a speech, but she waved them off.

"No speeches," she told them. "We're taking the night off, and getting drunk, and hopefully some of you are getting laid—" Everyone laughed uproariously again. They loved her. "And you'd best enjoy it, because in the morning we're back at it, this time full tilt. So don't fall overboard in the middle of the night."

Then they cheered, poured more champagne, and started on the hors d'oeuvres.

Defloria was there with some of his people, and she congratulated them.

"You're almost finished with the third tripod," she said. "Good work, thank you."

"We're ahead of schedule," Stefanato said, and he winked at her. "Nice bunch of kids. Smart."

"They are," Eve said.

Don went to get her more champagne and Defloria and Stefanato left, and a minute later McGarvey and Gail came over. They looked worn-out and Eve was uneasy. Cops and watchdogs were never supposed to be tired. But McGarvey was smiling. "You have a happy crew," he said.

"Most scientists are," Eve said. "At least most of the time. And they've been working pretty hard for the past eighteen months, so whenever they get the chance they like to blow off a little steam."

Gail nodded. "Understandable. But maybe tonight should be the last of it until we get to Hutchinson Island."

If someone was actually coming after them with the intention of sinking the platform, now or certainly in the next few days would be the time to do it. At these depths any sort of a recovery operation would be impractical. Once Vanessa was on the bottom she would stay there. At the very least, the project would be set back one year, probably longer. Funding would certainly dry up, Eve was sure of it, and depending on how many people got hurt, the entire project, concepts and all, might end up on the floor of the Gulf as well.

"So maybe now it's time to call for some help," she said, ignoring Gail, because lately she had felt nothing but animosity from the woman, and she didn't understand the change. "Once they start shooting missiles at us, or dropping bombs or whatever, it'll be too late."

"Nothing like that's going to happen, Doctor," Gail said.

"Are you sure?" Eve demanded, her voice rising a notch.

"No," McGarvey said. "We're not even one hundred percent sure that anyone's going to try to attack us, but if they do it'll only be a few people— maybe a half dozen. And they don't know that we're aboard so the advantage would be ours."

"Anyway it's a lot harder to hit a moving target than a stationary one," Gail said. "And there are a lot more people aboard than there'll be once you're at anchor. Defloria's guys wouldn't exactly be a knock over."

Don came back with the champagne. "Who wouldn't be a knock over and for what?" he asked, his eyes squinty.

He was angry again, and Eve understood why, he thought that he was in competition with McGarvey. The man-of-the-mind scientist versus the man-of-action warrior. And it also suddenly dawned on Eve that Gail Newby might be of the same mind, she could feel that she was in competition for McGarvey. The lady warrior versus the female egghead.

"Just speculating," Gail said, and she and McGarvey nodded pleasantly then headed away.

"What was she talking about?" Don asked. He was on the verge of arguing.

Eve shook her head. She didn't want to get into it with him. "I haven't a clue," she said. "Let's join the party, okay?"

FIFTY-NINE

From one hundred meters out, DeCamp and the others aboard *Forget It*, a forty-nine-foot Gulfstar extended aft deck charter motor yacht could hear the off-key music and singing on the main deck of Vanessa Explorer even over the noise of the boat horns, theirs included.

Wyner was dressed all in black, camouflaged greasepaint on his face, the same as DeCamp. He was hanging off the stern in the four-man

Avon RIB dinghy, the outboard idling. They'd painted the ten-foot rigid inflatable boat's hull and the engine cowling black on the way to join Schlagel's flotilla, keeping it out of sight until now, lest someone in the flotilla wonder why they'd done such a thing.

DeCamp handed him down a nylon bag with a pair of Heckler & Koch MP5 submachine guns in the SD6-silenced version, along with six thirty-round box magazines of 9mm x 19 Parabellum ammunition.

Helms, one of the four contractors from London, watched from just inside the bridge, and he waved when DeCamp looked up. Bob Lehr, one of the other new contractors, was at the wheel, and over the past few hours he'd slowly positioned them about twenty meters to the port of the *Pascagoula Trader*, which was the largest boat in the flotilla and the one with the small Bell Jet Ranger lashed to the after deck. His orders were to close the gap between the two boats as soon as DeCamp and Wyner were off.

Tony Ransom, one of Schlagel's top aides, more or less in charge of the "operation," as he called it, was aboard and DeCamp had been invited over for a drink a couple of nights ago. "You need anything, anything at all, Mr. Schlagel says to help you out. Says you met at the rally in Biloxi."

DeCamp had nodded. "Great man, the reverend," he'd said, smiling. "Maybe you can do me a favor, but later on. We'll see."

The seas were calm tonight, the wind relatively light, and as DeCamp hesitated at the back rail *Forget It*'s automatic foghorn sounded. When Gunther Wolfhardt had shown up at his home above Nice, he'd made the decision that when this job was completed he would walk away from the business. And from Martine. Yet at this moment his blood was up, had gotten up over the past few days and especially this afternoon after they'd passed forty-two-double-oh-three, and he was having second thoughts. This thing that was going to happen tonight was the very reason he'd been born. Being deserted by his parents had been his real birth in the sense that he'd not come alive until he'd been taken in by Colonel Frazer, and eventually the SADF, where he'd learn to kill, quietly if the need arose, but above all efficiently and without remorse. "The bastard who you kill would certainly not shed a tear if it was you instead of him dead," the tactical instructors drilled into them.

DeCamp climbed down into the dinghy, and Wyner released the painter and peeled off to the right in a straight line for the tug out ahead of Vanessa. For all practical purposes they were invisible from anyone aboard the platform or the fleet because the decks were all lit up—on the platform because work had been going on around the clock, and just now they were having a party, and aboard the boats because Schlagel wanted it that way. "He wants to make a statement, loud and clear, that we're out here," Ransom had explained.

The thirty-five horsepower four-stroke outboard was quiet enough to allow nearly normal conversation. DeCamp called Gurov on the sat phone. "Status?"

"They're having a bloody party just like you expected they would."

"Is Nikolai with you?"

"Here with me in my quarters."

"Start with the off-duty crew in their cabins, then the delivery crew on the bridge and the communications equipment. Then the sat phones."

"What about McGarvey and the broad?" Gurov asked, and he sounded excited; the past weeks without action had gone on too long.

"Take them if you can, but only after you disable the communications equipment," DeCamp told him. "We're on the way to the tug now. ETA back to the *Pascagoula Trader* three zero minutes. Call as soon as you're ready for us."

"Will do," Gurov said. "Good luck."

DeCamp broke the connection and smiled grimly. He'd never believed in luck.

Gurov and Kabatov used the 9mm Ingram MAC 10 because even with its suppressor tube the submachine gun was light and compact, which would make it much easier to conceal as they worked their way through the maze of corridors and spaces aboard Vanessa. And at a cyclic rate of more than one thousand rounds per minute it was devastating in small spaces.

Gurov's eyes were bright as he stuffed a half-dozen thirty-round magazines into his pockets and seated the seventh in the handle of the weapon. "Finally we have the green light," he said.

Kabatov was doing the same, and he was excited though his movements were steady and precise and the expression on his face was bland, even indifferent. "How much time do we have?"

"He wants our go or no-go in thirty minutes," Gurov said. He pulled on his dark blue Windbreaker, put the sat phone in a zippered pocket, and donned a hard hat.

"That's cutting it close," Kabatov said. "If they run into trouble aboard the tug our arses could be out in the wind without some additional muscle."

"If you're talking about McGarvey and his bitch, we've been given the green light to take them out if we get the chance."

Kabatov grinned, and to Gurov at that moment his friend reminded him of a wolf, a hungry wolf.

They'd spent the past week between work shifts wandering around the platform, sightseeing, getting some exercise and fresh air, away from the welding and pipe fitting—sometimes in tight, nearly airless quarters. They came across as men who'd rather spend their off time alone, which didn't make them much different from many of the other roustabouts and construction workers, so they'd not stuck out, nor had anyone made any real effort to engage either of them in conversation, ask them to play pool or poker or go fishing off one of the lower decks. Which is exactly the way they'd played it. But in their wanderings they'd pinpointed all the crew's quarters, including the wing where the scientists slept and hung out, had made handwritten copies of the deck crew's schedule, and had taken quick looks at the platform delivery captain's station with its communications gear, and mapped out plausible routes to the pair of satellite dishes on the roof of the control room.

The plan they'd worked out from the blueprints in Tripoli was straightforward. First they were to kill anyone asleep in their quarters—the roustabouts and construction workers first because they were the muscle. Next they were to tap Captain Lapides and whoever was on duty in the delivery station and destroy the radios. Finally Kabatov was to use the ladder on the backside of the control room, out of sight from anyone down on deck, and cut the coaxial cable leads to both dishes, while Gurov maintained watch. All that would be left after that were a couple of sat phones.

Their primary orders were stealth; eliminate as many of the crew as possible and destroy the comms gear, but do it without detection. If someone pushed the panic button and sent a Mayday the mission would be scratched.

"Ready?" Gurov asked.

Kabatov nodded. "I'll go left."

Gurov checked to make sure that the corridor was empty, then slipped out of his room and went to the next cabin on the right, eased open the door, and went inside.

A man—one of the welders, Gurov thought—was in bed reading, and he looked up, startled at first but then angry. "What the fuck—?"

Gurov hit him with a short burst, destroying most of his chest, blood spraying against the bulkhead behind him, the noise from the weapon acceptable.

Close up the *Tony Ryan* was much older and more decrepit-looking than DeCamp had expected. But on second thought the Vanessa Explorer had been ready for the breaker yard, and InterOil would not have diverted a new oceangoing tug for a job like this. Which in a way was a bit of good news; crews aboard junk heaps were usually second-string, not as sharp as those aboard newer vessels.

The pilothouse, crew's quarters, and galley were all forward, leaving three-fourths of the ship open deck. A massive hawser was connected to a bridle arrangement taut behind the tug, beyond which a thick steel cable snaked back nearly one hundred meters to another bridle arrangement connected to the platform at three points for maximum stability.

The tug was making less than two knots, so there was virtually no wake, though directly aft the wash from the twin props was dangerous, so Wyner maneuvered the dinghy to the port quarter and forward to a position just below the pilothouse. The entire hull from the gunwales to the waterline was festooned with large truck tires and frayed four inch rope hawsers used as fenders.

DeCamp gently tossed a grappling hook and line up to the deck railing ten feet above and made it fast to the dinghy's painter, and Wyner throttled back and put the outboard in neutral.

They took out their weapons, charged them, slung them over their shoulders, and DeCamp started up first, no words between them, none needed at this point. On deck they crouched in the shadows for just a moment or two to make sure they'd not been detected. But the deck lights didn't come on, and DeCamp headed up the portside ladder to the bridge while Wyner went through the hatch and headed below to the galley and crew's quarters.

The *Tony Ryan's* bridge, dimly lit only by the red night-lights on the two radar sets as well as the navigation and communications equipment in the control panels and the overheads, stretched the entire width of the superstructure. Two men, both in civilian clothes, were on duty at the moment, one of them at the wheel, the other looking through a pair of binoculars at their tow. The helmsman, seated in a tall chair, his hands not actually touching the wheel, was dark, slightly built and wiry, while the other was heavyset and bald.

The helmsman looked up when DeCamp opened the door and came in, and when he spotted the weapon he reared back and said something in a language that sounded like Greek.

DeCamp fired one short burst, hitting the man in the left side of his chest, his neck, and face, driving him off the chair to the deck, blood flying everywhere.

The man with the binoculars had reacted slowly and he was just turning around when DeCamp switched aim and shot him high in the back, at least one round hitting him at the base of his skull. He flew forward, his face smashing into the rear window and his legs folding as he slumped to the deck.

DeCamp studied the nav gear, making sure that the boat was operating on autopilot, then switched off the two single sideband transceivers and two VHF radios and put a couple of rounds into the front panels of each, rendering them totally inoperative.

At the door he looked back. It had been almost too easy. So far. And although he expected no trouble from the six people back aboard the *Pascagoula Trader* he was pretty sure that the mission would unfold a bit differently aboard the oil platform.

Wyner met him on deck and had a wild look in his eyes. "Two of them in the galley and one in the shitter," he said. He was enjoying himself.

"Problems?"

"No. You?"

DeCamp shook his head. "They weren't expecting us. Let's get back."

Twenty minutes later Gurov was crouched in the lee of the deserted control room, the music still loud below on the main deck as Kabatov scrambled up the ladder to the roof to cut the cables to the satellite dishes—the only remaining links to the outside world except for his and McGarvey's sat phones.

But it was only a matter of time now before someone discovered the bodies of the six crewmen in their bunks, Lapides plus two of his people on duty in the delivery station, or that of the young woman scientist who they'd caught in the transverse corridor on the way to the control room. She'd just come out of the bathroom and Kabatov had broken her neck before she could cry out, and then they had stuffed her body in an empty tool locker. Her name tag said, LISA.

Kabatov came down the ladder. "Done."

"Let's see if we can find McGarvey and the broad," Gurov said. So far everything had gone exactly according to plan, which in his mind was a little worrisome. McGarvey had a dangerous rep. He glanced at his watch. "Ten minutes."

Forget It was cruising easily just a few feet from the Pascagoula Trader's port side, the nearly dead idle speed they were making ensuring that the water between the hulls was just about calm without bow wakes.

Helms was outside on deck talking to someone on the larger vessel when DeCamp and Wyner pulled up unseen alongside, made the painter secure, switched off the outboard, and scrambled aboard.

Crouching low behind the coaming DeCamp rapped his knuckles on the bulkhead and Helms glanced over his shoulder. DeCamp nodded.

Helms turned back, took out his silenced 9mm Steyr GB pistol and shot the man twice in the chest.

Edwin Burt and Paul Mitchell, the other two recent hires, had been hiding in the darkness behind the bridge. An instant after Helms fired they rushed out on deck as Lehr maneuvered *Forget It* close enough for the three of them to jump across and head directly for the bridge.

"Get the dinghy under cover," DeCamp told Wyner and he went up to the bridge where he got a pair of binoculars and scoped the platform first, and then the flotilla boats nearest to them.

"How does it look?" Lehr asked. He'd been a top-flight cop with the German Federal police, and he knew how to take orders even though he'd admitted he hated the bureaucracy.

A good man to have in a mission like this one in which so many things could go wrong, DeCamp thought. All of them were comrades tonight. And once again he could feel a little of the satisfaction of leading good men into harm's way. "We're clear so far."

Wyner came up to the bridge at the same time Helms appeared on the *Pascagoula Trader's* deck and gave the thumbs-up.

"Prep the chopper," DeCamp said, and Wyner went out and crossed over to the bigger vessel.

"How did it go aboard the tug?" Lehr asked. Like most mercenaries he did not like loose ends.

"As planned," DeCamp said tersely. "Are you clear on your orders?"

"Stand by out here for pickup once the op is completed, and then get the hell out to our mother ship," Lehr said. "May I have the coordinates?"

DeCamp gave him a latitude and longitude about eighty nautical miles to the southwest where a Liberian-registered freighter was supposed to be standing by for them, and he programmed the numbers into the ship's GPS system.

"*Danke.*"

Everyone else was aboard the other ship and both vessels were on autopilot. DeCamp pulled out his pistol and fired one shot into Lehr's forehead, driving the man off the helmsman's chair.

He got on the sat phone and hit Send. The thirty minutes were up. "Status."

Gurov answered on the first ring. "We're holed up in a forward crew quarters passageway. Defloria and his construction foreman are having a powwow."

"Take them out."

"Not advisable. We haven't gotten to McGarvey's sat phone."

"Find a way now," DeCamp said. "Priority one. Our ETA is five minutes."

"Will do," Gurov replied and he broke the connection. "They'll be here in five," he told Kabatov. "Make sure the landing pad is secure. I'm going after McGarvey's phone."

"Watch yourself."

Gurov replaced the magazine in his weapon with a fresh one. "Even Superman couldn't stand up to this shit," he said.

SIXTY

McGarvey sent Gail back to the party that promised to run very late. Everyone down there was having a great time, blowing off a lot of pent-up energy and tension that had been transmitted to them through Eve's reaction to the possible threat they were facing. Some of them were likely to jump overboard if someone showed up and shouted "Boo!"

"You've got a hunch?" she'd asked. They were in his room away from the noise of the party and the constant din from the boat horns circling them, and she'd picked up his antsiness.

"This is the right place and the right time," he told her.

"Has Otto come up with something?"

"Not as of this afternoon, but I asked him to do a global satellite search for anything moving anywhere in the Gulf, especially anything heading this way."

"Foreign registry on the way to the Canal? Untouchables without clear evidence?"

"Something like that," McGarvey'd said, and before she'd left he told her to get her pistol. "Neither of us walks around unarmed from this point."

"One of those kids catches on that we're packing and they could start screaming bloody murder."

"That might be the least of our worries," McGarvey said.

She gave him an odd look and then left.

He called Otto on the sat phone. "Have you come up with anything new?"

"Nada," Otto said and he sounded dejected. "Rats in the attic?"

"Just a feeling."

"Me too, but honest injun, kemo sabe, there's nothing anywhere near you other than Schlagel's flotilla, and I'd be just about willing to bet the farm that if and when trouble comes your way it won't be from that direction. They're major jerks and Jesus freaks and full of themselves but they're not like the antiabortion crowd willing to kill for their beliefs. They're not even as bad as Greenpeace. None of them will try to stop you. They'll just hassle you all the way to Florida."

"No ships coming our way to or from Tampa or Port Manatee?"

"Nothing within a hundred miles—and even that close it would take 'em more than four hours to get to you. We could have the Coast Guard to you in one-fourth that time. My guess is if they're coming it'll either be by chopper from Tampa or someplace like that, flying low and slow under radar, either that or a go-fast boat, something like a Cigarette or hydrofoil. The timing might be a little tight for them to make the hit, and in any event they'd have to get away clean, because I don't think DeCamp is such a dedicated jihadist that he's willing to give his life for the mission."

"No," McGarvey said. The hairs on the back of his neck were bristling. "But we're missing something, goddamnit."

"Has anyone from the flotilla tried to make contact either with the delivery crew or with Eve Larsen?"

"I don't know about Eve or any of her people, but Defloria said they've been getting a steady stream of radio traffic on the VHF."

"If they're interfering with ship-to-ship channels, or tying up sixteen I can get the Coast Guard out there on a violation complaint."

"Except for the noise they haven't tried to interfere with operations so far," McGarvey said.

"I could ask Coast Guard Tampa to come out and make an inspection, sewage dumps overboard or something."

"No."

"You're not thinking straight. If something goes down out there and someone gets hurt you'll take the heat even though the Bureau and everyone else says no one is going to try anything. So let's make an end run."

McGarvey had thought about that very thing from the start. If an attack did come someone would get hurt—possibly a lot of people. Since the Bureau or the Coast Guard were officially hands off, the only alternatives would have been to postpone moving the platform to Florida or to cancel Eve's project altogether. The first might have given them time to find DeCamp, now that they knew his name, though there was no telling how long that might take. The man was a professional and he'd not made many mistakes in his career. It was possible they'd never find him. And it was equally possible that whoever was behind the threat might hire someone else and they would have to start their search all over again. And canceling the project was totally out of the question. Even if NOAA tried to pull the plug Eve wouldn't stand for it; and now as a Nobel laureate she carried a lot of weight.

Which left what?

At one point Otto had suggested smuggling a SEAL team aboard, or having a submarine trail them, but the Pentagon had declined, nor would pressuring the White House have worked either. The official stance was hands-off because the Saudis and other OPEC countries were becoming increasingly nervous with each step Eve's program came nearer to completion and the administration couldn't afford to antagonize its oil suppliers. If OPEC made sharp cutbacks the nation would be in serious trouble, much worse than the gas lines of the seventies because the U.S. had become ever more dependent on foreign oil.

The stakes had simply become too high for them to back away, and he said as much to Otto. "There's a real possibility that DeCamp won't try to pull anything off until Schlagel's flotilla is gone. Too many witnesses."

"But you don't believe it."

"To tell the truth, I don't know what the hell I believe anymore," McGarvey said, some bitterness welling up. He felt as if he were itching for a fight, wanting it to come, wanting to get it over with. "Gail and I are just along for the ride."

"I hear you, Mac," Otto said. He sounded subdued, as if he'd tried to talk some sense into a friend, but had failed. "But God help the bastards if they do try to hit you."

"Yeah," McGarvey said, and he switched off and laid the phone on the desk. He wanted to hurt someone.

Even here inside his cabin McGarvey could hear the boat whistles and horns and faintly the music and sounds of singing and laughter down on deck, and truly wondered if he had any other choice, if he'd ever had a choice from the moment he'd helped Eve get away from the power plant.

He checked the load in his pistol, holstered it at the small of his back, and pocketing a spare magazine he headed down one deck to the galley to get a cup of coffee, expecting to see at least a couple of Defloria's people, but the place was empty. It struck him as odd. There was always someone here

"Anyone home?" McGarvey called. He went across to the pass-through and looked inside. Nothing was on the grill and the kitchen was deserted, though a pot of something was steaming on one of the stoves.

No blood, nothing out of place, no reason whatsoever to be concerned. He turned and looked toward the open door to the corridor. Defloria had given his crew the evening off, and some of them would be up in the rec room, or catching up on sleep in their cabins. Some of them liked to fish from the lower decks during their time off. It was even possible a few of them had joined the party, especially Defloria and his construction foreman.

McGarvey used the house phone next to the galley door and called the delivery control room, but there was no answer after four rings, and the hairs at the nape of his neck bristled again.

Hanging up, he stood for several moments listening not only to the sounds of the rig, the distant sounds of the party on deck, and of the boat horns, but to some inner voice that his wife Katy had called his early warning detector. He'd been born with whatever it was that sometimes gave him an almost preternatural sense when something bad was about to happen. And he'd learned over the years to really listen as if his life depended on understanding what he was hearing, because on more than one occasion it had.

But just now nothing seemed to be out of the ordinary, except for the deserted galley.

"Goddamnit," he said, frustrated.

He had the almost overwhelming feeling that whatever was going to happen had already started.

He went across to the corridor door where he held up for just a moment, and suddenly he picked out another sound from the other noises, louder now and getting louder, and he realized that he had heard it earlier. A helicopter was incoming. It's what he'd been missing all along; it was the Jet Ranger on the aftdeck of one of boats in Schlagel's flotilla. The bastard was involved after all.

Drawing his pistol he peered around the door frame but the corridor was still empty, and he stepped out and hurried to the companionway where he took the stairs two at a time, mindful to make as little noise as possible.

The helicopter was much closer now, just about on top of them. But the chopper only carried a pilot plus four passengers, so unless DeCamp had managed to place some of his people aboard at Biloxi the odds weren't all that bad. But McGarvey had to consider the possibility that one or more of them were here and had already taken out some of the off-duty crew. And maybe any scientist or technician not at the party, maybe taking a break or something.

At the top McGarvey eased around the corner in time to see a stockily built man dressed in black coming down the corridor, a suppressed MAC-10 in his hand.

McGarvey ducked back behind the stairwell bulkhead, as the intruder opened fire, bullets ricocheting all over the place.

The ultracompact Ingram wasn't very accurate at any range over a few yards, even less accurate because of the long suppressor barrel, but its major disadvantage was its high rate of fire. A thirty-round magazine on full auto lasted less than two seconds.

McGarvey had this in a split second, and keeping flat against the bulkhead he fired two rounds against the corridor wall, the 9mm bullets ricocheting away with high-pitched whines.

The shooter sprayed the corridor, but the firing suddenly stopped and McGarvey heard the empty magazine hit the deck. He stepped up around the corner as the man slammed a fresh magazine into the handle.

"Raise your weapon and you'll die," McGarvey said.

The helicopter had landed, the noise of the rotors fading.

Gurov stood motionless, his eyes narrowed, and McGarvey thought he recognized the man as one of the new employees who'd been taken on just before the platform had gotten underway.

"How many of you came aboard at Biloxi?" McGarvey asked. The man looked Eastern European.

Gurov made no move to raise his weapon. But it was clear he was weighing his options, and just as clear he was willing to waste time here.

"Only five of your people came over aboard the helicopter, one of them Brian DeCamp. How about the others, Russian *pizdecs* like you?" At this point McGarvey figured knowledge was more valuable than time.

Gurov said nothing.

McGarvey suddenly walked directly toward the Russian, who at the last moment started to raise his weapon, but Mac shot him in the right knee, knocking him down. Before he could recover Mac bent down and jammed the muzzle of his pistol into the side of his head.

"Talk to me," McGarvey said.

"Fuck you," Gurov grunted. He batted the pistol away from his head with his left hand and raised the MAC with his right.

McGarvey grabbed the end of the still hot suppressor tube and twisted the muzzle under Gurov's chin as the weapon went off, completely destroying the man's head.

McGarvey took the man's weapon, removed the magazine, and jammed the suppresser barrel against the deck and, using his foot, bent it a few degrees rendering the submachine gun useless. He found a walkie-talkie that he pocketed as he ran down the corridor to his room. Otto could have an Air Force special ops team here from McDill in Tampa in under an hour. All McGarvey had to do was delay DeCamp and his team, and keep as many of the people aboard Vanessa alive for as long as possible.

But his sat phone lay in pieces on the floor of his room. One of the contractors had been here.

The music on deck had stopped but there'd been no shooting, no cries of alarm. It wouldn't last for long.

McGarvey took the Franchi twelve-bore shotgun from his equipment pack, quickly loaded it, stuffing a couple dozen shells in his pockets, along with several one hundred-gram packets of Semtex plastic explosives and a number of pencil fuses.

The equation had definitely changed, and he was going to change it further.

SIXTY-ONE

Brian DeCamp and the other three contractors got out of the Bell Ranger as Wyner completed the shutdown. Burt and Mitchell used two of the tie-down points on deck to secure the machine, while Helms ran to the edge of the pad to watch for someone coming up to investigate. It was Kabatov, who'd been waiting for them on the helipad. Like the others, he was dressed all in black, his face blackened, and he was armed with the silenced MP5 SD6.

Someone laughed below on the main deck but the music had stopped.

"Where is Boris?" DeCamp asked. The platform didn't feel right to him. Something was nagging at the back of his head. "Instinct is your best friend on the battlefield," Colonel Frazer had drummed into his head from day one. "Feed it good intel and then trust it, boyo."

"He went to look for McGarvey's sat phone," Kabatov said.

"How about the other communications equipment?"

"All of it disabled."

"Good," DeCamp said. Here aboard the rig they would communicate with low-powered Icom walkie-talkies. He pulled his out of his pocket and keyed the push to talk switch. "Boris, status."

"Someone's coming," Helms called from the dark. "Two men. Shall I take them out?"

"Help him," DeCamp told Mitchell. Gurov wasn't answering. "Status," DeCamp said again.

"What do you want me to do?" Helms called urgently.

DeCamp hesitated a moment, thinking about the situation. Either Gurov was down or he was in a situation where he couldn't answer. Kirk McGarvey was aboard because he'd suspected this attack, but DeCamp had been assured by his contacts that the U.S. government did not share the view; not the FBI, the CIA, or Homeland Security.

"Kill one, take the other hostage," DeCamp told him, and he turned back to the walkie-talkie. "Boris does not answer, so for the moment I have to assume that Mr. McGarvey has somehow gotten involved. Am I correct?"

Defloria came up the stairs onto the helicopter pad and Helms pointed the MP5 at him. "This way please," he said, motioning toward Mitchell who also held his weapon pointed at the OIM.

"Jesus," Defloria said, rearing back.

Stefanato came up right behind him, and when he saw the two men and the guns he tried to turn away but Helms tapped him twice in the side of the head at nearly point-blank range and the construction foreman pitched sideways and fell heavily ten feet to the first landing, dead before he'd hit it.

DeCamp walked over to the three men, and held out the walkie-talkie in front of their hostage. "What is your name, sir?" he asked.

Defloria had the look of a defeated man. He was large enough to have played professional football at some point in his life, but he wasn't a fighter. "Justin Defloria," he said.

"And your job here is?" DeCamp asked.

"I'm the Operations Installation Manager."

"Did you get that?" DeCamp said into the walkie-talkie.

"Yes," McGarvey said. "But I suggest that you get back in your helicopter and get out of here while you still can. Help is on the way from McDill."

"Oh, I doubt that seriously," DeCamp said. "If you want to avoid any further bloodshed this is what you are going to do for us, because my mission here is to destroy this platform and send it to the bottom, but not kill anyone unless absolutely necessary. Lay down your weapon and join the party on the main deck. We'll have everyone, including you and your assistant, loaded aboard the automatic lifeboats, and once you're all safely away we'll go about our business."

McGarvey didn't answer.

Wyner was finished securing the helicopter and he came over to the edge of the helipad with the other two men. Defloria was impressed.

"In that case, here is what we will do," DeCamp said. "We're going to secure all the personnel aboard this platform including the scientists, especially Dr. Larsen. If you make any overt move against us we will kill them all."

The walkie-talkie was silent, and after a couple of seconds DeCamp stuffed it in his pocket. "Mr. McGarvey prefers to make it difficult for us, so let's keep on our toes." He prodded Defloria with the muzzle of his MP5. "We'll join the party on deck. Whoever bags McGarvey will receive a fifty thousand euro bonus."

Defloria hesitated at the stairs. "The second your helicopter was spotted the delivery crew called for help."

"The radios have been disabled," DeCamp said. "No calls went out."

"You're forgetting the tug, you bastard."

There were parts of every job he'd ever been on that were DeCamp's favorite. Like these when the target began using up his chips to bargain for his life, never dreaming that he was facing a royal flush.

Kabatov took the lead because he knew the layout, Mitchell and Helms directly behind him, followed by Defloria, Burt, and Wyner. At the bottom DeCamp held them up behind one of the large pipe storage lockers welded to the main deck.

"Where is McGarvey's assistant?" he asked.

"Last I saw she was at the party on deck," Kabatov said.

"As soon as you spot her, kill her."

"Will do," Kabatov said.

"She and McGarvey are our primary high-priority targets," DeCamp said. "Same bonus applies to her. Clear, gentlemen?"

"Yes, sir," Kabatov and the others replied.

"Then let's proceed," DeCamp said. He prodded Defloria ahead. "After you, Mr. OIM."

They came around the corner, and DeCamp fired a sort burst into the air.

Eve Larsen, standing at one end of the long table that had been set up to hold the drinks and hors d'oeuvres, reared back, and her scientists and techs moved almost protectively around her. Even the musicians laid their instruments aside and moved toward her. It was clear by the looks on their faces, by their scared, nervous postures that they'd been expecting trouble, had probably been waiting for it ever since McGarvey and Gail Newby had shown up.

DeCamp's people immediately spread out, taking whatever cover they could behind the various storage lockers and equipment bolted or welded to the deck, their heads on swivels keeping an eye on the science team while searching the shadows above and especially behind them for any sign of McGarvey.

Eve stepped forward arrogantly, her lip out. "Who are you and what the fuck are you doing on my platform?" she demanded, her voice rock steady.

DeCamp had to admire her courage, at least a little, and he gave her a pleasant smile. "Oh, I think you know. I think Mr. McGarvey briefed you either before or after Oslo. And, congratulations on your prize, it must be a great vindication for your work."

"You'd know nothing about it," Eve said, her voice rising in anger. "We create, while you do nothing but destroy. And not even for principle, only for pay."

Kabatov came to DeCamp's side. "She's not here," he said, his voice low enough that Eve or the others could not have heard him.

"She's around someplace, unless she abandoned ship," DeCamp said. "We'll find her."

"She may be with McGarvey."

DeCamp nodded. "Ladies and gentlemen, please pay attention. Contrary to what you may have been told we mean you no personal harm. We have come here this evening merely to destroy the project."

"You son of a bitch," Eve said stepping past her people. She pulled up short when Kabatov pointed his MAC-10 directly at her. "You're one of the construction crew," she said, recognizing him. And she turned to Defloria. "He's one of yours?"

"I didn't know until now," Defloria said. "I'm sorry."

"We need to make certain preparations, during which you will have to be secured from causing any interference," DeCamp said. "Your experience will not be particularly pleasant, but it will last for less than an hour, after which you will be released and we will leave. From that moment you will have an additional thirty minutes to get aboard the lifeboats and abandon ship."

"You're going to kill us!" one of the young women shrieked.

"I assure you that is not my intention. No one who cooperates will be harmed."

Helms had opened one of the larger pipe lockers welded to the deck. About the size of a trailer for a semi; long and narrow, the storage bin was empty, and dark almost like a coffin.

"I'm not going in there," one of the techs said, shrinking back.

Don stepped forward, and before Eve could do or say anything to stop him he walked up to the blond man who obviously was the leader. The terrorists trained their weapons on him.

"No need for that," Don said. "I'm the man you know as William Bell, your contact here."

The scientists were shocked, and DeCamp suppressed a smile. None of them had suspected they'd had a traitor in their midst, especially not Eve Larsen who, this man had said, was in love with him. "She'll do anything I tell her to do," he had promised.

"Including not demanding a military escort?" DeCamp had asked several weeks ago.

"Especially not that. She thinks having that son of a bitch McGarvey aboard is all the protection she'll need."

DeCamp motioned for his men to train their weapons elsewhere, and he lowered his MP5. "You have been of some help, Mr. . . . . Bell."

"Dr. Don Price, actually, and I'm glad you're finally here."

"Why?" Eve asked, her voice strangled.

DeCamp almost laughed out loud. Price was a pompous ass, and the woman was naïve. Smart people with no common sense, and in the case of Price, no moral purpose.

"This is nothing but a stupid pipe dream with zero chance of success," Price said, turning to her and the others. "If you'd listened to me in the first place, if you had actually read my papers, studied my mathematics, you'd know that your experiments are dead ends. Failures. You won't be able to control the climate and you'll be the laughingstock of the scientific community—a position you've already just about hit. They handed you proof of that in Oslo by giving you the stupid Peace Prize, and not physics. Carbon capture is the future. The only future. My methods, my studies, my papers. My Nobel Prize in Physics."

"Christ, Don, is this what it's all about?" Eve asked. "Being famous? Professional jealousy, you dumb bastard?"

Price turned back to DeCamp. "That's the arrogant bullshit I've had to swallow all this time," he said.

"You could have come to me," Eve said plaintively.

"So now what can I do to help with the mission?" Don said.

"Why, die, of course," DeCamp said, and he raised his MP5 and shot the scientist in the face at point-blank range, driving the man backwards off his feet, and sending a spray of blood across the deck.

Some of the women techs screamed, but Eve stood her ground—her mouth open, her eyes wide.

Defloria shoved Mitchell away and bolted, but before he got five feet Wyner raised his weapon and fired two silenced shots, blowing the back of the InterOil manager's skull apart and sending him to the deck.

"All right!" DeCamp shouted. "Calm down! No one else needs to be hurt."

"You mean to kill us all," Eve said when her people finally quieted down.

"Not necessary," DeCamp said, and he motioned toward the open pipe locker. "If you will be so kind as to step inside, we'll lock you away for a bit, and you'll be out of the way and absolutely safe."

SIXTY-TWO

Gail reached the shadows behind one of the massive impeller cable tripods just as Eve and her postdocs and techs were herded into one of the pipe lockers about fifty feet away and the doors secured with a pry bar.

She'd been gone not much more than five minutes from the time she'd heard the incoming helicopter and slipped away from the party until now, and Defloria and Don Price both were lying dead on the deck, obviously shot in the head with powerful weapons. Silenced weapons, because up in the delivery control room where she'd gone to send the Mayday, she hadn't heard a thing. All she'd been concentrating on at that moment were the facts that Lapides and one of his crew were dead and the radios destroyed.

Mac had been right again, just as he had been right about an imminent attack. They'd apparently taken on one or more ringers from Biloxi. And when DeCamp's signal came they'd swept through the rig killing people. Maybe even Mac.

The slightly built man giving orders was DeCamp, the same man she'd seen in the second-floor corridor at Hutchinson Island. Although she couldn't hear his voice or see his eyes this time, she could tell he was the same man from the way he held himself, his self-assured manner, his apparent indifference. Nor could she clearly hear what he was saying, but she knew that he was issuing orders.

Watching them she felt more alone than she had ever felt, except the night she'd learned that her father had been shot to death. She had to assume the worst-case scenario now, that Mac was down and she was on her own. There were six of them, including DeCamp and possibly an additional one or more somewhere aboard, killing the rest of the construction and delivery crew, including Herb Stefanato who'd been at the party with Defloria.

She didn't think it was likely for her to take all of them out or even save the rig from destruction, but she figured they would be elsewhere engaged setting their explosives so that she would have a shot at getting Eve Larsen and her people out of the storage locker and into one of the automatic lifeboats and launch them into the sea.

DeCamp said something to his operators, two of whom immediately headed over to the outside stairs that led up to the helipad, while the others went with him to the main corridor hatch that led in one direction to the science control room and in the other across to the living quarters.

All that was left were the two bodies, the party table, the constant noise of the boat whistles and horns, and the pipe locker. Since her father's death and especially since what she considered were her failures at Hutchinson Island, Gail had come out here with the selfish motive of proving herself to Mac. It was important because the only other man she'd ever loved had been shot to death in downtown Minneapolis by a street bum, and she didn't want to lose Mac or disappoint him.

She waited a full two minutes after DeCamp and his operators were gone, then cocked the hammer of her SIG and stepped out of the shadows, hesitated just a moment longer to make sure no one had been left behind, then hurried across to the pipe locker. She could hear murmurs from inside, like pigeons in a hutch, and she leaned in close.

"Dr. Larsen, it's me."

The murmurs stopped and Eve was right there on the other side of the door. "Can you get us out of here?"

The broad muzzle of a suppressor tube touched the side of Gail's face and she started to bring her pistol up.

"No need to die here, Ms. Newby," Kabatov said. "Not now, not like this."

She was seething with anger. She'd let this happen. She'd walked right into it as if she'd been wearing a blindfold. Again she hadn't trusted her instincts that had been singing the tune loud and clear: De-Camp was a professional who hardly ever made mistakes. Price had been a traitor, so he would have informed DeCamp about Mac and about her. And setting the trap, which she'd walked into, had been child's play.

"Decock your weapon and raise it over your shoulder, handle first."

She'd been trained to suddenly move her head a couple of inches to the right, bat the muzzle of Kabatov's weapon to the left while firing her pistol over her shoulder into the man's face. But he was a pro and she didn't know if she had the luck.

So she did as she was told, her disappointment in herself raging as deeply and strongly as the grindingly heavy chip she'd been carrying on her shoulder for as long as she could remember.

"Bastard," she said.

Kabatov laughed and stepped back. "Pull the pry bar out and step inside, I'm sure you'll have plenty to talk about."

Gail turned to look at him, his face flat, his lips thick, a five o'clock shadow darkening his already swarthy features. He was a pit bull ready and willing to tear her throat out with the slightest provocation, and she shuddered inwardly.

She pulled the pry bar out of the latch, a momentary urge to hit him in the face with it, instead she handed it to him, opened the door, and stepped inside.

Eve and the others had backed away, and for just a moment seeing who it was they lit up, but then they spotted Kabatov and the door was closed, plunging them into near-total darkness, the only light coming through the seams at the corners.

"Where's McGarvey?" Eve demanded.

Gail was certain that Kabatov was still listening. "I think he's dead," she said for his benefit.

"Christ," Eve said.

And in that one word Gail found that she had genuine pity for the woman because she knew for certain that Eve was in love with Mac. Probably head over heels, judging by her despair. An even if they got out of this, both of them would end up disappointed.

They heard something rattle into the latch, and Gail knew that it wasn't the pry bar. It was a padlock. She put her ear to the door in time to hear footfalls moving away, and then nothing except the boat horns and the normal machinery sounds of the platform's various systems.

"Anyone got a flashlight?" she asked.

"On my key ring," someone said.

"Won't he see it through the cracks?" Eve asked.

"He's gone," Gail said.

A thin beam of light suddenly came on, enough so they at least could see each other. Eve and her techs and postdocs were frightened half out of their skulls.

"Is it true that Kirk is dead?" Eve asked. "Or did you just tell us that for his benefit in case he was listening?"

"I don't know," Gail said. "At least I hope he isn't. But in the meantime we're on our own. Everyone look around see if we can find something to use to get us out of here, and maybe a weapon of some sort."

"What good will that do?" one of the techs asked. "Someone on the bridge must have sent a Mayday by now."

"That's where I went when I heard the helicopter. But they're all dead and the radio gear has been destroyed."

"I say we don't antagonize them," the same young man said. "My God, look what they did to Don and Mr. Defloria. Let them do what they came to do, and when they're gone we'll take to the lifeboats. We can always come up with another oil platform."

"They're not going to let us out of here," Gail told them.

"But they said they're going to blow up the rig or something."

"Yes, and we'll ride it to the bottom of the Gulf," Eve said. "They have to make sure no one aboard survives."

"But why?" a young woman asked.

"There's no reason," someone else said.

"They can't let us live, we saw their faces," Eve said. She turned and looked at the others. "Where's Lisa?"

SIXTY-THREE

McGarvey's hands had been tied until this moment. Lying in the darkness on the platform that had once accommodated the workspace for the base of the exploration drilling rig about thirty feet above the main deck, he was in a position to see everything that had gone on below, plus the helipad one hundred feet to the left and ten feet above him.

His pistol and Franchi shotgun were all but useless at those distances, so he couldn't have risked trying to take his shot.

DeCamp and his people were all gone, two up to the helicopter where they'd retrieved two satchels and disappeared belowdecks, and the others into the main lateral corridor below and to McGarvey's right that ran the width of the platform with access not only to the living and recreation decks, but in one direction to the science control room and the other to the delivery bridge.

The contractor who'd locked Gail and the others inside the pipe locker had walked away and McGarvey was about to go down to the main deck when the man came back, obviously taking pains to conceal his return, and McGarvey eased back into the shadows.

But now the main deck was deserted, and so far as McGarvey could tell no sentries had been posted, though he was fairly sure that at least one or two of DeCamp's people were looking for him, while the two who'd carried the satchels from the helicopter were setting the explosives to sink the rig. Which made them priority one.

McGarvey crawled to the edge of the platform and took the ladder down to the main deck, where keeping to the deeper shadows as much as possible he made his way to the pipe locker that was secured with a heavy-duty padlock.

"Gail," he called softly.

"My God, Kirk, I didn't know what happened to you," Gail said. "Can you get us out of here?"

"Not without making a lot of noise. Is everyone okay?"

"No one's been hurt," Gail said. "Lapides and one of his people are dead up in the control room and the radios destroyed. I think they're going to try to sink us."

"That's exactly what they're going to do," McGarvey said. "They brought two satchels down from the helicopter, almost certainly explosives. They're going to take out two of the legs and capsize the rig. I'm going to take them out."

"What if you don't make it?" Eve asked. "We'll be stuck in here."

"It won't happen," Gail said, trying to override her.

"Goddamnit, there's six of them, all heavily armed, and it looked like they knew what they were doing."

"She's right," McGarvey said, taking one of the pencil fuses from his pocket. It just fit through the gap between the two halves of the door. "Here."

"Got it," Gail said.

He tore a lump about the size of book of matches from one of the blocks of Semtex and molded it around the body of the combination lock, making sure it was secure enough so that when Gail inserted the fuse through the gap it wouldn't get dislodged.

"Stay put until you hear the helicopter take off," he told them. "If I'm not back by then, blow the lock and get to the lifeboats."

"I'm sorry, Kirk," Gail said.

"You had lousy odds," McGarvey said. "Don't do anything to attract their attention. I don't want them to come back for some reason and spot the Semtex."

"I don't want to die," one of the young women cried softly.

"You're not going to die," Gail told her.

"Keep them quiet," McGarvey said, and he turned and headed for the hatch to the main corridor.

SIXTY-FOUR

In the delivery control room DeCamp was monitoring the VHF non-commercial channels sixty-eight and sixty-nine that the flotilla had used to communicate with one another to make sure that no one had noticed the activity aboard the oil platform. But the chatter was normal, mostly small talk heavily laced with religious mumbojumbo, the same as it had been all the way across from Biloxi.

To this point the operation was going according to plan with the exception of Gurov and his walkie-talkie now in McGarvey's hands, which made issuing orders to his people problematic. But not impossible. The odds were still definitely in their favor.

"He just went through the hatch into the main corridor," Wyner said from one of windows looking down on the deck.

Like clockwork, DeCamp thought, suppressing a slight smile. The trouble with professionals was their professionalism. By the training manual. Thinking out of the box was generally frowned on, especially by some of the unimaginative bastards who wrote those manuals. It was the same in just about every army or security service in the world. The good field officers remained in the field, while the failures were often the ones who made up rules. Hidebound government bureaucrats who couldn't see beyond their cubicles. Certainly in America no one had wanted to believe in a scenario in which al-Quaeda could mount such a devastating attack as 9/11. Most of them had been looking in the wrong direction—were still looking in the wrong direction—which made his work all the more easier.

DeCamp keyed his walkie-talkie. "Shall we make it one hundred thousand euros?" he said, effectively alerting his people that McGarvey was on the way.

The trap had been almost too easy. Locking Dr. Larsen and her scientists in the container and deserting the main deck had simply been too tempting a target for either McGarvey himself or the woman he'd brought with him—who turned out to be Gail Newby, the security officer from Hutchinson Island. He'd been only slightly disappointed that it had been Ms. Newby and not McGarvey but that didn't matter, because now he held the high ground. McGarvey was a dead man marching.

Wyner had been studying the pipe locker through a set of binoculars. "Looks like plastique around the lock," he said.

"About what I suspected," DeCamp said. "No doubt he managed to pass a fuse through to Ms. Newby."

"There's enough room for it between the doors."

"What's he carrying?"

"I'm sure he has a pistol, but he's got what looks like a Franchi slung over his shoulder," Wyner said.

It was a nasty weapon. DeCamp had seen firsthand what it was capable of doing in a confined space when he'd sent six of his men into the home of an Angolan army general outside Luanda, the capital city. All six had been cut down, but in the heat of battle the general had used all of his ammunition in one short firefight, leaving himself defenseless. In the end DeCamp had fired his American-made Colt Commando six times into the general's face—one round for each of his Buffalo Battalion troop—destroying the man's skull.

"Bring the two women up here," DeCamp said. "It's time we provided a little distraction for McGarvey. Perhaps give him pause."

SIXTY–FIVE

McGarvey held up at the corner before the mess hall one level down from his and Gail's rooms. The bodies of two construction crewmen lay sprawled on the deck, their blood smeared on the bulkhead. A third man lay in an open doorway, blood still pooling beneath his body. This had happened within the last few minutes.

"Goddamnit," he said under his breath. It was senseless. Had the Coast Guard been sent out to escort Vanessa to Florida where security might have been tediously long, none of this would have happened. Some good people had died here, and more would probably lose their lives before it was over. And he was a part of it.

But he'd seen this same kind of shit before; over and over again in his career. Timid bureaucrats, unwilling to stick their necks out. In this case because of someone with a vested interest in oil; someone whose back was against the wall, someone who could not allow an experiment like this to succeed.

Follow the money, he'd told Otto.

Someone shouted something farther down the corridor, and McGarvey heard what sounded like rounds richochetting off a steel bulkhead.

He had counted five operators in addition to DeCamp. Two had fetched the satchels from the helicopter and were somewhere below setting the charges. Which left two, possibly three, men working their way through the rig trying to find him and killing everyone they came across. No one was to be left alive, shot to death or locked away someplace to drown when the platform went to the bottom.

They were professionals. Almost certainly ex-military special services who for one reason or another became independent mercenaries, rather than go to work for a contracting service. It meant that by their very nature they were men who did not take orders very well.

They were in the business purely for the money. Their loyalty went to whoever had the biggest bank account, and only for however long they could see a clear escape route. These were not Islamic extremists willing to die for the cause. It was a weakness.

He keyed the walkie-talkie. "You've forgotten the helicopter, Colonel DeCamp," he said, as he started down the corridor toward the sounds of the gunfire. "I have something you may need."

Turning the receive volume way down so that he had to bring the handheld to his ear to hear if DeCamp answered, he hurried down the corridor, holding up at the open door to the galley. But the mess hall appeared to be deserted.

At the far corner he held up again, and keyed his walkie-talkie, but didn't speak.

From somewhere down the corridor, very close, he heard the distinct click of a handheld receiving his signal, and raising his shotgun he peered around the corner, when DeCamp's voice came over his walkie-talkie.

"Don't kill him yet."

Someone in one of the rooms a few feet farther down the corridor reached around the door frame with a silenced MAC-10 and fired a short burst. McGarvey snapped off three shots and ducked back, directly into the warm muzzle of a suppressor.

"You killed a friend of ours," Burt said, his British accent heavy.

"You have me," McGarvey said, dropping the walkie-talkie. He raised the shotgun up above his head, the muzzle pointed toward the overhead.

"Prick," Burt said, and he grabbed the Franchi, his pressure with the MP5 SDG against the back of McGarvey's head momentarily eased.

McGarvey ducked to the right, the Heckler & Koch firing an inch from the side of his head, and he slammed the Franchi's receiver into the man's face, breaking his nose and smashing out two teeth.

Burt grunted in pain as he stepped back and tried to bring the MP5 to bear, but McGarvey kept on him, batting his gun hand away, and yanking the shotgun out of his grasp.

"You should have turned down this job," McGarvey said, jamming the Franchi under Burt's chin. He pulled off one round, the twelve-bore taking off the back of the merc's skull and violently slamming his body against the bulkhead.

As Burt crumpled to the deck, McGarvey grabbed the submachine gun, pointed it around the corner and, one handed, sprayed the corridor, emptying the magazine.

There was no return fire.

"Get off this rig or I'll kill you," McGarvey called out, laying the weapon on the deck softly enough to make no noise. Picking up the walkie-talkie he hurried to the opposite end of the corridor where he ducked down the companionway, holding up on the first stair, and peering around the corner.

But no one was coming, or if they were they were being cautious about it.

McGarvey continued down five levels, taking the stairs two at a time, and making as little noise as possible. By now the explosive charges would have been set on two of the four legs, somewhere as close to the waterline as possible. But he didn't think DeCamp would push the button until the helicopter was secured. For the moment their primary concern was taking him down and finding out if he'd been telling the truth that he had something they needed.

At the bottom, below the main deck, but still forty feet above the surface of the Gulf, the platform's four massive legs, each thirty feet in diameter, were interconnected by a latticework of steel beams and girders and a catwalk with high railings.

Still no one had come after him, nor could he see anyone at or near the legs, which had to mean that the charges had already been set and the two men had gone topsides. But they had to know that he was down there. It was possible that DeCamp had sent someone to check out the helicopter and was at this moment getting set to fly off and push the button, but there was something else, McGarvey was certain of it.

DeCamp's escape. Once the rig went to the bottom he'd be stuck with the flotilla. His only way out was the Bell Ranger, but with a full load its range was limited. They'd never get out of the Gulf.

But DeCamp knew what he was doing. He had a plan, and he was confident in it. McGarvey had heard that much in the man's voice. There'd been no frustration, no fear, and especially no anger. He was a commander in control of the battlefield, and he had an escape route which he thought was foolproof.

But confident men made mistakes.

McGarvey turned up the walkie-talkie's volume to counteract the noise of the boat horns, the tug's massive engines out in front of them, and the wind tunneling through the substructure and the motion-induced waves sloshing against the legs, and pocketed it.

Keeping low, he headed to the leg on the front right corner of the rig relative to the direction it was being towed. He had a fifty-fifty chance at picking one of the two legs that had been sabotaged, but correct leg or not, he still had to find the explosives, while at the same time keep an eye over his shoulder for an attack he expected to come at any moment.

DeCamp knew where he was headed.

McGarvey hurried down the short ramp that led across from the main catwalk to another much narrower-railed walkway that circled the leg. An olive drab satchel, more like a small duffle bag, was shaped in an arc and jammed between the walkway and the curved steel plates of the leg.

Glancing over his shoulder to make sure one of DeCamp's shooters wasn't right behind him, McGarvey knelt down in front of the satchel. No wires came out of the thing, which meant its detonator was already in countdown mode, or the explosion would be radio-controlled once DeCamp and his people abandoned the rig. McGarvey gingerly released the snap catch and eased open the top flap. The duffle was half filled with a gray material that smelled faintly sour, like plumber's putty. It was Semtex, the same explosive he and Gail had brought with them.

Exceedingly stable—only an electrical charge would set it off—and extremely powerful. He figured the bag had to contain at least twenty kilos of the stuff, more than enough to take out a large section of the leg.

A radio-controlled detonator probe was stuck in the side of the mass, the light on a cell phone-sized unit green.

He glanced over his shoulder again, but if anyone was back there they were in the deeper shadows. Taking care not to disturb the detonator unit, which was possibly motion sensitive—too big a force or sudden movement would set it off—McGarvey prised the package out of the space between the narrow catwalk and the leg and set it down.

"Don't kill him just yet," DeCamp's voice came from McGarvey's walkie-talkie.

Kabatov unexpectedly came from around the curve of the leg, where he'd been waiting, and slammed the back plate of the MAC 10 into McGarvey's temple.

A shower of stars burst inside of McGarvey's head, and he went down heavily, banging his face on the steel grate.

These guys are good, the thought crystallized as he came around and could understand what he was hearing.

"He's down," Kabatov said.

"See if he's carrying anything," DeCamp's voice came from the walkie-talkie. "Joseph says the bird appears to be okay, but I want to be sure the bastard didn't take something we missed."

"Standby," Kabatov said.

McGarvey willed himself to remain loose, as if he were still unconscious, as Kabatov turned him over on his back, and began searching his pockets, finding and tossing the Semtex packets and fuses overboard.

"Semtex and acid fuses," Kabatov radioed.

"Nothing from the helicopter?"

"Nothing yet, but maybe he hid whatever it is," Kabatov said, and he laid the walkie-talkie and MAC-10 on the deck and grabbed the front of McGarvey's jacket so that he could pull him away from the duffle bag to make a more thorough search. It was a mistake.

McGarvey suddenly reared up, headbutting the Russian, driving the man backwards and off balance.

But Kabatov was quick and he slammed his left elbow into the side of

McGarvey's neck, pushing him back, and he dropped to one knee and reached for his weapon, grunting something in Russian.

As he fell back McGarvey managed to kick the submachine gun away, and Kabatov lunged for it as it went over the side of the catwalk into the Gulf forty feet below.

"Oops," McGarvey said, regaining his feet and charging before Kabatov could get out of the way. He wrapped his left arm around the Russian's neck from behind to stabilize it in one position, and using his right hand pulled Kabatov's head sharply to the right, the top of the man's spinal column snapping.

McGarvey let the man's body collapse onto the catwalk, and went back to the duffle bag, picked it up with great care, walked back up onto the main catwalk and well away from the leg and gingerly lifted the thing over the rail and let it fall into the sea. With a splash, not an explosion.

He turned as his walkie-talkie and Kabatov's lying near the leg came to life. It was DeCamp.

"Nikolai."

McGarvey keyed his walkie-talkie. "He's dead."

"How unfortunate," DeCamp said. "But I have someone with me who would like to speak to you."

SIXTY-SIX

□

Gail stood with Eve facing DeCamp, the man who'd fetched them from the pipe locker, and two others in the delivery control room whose windows gave a 360-degree view of the main deck below and the sea around them. Kirk was alive and that's all that mattered right now. They had a chance.

"Your numbers are dwindling," Gail said pleasantly. "Maybe you should think about gathering what's left of your merry mob and getting back into the helicopter."

DeCamp was on her in two strides and before she could lift a hand to defend herself, he casually punched her in the mouth, and she went backwards on her butt, a ringing in her ears. "Speak only when I ask you to speak, Ms. Newby. I have Dr. Larsen as a hostage, so there is almost no reason to stop me from putting a bullet in your head. Clear?"

"Yes, sir," Gail said, and Eve helped her to her feet.

"Don't antagonize them for God's sake," Eve said.

Gail winked at her, and for just an instant Eve seemed nonplussed, but then she nodded almost imperceptibly. A smart woman, Gail thought, and a little bit wise, too.

"Mr. McGarvey," DeCamp radioed.

"I'm waiting," McGarvey replied.

"Where are you just now?"

McGarvey keyed the walkie-talkie, and he laughed. "Coming to kill you," he said.

DeCamp's neutral stance and expression did not change, but he motioned for two of his operators to head out, and they left immediately.

He took a Steyr 9mm pistol out of his chest holster and pointed it at Eve, who flinched. Holding up his walkie-talkie he keyed the push-to-talk button. "Dr. Larsen would like to have a word with you. I have a gun pointed at her head."

"Get off the rig while you can!" Eve shouted.

DeCamp smiled. "Noble," he said, and he released the transmit button.

Mac was on his way up there and nothing that Eve could possibly say was going to stop him. She just hoped that he'd managed to find and disarm the explosives on the legs because otherwise his actions were nothing more than an exercise in futility.

McGarvey did not reply.

DeCamp keyed the walkie-talkie. "Give me a reason not to shoot her."

"You won't like the outcome," McGarvey said. "Yours, personally. Anyway, she would no longer be a hostage."

DeCamp showed the first signs of anger. He keyed the walkie-talkie again, but before he could speak, Gail grabbed Wyner, pulled his pistol from a holster high on his right hip, jammed the muzzle in the side of his head, and using him as a shield dragged him to the doorway.

"Two bad guys here in the control room, two headed your way!" she shouted.

DeCamp released the transmit switch and cocked his pistol, still pointed at Eve, which was an empty gesture as far as Gail was concerned. The pistol had no conventional safety and could be fired in the uncocked position. "I will kill her."

"Kirk was right, you need a hostage if you expect to get off this rig alive."

DeCamp seemed to consider her comment, and he nodded. "You won't get far."

Wyner tried to break free, but Gail jammed the pistol harder into his temple. "Behave or I'll blow your goddamned head off," she told him.

Eve was not moving a muscle, her eyes locked on Gail's. It was exactly the right thing for her to do.

"You won't get far," DeCamp repeated.

"Maybe not, Brian, but the odds are getting better by the minute," Gail said. She glanced over her shoulder out into the corridor, but the two DeCamp had sent to find McGarvey were gone.

"Don't leave me," Eve said, and she sounded frightened out of her mind, but the look in her eyes was steady.

"Do what he says, Dr. Larsen. He needs you alive, unless you make yourself a liability."

Gail stepped around the corner, pulling Wyner out of sight, but then she shouted, "Fuck it," fired one shot into the overhead and shoved him forward back into the doorway.

DeCamp fired in reaction, hitting Wyner, shoving him back out into the corridor before Gail got more than two steps toward the companionway. She fired three times over her shoulder, reaching the steps and ducking around the corner, taking the stairs down two at a time.

She hoped to Christ she'd done the right thing, leaving Eve back there, but she'd seen no other choice. And with one more of DeCamp's men down the odds had definitely improved.

SIXTY-SEVEN

McGarvey stopped at the bottom of the outside stairs that led up to the transverse corridor that crossed the back edge of the main deck. It was the logical route to and from the delivery control room and the helipad, and the quickest way down to the legs. To his left was the rig's workshop, though a lot of the tools and equipment had been removed at Biloxi, and directly above that, just below the main deck, was a maze of tanking and piping.

He'd debated finding the second shaped charge, removing it and tossing it overboard which was exactly what DeCamp wanted to prevent. But the man would not leave the rig until he'd killed or locked up everyone who'd seen his face. And he wouldn't send the detonate signal until he was aboard the helicopter and well away.

Eve was DeCamp's ticket out of there. And the two operators Gail had radioed were on their way down as a reception committee, knowing that McGarvey was on the way up.

But it still didn't make any sense. He was missing something, which all of a sudden came to him when he heard the sounds of the helicopter's engines grinding to life.

In all likelihood Gail was dead, and DeCamp had taken Eve to the helicopter and was about to abandon the remainder of his operators, plus the scientists and techs trapped in the pipe locker on deck and whoever else might still be alive or wounded aboard the rig.

DeCamp no longer cared if someone who knew his face—even his own men—survived this night, because he was going to ground. It was his ace in the hole. The only question was how he intended to get out of the Gulf.

McGarvey started up. His only hope was to reach the helicopter and disable it before it was fully warmed up and lifted off, when one of the mercs appeared at the head of the stairs, armed with an MP5.

"Here he is then," Helms said.

McGarvey stopped, absolutely no way of bringing his shotgun to bear before the merc pulled the trigger. "Sounds like your boss is deserting you."

"Just waiting for us to confirm we've bagged you, and then we're all getting out of here."

"Not enough room for all of you."

"Only the colonel, the broad, and three of us. Plenty of room."

The pitch of the helicopter rotors deepened.

"Are you sure?" McGarvey asked.

Helms pulled out his walkie-talkie and keyed it. "We've got him!"

DeCamp did not reply.

Helms turned to look over toward the helipad, which was blocked from view by the edge of the superstructure containing the project control room. "Goddamnit, wait!" he radioed.

McGarvey raised the Franchi and pulled off two shots, destroying the front of the operator's face and torso and shoving him backwards, the MP5 briefly firing overhead before it was flung away.

The helicopter sounded as if it were taking off, and McGarvey started up the stairs when five pistol shots, pulled off in rapid succession, came from inside the workshop. He spun around, bringing the Franchi to bear, prepared to fire from the hip, when the body of one of DeCamp's mercs slumped out of the doorway, blood immediately spreading from his head and the back of his neck.

"Clear!" Gail shouted from inside.

"Clear!" McGarvey shouted back.

Gail appeared in the doorway, a pistol, but not her SIG-Sauer, in hand. Even in the harsh light from the overheads McGarvey could see that she was out of breath and flushed.

"They separated," she said. "I figured you could handle one and I'd cover the other guy on your back."

"Good job," McGarvey told her. "But we need to get to the helipad right now before DeCamp lifts off." He turned and raced up the stairs.

In the corridor he could hear the helicopter, and he knew damned well it was already away and accelerating, but he redoubled his efforts, emerging from the hatch just below the pad in time to see the Bell Ranger dip down out of sight to the west.

Gail was right behind him as he dashed across the lower landing, took the stairs up to the helipad two at a time and ran immediately to the edge, but the helicopter was already out of range for his Walther and certainly for the shotgun.

"Christ," he said, a rage building. He'd failed. Again.

"Eve's aboard with him," Gail said. "Did you get to the explosives?"

"Just one of them, and he's going to pull the trigger on the other any second now."

Gail turned to look down at the main deck. "The techs are still locked in down there."

"Get them out, and down to the lifeboats."

"I'll need Semtex to blow the lock."

"Mine's gone," McGarvey said. He was watching to see if the helicopter would turn to the east, toward Florida, when he spotted something drop out of the hatch and fall to the Gulf sixty feet below.

And he got the momentary impression of flailing arms and legs at the same instant a tremendous explosion rocked the entire platform, and Vanessa began to slowly list to port.

SIXTY-EIGHT

□

McGarvey sent Gail below to get the Semtex and fuses from her room so that she could blow the lock on the pipe storage container and release Eve's people, promising to be with her in five minutes. Standing now just down the slanting corridor from the delivery control room, Franchi in hand, he stopped to listen.

Blood had pooled in the doorway, but there was no body. Two pairs of footprints, one set larger than the other, led down the corridor to the hatch. DeCamp's and Eve's.

Gail had told him how she'd managed to escape. "DeCamp shot him and the last I saw the guy was on the deck. Looked dead to me."

All the boat horns and whistles were shrieking loudly now. Schlagel's followers had finally gotten what they wanted and the hell with the loss of lives they had to know was inevitable. They had to have seen and heard the explosion, and he could only hope that someone had the decency to send a Mayday.

But there were no other sounds, and McGarvey approached the doorway with caution, careful not to step in the blood, and he looked inside. The control room was deserted, the SSB radios had been destroyed, leaving only a short-range VHF unit intact, exactly what he'd hoped to find.

He stepped inside, sweeping the Franchi left to right, when Wyner stepped out from a dark corner. The merc was badly wounded, and barely able to stand, blood frothing from a hole in his chest. He held a small pistol, what McGarvey recognized as a 5.45 mm Soviet-made PSM semiautomatic, but his aim kept wavering, as if simply holding the weapon was at the extreme limit of his strength.

"The son of a bitch left me," he croaked.

"He left all of you," McGarvey said. "It was his plan from the beginning."

"We're sinking. Why the hell did you come back? You can't call for help, we shot the radios all to hell."

"Not the VHF," McGarvey said, his shotgun steady. "I need to call the tug, tell them to back off."

Wyner shook his head. "They're all dead. Tug's on autopilot."

It was a possibility McGarvey had considered. If this had been his operation it's exactly what he would have done.

A small, sharp explosion went off below on the main deck, and Wyner looked toward the window. "She made it," he said, a touch of admiration in his ragged voice, and he had to hold on to the port radar cabinet to remain standing. "Tough broad. Knows what she's doing." He turned to look at McGarvey and he let the pistol drop to the deck. "Get the fuck out of here before it's too late."

"I'll take you out of here, maybe you can make a plea bargain," McGarvey said. "We'll want to find DeCamp and you can help."

Wyner shook his head again. "Even if I survived, which you and I both know is impossible without medical help right now, there's no way in hell I'm going to spend the rest of my life in prison."

"Why?" McGarvey asked, even though he knew the answer.

"I'm a merc because it's what I do. How about you? You've killed a fair share this evening."

"It's what I do," McGarvey said.

Wyner smiled. "Too bad you're on the wrong side," he said. "We could have used you." He crumpled to the deck, and before McGarvey could reach him his breathing stopped.

The rig slipped a few feet to the right, as if it were an airliner suddenly hitting a downdraft, but then it stabilized, but at a greater angle of list.

McGarvey first made sure that Gail had gotten Eve's people out of the pipe locker and was hustling them below to the lifeboats, then he switched the VHF radio to channel sixteen, the calling and emergency frequency. "Any vessel hearing my voice, I'm aboard the Vanessa Explorer. We've have casualties and we are abandoning the rig. Please relay a Mayday for us."

"Vanessa Explorer, this is *Holy Girl*, we copy. The Mayday has been sent. Coast Guard Tampa has advised they are sending the helo out along with a cutter. We're standing by to take on your survivors."

"Thank you," McGarvey said. "You've won. Shut off your horns and whistles."

Another voice came on. "Not until that godless abomination is on the bottom, Mr. McGarvey."

"You know my name, but I don't know yours."

"Oh, yes, we know you. And your harlot. We pulled her out of the water, like a dead fish."

"Mr. McGarvey, this is the *Holy Girl*. No harm will come to Dr. Larsen, or any of your people. We'll take you aboard from your lifeboats. But I suggest you get clear as quickly as possible."

"Have Dr. Larsen ready to be transferred to our lifeboats," McGarvey said. "We don't want to interfere with your celebration because of the people who lost their lives tonight. We'll wait for the Coast Guard."

"You don't understand," the man said, but McGarvey had already turned and was out in the corridor, racing for the lifeboat deck.

SIXTY-NINE

☐

As the lifeboat approached the fifty-foot twin flybridge cruiser *Holy Girl* out of Mobile, Alabama, McGarvey stood up above the open hatch and waved at Eve who was at the stern, a blanket over her shoulders. She waved back.

All eleven of the survivors from Eve's team were aboard one of the motorized lifeboats. They were frightened and elated and sad and subdued all at the same time, some of them looking back at the spectacle of the badly listing oil exploration platform.

"You're all welcome aboard," a short, squat man in jeans, a polo shirt, and a captain's cap called across. "Plenty of room."

"Thanks for pulling me out of the water," Eve told him. "But I'd prefer to be with my friends."

One of the young techs heard her voice and she jumped up. "My God, it's Eve!" she shrieked

The *Holy Girl*'s skipper gave her a sad look and shook his head ruefully. He glanced up at the bridge where some of his people were watching. "Frankly we'd just as soon not have you aboard. You're a godless woman who has no conception of the terror your science is about to unleash on the world. And we're dedicated—I'm dedicated—to seeing you fail."

Eve pointed toward *Vanessa Explorer*. "Including damaging property that's not yours? Including killing innocent people? Is that what your god tells you to do?"

The skipper was stricken. "No, we did no harm. We hurt no one."

"But you stood by and let it happen!"

"We didn't know!"

"The helicopter that brought over our attackers, the one from which I had to jump to save my life, was off one of your boats!"

"We didn't know what was going on. I swear—"

"You swear to whom?" Eve spat. "Your kind, loving god? Because if that's the case, you've got to be talking to a different god than the one I was raised with in Birmingham."

She took off the blanket, tossed it in the skipper's face, and jumped down into the lifeboat.

"You'll rot in hell," the skipper said.

"That's funny, because from my perspective that's where all of you and your reverend Schlagel already are! Hanging right over the abyss."

Gail was operating the lifeboat, and as the techs swarmed around Eve, McGarvey motioned for her to head out to the tug. The engines needed to be shut down before the deeply listing platform was pulled apart because of the stress.

At one point all of them stopped and stared with Eve at Vanessa, and she glanced at McGarvey and Gail and then back at the rig. "What a terrible waste."

"Maybe it can still be salvaged," McGarvey said.

Eve shook her head. "I meant all the people, Defloria and Lapides and the men who worked for them. For us."

"And Lisa," one of the techs said. "She never came back."

"And Don," someone else said, sobbing. "He was helping them."

An infinite weariness seemed to come over Eve, as if she were on the verge of collapse, as if she could not go on, as if she could no longer see the necessity of going on. "From the start," she said. "Maybe aboard the Big G." And she began to cry.

McGarvey put a hand on her shoulder, and she looked at him, tears streaming down her cheeks. "I'm not going to leave you," he promised. "Not until you're set up and in business in the Gulf Stream."

☐

SEVENTY

DeCamp had been flying for a little more than an hour at full throttle less than fifty feet from the surface when he spotted the Cuban gunboat stopped in the water off to the starboard where he expected it to be. He'd been running without lights, but he flashed them twice, and when the Cubans responded in kind he throttled back and made a wide, lazy circle around the ship.

They were in international waters here, about sixty miles northeast of the western tip of Cuba, just far enough away from the Yucatán Channel busy with ships coming from or heading to the Panama Canal to be relatively safe from detection. And the fact that the Cubans had shown up as promised, meant they'd not been illuminated by the radar of any American warship.

As he came to within one hundred yards of the gunboat a small launch headed out to meet him. He unlatched the door, shut down the engines, and released the blades so that they would autorotate. The helicopter immediately lost most of its lift and settled toward the surface of the water, DeCamp carefully maneuvering the collective and cyclic pitch to keep the machine on an even keel so that the tips of its rotors would not hit first and tear the machine apart. It was one of the hardest skills he'd had to learn in the Buffalo Battalion.

The landing gear touched and the machine settled, water pouring through the hatch, when the rotors hit the surface and came to a stop after only another half turn.

DeCamp climbed out and swam directly away until he was well out of range as the helicopter settled onto its port side and submerged within a few seconds.

Five minutes later he was scrambling up the gunboat's boarding ladder to the deck where a smiling Captain Rodriguez was waiting for him, and they shook hands. "A skillful landing, señor."

"Anything on radar?"

"Nothing of any importance within one hundred and fifty kilometers," the Cuban said. "But come to my quarters where I have dry clothing and a good cognac, and I can tell you what news we have been picking up on the radio."

"Did it sink?" DeCamp asked.

"Not yet, but it is heavily damaged and in immediate danger of capsizing," Rodriguez said, no need to ask if that was DeCamp's mission. "So let's celebrate at least a partial success, shall we?"

McGarvey, the single name crystallized in DeCamp's mind, as he followed the Cuban below decks, and he began to turn over the mechanics of three possibilities open to him: revenge, disappearance, or both.

That Night

They had been standing off from the flotilla waiting for Vanessa to capsize, expecting it to, not quite believing that its list had stopped increasing and there was just an off chance that it might be saved, when the Coast Guard showed up. First one of the helos out of Saint Petersburg and then the 110-foot cutter *Ocracoke*. McGarvey had gone aboard, leaving Eve terrified that he had lied to her. But Gail had remained and she had been a comfort to them all, her hand steady, her words kind, her confidence infectious. "We've survived the worst of it," she'd said. "We're safe now."

This was a major crime scene, and the Coast Guard had taken over, ordering the flotilla to stand well off, and most of the boats had simply turned around and headed home, but the horns and whistles kept up in a sort of angry triumph, because the bodies aboard the *Pascagoula Trader* had been found. People aboard the oil rig had died, but God's flotilla had suffered its own casualties for a righteous cause, which in a lot of minds evened the score.

A couple of hours before dawn the Carnival Cruise Line ship *Inspiration* on its way back to Tampa from Cozumel had stopped at the Coast Guard's request to take on survivors. One of her motorized launches had been dispatched and Eve, Gail, and the others had been transferred from the lifeboat to a boarding hatch just above the cruise ship's waterline. Passengers had gotten up from bed, and in their pajamas lined the rail to stare at the unfolding drama, flash cameras pointed at Vanessa like so many fireflies on a warm summer evening. Under ordinary circumstances Eve would have been irritated by the lack of sensitivity, but she was tired and strung out, and anyway the passengers taking the pictures had no idea of the carnage. They had never met Lisa, and they hadn't known Don, like she thought she had.

The crew gave her a pair of white coveralls and sneakers that fit reasonably well, and when they found out who she was, the captain had come down to the ship's clinic to personally welcome her and the others aboard. They were only a few hours out of Tampa, but they were put up in some nice cabins, Eve and Gail in one of the first-class suites and urged by the doctor to at least try to get some rest.

He'd offered them a sedative, but Eve had refused, and lying in bed alone with her thoughts, listening to one side of Gail's sat phone conversation in the sitting room with McGarvey, still working with the Coast Guard on scene, she wondered if her refusal had been such a good idea after all.

She was having a lot of trouble, for some reason, seeing an image of Don's face in her head, or to remember what his voice sounded like or feel his arms around her. But she could remember the times he'd been there for her, his steady presence, his precise work; he was a better mathematician than her, and she thought he'd been proud to check her calculations, especially so when he told her that she'd been spot-on, no errors.

But it had all been a horrible mistake on her part, and she felt like a complete fool. She had failed as completely, probably even more so, with Don than she had with her husband, father, and brothers.

And with Kirk, she thought, hearing Gail say his name.

But her science was sound, despite what Don had said to her on Vanessa. And if the rig could be salvaged, which McGarvey had told her was a real possibility, and if she could somehow come up with the money for the salvage operation, and if she could stay out of Schlagel's sights long enough to get back on track, the damn thing might work.

Nor could she dredge up Lisa's face or hear her voice, though she could remember some of the kid's quips, calling Eve the boss lady, slave driver, or taskmaster, and it bothered her tremendously. It was as if all the lights that had brightened her work had gone out of her head, leaving her with nothing but the cold, hard calculations of her theories, and she was more afraid that she was losing, not her mind, but her interest, her enthusiasm. Which after all, she reminded herself, was all she'd ever really had since she'd fully understood that her family in Birmingham genuinely did not like her. In fact they had been afraid of her, as had the kids and the teachers in school.

She thought about Krantz and what he would say to her when she got back to Washington. NOAA was just another governmental agency that could be and often had been swayed by public opinion. It was more than possible that Schlagel's followers could do just that, especially after their partial triumph in the Gulf. They would be calling the incident God's will, and it made her skin crawl.

But it hadn't been the hand of some God-directed group of terrorists or whatever they were, that had come aboard Vanessa, killed her crew and attempted to destroy the platform and send it to the bottom. They were men, according to Kirk, who did such things for a fee; it's what they did for a living. Someone had paid them to destroy Vanessa and stop work on the project. Not Schlagel, but someone with a strong financial purpose, for whom Eve's work was a threat.

Gail came to the partially open door and knocked softly. "Eve?"

"I'm awake," Eve said, sitting up and switching on the bedside lamp.

"Kirk wants to talk to you," Gail said, coming and handing the sat phone she'd borrowed from one of the officers to Eve. She smiled and went back out.

"Hello?"

"How are you doing?" McGarvey asked.

"I've been better," Eve said. "I don't have any idea what comes next, though."

"InterOil is sending out a salvage crew, and the Coast Guard people say that it looks like the rig can be repaired."

"Back to fund-raising," Eve said with a little measure of bitterness, though she knew that she should be grateful.

"The company is picking up the tab," McGarvey said. "It may take a little longer than you wanted, but your rig will make it to Hutchinson Island."

"How?" was all Eve could think to ask.

"Something about towing a spare leg structure out here, filling it with water so that it can be positioned under the rig and then slowly pumping the water out so that it'll rise up into the correct position."

"They're smarter than me," Eve said, and she could hear Stefanato holding his own against Don and the other eggheads.

"Me, too," McGarvey said.

"When will I see you?"

"Not for a bit, but I'll catch up with you as soon as I can."

Eve suddenly panicked. "What if he comes after us again?"

"That's what I'm going to try to prevent. But Gail will hang around to see that you're okay. She's good at what she does."

"Yes, I think that you're right," Eve said. "I'll miss you."

"Not a chance, Doc, you've got work to do," McGarvey told her. "And besides, the media is already all over this thing. The Nobel laureate versus the preacher's flock. You'll have a reception committee when you get to Tampa, so I suggest you try to get a couple hours of sleep."

"It doesn't seem real to me. None of it."

Later the Same Day

Anne Marie's hand shook as she set down her teacup, Parkinson's the first thought in her head, absolutely terrifying her, all the more because she'd been expecting the first symptoms for years. It was a fear she'd harbored in secret—in secret most of the time even from herself—since a couple of months after she'd buried her father and had lunch with Bob Calhoun, the old man's longtime personal physician and friend.

They'd met at the downtown Boston Harvard Club on his suggestion, a bright sunny fall day, Anne Marie's hedge fund roaring along at the start of the dot-com buildup, the world completely her oyster, and she'd simply not been prepared for what he'd had to say to her.

"You'll need to watch for the symptoms, of course," he'd told her after their second martini and after they'd ordered the boeuf bourguignon.

"I don't understand."

Calhoun was an old man on the verge of retirement from his GP practice and he gave Anne Marie a patient smile. "Do you know why your father chose to end his own life?"

"Business reverses."

"He was losing his shirt, he and I talked about it. But it wasn't the real reason he decided to go out that way. He had developed Parkinson's and he was damned if he was going to end up some doddering old son of a bitch strapped to a wheelchair and drooling. 'I'm not going to spend my last days with a bedpan strapped to my ass so I won't shit in my pants,' his exact words."

Anne Marie could hear the old man's voice as if he'd been sitting right there with them at the window table looking out across the city's financial district. "Do you think that the disease affected his judgment?"

"Not directly. But I suspect he was distracted by it."

"Enough to make mistakes?"

"Possibly," Dr. Calhoun had told her.

"And realize that he was making mistakes?" Anne Marie had wanted to know, but the doctor had been unable to answer that question exactly except to say that the disease had probably disgusted him.

"Your father never accepted failures in others, and I expect that he thought his body was failing him, so he would have been upset." Dr. Calhoun spread his hands. "It had been three months since I'd seen him before he killed himself, so I don't know his state of mind. But you need to start keeping track of your own health."

Her own doctor had told her what she had was nothing more than benign essential tremors, a common condition. But she hadn't believed him six months ago when she'd first noticed she was developing the shakes, or now this afternoon in her penthouse apartment waiting for Wolfhardt to show up.

She was convinced that rather than face an uncertain future with the disease her father had put the pistol to his head and blew his brains out, an option she would never consider. Anyway if she had Parkinson's, it was in the early stages, which left her plenty of time to plan her next move, stay and fight or run. But it was fast becoming crunch time now; she could feel it viscerally just as she had felt when it was time to bail out of the dot-com bubble and a few years later the real estate boom and get out of Dodge.

The television behind her, tuned to Fox, had been covering two stories all morning, one they called "the Tragedy in the Gulf," and the other the Reverend Schlagel's take from his headquarters in McPherson, Kansas, in his sermon, "God Has Spoken, Are We Ready to Listen?"

DeCamp had failed again. For the third time. The oil platform had been crippled, but not sunk, and Dr. Larsen and most of her technicians and postdocs had survived, rescued by Kirk McGarvey, a former director of the CIA. Drama at sea in the high-stakes contest of big oil's interest in the status quo versus the green revolutionaries who warned that the planet was at the tipping point and the only way for humankind's salvation was to stop all carbon dioxide emissions immediately. Alternative sources of clean power from nuclear energy for the time being and then from the wind, the sun, and Nobel laureate Dr. Larsen's World Energy Needs project. The World Energy Needs project in Eve Larsen's words; the God Project in Schagel's.

Wolfhardt had telephoned an hour ago. "Turn on the television. There's been a development."

She'd done so while he was still on the line, and she'd immediately realized that her decision not to follow al-Naimi's warning about her security chief until after the oil platform had been destroyed had been the correct one. Insurance, her father had once told her, is not necessarily a waste of money in itself. And thus had been born, at least in his mind and in the minds of others, exotics and semi-exotic financial instruments, among them credit default swaps, a sort of insurance in a negative sense. Cashing in on failure.

Rightfully she'd made the decision to keep Wolfhardt in play as a credit default swap against DeCamp's failure, because something would have to be done about the mercenary before he was caught. She could not afford for him to be arrested because the leads would come back to Schlagel and very possibly to her. And whatever else he was, whatever his other agendas might be, Wolfhardt knew what he was about.

"Come here," she'd told Wolfhardt. "I have another job for you."

"I expect you do," he'd said. "I'll be there within the hour."

And Octavio had seen the same news stories and had telephoned her from Caracas twenty minutes after Wolfhardt's call. They spoke via encrypted sat phone and so could be totally open with each other.

"The president has agreed to extend his invitation for you to transfer your MG operation here as soon as you desire," he told her.

"The CIA has a strong presence in Venezuela."

"Not so strong as you'd think these days," he said. "More bluster, perhaps, than actual effectiveness."

Anne Marie chuckled. Money bought strange bedfellows, usually for the most transparent of reasons. But Chávez was in trouble, and the country was on the verge of becoming unstable and possibly even collapsing. China, on the other hand, was growing exponentially and desperately needed two things that she could supply: oil for that growth and money management services for the more than one trillion U.S. dollars of foreign debt it owned. And Hong Kong, with immunity, was much more to her liking than Caracas with the CIA breathing down her neck.

"The offer is kind," she said pleasantly. "Please thank the president for me, and tell him that I'm sincerely considering his generosity."

"My pleasure," Octavio said, and he dropped his voice. "Be careful, Anne."

"Langley is no threat to me here."

"I'm talking about the Saudis. Al-Naimi has a long reach in the region. Longer than yours."

"I understand," she said, suddenly feeling chilly. At her level of play she could not defend herself on her own, for that she needed the backing of a government. And Octavio had just offered it in the form of protection from Saudi Arabia. "First I have a few loose ends to clear up."

"Quickly," Octavio said and he was gone.

She looked at her hand, it had stopped shaking, and she felt as if she were settling down. Really settling down now for a fight, and she felt the first glimmerings of interest, not dread, about what might be coming next. She wasn't exactly as rich as Bill Gates, but she was wasn't all that far away, and at least in her mind that kind of money carried a certain clout. She didn't know where the threshold of importance started, but it was certainly more than a couple hundred million, or even a few billion, and it had something to do with influence. So since she'd left Florida she'd worked on that principle, easing her way—sometimes bullying her way—into the bank accounts of a diverse group of individuals, corporations, local as well as international, and even a few governments—or at least governmental agencies. It was why she'd felt reasonably safe cruising the Med for the first time, and why she wasn't convinced that she should head for the hills just yet. Perhaps staying to fight might be the better course after all.

Ramirez buzzed her. "Mr. Wolfhardt is here."

"Send him up," she told her bodyguard. Her chief of security hadn't been pleased about the extra layer of personal protection she'd put in place after her talk with al-Naimi, and she expected that he'd simply put it down to female paranoia. But he'd accepted the change without protest, though a distance had been created between them.

Wolfhardt, dressed in a white linen suit, no tie, stepped off the elevator, came across the hall, and walked directly out to where Anne Marie was seated on the balcony. "Good morning," he said, not sitting down.

"Would you care for coffee or tea?"

"I don't believe there's time."

"Mr. DeCamp has failed for the last time. I want him eliminated."

"That may not be easy," Wolfhardt said. "Most likely he's gone to ground somewhere to wait and see which way the wind blows."

"Are you telling me that you cannot find him?"

"No, madam, I'm telling you there will be no need because within the next twenty-four hours he'll come to me and I'll kill him."

For just a moment Anne Marie was vexed. She did not enjoy riddles when it was straight answers she was looking for, but then she understood, and she smiled despite herself. "I see," she said. "If something were to happen to his woman in Nice he would have the motivation to find you."

"Exactly."

Stay and fight indeed, Anne Marie thought. It was her nature after all.

PART

FOUR

The Next Few Days

It was nine in the morning in Washington when Eduardo Estevez, the president's adviser on national security affairs, walked into the Oval Office, a scowl on his broad Latin face. Lord's chief of staff, Robert Russell, his press secretary, Paul S. Green, and his chief science adviser, George Mills, were all watching CNN's reporting on the attack in the Gulf while the White House photographer snapped pictures. They all looked up.

"With that kind of expression on your face this can't be good news," Lord said.

When he had been awakened earlier and told of the developing situation in the Gulf, he'd refused to call a cabinet meeting, demanding instead that he be supplied with constant updates. "This will not be allowed to get out of hand, like Hutchinson Island has," he'd told Russell. "No more fodder for Schlagel."

"Kirk McGarvey is on the line from the Coast Guard cutter *Ocracoke* on scene," Estevez said. "It's a video link."

Lord went to his desk console, pressed a couple of buttons and the CNN broadcast was replaced by the image of a weary-looking McGarvey seated at a small conference table. It appeared as if he were alone.

"Good morning, Mr. McGarvey," Lord said. "From what I understand congratulations are in order." His image was being picked up by the camera in his computer monitor.

"Not yet, Mr. President, because we're not out of the woods," McGarvey said. "Is it just you and Mr. Estevez?"

"That's not important. What do you have for me?"

"As you wish," McGarvey said. "The same man who hit Hutchinson

Island was behind this attack. Which means he's being directed either by Schlagel, Marinaccio, Octavio, or the UAE International Bank of Commerce, or some combination of all four—and very likely the Saudis are somehow involved."

"Goddamnit, we've been down this path before," Estevez said, but the president held him off.

"Do you have any proof?"

"Gail Newby was chief of security at Hutchinson Island, and she came face-to-face with him just before the explosion. He was only a suspect at that time, and in fact we'd not been able to identify him until a couple of days ago. But he was there on the rig directing the attack and Gail saw him."

"You say that you identified him?"

"Yes, sir. His name is Brian DeCamp, an ex-South African Defense Force colonel in the Buffalo Battalion. Evidently he turned freelance and apparently worked a number of operations over the past several years. He's good, just about the best I've ever heard of."

"Now he's dead, and that part of the problem has been solved," Lord said. "For that we also offer our thanks."

"He got away aboard a helicopter from Schlagel's flotilla."

The president's anger spiked. "That's proof enough for me."

"No, sir, it's not that easy," McGarvey said. "There's more."

"There always is."

"The helicopter came off the yacht *Pascagoula Trader*, with a crew of six, one of them identified as Anthony Ransom, a top aide to Schlagel. We think he was directing the flotilla. But he and the rest of the crew aboard, along with one of the mercenaries DeCamp left behind to act as a rear guard, were shot to death."

"How about his other people?"

"All dead."

"Did you actually see him take off?" Estevez asked.

"Yes, and he was heading west toward the coast of Florida," McGarvey said.

"Then we have the bastard," Estevez said. "He must have shown up on someone's radar."

"No," McGarvey said, and in that one word Lord knew this situation had the possibility of turning out even worse than Hutchinson Island, much worse.

"Why do you say that?"

"Because he's smarter than that. And he's not a martyr, which means he'd planned his escape from the beginning. My guess is that he made a deal with someone in the Cuban Navy to meet him somewhere inside Cuban waters, or very close, where he ditched the helicopter."

The president, who'd been standing hunched over his desk, sat down. "You think that it's not over? He'll strike again?"

"We saw his face, so I think he'll go to ground. Maybe plastic surgery, but that would take months, maybe longer."

"I'm not following you, Mr. McGarvey. Are we out of the woods or will someone else come after Dr. Larsen and her project?"

"And don't tell us that Saudi intelligence agents are going to try next," Estevez said. "Because I just don't believe they're stupid enough to take that kind of a risk."

"It won't be the Saudis," McGarvey said. "At least not directly. But they funnel money into the IBC in Dubai, which has connections with Marinaccio and Octavio, we know that much for a fact. And no, Mr. President, we are not out of the woods yet, and probably won't be for a long time."

"It's agreed that none of them, especially the Saudi government, can afford to allow Dr. Larsen's project to succeed," the president said. "So we can be fairly certain about the why, but you still don't have proof who hired this mercenary."

"We're working on it, and if we do come up with something the ball will be back in your court, Mr. President. You might want to give someone at Justice the heads-up."

Lord bridled for just a moment, and he almost shot back that he took advice but not orders. Instead he held himself in check. "But somebody else will be coming after her."

"Yes, sir."

"Who?"

"Schlagel."

It was the worst possible news for Lord. While his own numbers in the polls had dropped from an approval rating of 67 percent to a dismal 43, Schlagel's, even though he had not yet announced his candidacy, had risen from nothing to a respectable 29 percent. And it had begun with the incident at the Hutchinson Island Nuclear Power Plant. The bastard had done nothing but hammer home his message of fear; fear of nukes and especially fear of Dr. Larsen's God Project, which spilled over to the populist message of fear of all scientists.

"Tinkerers with God's designs!" Schlagel shouted from his pulpit in McPherson, and just about everywhere else as he crisscrossed the country, all of his appearances as well prepared and stage-managed as the Reverend Billy Graham's had been at the height of his ministry. But Schlagel was even better than Graham had been; his sermons were more firey, yet simpler and even more real and current. "Americans," he preached, "are frightened out of their wits, and believe me they have every reason to be."

"You say that he was personally behind the attack against Dr. Larsen's project?" Lord said.

"No, but his followers were."

"Then he's already won. As long as he keeps his hands clean."

"Unless he's pushed," McGarvey said.

"I'm listening," Lord said, his interest piqued.

"He's campaigning for your job, even though he hasn't come out and said it in so many words yet. So you need to do two things."

Estevez started to object, but Lord waved him off. "I'm still listening."

"Campaign back. You're very good at it. You're smart, you're articulate, and you photograph well. Take him on the issues. Green energy will be our ultimate salvation. Give the public Eve Larsen's message in plain language that everyone—especially Schlagel's followers—will understand. And he's right, you know. Americans are frightened and they do have a right to be. So fight back."

"And the second thing?"

"The media is all over the attack in the Gulf, so you need to hold a news conference as quickly as possible, today or better yet tonight when you can address the nation on all the networks. Your administration will make sure that Vanessa Explorer will be repaired and towed to Hutchinson Island, and Dr. Larsen's project will get the highest priority."

"That would certainly put me head-to-head with Schlagel."

"It'd be risky," McGarvey admitted. "But not as risky as having someone like him in the White House."

Lord figured that his advisers would tell him that he was committing political suicide; he could see it already in Estevez's eyes. But they were talking about his political suicide, not the nation's.

"In the meantime what will you be doing, Mr. McGarvey?"

"Waiting for Schlagel to make a mistake."

"Are you so sure that he will?" Lord asked.

"Oh, yes, sir, he'll have to stick his neck out if he wants to be president, and you already know what that's like."

"And then what?"

"I'll nail him," McGarvey promised.

It was about what Lord had expected and he exchanged a glance with Estevez. "You understand, Mr. McGarvey, that I can't become personally involved with an action like that. I can't sanction it. My critics would have a field day."

Estevez nodded his approval.

"We never discussed this aspect, Mr. President," McGarvey said.

SEVENTY-TWO

□

In the *Ocracoke*'s officer's mess, McGarvey clicked the shutdown tab on the laptop computer he'd used to talk to the president, and sat back to gather his thoughts. He'd been given all but a carte blanche to pursue whoever was behind the attacks on Hutchinson Island and here in the Gulf, but this now would not be the same as chasing after someone like DeCamp, who if he managed to go completely to ground would be all but impossible to find.

Schlagel was a different problem altogether, because unlike DeCamp, who either worked alone or with a very few handpicked operators, Schlagel's followers were a sizeable portion of the American voting public. Millions of people were backing him, and the number was growing daily. Isolating him from his supporters in such a way that making a mistake large enough to topple him, expose him for who and what he really was, would be next to impossible.

But until the good reverend was brought down, Eve Larsen and her project were in imminent danger, although Schlagel was already denying any involvement in the attack.

"In fact," he told his flock, "it was members of my flotilla who actually saved lives, at great risk to their own. In fact some of my faithful lost their lives. Let us use the power of prayer but never, never forget the power of action to do the work God has set before us."

The argument was the same among antiabortionists: killing abortion doctors saved lives!

Lieutenant Craig Moon, the cutter's skipper, came to the doorway and knocked on the frame. "Are you finished, sir?"

McGarvey looked up. "Just about, thank you. Have your people finished bagging the bodies?"

"No, sir, the FBI is still doing forensics, could be another six hours or longer. But they've asked that you stick around a bit longer, they have a few more questions."

"They can catch up with me in Washington. What're the chances of getting me ashore?"

The lieutenant had his orders, but Marc Morgan was only the special agent in charge of the Bureau's on site team while Kirk McGarvey was a former director of the CIA. And it was he who had almost single-handedly put down the attack and killed most of the bad guys. "I can have a helo out here within the hour. Where do you want to go?"

"Tampa International."

"Will do," the lieutenant said.

"And I need to make a couple more calls. Can I connect to ordinary phones ashore from here? A landline as well as cell?"

"Yes, sir. I'll have someone come down to show you."

"No need, I'll figure it out," McGarvey said, and after the lieutenant left he found a phone tab on the laptop's screen and entered Gail's cell phone number. After twenty seconds or so, it rang and Gail answered.

"My number's blocked, so this has to be Kirk, Eric, or Otto."

"It's me, where are you?"

"We just landed at Dulles. How's it going?"

"The Bureau is working the issue. How about you and Eve?"

Gail chuckled. "Not bad for a couple of women who've been through what we've been through. Especially Eve and her high-dive act." She got serious. "What's next?"

McGarvey quickly explained his conversation with the president. "Officially Otto and I are looking for our contractor, and we're going to make a good show of it."

"Unofficially?"

"You and Eve are going to draw Schlagel down from his podium while I keep watch from the sidelines."

"DeCamp's not coming back?" Gail asked.

"I think he's going to ground."

"Revenge?"

"He's a pro, and Hutchinson Island and Vanessa were nothing more than assignments that didn't go quite the way he'd planned them. No revenge motive there. Neither operation was personal enough."

"I meant on the part of his paymasters. From their standpoint he botched Hutchinson Island, and now this."

McGarvey had already thought about it. "They'll probably withhold a final payment, but Hutchinson Island was enough of a partial success that they gave him another chance."

"And you were the monkey wrench in both operations. Might make you their next best target."

"It's a possibility," McGarvey conceded because he had thought of that, too. "Otto's keeping track of Marinaccio and Octavio, but they'd have to hire someone to come after me, so I'll watch my back. In the meantime my bet's on Schlagel because I'm about one hundred percent convinced that he and Marinaccio are connected through the IBC in Dubai. If Schlagel were to make it to the White House he'd be the perfect president for big oil. Be in her best interest to support him."

"Okay, what's the next step? What do you want me to do?"

"Is Eve sitting next to you?"

"We're scattered all over the plane. She's about six rows back."

"How is she?"

"Awed by the violence, by all the people killed. A little confused, I think, about Don Price, and saddened by Lisa's death. She was one of the bright sparks on the team."

"Intimidated?"

"Angry, but so far as I can tell all the more determined to get on with it."

"The White House is going to support her project. Publicly. Which means the Coast Guard will provide around-the-clock security."

"So Lord is finally taking Schlagel seriously."

"Something like that. Which makes Eve the primary target. If she can't be bullied into backing away, or if NOAA can't be convinced by public opposition, or if InterOil continues to support her, she could be in some physical danger again. Probably worse than Oslo."

"I don't think that she's going to run and hide," Gail said. "She's pretty tough."

"How was her reception in Tampa?"

"She was mobbed, and it'll probably be the same here."

"I want you to stick with her, even if she objects. And I want you to convince her to return to Hutchinson Island to talk with the SSP and L people about the power connection with her platform. I want it to be business as usual for her, as if what happened in the Gulf was only a little speed bump."

"That should be an irresistible draw for Schlagel and his people. How soon do you want her there?"

"Within the next day or two, I want to give Schlagel as little time as possible to capitalize on what happened in the Gulf."

"Where will you be during all of this?"

"Right behind you," McGarvey said. "But don't try to spot me. And, Gail?"

"Yes?"

"Carry a weapon and stay sharp."

McGarvey broke the connection and phoned Otto, telling him essentially the same thing he'd told Gail, and repeating the conversation he'd had with the president.

"How are you planning on going about it, kemo sabe? Schlagel's people were willing to put their lives on the line out in the Gulf, and they sure as hell wouldn't hesitate to run over you if they thought you were a threat to him.

And McGarvey told him.

Otto laughed. "Devious, but I think I can put something together that'll get his attention. May I share this with Yablonski?"

"Only if he promises to keep it between the two of you. No leaks."

SEVENTY-THREE

It was late, nearly midnight, when DeCamp stopped his rental Peugeot along the side of the narrow D2204 corniche highway above Nice, shut off the lights, and got out. It was a moonless night, but the sky was bright enough with the glow from the city below for him to see the blackened remains of his house.

He'd arrived in Nice late this afternoon, but instead of taking a taxi straight to his house he had rented the car at the airport and driven up to the L'auberge de Col de Braus, a small country inn of six rooms and a good kitchen near the village of L'Escarene ten kilometers up in the hills. He'd been spooked ever since the German had shown up on his doorstep, knowing his real name. And after his encounter with McGarvey on the platform, he was taking nothing for granted.

But this now, what he was seeing, was far worse than he'd feared, and he had to pace back and forth to somehow put a cap on his rage. He expected maybe to see the house dark, and Martine gone to Paris as she'd told him she often did when he was away. But not this. Anything but this, his house destroyed and Martine almost certainly dead, her body in the morgue.

Hutchinson Island had only been a partial success, but the business in the Gulf had ended in disaster. The edition of the *International Herald*

Tribune he'd picked up during his layover in Paris had a two-page photo spread of "*Le terroisme dans le Golfe de Mexique.*" Loss of life was minimal, thanks in part to the efforts of Kirk McGarvey, a former director of the CIA, and most important the life of Nobel Peace Prize laureate Dr. Evelyn Larsen was saved as was her project aboard the oil exploration platform *Vanessa Explorer.* Photos of the badly listing platform with U.S. Coast Guard gunships standing by were in full color. So far the terrorist leader remained unnamed and no group had come forward claiming responsibility.

He had failed, and this was Wolfhardt's demonstration of the client's displeasure.

DeCamp stopped pacing, and stared at the burned-out ruins. This act was much more than a simple message passed to him; he'd stopped at an Internet café in DeGaulle Airport to check his bank balance. The ten million euros had been deposited during the night. The money was meaningless to them, completely trivial.

Go away, hide under a rock, enjoy your money if you can. Or find us and try to take your revenge. Either way Mr. DeCamp you are totally out of the business, superfluous, ineffective, nothing more than a swatted bug whose very existence is nothing more than a minor offense to the larger scheme of things.

And DeCamp had always thought that tales of revenge were stupid, but until this moment he hadn't realized just how much he'd loved Martine and had come to depend on her presence at his side. He'd always planned on retiring, but with her, not by himself.

He heard her laughter and he suddenly turned and tried to find out where it had come from, but then he realized the sound was nothing more than a siren or car horn in the very far distance, distorted by the light breeze.

Wolfhardt had done this in retaliation for Hutchinson Island and the Gulf, and the man was a professional. He would have made certain that Martine was dead before he'd set fire to the place.

But Colonel Frazer had taught him from the beginning to always go into a battle with dispassion. "Let the other soldier shout his war cries, while you approach from behind and silently slit his throat."

Be prepared.

Be fearless.

Life without honor is possible, but honor without life is fruitless.

Remembering four thousand days of lessons with the colonel and nearly ten thousand days of experience in the field finally calmed De-Camp down enough so that he could go back to the car and drive away.

In the morning he would take the train to Zurich where he could access one of his bank accounts, and where he could contact his friend in the SADF who had warned him about Wolfhardt and who presumably knew where the man operated from.

Then once he had the information he needed, he would change his appearance, gather his weapons, and make his strike. Clean, surgical, decisive. You have given me your message, now I will give you mine.

SEVENTY-FOUR

□

Eve had said a few words about her postdoc Lisa Harkness in the stone chapel at the Swan Point Cemetery along the Seekonk River in Providence, Rhode Island, but standing now at the graveside, in the midst of her other postdocs and techs, Gail standing just behind, she wanted to shout what a terrible waste it had been.

She couldn't, of course. Lisa had been an only child and her parents, who'd sent her off to Princeton to become a famous scientist, someone who would do good in a world that needed mending, were devastated and had hung on every word Eve had said about their daughter.

"Lisa taught us how to text so that she could send us messages many times every day," her mother, a local high school math teacher, had told Eve before the service. "Once she got into your graduate program, and then began working with you, she couldn't talk about anything or anyone else."

"She was a wonderful girl," Eve said, choking back tears. "Everyone loved her. You couldn't help not to."

The funeral was large. More than one hundred of Lisa's family and friends had shown up, including aunts and uncles and both sets of her grandparents, which brought home hard just how alone Eve had always been. This was the family she'd dreamed about having all of her life.

"Everyone felt that way, Dr. Larsen. So who would want to kill her and why?"

"It wasn't her, it was me and my project they wanted to stop," Eve said, not knowing what she could say to offer Lisa's parents any sort of comfort.

"We know that," Lisa's father said, squinting. He taught history of philosophy at Brown University and Lisa had once described him as a gentle bear with clothing. "But what are they so afraid of that would drive them to commit murder—mass murder?"

"Losing money, I'm told."

"Money," Mrs. Harkness said, but not as a question.

And after the funeral and the reception on the big back lawn of the Harknesses' home, during which just about everyone had stared at Eve and her team, but especially Eve as if she were some mysterious goddess who'd stepped down from Mount Olympus, it was a bittersweet relief for all of them to be on their flights home—to Princeton for most, and to Washington for Eve and Gail.

"They'd never met someone who'd won a Nobel Prize," Gail said. "And for a person like you to come all the way to Rhode Island for the funeral of one of your students was a big honor."

"I was afraid that I'd say something that would hurt them ever more."

"But you didn't, and they loved having you there."

Eve felt a nearly overwhelming sense of bleakness, as if it were the black of night now and would always stay the black of night for her. "At times like this I don't know if I'm doing the right thing," she said. "I mean I believe the science is on track, but maybe there are other issues, larger issues, social issues that I just don't get." She wanted Gail to reassure her.

"I think the social issues are exactly what your project is all about."

Eve turned away, a little embarrassed by revealing an inner portion of herself. She'd never become comfortable with such things. British reserve

and all that, but mostly what she considered to have been a crappy upbringing. Don had told her once that she should stop blaming her past for
what she had become: "For better or worse you are who you made yourself to be. Your parents gave you life. The rest is your doing, so get on
with it, and stop complaining." Good advice, even from a bad man.

"You're right," she said after a while. "We just have to make it work,
and screw the bastards who want to stop me."

Gail smiled. "You scared me there for a minute. If you've lost confidence I don't know what the rest of us are supposed to do. After all, you're
the Nobel doc."

Her boss, Brian Landsberg, had told her essentially the same thing in
his office at Princeton the day before. "I can't speak for Bob Krantz and
the other NOAA people the day before in Washington, but despite what
happened in the Gulf the science has not changed. The Nobel Prize com-
mittees are not composed of idiots—or at least not entirely composed—
and like the rest of us they saw that you were right."

"Somebody doesn't think so," she'd replied, still thinking mostly
about Lisa's death and Don's perfidy.

"If they didn't they wouldn't be so desperate to stop you," Landsberg
said. "Think about it."

And next for her was convincing Krantz that she had to be allowed to
continue despite the deaths. And he was the last hurdle because her team
was raring to go now, ready to meet Vanessa off Hutchinson Island as
soon as she was repaired and towed the rest of the way. This time the
Coast Guard was providing the security, and that fact alone gave them all
the assurance they needed to get back aboard the platform and finish
their work. The real beginning.

"We can be on Hutchinson Island the day after tomorrow," she told
Gail.

"I'll let Kirk know," Gail said.

"Where is he?"

Gail spread her hands. "Around somewhere. Watching us."

And Eve felt a warm sense of comfort. They were not out of the woods
yet, not by a long shot, but McGarvey was close and it was enough for her.

SEVENTY-FIVE

☐

At Abu Dhabi's International Airport, DeCamp, dressed in a plain light business suit and traveling under the work name Howard Beckwith, presented his passport to the immigration official who compared the photograph to his face. "The purpose of your visit to the United Arab Emirates?"

"Business."

The officer looked up. "What business would that be, sir?"

"Oil futures trading."

"Ah," the officer said, smiling as he stamped the passport and handed it back. Oil was something everyone in the UAE understood and approved of. "I hope that your stay will be a profitable one."

In the customs hall he retrieved his single bag, and brought it to one of the officers serving the Etihad flight that had just arrived from Geneva. The man checked the passport and declarations slip DeCamp had filled out just before landing, placed an invisible check mark on the leather bag that would show up on scanners on the way out to the departure area, and waved him on.

It was a little after eight in the evening, and heading across to the exits he thought how nice it would be to finish here and then return home to have a dinner and a good bottle of wine on the veranda with Martine. A simple pleasure he'd enjoyed for a number of years that had been taken from him.

For no reason. It was merely business, and could have been handled equitably between them. He would even have been willing to return all the money, less expenses, if Wolfhardt had talked to him.

But even that sort of a possibility had been made impossible on the day Wolfhardt had shown up in Nice. They had known where he lived, and they had known Martine made him vulnerable.

"If we should have to leave our bleached bones on the desert sands in vain, then beware the anger of the legions!"

Outside, George Marks, one of his top sergeants from the Buffalo Battalion, was waiting for him with a Land Rover, and he had to do a double take before he recognized DeCamp. Short and stocky, with arms like a gorilla's and the speed of a gazelle, Marks had ended his career in the Batallion as the chief hand-to-hand combat instructor. Afterwards he'd moved to Capetown where he opened a mercenary consulting business with his nineteen-year-old son Kevin, who was a computer whiz. Together they helped clients find contractors and do the logistical planning for operations, something DeCamp had preferred to do on his own until now.

"You're looking fit, Colonel," he said.

"You, too, Sergeant," DeCamp said. "When did you get here?"

"Yesterday, early. I had a few things to check out on the ground before I could be completely sure you wouldn't be running into a buzz saw, if you know what I mean."

They got into the Land Rover, Marks behind the wheel, and headed away from the airport. "I've booked you a suite in the InterContintenal for three days, though I expect you'll be gone before that."

"I'm heading up tonight, and taking the morning flight to Geneva if all goes well," DeCamp said. "What about weapons?"

"You specified the 9mm Steyr GB for your handgun. It's in your kit along with four eighteen-round mags, and a suppressor. But I also brought a Knight PDW with four thirty-round mags. It's been modified to pull down the muzzle velocity to subsonic so it can be silenced as well. It's short, lightweight, and capable of putting up to seven hundred rounds per minute on target."

"I know the weapon," DeCamp said. "It's a good choice."

"I didn't know if breaking and entering or shock-and-awe tactics might be a consideration, but I brought a mixed bag of small Semtex packets and the appropriate fuses, plus a pair of Haley and Weller multiburst stun grenades that make no sound as the cap fires, a K-BAR knife and a night-vision ocular. All of it is untraceable of course, so when your op is completed you can drop it in place."

"The pistol and perhaps the knife may be all I'll need," DeCamp said. "Clothing?"

"Nothing military, of course. But knowing your sizes helped. Dark jeans, a black polo shirt, and a reversible Windbreaker. White on the outside so you won't attract attention on the drive up, and black on the inside. Dark Nikes."

"Transportation?"

"You'll take this machine. It's a bit less than five hundred klicks round-trip, so you'll have plenty of petrol, and the registration is also untraceable, so if the need should arise, you can simply park it and walk away. Otherwise bring it back to the hotel and leave it with the valet."

"Coms?

"An encrypted Nokia, my number programmed in. After twenty-four hours its memory will be erased. And soon as you're gone I'll sterilize your track."

They were coming into the capital city and traffic on Highway 33, Airport Road, was heavy with Mercedes and BMWs plus a smattering of Rolls and Bentleys. The UAE, despite Dubai's financial meltdown a couple of years before, was in very good shape. And as long as oil continued at seventy dollars per barrel or higher, life there was good.

"I could have used you on my last op," DeCamp said. "Wouldn't have to be wasting my time here."

Marks glanced at him. "When you called for backup, I figured it might have been you involved in that dustup in the Gulf of Mexico. Was it a double-cross?"

DeCamp had debated how deeply to involve Marks beyond the logistics, and yet other than Martine and before her Colonel Frazer, he'd never had anyone to talk to. And he was already missing it.

"It didn't go exactly as planned, but instead of coming after me they hit someone very close. Someone defenseless."

Marks drove the rest of the way in silence until they were within sight of the hotel. "Revenge is not always the best course, Colonel."

"I agree, Sergeant, but this time it's necessary," DeCamp said. "Now tell me where you got your intel."

And Marks did. Both sources.

SEVENTY-SIX

□

It was already four in the afternoon when Gail walked back across A1A
from the South Service Building, the containment wall that blocked reactor one looming ominously into the clear blue Florida sky, and she felt
the deepest sense of failure in her entire life since her father's death. She
hadn't been there for him, just as she hadn't been there for her partner.
And coming back now brought everything into her mind in living color,
and it wasn't pleasant.

Most of the work was being done on the north side of the facility,
where power from Vanessa, when and if it ever got here and was put
into service, would be led to the transformer yard, and from there connected to the grid. That side of the plant had been saved any radiation
damage so the linemen and engineers were able to work without hazmat
suits.

The decontamination tent was up and running, empty of personnel
just now, and Gail stopped a moment to look toward the south down the
highway where Schlagel's followers by the thousands had begun showing up early that morning. Some of them had set up tents, while others
had parked their motor homes or travel trailers just off the side of the
road within a few feet of the National Guardsmen manning the barriers.
A1A was supposed to open for normal traffic within the week, but for
now only people essential to the decontamination and rebuilding programs were being allowed through.

Yesterday was Sunday and Schlagel had been in Washington, making
all the morning news shows including *Face the Nation* and *Meet the Press*,
arguing that nuclear power was not the future of America's desperate
energy situation, nor was it a viable answer to the carbon dioxide issue
and global warming. He was sorry for the tragedy in the Gulf, the loss of
lives among his followers as well as those aboard Vanessa Explorer, but
that abomination to God's will was currently under repairs and the

Hutchinson Island power station, which would never produce nuclear electricity again—thank the Lord God Almighty—was making preparations to receive energy from the God Project.

"You can laugh at the coming Armageddon or the apocalypse if you want—and at your own peril—but the seed of our destruction is at this moment making its way to Florida!" Schlagel had preached. "It must be stopped at all costs. Save your lives, save America's life, believe in God, and your salvation will be assured. Turn your back on His holy will at your peril!"

And they were coming. The last estimates Gail had gotten from Eric was that 100,000 or more people were on the move across the U.S., all of them converging on Florida's east coast. Fox was calling it the greatest mass exodus in the history of the United States, and one of Schlagel's SOS network commentators said that "God's hammer was poised to strike, so sinners beware."

The reverend himself flitted here and there, showing up with a lot of fanfare to talk to members of his "flock" as he called them in Kansas, then Ohio, in Michigan and Missouri, Tennessee, and Georgia, and last night in Orlando, Florida. His people were on the move and so was he.

Eve was at the north end of the plant working with the engineers, and now that she was back at it Gail thought the lady scientist was happy again. They'd gotten a suite at the Hotel Indigo up in Vero Beach but in the two days they'd been down there neither of them had watched television, Eve because she only came back to the suite to shower and sleep, and Gail because she was getting the real news from Eric. So to this point Eve was all but unaware of the true size and seriousness of the gathering storm.

She turned and looked back toward the South Service Building, wondering why she had bothered to suit up and go inside, because very little was left. The control room, along with all the offices on the second floor had been gutted, the slightly radioactive debris bagged and taken away. Even the walls had been stripped bare, the floor tiles taken up, and the engineers were working out ways to seal the concrete that would cost the company less money than tearing the building down and starting from scratch.

The facility's chief engineer, Chris Strasser, had confided in her yesterday that he thought the power plant would never reopen. "It won't be safe to tear down reactor two for a thousand years," he'd said. "And there's the problem with South Service."

"The mood of the country is against nukes right now, so you might have a tough time getting the necessary permits anyway," she'd told him, but he'd given her a blank look. He was a nuclear engineer, after all, not a politician.

"It's the only reason the company's giving Dr. Larsen a shot. If her project works, and if the security concerns are taken care of, it could save us a considerable amount of money. In the tens of millions."

Money. Everything was about money, and right now some of the major players were beginning to step up to the plate to take their shots; either to protect big oil for as long as possible by delaying nuclear permitting and stopping Eve, or by positioning themselves to look as if they were supporting her. Because if her final experiment actually worked, and electricity began flowing into the Eastern Interconnect, which supplied power to the eastern third of the country, the full project would be worth somewhere in the range of fifty trillion dollars, and possibly more by the time it was finished. Bigger than the Panama Canal by some order of magnitude. And that was some serious money.

Inside the tent Gail went through the automatic showers, foam baths and showers again, before stripping off her hazmat suit and placing it in one of the barrels, then she went through another series of showers, taking special care to clean under her fingernails and toenails.

When she was done she padded naked, except for a towel around her neck, into the locker room, and McGarvey was there smiling at her. And his being there took her breath away.

"Hi," he said.

"Oh, shit," she said, and she began to shiver, though it wasn't cold, not realizing until just that moment how much she had missed him. She went to him and he held her until she began to calm down.

"Are you okay?" he asked.

"Now I am," she told him honestly. "Where have you been? Otto wouldn't tell me."

"I came down from Atlanta last night in a convoy with some of Schalgel's people, trying to find out what was coming and how soon it was going to happen. I figured that you and Eve were safe as long as you stuck it out here."

"Eve is at the north end of the plant."

"I know," McGarvey said. "But you need to get dressed because we have a lot to do and only a couple of hours to get it done."

"Is it going to happen tonight?"

"The word in the mob is that Schlagel will be showing up around six, and his people are being told to get ready for action."

"Shit," Gail said, pulling her clothes out of a locker. "What about the National Guard and the Bureau guys?"

"The Bureau will stay out of sight, and Colonel Scofield's people are going to fire some guns into the air, but when crunch time comes they're going to back off and let the crowd through."

"To where?"

"All the way to the main gate in front of the South Service Building."

Gail was slipping on her sneakers and tying the laces, but she stopped and looked up at McGarvey. "You figured out a way to stop him?"

McGarvey nodded. "He's going to do it to himself."

SEVENTY-SEVEN

It was ten minutes past two in the morning when DeCamp arrived at the Marina Tower apartments in Dubai and entered the six-digit security code at the entrance to the underground parking ramp. During the day an attendant was on duty, but after midnight a hardened steel link gate dropped down from the ceiling. Security codes were changed on a random basis, texted to tenants an hour before they went into effect.

This was to be the first test of the sergeant's sources, and when the gate rose DeCamp's skepticism was dampened somewhat. The problem had been the fantastical and dangerous nature of the sergeant's informant.

"Money is a powerful motivator, Colonel," Marks had offered as an explanation. "For some, the most powerful. And in this instance I had a hunch the woman's position could be compromised by the very nature of her business dealings. The U.S. Securities and Exchange Commission considers her a person of extreme interest. Something the UAE government became indifferent to once they had received help with civilian nuclear technology from the States. I thought that since she is all but a fugitive from her own country, perhaps she has stepped on other toes."

"Devious," DeCamp had said with admiration, and Marks had smiled.

"Ah, the ways of mortal man—or woman—on the path to Mammon," Marks said. "My mum read the Bible to me till it came out of my ears. You can't serve two masters. Both Luke and Matthew wrote it in their gospels."

DeCamp had smiled inwardly. His mother, on the other hand, had only ever cared for a few things: where her next bottle of booze or fix were coming from and occasionally what particular man she was going to allow between her legs and why.

Only Martine had ever really cared.

DeCamp drove inside the garage and took the ramp three levels down, switching off the headlights before he reached the bottom, and holding up at the end of the lane that went directly to the penthouse parking slot and private elevator.

Marks had promised that the guard, normally stationed in a dark blue E-class Mercedes four positions on the right from the elevator, would be away from the building for exactly sixty minutes starting at 2:00 A.M.

The only other cars were a black Mercedes Maybach and a ten-year-old white Lamborghini Countach that had been totally restored at the factory in SantAgata Bolognese, belonging to Anne Marie, and a smoke silver Mercedes SL 65 AMG Black, belonging to Wolfhardt.

DeCamp drove the rest of the way down the lane and backed the Land Rover into the empty fourth slot. Shutting off the engine, he got out, reversed his jacket, screwed the silencer on to the end of the Steyr's barrel, and walked to the elevator. He moved on the balls of his feet making absolutely no noise as he listened for a sound, any sound to warn him that he had been betrayed and that Marks had sold him out. But there was nothing.

The elevator car was there, which meant that the last person to use it had come down from the penthouse. Possibly the guard who'd left his post for whatever reason.

Moving to the side so as to be out of the line of fire, he pushed the call button and as the door slid open he swept his aim across the interior of the empty car.

One of the old jokes from the Battalion days was that if everything was going according to the operational plan, you were probably heading into a trap. The men didn't care that special forces just about everywhere had the same jokes, Murphy's Laws, because they fit.

The elevator stopped only at the lobby and the penthouse apartment and required a key card, which, as Marks had promised, was in its slot, ready to be swiped, and once again DeCamp paused. The setup was too easy, the information too pat, and every instinct was telling him to turn around and get out while he could. But then he remembered the look on Martine's face when she knew that he was leaving again, and he could feel and taste her body when they made love, her exotic scent still in his nose.

He swiped the card, pressed the button for the penthouse, and the car headed up. At the most there should only be three people in the apartment: the Marinaccio woman, possibly one of her personnel security people, and Wolfhardt. The house staff did not live on site so there would be no danger of collateral damage, though for DeCamp that consideration had always been meaningless.

At the top the elevator slowed to a halt and the doors slid open onto a marble-tiled vestibule, an ornate Italianate fountain softly spewing water from the penis of a small boy.

Marks had given him a simple sketch diagram of the floor plan. The living room, dining room, conservatory and beyond, the kitchen and pantries were off to the left, while the five bedrooms were straight ahead and to the right. At this hour the woman would almost certainly be in her bedroom at the end of the hall.

He switched the elevator off, and gingerly stepped out into the vestibule as a dark figure came down the corridor from the left.

"Phillipe, what the hell are you doing up here?"

DeCamp turned, catching the image of a short, wiry man in jeans and a white T-shirt standing in the middle of the corridor five meters away reaching for something, and he shot him twice in the middle of the chest, driving him backwards with a soft grunt.

The sounds of the silenced shots, though muted, seemed loud even over the noise of the water fountain, and DeCamp waited for a full ten seconds to make sure that no one else was coming to investigate. But the penthouse remained quiet.

DeCamp went to the downed man to make sure he was dead, careful not to step in the blood, then hurried to the end of the hall where again he stopped for a moment to listen at the door to the woman's bedroom suite before he went in.

The large sitting room was straight ahead, the sliding glass doors open to the night breezes off the Persian Gulf. The bedroom, walk in closets, powder room, and bathroom were to the left.

Anne Marie's head appeared over the back of the couch, and DeCamp almost shot her on instinct.

"We were expecting you, Mr. DeCamp," she said, apparently completely at ease.

DeCamp stepped back into the deeper shadows by the door, trying to detect where Wolfhardt was hiding, checking firing angles and lines of sight.

"Gunther's not here at the moment, and I have to assume that you have already disposed of my bodyguard Carlos, so it's just you and me. May we talk, or do you intend to shoot me right now?"

"Why was my house destroyed and why was Martine murdered?" DeCamp asked. He'd almost said "my woman" instead of Martine.

"It was a dreadful mistake, believe me," Anne Marie said. "I merely wanted your house leveled so that you would understand that I can't countenance failure. We thought Ms. Renault was in Paris, and that when you returned you would first find her a safe house, and then come here. I don't want the money returned, it's yours to keep. But I was hoping to offer you redemption. I still am, if you are willing to lower your weapon and hold out your hand."

Wolfhardt was close. DeCamp could almost feel the man's presence

like an approaching low pressure system bringing with it a storm. But
Wolfhardt had been one of Sergeant Marks's sources at the behest of the
other source, Abdullah al-Naimi. Money indeed.

"Who killed her?" he demanded.

"It wasn't Gunther himself, if that's what you thought. He hired a
pair of small-time hoods from Marseilles, and when he found out that
they'd bungled the job he killed them both. It's the only blood on his
hands." Anne Marie shrugged. "On my hands, too, I'm willing to admit.
But then yours are none too tidy."

"But you ordered it."

"The house, not the woman," Anne Marie said. "And now I want to
make it up to you." She stood up and came around the couch, dressed in
a nearly sheer negligee, her legs outlined in the dim light coming from
outside.

"How?"

"I'm worth a great deal of money—"

"How will you bring Martine back to life?"

"My dear boy, that is quite impossible," Anne Marie said, almost
laughing but stopped. "There are other women. The world is full of us."

DeCamp had learned dispassion from Colonel Frazer and later it had
been drummed into his head in the Battalion. The man who kills with
precision but without passion is the man who will live to walk from the
battlefield. But at this moment the blackest of rages that he'd ever imagined could hit a human being threatened to blot out nearly everything
he'd ever learned on and off the battlefield.

Anne Marie, sensing some of this, raised a hand. "Don't be a fool.
Think of the money you'd be throwing away by killing me. Fabulous
money beyond your wildest dreams."

"Beware the anger of the legions," DeCamp mumbled before he
raised his pistol and fired one round, catching Anne Marie in the center
of her forehead, driving her body backwards onto a glass coffee table
that shattered.

"Well done," Wolfhardt's voice came from a speakerphone across the
room. "She was telling the truth, it was an accident. And she was telling
the truth about the money. May we talk?"

DeCamp stepped away from the door. "Where are you?"

"In the bedroom to your left. May we talk?"

"Yes."

"Toss your pistol straight ahead over the back of the couch."

DeCamp hesitated for just a second but did as he was told.

The hall door behind DeCamp opened and Wolfhardt, holding a 9mm SIG-Sauer pistol expertly in his left hand, came in. "Considering your abilities I thought it best to lie about where I was," he said.

"An advantage," DeCamp told him. "Now what?"

"She was telling the truth about Ms. Renault. We thought she was still in Paris. It wasn't our intention to kill her."

"Now what?" DeCamp asked again.

"More work, if you'll cooperate."

"For the Saudis? Al-Naimi?"

"Yes, and they have even more money than her," Wolfhardt said, nodding toward Anne Marie's body. "And a longer reach, and collectively a greater intelligence, more connections, more power here in the Middle East and everywhere else."

"Including Washington?" DeCamp asked, wanting to keep Wolfhardt engaged.

The German laughed. "Of course. Why do you ask?"

"I was thinking about disappearing there."

"You are a clever bastard," Wolfhardt said. "What else are you carrying?"

DeCamp started to move away, drawing the German half a step forward, and he pulled out his KA-BAR knife with his right hand and turned back, parrying Wolfhardt's gun hand, the single silenced shot popping into one of the sliding glass doors, and plunged the knife into the man's chest, between the ribs, hitting the heart center mass.

He stepped back to avoid the initial gush of blood and looked into Wolfhardt's eyes as the man sank dead to the floor.

"As I told your boss, beware the anger of the legions," DeCamp said.

He left the penthouse, careful not to step in any of the blood, and took the elevator down to the garage. A few minutes later he was driving away from the building and heading for the highway back to Abu Dhabi, his work finished. Melbourne, he thought. He would go to ground in Australia where he would wait to see what shook out.

□

SEVENTY-EIGHT

McGarvey and Gail, dressed in hazmat suits, took a golf cart up A1A to the north end of the plant where Eve was inside one of the construction trailers poring over blueprints of the transformer yard with Townsend and Strasser. They looked up, startled, when the door opened.

"Do we have breakout up here?" Townsend demanded, and Eve looked as if she were a deer caught in some headlights.

McGarvey took off his hood. "You're clean, I didn't want to be recognized."

"Mac," Eve said with obvious relief and pleasure. "I was getting worried. Have you seen the crowd?"

"A hundred thousand people are on their way, and it's why I'm here."

Gail had taken off her hood. "Before anything happens we need to get you back up to Vero. But just for tonight."

Townsend was angry. "What the hell are you talking about? Will there be another attack?"

"Schlagel is supposed to be here around six, and once he gets his people fired up there's no telling what might happen," McGarvey explained. "But Eve is one of his main targets, so I want her out of the line of fire. And if I could move the power plant I'd do that too."

"Well, I'm sure as hell not leaving," Townsend said, and Strasser nodded but he didn't seem to be quite as enthusiastic.

"I can't leave like this," Eve said. "I mean how long is this supposed to go on? Vanessa is under repairs right now and InterOil is promising they should have her up here within a week. Are those crazy people going to keep on attacking? Killing more people?"

"It stops tonight," McGarvey said.

"We've lost Lisa and Don already, and all the others. I'm not going to put more of my people in harm's way," Eve said, her voice rising.

"It ends tonight," McGarvey said again, and it finally penetrated for her and for Townsend and Strasser.

"The National Guard isn't going to stop a crowd that big, not unless they mean to block the road with tanks and actually fire into them," Townsend said. "And getting Dr. Larsen up to Vero is out, because Schlagel's people are blocking A1A from the north as well."

"Actually Colonel Scofield is going to pull back and let them past the barriers."

"Gives them access to South Service," Gail said.

"And everywhere else," Strasser said. "Including places that are contaminated. A lot of people will get hurt. We can't allow that to happen under any circumstance."

"I agree," McGarvey said. "But at the right moment we're going to have Schlagel dress in a hazmat suit and meet me in the South Service lobby."

Townsend was skeptical. "What makes you think he'll agree to something like that? What's in it for him?"

"I've been a thorn in his side ever since the first attack here, and the attack on Vanessa Explorer."

"Goddamnit, stop right there," Townsend said. "Because if I'm reading you right, you're telling us that Schalgel was somehow involved. And I'm just not buying it. The man wants to be president, and the media is all over him. He can't take a dump without it being reported on."

"He's involved," McGarvey said. "And I'm going to prove it tonight."

"How?" Townsend asked.

And McGarvey explained it to them, getting the same initially incredulous reaction that Gail had given him.

"You think he'll fall for a cheap stunt like that?" Townsend asked. "It makes no sense."

"He'll have no other choice. His ego will demand it."

Townsend and Strasser weren't seeing it, but Eve was.

"I'm a bigger issue to him than you are," she said. "All the more reason for me to stick around."

But McGarvey disagreed. "He's getting desperate now that his people failed to stop your project."

"And desperate people do desperate things," Gail said. "Without us, the project goes on. But if something should happen to you, it's over."

Eve wasn't happy, but she nodded. She'd seen firsthand what people opposed to her project were willing to do. "Still leaves us with the problem of how to get me out of here."

"A police helicopter is coming up from Miami with a couple of FBI agents who'll take you up to Vero and stick around until morning. If things go bad down here they'll make sure that you get back to Washington."

"If things go bad here tonight, we'll have bigger problems than getting Dr. Larsen to safety, because it'll mean that Schlagel has won and nothing will stop him," Townsend said. "Everyone loses, including us."

Strasser shook his head in wonderment. "One man against a mob of one hundred thousand?"

McGarvey smiled. "I'll have Gail with me. Cuts the odds in half."

"What about us?"

"Anywhere but South Service," McGarvey said. "If he sees anyone else he'll take it as a trap and won't play along."

SEVENTY-NINE

☐

Twenty minutes after Eve was safely away with her minders, Mac and Gail were back at the decontamination tent preparing the hazmat suit Schlagel would wear if he took the bait, when Colonel Scofield radioed.

"You're going to have company in about three minutes."

McGarvey keyed the National Guard walkie-talkie. "Schalgel already?"

It was nearly five thirty, a half hour early, but already the crowd outside was huge at both the north and south barriers, and was growing exponentially by the minute, already stretching for miles in both directions. Widescreen hi-def video monitors and loudspeakers had been set up along the side of A1A at intervals of a couple hundred feet so the faithful would be able to see and hear the reverend's sermon, as Fox called it: "Not from the Mount but from Ground Zero." The media had shown up several hours ago, positioning their vans, bristling with microwave antennas and satellite dishes, at the south barrier, which apparently was where Schlagel would speak.

"Negative, it's one of our birds from Miami transporting some of your people. Where do you want them?"

"I didn't ask for any help," McGarvey said, but he knew who it was and why he and his team were coming here. The problem was who had ordered it. "Have them set down on the road in front of the gate. But I want the chopper to stand by, I'm sending them back."

"They said that they had orders."

"I don't care. Just make sure the pilot holds here."

"Roger that," Colonel Scofield replied.

And then they could hear the noise of the incoming helicopter over the growing sounds of the mob. "Is that who I think it is?" Gail asked.

"Unless I miss my guess it's Carlos coming up from Miami, the question is who sent him here and why, because he sure as hell didn't make that kind of a decision on his own."

"It wasn't Admiral French."

"Someone higher up," McGarvey said. "Probably Caldwell at DOE. Guy's a grandstander."

The helicopter was settling in for a landing, the rotor wash buffeting the decontamination tent, and McGarvey had to shout for Gail to hear him.

"Put on your hazmat suit, and go get him. Tell his team to stand by, and I don't give a shit what objections he gives you. Tell him that someone from Washington wants to have a word before he sets up shop."

Gail was almost laughing now, but she quickly donned the suit, and went outside. And less than three minutes later she was back with a fuming Carlos Gruen, who pulled up short when he saw McGarvey.

"I was told A1A was clean!" he shouted. "And what the fuck are you doing here in my situation site?"

"What situation is that, Carlos?" McGarvey asked.

Gruen looked nervously to Gail who'd taken off her hood. "Is this place clean or not?"

"It's clean for now," McGarvey said. "What are you doing here?"

"Preventing another attack."

"On whose orders?"

Gruen puffed up self-importantly. "Deputy Secretary Caldwell asked that I personally take charge."

McGarvey nodded. "Glad to have you," he said. "But would you mind telling us how you plan to stop one hundred thousand people from marching into the plant and causing a lot of damage, but mostly to themselves when they start taking radiation?"

"Not my concern," Gruen said. "All I'm interested in is the presence of radiological devices."

"Do you actually think that Schlagel's followers will try to smuggle a nuclear device into a wrecked nuclear power station?" Gail asked.

Gruen looked smug. "You could hide an entire platoon of saboteurs in plain sight inside a crowd that big, and the only way to tell who's who and neutralize the threat is with our equipment. You of all people should know the drill, Ms. Newby," the last said with sarcasm.

And Gail reacted, but McGarvey held her back. "What happens afterwards, when the rest of the crowd decides to tear you and your team apart?"

"Won't happen."

They were running out of time. Schlagel was due soon, and there was no telling how he might react, seeing a National Guard helicopter parked in the middle of the road. "Go back to Miami," McGarvey told him. "Or at least go out to the perimeter of the crowd and stand by in case the situation gets out of hand."

"Not a chance in hell. You two bungled the first attack on this facility, and I'm here to see that there isn't a repeat."

"You pompous ass," Gail said angrily, and McGarvey waved her back, but she wouldn't be silenced. "All you're trying to do here is make a name for yourself." She gestured toward the tent flap. "Have the media take notice, get your picture in the *Times* or the *Post*, maybe a sound bite on ABC. Thank God none of the other Rapid Response team leaders aren't guys like you with their heads firmly planted up their rectums."

"Screw you, Newby, you're fired," Gruen said and he pulled a cell phone out of his pocket, but before he could press the speed dial button McGarvey snatched it out of his hand.

"You can fire both of us later. But right now I want you to get the hell out of here."

"This is my incident site, goddamnit!"

"I don't have time," McGarvey said and he pulled out his pistol.

Gruen's eyes went wide and he stepped back a pace. "You're a fucking maniac."

"Absolutely unhinged."

"No way in hell you'll shoot me."

"Are you sure?" McGarvey said, advancing but keeping his aim down and away.

"Kill me and you'll go to jail for the rest of your life."

"Makes you wonder what I'd get for a kneecap."

Gruen looked to Gail but she shrugged, and he stepped back another pace.

McGarvey handed back the cell phone. "I want you to get the hell out of here right now. I just need one hour."

"It could be all over by then," Gruen said, almost plaintively.

And McGarvey almost laughed, because the man might be a jerk, but he was a jerk who was sincere in his desire to do good deeds and to get the recognition he figured he so richly deserved; he saw himself as the dedicated public servant. "I hope it is," McGarvey said. "But if things go south here, you can come back and straighten out my mess. And I'll even apologize, in public."

"Me, too," Gail said.

"We'll see about that," Gruen said and he left the tent and walked back to the helicopter and climbed aboard. Moments later the chopper lifted off and headed north along A1A, finally turning west over the Intracoastal Waterway to the mainland.

"He'll probably have my job," Gail said.

"Not if we pull this off," McGarvey told her, but she grinned.

"And I meant to say, he's welcome to it."

McGarvey called Otto on the encrypted Nokia. "Where's Schlagel?"

"In the back of a pickup truck about a hundred yards south of you on A1A," Otto said. "I have a Keyhole bird on him. Louise is giving me the feed. Looks like Moses parting the Red Sea. Who was in the chopper that just left?"

"Gruen."

"Surprise, surprise. What did you have to do to make him leave? Threaten to shoot him?"

"Something like that. How's my feed?"

"Up and ready to roll. If you can get Schlagel to take the bait, every-thing he does and says inside the South Service lobby will connect not only to his public address system and hi-def screens, but to the satellite uplinks of every major television and radio network. The good reverend wants an audience, we'll give him one."

"Will he know what's happening?"

"Depends on the volume of his speaker system. But if you can get him inside and keep him there it's not likely he'll hear that what he's saying to you is being broadcast to his faithful. Knowing about last night in Orlando and having the video to prove it is gonna blow him away big-time."

"No chance he suspected the setup?"

"Nada," Otto said.

"That's all I need to know," McGarvey said. "We're wiring his suit and mine right now."

"One other thing. I just found out that Anne Marie Marinaccio and two of her people were assassinated in Dubai. No suspects. Thought you'd want to know."

"DeCamp?"

"We'll probably never know."

EIGHTY

□

Schlagel's magnified voice had started to roll over the crowd from the south a few minutes before McGarvey, dressed in a hazmat suit, the hood covering his head, darted across the street to the main gate, where he paused for just a moment.

According to Otto the mass exodus from all across the country was still flowing across Florida's borders to this very spot with no end in sight even though Schlagel was on the verge of what was being hailed as his most important sermon ever. Hundreds, perhaps as many as one thousand boats stood offshore from the nuclear power station, some within shouting distance of the beach. A pair of Coast Guard cutters from Miami were standing by with orders not to interfere except in an emergency. Helicopters from the local affiliates of all the major television networks hovered overhead like paparazzi around royalty. The collective murmur of the crowd was that of an eager audience waiting for the show to begin.

A circus, McGarvey thought as he turned and went across the parking lot and inside the South Service Building's lobby where he held up at the open door. He took off his hood and laid it on the bare concrete floor.

"You copy?" he asked.

"Yes," Otto's voice came back in his earpiece. "Are you in place?"

"I'm here," McGarvey said. "Stand by."

With the door open he could hear Schlagel's voice, but it was difficult to make out what the man was saying, because the speakers were all turned toward the crowd. He closed the heavy glass doors and the noises from outside were sharply muted, all but inaudible.

He opened the doors again. "Good enough," he said. "We have a shot, I think."

"Only if his ego is as big as we think it is," Otto came back. "And you'll have a feed to your cell phone when you need it."

"Have you ever known a man in his position whose ego wasn't off the chart?" McGarvey asked rhetorically. "Gail?"

"Here."

"He's on his way."

"I can hear him, he's getting close," Gail radioed.

"You need to be obsequious."

"I know the word, doesn't mean I have to like it."

"Is Eric linked with us?" McGarvey asked Otto.

"Here," Yablonski said from his computer center. "And I've known Gail a lot longer than you guys and I can tell you with near one hundred percent confidence that she might know the word, but there's never been a subservient bone in her body."

"Okay, people, showtime," Otto broke in. "Gail, you ready?"

"I'm outside the hazmat tent, no suit," Gail replied. "He just pulled up

on the other side of the barrier, about fifty yards away. I'm on my obsequious way. As if any of you sexist pigs ever knew the meaning of the word."

"Are you armed?" Yablonski asked.

"Negative. My magazine only holds seventeen rounds, not a hundred
thousand. This is Kirk's show not mine."

McGarvey could hear the strain in her voice.

Schlagel was shouting something but his words were no less clear
now than they had been earlier. But from McGarvey's vantage point at
the lobby doors he could make out the reverend's figure standing above
the heads of the vast crowd, the nervous National Guard troops who
were already starting to edge away, and Gail in a light sweatshirt and
jeans walking up the middle of A1A.

"I can't make out what he's saying," McGarvey radioed.

"He's thanking his faithful for making this important pilgrimage,"
Gail said. "God's righteous work. 'Let it begin here and now.'"

Then Schlagel's voice was being picked up by Gail's comms unit, the
microphone of which was concealed inside her NNSA dark blue windbreaker, but what he was saying made little or no sense to McGarvey,
something about swift justice and then peace and bliss would cover the
land as if "directed by a booming voice come down from the heavens."

"Okay, I'm hearing him now," McGarvey said. "Does he have a security detail?"

"Four of them. Looks like they know what they're doing. Sharp."

"He has to come in alone."

"Reverend Schlagel!" Gail shouted. "Reverend!"

Someone yelled something that McGarvey couldn't make out, and suddenly there was a lot of noise, more people shouting, and what sounded like
scuffling, heavy breathing.

"Just a moment, just a moment!" Schlagel shouted.

"Gail Newby, National Nuclear Security Administration. Someone here
from Washington needs to speak with you, sir. It's extremely urgent."

Gail's comms unit was picking up other voices, but they were garbled,
and McGarvey could only make out a word here and there, something
about risk, no necessity, no reason for it."

"I can personally guarantee your safety, sir," Gail said.

Someone, maybe Schalgel, asked who it was.

"I'm not at liberty to say."

"The hell with that."

"He's indirectly from the White House, sir. And as I said, this is extremely urgent. National importance. In fact he's begging you for your help."

"Nice touch," McGarvey said.

"I'm not armed," Gail said. "Besides the National Guard is here along with the media. You'd be perfectly safe."

"Where is this meeting to be held?" Schalgel asked, his voice suddenly clear.

"The lobby of the South Service Building," Gail said. "You'd have to wear a hazmat suit, but the radiation is minimal, and the meeting will only take a minute or two."

"This representative from President Lord is waiting for me now?"

"He took the bait," Otto said.

"Yes, sir," Gail said. "He arrived just a few minutes ago, aboard a National Guard helicopter. You might have seen it."

Schlagel's voice became indistinct again, mixed with other urgent voices, but it was clear enough in McGarvey's earbud that the reverend was arguing with his minders. And it only lasted for a minute.

"I have a sermon to finish, so let's make this quick," Schlagel said.

"Just this way, sir, to the decontamination tent," Gail said.

Someone else had taken up the microphone and was speaking to the crowd now, though McGarvey could no longer make out what was being said as Gail and Schlagel headed past the barrier.

"Okay, he's taken the bait," Otto said. "Mac, are you set?"

"Yes, but don't enable the links until ten seconds after you hear me say, I'll close the doors."

"Roger that."

McGarvey watched from the relative darkness just inside the lobby but it seemed to take forever before Gail and Schlagel appeared on the roadway and went into the decontamination tent. And even longer before the reverend, dressed in a full hazmat suit, came out alone and without hesitation strode across A1A and through the main gate.

"Okay, showtime," McGarvey said. He pulled on his hood and stepped outside.

Schlagel pulled up short about ten yards away, maybe sensing that something was wrong. "Who are you?" he shouted.

"I'll explain inside!" McGarvey shouted back.

"Why here, like this?"

"Privacy, Reverend. No one will bother us here."

Schlagel didn't like the situation, it was clear from his suddenly tense body language. He looked back the way he had come, and he half turned.

"Please," McGarvey said, letting a trace of fear creep into his voice. "Sir, I'm begging you, on behalf of the president. Just hear me out. My God, you can't begin to realize how important this is."

"To me?"

"For the entire nation," McGarvey said. "Only you can help now."

Schlagel hesitated a moment longer, but then as McGarvey had counted on, his ego got the better of his judgment and he came the rest of the way. "I'm all ears," he said. "Whoever the hell you are."

At the steps he turned and waved to his people, and then followed McGarvey inside.

"Thank you, sir," McGarvey said. "I'll close the doors, so we'll have a little more privacy."

"If you think it's necessary," Schalgel said.

When the doors were closed, McGarvey turned around, took off his hood, and dropped it on the floor.

"You're live," Otto said.

Schlagel was taken aback at first, but then he took off his hood and smiled, almost in admiration. "You son of a bitch," he said. "Lord didn't send you. This is one of your schemes. And what now? Are you going to shoot me?"

"Wouldn't dream of it," McGarvey said.

"Glad to hear it," Schlagel said, still amused. "But, if you don't mind, my people are waiting for me."

"Your choice, Mr. Deutsch, but you might want to stick around for a couple of minutes, just to hear me out."

Schlagel was suddenly wary, but not concerned. "Now that's a name I haven't heard for a very long time."

"We have your background in Milwaukee, as well as your real service record—cigarettes, gambling, sex."

"Youthful indiscretions, along with my arrest and incarceration in California. All of which brought me face-to-face with Jesus Christ our Savior, who I took into my soul and to whom I promised my life's works."

"Including the Marinaccio Group in Dubai?"

Schlagel said nothing.

"It's an oil futures hedge and derivative fund and you know the woman who runs it. Anne Marie Marinaccio."

"Never heard the name."

"Then you probably don't know that she and two of her people were assassinated last night," McGarvey said. "No one knows what's to become of her holdings."

"It has nothing to do with me."

"You're heavily invested in the fund, to the tune of at least fifty million dollars, probably a lot more. We know that much. We even have your account numbers. Your ministry's funds. Your church and network are big, but that'll be a major hit."

"I have no idea what you're talking about," Schlagel said. "Nothing but a cheap trick, a smear campaign. And all this time I thought the bastard in the Oval Office was above this kind of crap."

"I think we can come up with the names of a number of mistresses and whores you've been involved with over the past few years."

Schlagel looked over his shoulder, but then shook his head. "In the past, before I took Jesus into my heart," he said.

"Offshore accounts in the Caymans and Channel Islands."

"Liar," Schlagel said.

"How about the International Bank of Commerce in Dubai? You have money there, too."

"If you had any proof of that sort of nonsense you would have turned it over to the FBI by now. Lord would have made sure of it."

"Did you know that the bank funds terrorist groups like al-Quaeda? I wonder what your faithful flock would say if they knew."

"Listen to me, you prick, if you and your pals in the Bureau had any proof you would have arrested me by now."

"Maybe you should take a look at this," McGarvey said and he opened his cell phone and held it up. "Orlando, Mariott, last night." The prostitute Otto had arranged was twenty-three but she looked sixteen, and the hidden cameras the techs from Special Projects had set up caught everything in high-def living color; including the reverend, the girl, and the sounds of their sex, which at one point had gotten a little rough, almost so much so that Otto had been about to order the girl be rescued.

Schlagel didn't care. "The recording was fabricated, so go ahead and show it to whoever you want. But let me tell you shit like that is done all the time. Christ, we even have the facilities for parlor tricks like that and a lot more out at McPherson. What do you think we are, a bunch of Kansas Bible Belt hicks? But you did hit the nail on the fucking head when you called them my 'faithful flock,' because that's exactly what they are. Faithful, because I molded them that way, and a flock of sheep because that's how I lead the dumb bastards."

"It can't be easy, being in the spotlight like that."

"You can't imagine how easy it is."

McGarvey nodded. "I have to hand it to you, Reverend, you're good. But if you mean to get those people out there excited enough to storm this place a lot of them could get hurt."

"If one hundred die tonight, if one thousand are wounded and horribly maimed either by radiation or by National Guard bullets, it will only advance my cause."

"Your cause?"

"Prove to the world that I alone have the vision to take us out of this terrible mess we're in."

"And you think your flock will believe it?"

"They'll believe anything I tell them," Schlagel said.

McGarvey went to the doors and threw them open. "Then go, Reverend, tell them," he said, and someone had turned one of the loudspeakers around, so his voice echoed off the side of South Service. Along with the moans and cries of the prostitute and Schlagel's grunts.

"What?" Schlagel said, his voice booming. "You son of a bitch," he said, his words rolling over the crowd. "Lies!" he shouted, brushing past McGarvey and walking out the door to his waiting flock.

One Year Later

Tents had been set up in the visitors center's parking lot at the Hutchinson Island power station and more than two hundred and fifty dignitaries from Sunshine State Power & Light; county and state governments, plus Washington, D.C.—including a sprinkling of influential green congressmen who in the beginning had been dead set against Eve's project because of the tremendous costs and the possible bad effects on the earth's climate, unintended consequences indeed—a few from Princeton, among them all of Eve's team; from NASA, including Krantz; from Commerce and DOE, including Caldwell, and even Vice President Robert Holden was there, as well as the Committee of Six for the Ethical Treatment of the Planet, and celebrities from Hollywood—some of the top movie stars, actually—were all there waiting for sunset, and for the switching on ceremony. Power from the impellers in the Gulf Stream would be sent ashore along the underwater cable where it would pass through the station's transformer yard and from there out to the Eastern Interconnect.

McGarvey was looking out at the crowd seated in the tent and Gail came over. "Hi, Kirk. I'm happy you could make it back for this."

McGarvey smiled. He was weary but not tired. The last year, alone in his house on the Greek island of Seriphos, had been a time of healing, he supposed. But it hadn't really worked the way he'd wanted it to. The days had passed, but far too slowly for his liking. His wife, Katy, would have told him to get on with it. "Stop moping, Kirk. It's not becoming."

And now, he wondered, what was next? "Wouldn't have missed it," he said.

"It'll mean tons to our lady scientist."

McGarvey smiled inwardly. Gail had gone from referring to Eve as "his lady scientist," to "our lady scientist," mostly because of what the three of them had gone through together. But in a good part, he thought, because Gail had finally accepted the likelihood that he would never set up house with either of them. Eve had her work on the project, and Gail was head of field training for the NNSA. Both of them were busy and McGarvey had dropped out.

"I haven't seen her yet," he said. "How is she?"

"Nervous. She hates public speaking, you know. Especially since Vanessa. She keeps going around saying, 'The damned thing works,' as if she's had her doubts all along."

"But it does."

"This part at least," Gail said. "But she says it'll be at least ten years before enough impellers are online to see if there's any effect on the Gulf Stream and on the Atlantic temperature distribution. That's the key."

Schlagel was gone, totally dropped out of sight, his ministry and SOS network all but defunct. DeCamp had disappeared, dead for all anyone knew, and the Marinaccio Group had been absorbed into Dubai's finance ministry in the form of taxes, though a court battle was looming between the Emirates, her investors, many of them Saudi royalty, and the U.S. government. Everyone wanted a piece of the action.

"Then she'll have to wait and see."

"Anyway, when did you get here?"

"About an hour ago," McGarvey said. "I wanted a chance to look around."

Gail gave him a nervous look. "And?"

"Everything looks fine," McGarvey said. "And when this is done, I'm taking you to dinner."

"Can you handle two hyper women at the same time?" Eve asked, coming around the corner, a big, though nervous, grin on her face.

She and McGarvey embraced. "I don't know if I can handle one of you, so I suppose it won't make any difference if it's both."

"I missed you," Eve said.

McGarvey shook his head. "Nice of you to say so, Doc, but you've been too busy."

"The name is Eve. Now I have a speech to make, a switch to throw, and some hands to shake, so neither of you go anywhere until I'm done."

McGarvey smiled. "The damned thing works."

The oddest expression came over Eve's face, and her lips pursed for just a second, but then she smiled and nodded, too. "Yup, the damned thing works. And it better after all we've gone through, and still have to go through, because we're hanging on the edge of an abyss at the bottom of which is nothing but darkness. Maybe even death."

"Dramatic," Gail said.

"No, not at all," Eve replied bleakly even though she was smiling. "We either fix things now within the next decade, or it'll be too late."

Abyss, indeed, McGarvey thought, as Eve walked to the podium to give her speech and turn the switch.